AF279283

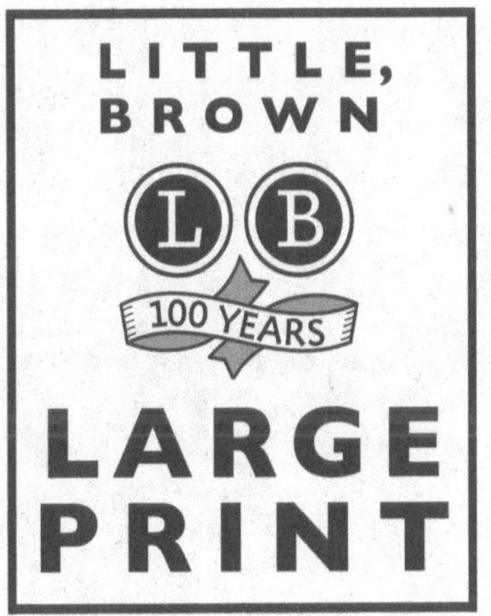

LITTLE,
BROWN
L B
100 YEARS
LARGE
PRINT

The Neon Sky

Alyssa Villaire

LITTLE, BROWN AND COMPANY

LARGE PRINT EDITION

Little, Brown and Company
Hachette Book Group
1290 Avenue of the Americas, New York, NY 10104
LBYR.com

First Edition: May 2026

Little, Brown and Company is a division of Hachette Book Group, Inc. The Little, Brown name and logo are registered trademarks of Hachette Book Group, Inc.

The publisher is not responsible for websites (or their content) that are not owned by the publisher.

Little, Brown and Company books may be purchased in bulk for business, educational, or promotional use. For information, please contact your local bookseller or the Hachette Book Group Special Markets Department at special.markets@hbgusa.com.

Library of Congress Cataloging-in-Publication Data
Names: Villaire, Alyssa author
Title: The neon sky / by Alyssa Villaire.
Description: First edition. | New York, NY : Little, Brown and Company, 2026. | Series: The glittering edge ; [book 2] | Audience: Ages 12 and up | Summary: Friends Penny, Alonso, and Corey must once again join forces to stave off a nefarious magical force that threatens to drive them apart, as Corey battles with a seemingly impossible choice and Alonso pushes the limits of his magic.
Identifiers: LCCN 2025039185 | ISBN 9780316574983 hardcover | ISBN 9780316575126 ebook
Subjects: CYAC: Fantasy | Magic—Fiction | Friendship—Fiction | LCGFT: Fantasy fiction | Novels
Classification: LCC PZ7.1.V5395 Ne 2026 | DDC [Fic]—dc23
LC record available at https://lccn.loc.gov/2025039185

ISBNs: 978-0-316-57498-3 (hardcover), 978-0-316-57512-6 (ebook),
978-0-316-61079-7 (large print)

For Mom, who believed in me first

Cozy Mystery Book Club

OCTOBER 30, 5:06 PM

Penny Emberly

THE TEENAGE WEREWOLVES

**PLAYING
ALL HALLOWS' EVE!**

Boxer's Irish Pub • Idlewood, Indiana
9 PM • 18 and up

AD Alonso De Luca

oh hell yeah

CB Corey Barrion
Sounds fun but I can't make it.

Nooooo why??

NS Naomi Salazar
I thought tickets were sold out???

Sly is working the door!
She'll get us in.

NS Naomi Salazar
Omg yes! I'll be there!

Dylan, you should join us!

OCTOBER 31, 9:10 AM

Dylan?

MP Milton Pierre
don't think I need to be in this chat
so I'll show myself out

MILTON PIERRE has left the group chat.

Oops sorry Milton!

Oh he's already gone.

AD Alonso De Luca

got a surprise for you ladies tonight

NS Naomi Salazar

That sounds ominous.

AD Alonso De Luca

thank you

here's a question

why can't corey barrion spare thirty minutes for us on a friday night

even he's not too cool for halloween

CB Corey Barrion

I literally can't make it. Family stuff.

NS Naomi Salazar

I'll bet money the Barrions give out full-size candy bars to the trick-or-treaters.

CB Corey Barrion

Just doing our civic duty.

I'll save some for you.

NS Naomi Salazar

An angel!!!

CB Corey Barrion

Happy Halloween! Don't let any ghosts across the Veil, Alonso.

AD Alonso De Luca

ghosts are no match for me 😉

Corey

COREY SHOULDN'T MAKE PROMISES HE CAN'T keep.

Boxer's Irish Pub is already full to the brim by the time he gets there. Everyone is dressed up in shiny polyester, horror movie masks, and tangled wigs. Old pop-EDM crossover hits from the 2010s are barely audible over clinking glasses and too-loud laughter.

From his vantage point near the makeshift stage, Corey shifts in his plastic chainmail. Every few minutes his football teammates remember they dragged him here, and they pull him into the conversation like he's a balloon threatening to drift away. He nods and smiles as he marvels for the tenth time that night that nodding and smiling might be his only valuable skills.

Every time the conversation loses him, Corey's

eyes wander back to the door—where, any minute now, Penny Emberly is going to appear.

He didn't tell her he changed his mind about tonight. He'll make excuses, but she won't be mad anyway. Especially once Alonso arrives to distract her.

That thought makes Corey's stomach twist.

He tries to focus on watching the band set up onstage instead. There are cords being hooked into amps, mics being tested, plugs being inserted into ears. It's chaotic and at least one of the band members is rolling their eyes, visibly stressed and anxious. But something about it brings Corey comfort.

Before long, though, Corey glances at the door again—just as it opens, letting in a blast of wind from outside. And with that wind comes Penny.

Corey cranes his neck to see her through the bodies. She's wearing a short black dress, and she's got some kind of prop in her hand. She stops to talk to the bouncer, who shouts and gives her an enthusiastic hug. This must be Sly. She's recognizable from her place behind a drum set in the numerous Quicklime posters that are scattered on the walls of the bar:

QUICKLIME RETURNS FOR A
TWO-WEEK RESIDENCY IN IDLEWOOD!
ALBUM RELEASE PARTY!
Y2K CONCERT—
COME CELEBRATE THE END OF THE WORLD!

Corey takes a long pull from his beer bottle. He'll say hi to Penny later. Ideally as he's on his way out the door.

"Hey."

At first, Corey doesn't recognize the petite woman in the black wig. Then she glances up, and Corey's composure cracks like glass.

It's Dylan Mayberry. His ex-girlfriend.

"Oh," he chokes out. "Hi."

She sips a bright blue beverage and doesn't say anything. She doesn't leave, either, so Corey clears his throat and continues. "How are you?"

She eyes the band's lead singer, a guy wearing what some people might call a tank top but which Corey would call two pieces of fabric barely held together at the seams. "Single. You?"

"Also single." He pauses. "I knew you'd be here."

"You almost sound happy."

Corey can't help it; he smiles. "I am. It's good to see you."

Whatever Dylan thinks of this comment, she shrugs it off. "You know me. I hate to miss a party."

"Any bullying planned?"

Dylan's smile fades. "Come on."

"It's a valid question."

"No, Corey. I'm trying this thing where I don't get drunk and do stuff like that." She lifts up her glass. "This is nonalcoholic."

"Cool," Corey says, and he means it.

The tension between them dissipates for a moment. It would be so easy for them to fall back into old habits. To dance together, to fit their lips against each other's like they've done thousands of times before. The thought might've been comforting to Corey last summer.

Not anymore.

Royce Montalban appears beside Dylan and whispers something in her ear. Dylan looks unenthused, but she shrugs and follows him. Just like that, she's gone.

A guitar growls, and Corey turns around just as the band members are pulling on werewolf masks. A few ancient stage lights change from white to red. The lead singer has to put the mic halfway into the werewolf mask's mouth to be heard over the crowd.

"*Idlewood!* Our favorite dump!"

A wave of sound rises—boos and cheers melding into a roar. The guitarist begins a descending riff that quickly turns hypnotic as the rest of the instruments join in. The sound quality is so bad that the lyrics are mostly inaudible, but people start dancing anyway.

Someone elbows him in the side, and for a second Corey wonders if he's going to be in the middle of a mosh pit. Then the person who elbowed him yells, "BOO!" and Corey realizes he's standing next to the human version of a mosh pit.

Alonso De Luca grins from under a pair of devil horns attached to a headband. His entire outfit is red: button-up shirt, pleather pants, and even his shoes have been spray-painted. Alonso holds out a hand, and Corey grins as he grabs it and claps him on the back. "Hey, man."

"You came out!" Alonso nods at the stage. "You're really into the band, huh?"

"Not really." The moment the words come out of his mouth, Corey doesn't know why he denied it. "It's a good song."

"Of course it is. It's The Cramps."

"Who?" Corey shouts over the noise.

"The Cramps! 'Human Fly'? You've never heard this before?"

Corey shakes his head, but he makes a mental note to look them up when he gets home. This song almost makes him feel guilty, like he's not supposed to enjoy it, even though he's the one who decides what he does and doesn't like. But Corey's life is orderly, and this song is loose and angry and messy.

Maybe that's why he's drawn to it, though. What would it feel like to be onstage performing a song like this? To sway to the music and ignore the shocked faces in the crowd? To not care that anyone might be judging him?

Good, Corey thinks. *It would feel good.*

Alonso's grin fades. "So how've you been? Since…"

Corey is saved from having to answer by the song ending. The bar erupts in cheers, and Corey claps, pretending he didn't hear the question. Either Alonso is easily distracted or he got the hint, because he lets it drop as the next song starts up.

It's weird, just existing around Alonso like this. Corey isn't used to it, but he's getting there.

Idlewood, though? They don't know what to make of the enemies-turned-almost-friends. From the corner of his eye, Corey can see the phones raised in their direction, as if there isn't a much more interesting werewolf band playing three feet in front of them.

If Alonso notices the attention from the crowd, he doesn't care. Or maybe he's basking in it. He looks around them with a small grin on his face, and then he does a double take.

"Hide me, hide me," he says, ducking around Corey and crouching down.

The crowd shifts, and a straw broom emerges from between the bodies. "Sorry!" comes Penny's voice as she and Naomi appear. Naomi has used makeup to turn herself into one of the blue aliens from the *Avatar* movies, but Penny's costume is more subtle. Unless you happened to spend the summer doing magic with her.

"You're a witch?" Corey asks, grinning.

"I already had a black dress in my closet." Penny beams up at him. "You made it!" She shifts to give him a one-armed hug, and he doesn't look at her as he wraps an arm around her shoulders, barely touching her before he lets go and steps back.

Except he forgets that Alonso is behind him.

Corey gasps as he bumps into him. There's a yelp as Alonso falls, narrowly missing the lead singer. The guitars screech to a halt.

"Whoa!" The singer jumps back. "Hey, it's our stage, man!"

Corey shouts an apology and leans forward, reaching out to help Alonso up. But Alonso grins and gets to his feet onstage.

"Alonso?" Penny says, a hint of panic in her voice. "What are you doing?"

Alonso grabs the mic from the singer, who starts yelling something about getting security. But Alonso ignores him, and he leans into the red light as a grin spreads over his face.

"I just wanted to say something!" Alonso's eyes lock on Penny. His grin flickers, and for a moment he looks like he's forgotten that he just interrupted a band's set.

"Hey," he says, "I love you."

Corey rolls his eyes as the crowd screams. Alonso lets the mic stand fall back into the singer's hands as he hops off the stage.

"Such a drama queen," Naomi shouts at Alonso, but Penny pulls him against her.

"That was embarrassing," Penny mutters, but

she's smiling. He wraps his arms around her and presses his lips to the top of her head.

Corey clears his throat and tries to ignore the strange tightness in his chest. The longing for this thing he still can't have.

This is why he shouldn't have come tonight. He doesn't want to be angry at anyone else for being happy. And if this past summer taught him anything, it's that Corey can't trust himself. Not his words, and not his actions.

Especially where Penny and Alonso are concerned.

"Your hair!" Naomi says.

Corey glances back at Alonso, and that's when he notices it.

"Whoa," Corey says. "It's red."

Alonso reaches up and touches the neon red ends of his hair. The blue is still visible in a couple spots, but mostly, Alonso's hair is as bright as the stage lights.

Penny gasps. "It was blue at school today! When did you do it?"

"An hour ago. You like it?"

"I know you're only asking Penny," Naomi says, "but I think it makes you look deranged."

"Nice."

The Teenage Werewolves launch into their next song as if people interrupt them to give declarations of love during every show. Penny runs her fingers through the ends of Alonso's hair, her eyes soft.

"I love it," Penny says. "And you."

"I know," Alonso says, beaming.

"No making out," Naomi says. "It's too hetero in here already."

Alonso laughs as he and Penny disentangle themselves. Then he bumps Corey's shoulder. "I'm going to get some root beer. Want to come with me?"

"Sure," Corey says.

As he follows Alonso through the crowd and puts space between himself and Penny, the knots in Corey's stomach begin to unfurl. When they have their drinks, Alonso rests his back against the edge of the bar and considers Corey. "So what's up with you?"

"Huh?"

"I mean, what's going on? Penny and I barely hear from you anymore."

Corey tries to laugh it off, but dread encroaches, crawling up his body like a million tiny spiders.

"Just busy. Lots of stuff happening with the company."

"She's worried about you." Alonso looks off into the crowd. "So am I."

Corey snorts. "Really?"

But Alonso doesn't smile. "I hated your grandfather, but I never wanted him to die."

Corey stares at the floor. Ever since the murder of his grandfather, Charles Barrion, at the end of the summer, people have treated him like he's fragile, just like they did when his mom died. Everyone talks around it as if acknowledging it directly will cause Corey to have a breakdown. He wishes people could just say what they're thinking.

But now, hearing Alonso's blunt words, Corey isn't so sure that's what he wants after all.

"We're dealing with it," Corey says.

"You want us to come over? See if we can find the spell?"

When they learned his grandfather had created a bargain sacrificing the lives of Barrion loved ones in exchange for the success of their company, they also found out that the only way to undo it is to create another bargain that cancels it out. Corey will have to make a sacrifice to set it in motion, just like his grandfather did.

And his grandfather killed someone.

Corey's entire body buzzes with anxiety, as if he can run from the reality of what he has to do. But of course he can't.

If Corey wants to save his family, he'll have to kill someone, too. Someone important to him.

"I can't think about that yet," Corey says.

"Hey," Alonso says, "maybe there's another way."

"If Milton says there isn't, I believe him." Milton Pierre is another witch who helped them save Penny's mom last summer. The scion of the Pierre coven, one of the most powerful witch families in the world, Milton knows his way around magic in a way Alonso doesn't. And according to him, bargains can only be counteracted. Not broken, like curses.

Alonso opens his mouth to say something else, but a short man with greasy hair appears from the crowd and shoves Alonso to get to the bar. Alonso jerks aside, his root beer bottle falling from his hand and crashing into a million shards on the floor.

The guy who pushed him doesn't even look up.

Alonso stares at the broken bottle for half a second. Corey's hands are up, as if he's about to defuse a very fragile, very deadly bomb. But Alonso doesn't explode. He just leans back against the bar like nothing happened.

"I'll get you another one," Corey says.

But Alonso sighs, and suddenly he doesn't seem angry at all. "It was empty anyway. Let's find Penny and Naomi?"

People do change, apparently. Corey grins, and he's about to say yes, they should go back into the swarm.

Until slurred words cut into their conversation.

"Well. It's Corey Barrion." The drunk man steps back from the bar and sizes Corey up. "Out spending daddy's money, are you?"

The man's words send a prickle of unease over Corey's skin. "Excuse me?"

"Must be nice," the man says, "sitting in your pretty house while the people who work for you suffer."

"Whoa, Keith," the bartender says, and then she turns to Corey. "He's had too many drinks, Mr. Barrion. I'm sorry, just ignore him!"

Mr. Barrion. That makes Corey squirm. This bartender is at least twenty years older than him.

Keith sneers. "You get to ignore me every other day of your life. Not today, though." He steps closer to Corey. Alonso is a foot away, still leaning back on the bar. His eyes are closed, and he looks like he's doing an elaborate breathing exercise.

Stay out of this, Corey wants to tell him, but already Keith is grabbing the collar of Corey's shirt.

"I lost my job because of your old man," Keith spits. "Thirty years I worked on that manufacturing floor, and then my job becomes obsolete. I've got nothing now, and you still have everything! Does that sound right to you?"

The heat in the bar becomes unbearable. This isn't just some belligerent stranger who's had too many drinks; he was laid off from Barrion Heating & Cooling.

Freshman year of high school, Corey arrived at his locker to see that someone had written on it with permanent marker: **THERE R NO ETHICAL BILLIONAIRES.**

He'd wanted to find the culprit more than anything. To tell them what his family suffered as a result of this curse, but how they persevered.

How, despite everything, they kept Idlewood afloat when all other companies shut down or left. Most billionaires seemed bad, it was true. But the Barrions were the exception.

Corey is glad he never found out who graffitied his locker. Because after he learned what his grandfather did to their family, Corey realized the Barrions aren't the exception after all.

Corey almost wants to apologize, but through the haze of his panic he knows that would be the worst thing he could say. What does it matter if he's sorry? That won't get Keith his job back.

"Sly!" the bartender calls, running out from behind the bar. More people are looking at them now, whispering and laughing and staring with wide eyes.

"You need to let go of me," Corey says, trying to keep his voice even.

"Or what? You'll start crying?" Keith scoffs. "Bet you've never felt any pain your entire life."

Whatever Corey was going to say next disappears from his mind like this man reached down his throat and stole the words. All Corey can do is gape at him.

Corey's mom. His uncle Jason. His cousin's genius husband, Ramón. And everything that happened this past summer—all the fear and risks taken and lives almost lost.

Please see it when you look at me, Corey thinks. *See how wrong you are.*

Keith just grins, the red lights from the bar reflecting off his teeth. "How about I introduce you to the real world?" he says, and he lifts his fist to throw a punch.

There's a blur of motion, and Corey is shoved back, stumbling a few steps before he catches himself on the bar.

Keith is on the floor, wailing as he clutches his nose. Blood gushes from between his fingers.

Alonso stands in front of him, shaking out his fist. He throws a look over his shoulder. "You good?"

"Fine," Corey manages to say.

Sly appears in front of them. Her eyes aren't on the injured man; they're just on Alonso. "De Luca. You promised to behave."

"I know." Alonso runs a hand through his hair. "I'll leave."

Alonso sweeps by Corey, clapping him on the shoulder before he disappears into the night, leaving only a gust of cold air in his wake.

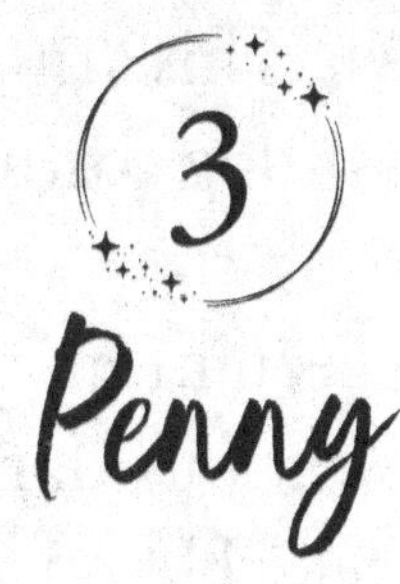 Penny

PENNY BURSTS ONTO THE SIDEWALK IN FRONT of Boxer's. A few people stand outside smoking, and they glance up at her before quickly returning to their conversations. Penny is still holding her broom, but she lost her witch's hat in the crowd. It belongs to Boxer's now.

"Alonso!" she shouts, looking all around. But he's nowhere.

Corey found her in the crowd after the fight, if you want to call it that. And when Penny checked her texts, there was one message from Alonso:

> i'll meet you outside.

"Alonso!" Penny calls again.

"Penny?" someone says. It's Aidan Lostis,

Alonso's friend. He has his arms wrapped around a thin person in a hot dog costume. "You looking for Alonso?"

"Yeah, have you seen him?"

"He went that way." Aidan gestures behind them, up the street. He gives her a sympathetic smile. "I recognize that look. Did he do something?"

"Corey was attacked," Penny says. "I guess Alonso stepped in."

"Look at him, being all noble," Aidan says.

Penny tries to smile, but she can't ignore the anxious feeling in her stomach. This is the first fight Alonso has been in since the summer. Part of her wants to defend him even though nobody asked for that, and the other part of her wants to apologize on his behalf.

"I'm going to find him," Penny says. "See you at school?"

"See you," Aidan says, already pulling his date down for a kiss.

Penny runs past Village Blues Records and through downtown Idlewood. As she reaches Horizon Café—a periwinkle hole-in-the-wall that her mom and godfather have owned and operated for over a decade—she stops. In the dark windows of the café, she sees herself: hair permanently disheveled, tight dress riding up, eyeliner making her look less like a sexy witch and more like a shocked mouse. She wipes the black smudges from beneath her eyes and then wipes her hands on her dress.

"Smooth."

Penny gasps. Reflected in the window, Alonso stands a few feet behind her with a small smile on his face. His devil-horn headband is gone, and a few more buttons on his red shirt have come undone, revealing a sliver of his chest.

"There you are," she says, turning around. "I thought you'd—"

She stops. There's nobody there.

Penny's eyes move from side to side. She can already feel herself smiling, but she tries not to let it show. "Huh. I thought I saw my boyfriend." She shrugs. "Guess I'll go home!"

She turns on her heel to leave, but she immediately bumps into Alonso's chest, which materializes out of thin air. He wraps his arms around her, and she does the same. She doesn't even think about touching him anymore; it's like a reflex. Instinct.

"Invisibility spell?" Penny says.

"Yeah." Alonso rests his chin on top of her head. "I switched out the amaranth for chicory. Lets me be visible in mirrors and windows. Creepy, right?"

"If by creepy you mean *hot*…"

Alonso lifts her chin. In the low light from the streetlamps, there's a blush barely visible on his cheeks. *I did that*, Penny thinks.

"I would tell you creepy shouldn't be hot," Alonso says, "but in this case, I'll allow it."

The memory of the events at Boxer's interrupts Penny's reverie, and her smile falls. "Are you—"

Alonso puts a finger to her lips. It makes whatever she was about to ask—*are you okay, did you hurt yourself, why did you have to hurt that man*—evaporate. All she can think about is the feel of his strong hand, so much bigger than her own, as it touches her mouth. Heat floods her limbs, making her lightheaded.

"I have something to show you," Alonso says.

His hand drops to grab hers, and then they're weaving through Idlewood at night.

The streets are abandoned. Not a single car drives by, and trick-or-treaters have gone home for the night. As Penny and Alonso move from Main Street into Penny's neighborhood, the laughter and music of Halloween parties occasionally interrupt the crickets. When they hear a slow, mournful song coming through someone's screen door, Alonso stops and blinks as if he's just woken up from a dream. The song is fuzzy, like the recording is from the early days of music, but the voice is soaring.

"What is it?" Penny asks.

"The Ink Spots."

Penny doesn't get a chance to ask who that is; already Alonso is pulling her close, wrapping one arm around her waist.

And just like that, they're dancing in the street.

Alonso whispers the lyrics to her. Penny has never heard the song before, but she closes her eyes and lets the words wash over her: something about setting the world on fire, and burning flames in hearts, and having only one desire.

When the song ends, they keep walking. Alonso holds her hand against his chest, keeping it warm.

Is this real life? Penny wonders, but she can't question it. She just breathes in the chilly night air until it makes her lungs sting.

Gradually, the houses give way to trees and

the rush of water. They stop by the Porter River, which divides central and northern Idlewood. The water is thirty feet below them. Running across the river is a railway bridge, massive and rusting and echoing with eerie whispers as the wind moves through the tangle of metal beams that hold it in the air.

"We're here," Alonso says.

Penny looks around, trying to figure out what he so desperately wants to show her. Before she finds it, Alonso takes off running toward the bridge.

Penny laughs as she follows him, but when he starts running on the bridge itself, she stops. There's a rotting wooden guardrail on either side that will save literally nobody. This close to the edge, the drop into the foaming river looks much higher. Penny's heart pounds painfully against her ribs.

Alonso doesn't stop until he gets to the middle of the bridge. He looks up at the night sky, beaming like a little boy. Above them, a gibbous moon glows behind smoky clouds.

A low call disrupts Penny's thoughts, and she squints into the distance as she listens. There it is again, and this time, she recognizes it.

A train whistle.

Alonso is too far out. He'll get trapped.

"Come back!" Penny calls. "There's a train!"

Alonso grins at her. Then he ducks under the guardrail.

That's what it takes for Penny to run onto the bridge. By the time she reaches the spot where Alonso stood, he's disappeared.

Penny leans over the edge, looking down into the churning water. "ALONSO!" she screams, searching desperately for him. He could've survived this fall, right? If he jumped, he must've known that he would be okay.

Then his head appears from only a few feet underneath her, and Penny lets out a truncated yell. "What are you doing?!"

"There's a platform," Alonso says. "Come on!"

Penny grits her teeth. The train is getting closer by the minute, and the chill in the autumn air is making her hands go numb. Or maybe that's the stress.

"You'll catch me?"

Alonso's smile fades. "Always, Penny."

And she believes him.

She moves slowly: ducking under the rail, kneeling down, dangling one leg. There's a warm pressure on her calf: Alonso's hand, holding her steady, reassuring her. She activates the little bit of upper body strength she has, and Alonso's arms wrap around her, lowering her slowly until her feet touch the floor. Then he grabs her around the ribs, and she lets go of the bridge as he guides her underneath it.

Penny looks down and she gasps, clinging to the metal beam closest to her. What Alonso described as a "platform" is really a strip of metal between the support beams underneath the bridge. The metal doesn't extend all the way across, and one wrong step in either direction will send them careening into the river.

The train whistle blows again, still a ways off.

"You hang out here a lot?" Penny asks in a shaky voice.

Alonso laughs. "Heard about it from some people at bike polo." He points to some scratches in the metal: MOLLY WAS HERE!!!, J + A FOREVER, DIAL THIS NUMBER FOR SEX XOXOXO. Penny blushes and drags her eyes back up to Alonso's face. The wind down here is much more intense, and Alonso's newly red hair blows around his face. He holds on to the beams above him, and the necklaces he always wears make light, musical sounds as they clink against each other.

"You're beautiful," he says.

Penny blushes. "I was thinking the same thing about you."

He steps closer until Penny's back is pressed against the beam behind her.

Against her will, Penny thinks about the looks they got at Boxer's. It happens every day at school, too: people laughing behind their hands or whispering to each other as Penny and Alonso walk by. She tries to ignore all of it, but when she lies down at night, sleep doesn't come. She just hears their whispers.

They're really *dating?*

Six months ago, Penny wouldn't have believed it, either. But for some reason, when other people say it, it hurts so much more.

Every day, Penny wonders if Alonso will realize they're right. Now that they're together and Alonso has stopped the boxing matches with Corey, people aren't as afraid of him as they once were. She sees the way girls look at him. Alonso could have anyone he wanted.

So why would he choose her?

"Hey."

Reluctantly, she looks up at him.

"Where'd you go?" Alonso whispers. His

voice gets carried away by the wind, but Penny can read his lips.

"Nowhere."

Alonso contemplates her. She expects him to push for a real answer, but he just reaches up with both hands and brushes her hair away from her face. She glances at his mouth, and then she can't look away. Alonso lets out a low breath.

"You can't look at me like that," he mutters.

"Why not?"

Instead of answering her, Alonso leans in and presses his lips to hers.

The kiss is slow at first. Steady. Reassuring. But the wind picks up, and Penny pulls him closer, opening her mouth to breathe him in. He gasps, and Penny can feel his tongue against hers. He uses one hand to tilt her head up, and he moves his mouth down to her chin, her neck, and Penny's breathing grows ragged.

"I want you," he whispers into her neck. "You're all I think about. Every day…"

"That's not—" *True.* She manages to stop that final word before it leaves her lips. But Alonso is already pulling back, letting the cold wind in between them.

"Not what?"

Penny sighs, pushing her curls out of her eyes. "I don't know."

"Yeah, you do. So tell me."

The words spill from her like water. "I don't know why! Why you want *me*."

Alonso narrows his eyes at her. Then he turns his gaze to the river below them.

"You make me want to be better," he says. "Better than I am."

Hesitantly, Penny reaches out and grabs a fistful of his red silk shirt. "You're already good, Alonso. With or without me."

Alonso lifts his hand so she can see his bruised knuckles. "I don't think so."

Penny lets her eyes run over his hand. Then she grabs it and brings his knuckles to her lips. Alonso softens, stepping closer to her again.

"It's hard for me to believe, too," he whispers. "That you want this."

"I do," Penny says.

He presses his lips together. "It didn't feel good, hurting that guy. But he deserved it."

There's a surety to his words that makes Penny shiver. She believes him, though. As she learned over the summer, Alonso isn't the person she thought he was. He doesn't go looking for violence.

Still.

"Even if he deserved it," Penny begins, "you're strong. You have the power to really hurt people." Because fistfights aren't the only weapon in Alonso's arsenal. According to Milton, Alonso is also one of the most powerful witches alive. Penny would be lying if she said that didn't scare her. But she won't tell Alonso that. Believing in someone isn't always easy. It's a choice.

Alonso considers her, his gaze unrelenting. Then he nods. "Yeah. You're right. I—"

His words are cut off by the train whistle. Penny looks around, suddenly remembering where they are. "We should get back onto the sidewalk."

"Too late," Alonso says.

"But the bridge—"

"It'll hold us," Alonso says. Then he leans closer. "I have something for you."

"What is it?"

"A spell."

Penny's breath catches. She spent her summer doing magic with Alonso. She even crossed the Veil and confronted ghosts and poltergeists.

But she's still not used to it.

"This is a spell that will allow me to find you," Alonso says. "Always."

Penny smirks. "We're already sharing our locations."

"That doesn't work across the Veil."

"I'm not planning on going back there."

"I know. But you're dating me. And I don't want to take any chances."

What do you think will happen? Penny wants to ask, but she stops herself. Alonso is right. Being with him creates risks that she wouldn't have with another boyfriend. A *mortal* boyfriend.

"No matter what city or country or realm you find yourself in," Alonso says, "this spell will guide me to where you are. If you need me."

Alonso holds out a hand, fingers pointed up. Penny reaches out and grabs it in her own.

"Repeat after me," Alonso says, and he closes his eyes. Penny does the same, and she repeats the words he speaks in a low, clear voice:

> *"Harvest moon, lend your gravity,*
> *Ocean waves, tremors of earth*
> *Echo loudly underfoot*
> *So this witch's ear can hear."*

From the first syllables, Alonso's magic is palpable. It lifts the hairs at the back of Penny's neck and builds pressure behind her eyes, but she doesn't want it to stop.

After they speak the final words, the bridge begins to rumble. Penny's eyes shoot open, and she presses herself back against the metal beam. The train whistle sounds, so close now.

Alonso steps closer to Penny, clutches the beam behind her so that his arms encircle her. Protecting her. She grabs his forearms as the bridge begins to quake, barely holding back a scream as the train passes overhead.

"Look at me," Alonso yells over the noise. And she does.

The noise and the shaking fade. In Alonso's eyes, there's an entire universe. Penny wants to explore every corner of it, no matter how dark. No matter how dangerous.

Alonso presses his forehead to hers. "Doesn't it feel like the world is ending?"

If it was, this is how Penny would choose to go.

4

Alonso

AFTER HE DROPS PENNY OFF, ALONSO ROLLS
down the windows of his car and turns the
heater on blast. He was born in the spring, but
aesthetically, fall is his season. It's a cliché since
he's a witch, but he doesn't care. The orange and
yellow and red color palette, the bright moon,
the smell of cinnamon on the air—all of it makes
him feel alive.

And during autumn, the Veil and the Second
World feel closer than ever. It makes the magic
thrum in Alonso's veins.

He pulls into the driveway at eleven PM. A
candle flickers behind the stained glass of the
front window, and the upstairs lights are on. All
the De Lucas are night owls, so Alonso expected
this. What he doesn't expect is the deathly silence
that greets him when he walks through the front

door. His family isn't what anyone would call quiet.

"Hello?" Alonso calls.

"In here," comes his mother's voice.

Alonso follows the sound of it to the back of the house. In the solarium, his mother, Vera De Luca, stands among their overgrown plants with Alonso's aunts, Emilia and Donna. One small window is open, and a breeze rustles the leaves on unnaturally tall cat palms and pothos and birds of paradise. Alonso's mom and aunts stand clustered with their backs to Alonso, whispering to each other.

"What'd I miss?" Alonso says.

They all turn around, their gazes bright. Alonso's familiar, Nimble, sits in Emilia's arms, her orange tail swishing back and forth.

"Look," Alonso's mom says, and all three of them turn to stare out the window.

Alonso gazes into the dark. The gibbous moon lends a glow to their densely forested backyard, and Donna points a finger to a patch of lawn just outside their window.

There's something on the grass.

Alonso squints. No, not something. Some-*things*. Four small bodies lay motionless in the light cast from the solarium's windows, moon-light glinting off black feathers.

"Crows?" Alonso breathes.

"Crows," Aunt Donna says.

"They flew into the window, one after the other," says Alonso's mother. "We heard them from the dining room."

"An omen," Aunt Emilia whispers, clutching Nimble tighter to her chest.

"A bad omen," Aunt Donna agrees. "You never want anything to come in fours."

Alonso wants to argue, but he can feel it as he stares at the dead crows. There's something emanating from them. A message? A warning? Alonso focuses his magic on the crows, and he listens. The message almost forms into words…

And that's when Alonso's head starts pounding. He steps back, clutching at his temples. He's been getting a lot of migraines recently. Before this summer, he barely even got sick.

His mom and aunts turn to look at him. Since the Council of Witches restored their magic this summer, his entire family has become attuned to each other on a new, primal level. Last week, Alonso stubbed his toe in his attic bedroom, and Emilia felt the pain in her own foot two floors down. And when Alonso's mom got a call that one of her clients at her social work job was getting off probation, Donna apparently heard her happy gasp at the grocery store, which made her drop a spaghetti squash that splattered everywhere.

It's freaky. But Alonso kind of loves it. They aren't just a family anymore; they're a coven. And he'll do anything to keep his coven safe.

So he volunteers to take care of the crows.

"Maybe you should wait until morning," Emilia calls after him as he grabs some matches and lighter fluid from the kitchen.

"And let that bad energy hang out in the backyard all night? No, thanks." As Alonso walks by Aunt Emilia, he reaches out to scratch Nimble's head. She hisses and swats at him.

"Wow," Alonso says. "Some familiar you are."

"She's been grumpy with you lately," his mother says, eyes trained on Alonso's face. "Any idea why that is?"

"Nope. She'll only let me pet her when I give her food." Alonso narrows his eyes at Nimble. She narrows her eyes back. He could make a snide comment, but he's too tired to fight with her, so he gives up and goes outside.

They don't clean their yard often, so it only takes a minute to gather enough sticks for a small fire. Alonso digs a shallow hole, dumps the sticks inside, then uses the shovel to transfer each of the four crows onto his makeshift pyre.

Once the fire is really going, Alonso watches the crows burn. He needs to make sure they're ash. When he starts to get impatient, he aims the bottle of lighter fluid directly at the blaze.

Instead of flaring up, the fire shoots out—directly at Alonso's legs.

"Holy shit!" he yells, falling back. The fire has already shrunk back, and Alonso wonders if he was seeing things. He pushes onto his feet again. One of the crows is angled in his direction, and the way the fire glints in its beady eye, it looks as if it's still alive. Watching him.

"What did you kill yourself for?" Alonso whispers.

The crows don't answer. But, from up in the trees, there's an earsplitting *caw*.

Standing on the top branch of a maple tree is another crow. It's completely still, and though it's impossible to tell where it's looking, Alonso feels its eyes on him.

So he waves at it.

"Caw!" says the crow again. Then it takes off and flies into the night.

It's hard to tell. Maybe it's a trick of the light. But this crow looks much larger than the birds that are burning at Alonso's feet.

Corey

COREY IS AWAKE BEFORE DAWN. HE LIES IN BED as the sun comes up and casts the room in a hazy blue glow. The bright summer sun is gone; this is the autumn sun, the one that bounces off dying leaves and struggles to be seen through layers of cloud cover.

Corey tugs off his headphones, which are still blasting The Cramps. Not exactly a lullaby, but the only thing that helps Corey sleep these days is music loud enough to drown out his thoughts. There are at least thirty tabs open on his laptop and half of them have to do with insomnia. He can recite from memory the definitions of *sleep debt, chronic deprivation, sleep hygiene.* No matter how much he reads about it, it doesn't change the fact that he's tired all the time but never tired enough to sleep at night.

Corey throws back his covers and pads out of

his room. Across the hall, Julian's door is open. Corey almost walks past it, but at the last second, he peeks inside.

Corey's cousin is splayed on his bed at an awkward angle, like roadkill. Corey's heart rate picks up at the sight—*is he okay?*—but then he sees Julian's chest rise and fall.

Just because you love someone doesn't mean they're going to die, Corey reminds himself. Rationally, he knows this. But his nervous system doesn't.

Corey wipes his sweaty palms on his pants as he walks over to the bed. Julian's comforter is threadbare in places; he's had it since they were kids, and he refuses to get rid of it. Corey pulls it over Julian's shoulders. Then he stands back, arms crossed, and considers Julian's desk.

For fifty years, Corey's family blamed Alonso's coven for the curse that killed a dozen of Corey's relatives. At the end of the summer, Penny crossed the Veil and discovered the truth: that it wasn't a curse that killed Corey's mother and their other family members. It was a bargain created by Corey's grandfather—a bargain that exchanged the lives of anyone loved by the Barrions for the success of their family's company. All along, the De Luca coven had been blamed—and ostracized—for something they didn't do.

Corey swore he would find a way to undo his grandfather's bargain as quickly as possible, and the first thing he intended to do was confront his grandfather in front of his entire family. To put the truth out in the open.

Then his grandfather was brutally murdered in a home invasion.

It happened in August, after Penny's mom was sent home from the hospital. This experience of death was different from what happened every time the bargain killed somebody. Back then, grief would create a silence so thick that it stayed in Meredith House for weeks. They grieved quietly, in their own chosen ways.

This time, Corey arrived home to an array of police cars and fire trucks and an ambulance. When his dad told him what had happened, Corey almost couldn't believe it. People only died because of the bargain. It wasn't random. But there was his grandfather, being rolled out of his house in a body bag. It wasn't until the ambulance left that his dad told him how it happened: a single gunshot to the head.

And it was Julian who found him.

He was bringing their grandpa something. Maybe food. Maybe his daily newspaper. But when Julian got there, the door was wide open—and it was too late.

More than anyone else, it was Julian who worshipped their grandfather. He craved Charles Barrion's approval like he needed it to live, and Charles refused to give it to him.

And then their grandfather was gone, leaving Julian haunted. Obsessed.

The desk in Julian's room is covered with printed articles about the murder, email exchanges between his grandfather and business associates, screenshots from the security footage that had been scrambled by the intruders to the point of uselessness. If Corey opened Julian's tablet, he'd find more of the same.

Julian shifts in his sleep. "Grandpa," he mutters before rolling over onto his side and curling into a ball, face buried in the mattress.

Corey doesn't know how to tell Julian—or the rest of his family—that the man they're mourning wasn't who they thought he was. The only person who knows about the bargain and what kind of sacrifice it will take to fix it is Corey.

He's being a martyr by not telling them. He

also can't physically make his mouth form the words.

Corey sighs. Then he leaves, closing Julian's door quietly behind him.

"Corey. You're up early."

His dad, James Barrion, stands a few feet away. This early, James doesn't have his blazer on yet, but his freshly ironed shirt is tucked into a pair of gray dress pants.

"I was just checking on Julian," Corey says.

His dad nods. "You slept well?"

"Yeah. You?"

"Fine."

They're silent for a long moment. Corey is about to make some excuse when James clears his throat. "I wanted to talk to you about something."

Hope flutters its wings in Corey's chest. *Dad knows about the bargain. I won't have to fix this by myself. I won't have to . . .*

Kill.

"Yeah?" Corey says, too eager.

"I know it's been a hectic time. But I'll need your analysis on those year-end projections by our meeting tomorrow morning."

Anything resembling hope disappears, and

Corey is once again painfully, unavoidably alone. He's officially the heir to Barrion Heating & Cooling, which means he's in a never-ending internship. That would be bad enough, but his dad is also his boss. That means early meetings on days when he has football, late meetings at home on days when he doesn't, and the ever-present specter of his family's expectations following him around.

From James Barrion's perspective, grief is for people with free time. They've never really talked about the murder except for right after it happened, when Corey's dad delivered the facts like a court reporter. After that, he expected Corey to move on.

Capitalism waits for nobody, after all.

"Right," Corey says. "I'm really sorry about that."

James shifts, but Corey doesn't look at him. "Just do it when you have time."

That's supposed to be comforting, which makes it even worse. Corey can't hold back a scoff. "Thanks, Dad, but I'll get it done today."

James watches Corey walk away. He looks like he wants to say something else, but he doesn't, so Corey closes his door.

After school, Corey walks across the property to Charles Barrion's house, which is near the tree line. Penny is already there, staring at the house with an unreadable expression.

There it is again—that *zap* Corey feels every time he sees her. He isn't sure when it started. Maybe it was watching her show surprising bravery in the face of witchcraft. Maybe it was that night she confronted him in the hospital parking lot, voice shaking even as it became clear she was determined to save her mom despite the odds being stacked against her.

As usual, Corey does his best to suppress the memories. The feelings.

It would be one thing if the bargain didn't exist. Then Corey could let himself have feelings for anyone, even if they'd never amount to anything real. But he learned at a young age that if he fell in love with someone, that person would die.

He doesn't love Penny. He hasn't allowed himself to get that close. But every time he's near her, he feels the risk of it—of *her*. Already he's beating himself up for letting her come over, but Alonso will be here soon. It's easier to ignore his own feelings when he remembers that Penny loves someone else—someone Corey also considers a friend.

"Hey," Corey says.

Penny jumps. "Hey. Sorry."

"For what?"

"I was lost in thought." She glances at the house again, her eyes a striking blue against the autumn leaves hanging around her.

Corey gets it without her having to say anything: *I can't believe it happened there.* Neither can he. For the first time in his life, Corey almost sees the appeal of true crime shows and podcasts. When you're faced with the echoes of horror, it's hard to look away, even if you want to.

"Alonso is running late," Penny says. "He wasn't at school today. He said he has another headache."

"Another?"

"It's been happening a lot lately." Penny shrugs. "I think it has something to do with his magic. Maybe he's using it too much?"

"Seems like he's doing pretty well, though. Like he has it under control."

Penny smiles. "He does. It's amazing, actually,

how the whole coven has adjusted to having magic." She flinches and quickly adds, "Sorry, is this a sore subject?"

"I'm glad they have their magic back. It's the reason we're here." Alonso agreed to use a finding spell to locate a page Corey's grandfather stole from *The Blackfire Grimoire*, the De Lucas' most dangerous spellbook. This is the same spell Charles Barrion used to create his bargain, and it's the one Corey will use to fix everything.

Penny watches him, her gaze steady. "Have you been inside the house since…?"

Corey's smile fades. "No."

He should've gone in. As soon as he got home, Corey should've looked for the spell. He even came out here after the police were done with the house and stood at the doorway, key in hand.

But Corey couldn't make himself go inside.

He can't put this off forever. Knowing Penny and Alonso would be here—and that Alonso has a spell to help them find what they need quickly—is the only thing that's making this bearable.

Both of their phones buzz. Corey opens up the Cozy Mystery Book Club thread.

Corey grimaces.

"Maybe we can do this tomorrow instead?" Penny asks.

But Corey is already here. He's built up his courage. He has to do *something*.

"I want to search," he says. "You don't have to stay."

"Of course I'll stay—"

"If I don't do this now, it means I'll keep dreading it. And I just…can't."

"Corey."

He looks up. Penny is standing a few feet away, considering him. A cold wind rustles a silver wind chime hanging from a nearby tree.

"I already said I'll stay," Penny says.

"Oh." Corey nods. "Okay."

But Penny hesitates. "I noticed you didn't offer to drive me here after school."

Heat stings under Corey's skin. "I—yeah, I just thought it'd be easier if you had your car."

"Is that also why you asked me to park at Alonso's house and come straight back here? You didn't want me to knock at the front door."

Corey runs a hand over his hair. He really hates this. The way Penny can read him makes him feel like someone has sliced him open and taken out all his feelings and memories, laying them out for careful inspection.

"You haven't told your family about the bargain," Penny says, and it's a statement. She already knows she's right.

"No," Corey admits. He doesn't plan on saying anything else, but Penny looks at him without judgment. Without pity. She's just listening.

And suddenly he's spilling everything.

"I don't know how to tell them. Everyone is still reeling from what happened, and if they find out what my grandpa did to us? How much worse will that make the pain? At least right now they think he loved us."

"He might've loved all of you. Just because you love someone doesn't mean you're not going to hurt them."

"I guess that's the theme of my entire life." Corey turns back to the house.

It's too still. The blinds are all drawn. There's

no hum of air conditioning or sound of his grandpa clearing his throat from somewhere inside. It makes Corey's skin crawl.

As if she can read his mind, Penny steps forward. "I'll go in first."

Penny

THE AIR INSIDE CHARLES BARRION'S HOUSE IS dark and stale. Penny fights the urge to hold her breath as she flicks the nearest light switch. The yellow glow struggling to be seen through the dusty light fixture somehow makes the house even lonelier. She deliberately avoids looking at the floor around the entryway—the place where Charles Barrion's body was found.

Corey stands at the threshold, eyes blank.

"You don't have to come in," Penny says. "Just tell me where to look—"

"No," Corey says. "I'm fine." He sniffs and rubs his nose once, hard, before he walks past her into what must be the living room.

Penny swallows. "I'll search the kitchen?"

"Sure," Corey calls from the other room. A second later there's the *thwop* of what sounds like papers and magazines being dropped onto the floor.

Penny walks into the kitchen.

She's not sure what she expected. This is the home of the man who murdered Giovanni De Luca and his own wife in exchange for success. Surely his house would be opulent. Lots of gold filigree, right? Maybe a statue of himself?

Except there's none of that. This just feels like an old person's house. A middle-class old person, at that, even though some of the art on the walls is probably worth enough money to pay for someone's college tuition.

The kitchen tiles are old but clean, like they were taken care of for decades. The counter is tiny, the oven tinier, with a yellowed stovetop. Instead of curtains, white blinds cover the window, letting in the last slivers of evening light. A loud clock marks each passing second like a death knell.

Penny shivers, wrapping her arms around herself. Then she gets to searching.

If Corey is going to create a bargain, he needs the missing page from the very much illegal spell book they found in Alonso's basement. *The Blackfire Grimoire* is as dangerous as it sounds, full of dark magic that can hex and curse and, yes, trade human life for success and riches. But according to Milton Pierre, bargains can be made for good, too. The problem isn't the spell; the problem is people.

But Corey is good. Not perfect—though that's what Penny used to think. No, Corey is as human as the rest of them, but his intentions are good. He might be Charles Barrion's grandson, but Corey is nothing like him. Which is why Penny is certain he'll be able to create a new bargain.

He'll have to kill, a voice whispers.

Penny shakes her head to get rid of that thought. Unlike Corey, Penny wants to believe they can find another way. They have to. Corey can't become a murderer.

Penny continues digging through drawers, sorting through tiny address books and recipes on index cards and bills for a landline that's probably been disconnected by now. She looks in every cupboard, piling glasses and plates on the counters to see if the laminate liners are loose. She checks the garbage.

Nothing.

Penny sighs and goes to find Corey. He's

sitting on the floor in the middle of the living room, going through a stack of papers.

"Any luck?" Penny asks, but his furrowed brow tells her the answer.

"It should stand out," Corey says.

He's right. All the pages in *The Blackfire Grimoire* are made of animal hide—though what kind of animal, Penny doesn't want to know.

"Yeah." Penny sucks in a breath. "Let's keep looking?"

They move on, together this time. They look in the office, then the guest room. They search under the bathroom sink and in the linen closet.

Last is Charles Barrion's bedroom.

Penny takes the nightstand and Corey takes the dresser. Penny is torn between making conversation to distract from the horrors of what they're doing and staying silent out of respect for the dead, even if this particular dead person didn't respect her. But she gets distracted when she pulls a stack of letters from the nightstand.

She opens one, unfolding the letter. *Dear Charles…* it begins, and when Penny's eyes find the sign-off, she gasps.

This is a letter from Corey's grandmother, Ellie Barrion.

She almost puts them back, because knowing what she knows about how Ellie Barrion's life ended, reading these might make her physically ill. But no stone can be left unturned, so Penny looks through them one by one.

They're love letters starting in the early 1970s, with the final letter dated 1975, four years before Ellie died. By then, Charles and Ellie were married, and Helen was about to be born. There's probably no need to write love letters when you're in bed next to each other.

Penny sifts through them just in case the spell is hidden inside. All she finds are pages so worn with reading that the creases are see-through in some places. She sighs, tucking the letters back into the envelopes and closing the nightstand. She turns to Corey, about to ask what she can help with.

But Corey isn't moving. He's standing in front of an open drawer, gripping its edge so hard his hand is shaking.

"Corey?" Penny says, walking up to him. "What's wrong?"

Corey swallows, and that's when Penny sees his eyes. They glimmer in the dim light, wet with tears. But his jaw is clenched shut, and he doesn't make a sound.

Penny follows his gaze to the framed photos on the dresser. There's a photo of Ellie, and at first Penny is convinced this is what Corey is looking at. Then she sees the small frame behind it. In it is a photo of Charles, a little younger, beaming as he holds a tiny Black boy in his lap. Corey can't be more than four or five, and he's laughing, his big smile infectious.

"Is it wrong to be sad about this?" Corey asks.

Penny's own eyes begin to sting. "Grief isn't about right and wrong."

"He hurt all of us. And he could still look us in the eyes afterward and pretend none of it was his fault." Corey lets out a low, pained breath. "Why do I care that he's gone?"

Penny doesn't answer. She just puts a hand on Corey's forearm, and they stand there until the sun is gone for the night.

7

Corey

COREY WAVES FROM THE PORCH OF MEREDITH House as Penny backs out of the De Lucas' driveway. When she's out of sight, Corey slumps over, pinching the bridge of his nose.

There was no sign of the spell: not in cabinets, not under mattresses or loose floorboards. They checked for false bottoms in all the drawers. They took every book off every shelf and flipped through the pages. If the spell had been in Grandpa's house, they would've found it.

Which means it's time for Corey to make a phone call.

As Corey is walking up the stairs, someone clears their throat behind him. It's Aunt Helen, Julian's mom. She's standing in the foyer holding her laptop and a few legal journals, her reading glasses perched on her head.

"Was Penny here?" Aunt Helen asks.

"She stopped by." Not a lie, but definitely not the full truth.

"I see." But Aunt Helen lingers. "Her mom is . . . ?"

Corey gives what he hopes is an encouraging smile. "She's good, I think."

Aunt Helen's shoulders sag, maybe with relief, maybe with sadness. Corey's aunt was dating Penny's mom in secret earlier this year. When Mrs. Emberly was in an accident at Elkie Lake that put her into a coma, Corey told Penny about the magic that had plagued his family for decades. Penny, Corey, and Alonso were able to save Mrs. Emberly, but after that, her relationship with Aunt Helen was over. Aunt Helen had already lost Uncle Jason, Julian's dad; after Mrs. Emberly almost died, she threw herself into work again, not unlike Corey's dad. She's started taking on legal clients for the first time since her husband died, and it's become her entire life—or just a big distraction.

Corey can't blame her. This is why most of the people in his family don't date. But he also understands you can't help loving people sometimes—which is exactly what he's afraid of.

"I'm glad to hear it," Aunt Helen says before heading into the library.

Corey looks after her, pain welling in his chest. Determination renewed, he locks himself in his room and calls Milton Pierre.

"Corey!" Milton says when he picks up, his voice bright. "How are you, man?"

Corey smiles. "Doing okay. You sound happy."

"Big day over here."

"What's happening?"

Milton's voice is full of pride. "You are talking to the newest member of the Council of Witches."

Corey's jaw drops. "Whoa, really? Congratulations!"

As far as Corey can tell, the Council of Witches is the only group that provides rules for witches across the world. It's made up of members of the most prestigious covens, which includes Milton's family. Milton was a huge part of their efforts to save Penny's mom the summer before, but he wasn't on the Council yet. There are only thirteen witches in the group, which includes Milton's grandmother—

"Wait," Corey says, "is your grandma okay?"

"Oh yeah, she's fine. Just retired. She's served

for sixty years, so she deserves a break. Listen, I can't talk for too long because there's a family party I gotta get to, but did you need something?"

Maybe Milton being on the Council is good news. It means he has more power, more influence—and maybe he'll be more willing to help Corey.

"Yeah, actually," Corey says, "I need a copy of *The Blackfire Grimoire*."

The words are met with silence, and Corey's stomach drops.

"You need that bargain spell," Milton finally says.

"Yeah. It was stolen from the De Lucas' copy."

"By . . . ?"

Corey sighs. "My grandfather, probably."

"Right. I was sorry to hear what happened there. Did they find out who did it?"

"Not yet. There are no leads, as far as I know."

Milton pauses. "None at all? He must've had security cameras, right?"

Corey doesn't want to talk about this, but he forces the words out anyway. "There was nothing salvageable. Whoever did it, they messed with the cameras."

"Huh." Milton pauses again, as if there's something he's not saying.

"I'm not asking for help with that," Corey says.

"Well, I hope they find whoever did it, and fast. But back to the book…" Milton sighs. "I hate to tell you this, Corey, but *The Blackfire Grimoire* is hard to find. My coven doesn't even keep a copy."

Corey tries to ignore the rising panic that's making his eyes lose focus. He hadn't even considered this as a possibility. If anyone had *The Blackfire Grimoire*, shouldn't it be a member of one of the most powerful covens in the world? Corey pushes him. "But the De Lucas had a copy, and they were in exile for decades."

"That's actually *why* they had a copy. The Council issued an order that every single one of them had to be destroyed back in the nineties. The spells in that book were causing too much trouble, giving witches all over the world a bad name. The De Lucas should've handed theirs over to the Council, but they probably weren't on that mailing list, and there's no reason the Council would've followed up with them. The truth is that you'll be hard-pressed to find an intact copy."

"Right," Corey mutters, his voice small. "So how do I... I mean, there's got to be something I can do, right? Because the bargain..." He trails off, hoping Milton hears what he's not saying: that he's scared. That, as the days go on, Corey feels more and more urgency to create his own bargain and save his family—and himself—from whatever the future holds for them.

There's a long silence on the other end of the call. Eventually, Milton says, "I'm real busy the next few weeks with Council stuff, but let me see what I can do. I'll text you."

"Okay. Thank you."

What he doesn't say before they get off the phone is that even weeks feels like too long. Corey tosses his phone onto the bed, his mind desperately searching for a way out of this. He'll have to look for that spell one more time. And he'll need Alonso with him.

Milton

WHEN MILTON GETS OFF THE PHONE WITH Corey, he stares at the screen for a beat. Then he shouts, "Marley!"

He waits.

And waits.

"MARLEY!"

There's a rustle from the front of Second World Emporium, and Marley appears in the doorway to the stockroom. Music blasts from her phone, and she makes no move to turn it off. As usual, she's dressed in bright primary colors. Today it's a blue pleated skirt with a matching oversized sweater. Her dusty apron doesn't look like a work uniform; it looks like punishment.

Which it is.

"Having dinner in a closet again?" Marley says, smirking. "Did you forget we have a break room?"

Milton glances down at the cardboard box he's sitting on, which may or may not be structurally sound. "I needed space to think." He nods at the pocket of her apron. "Can Biggie give us a few minutes to talk?"

Marley sighs, but she pauses her music.

"Close the door."

From the look on her face, Marley probably wants to make a shitty remark, but something—maybe curiosity—stops her. She closes the door. "You can't boss me around just because you're Council now."

"I can boss you around because I'm your older brother." Milton tries to make his tone casual as he asks, "You heard from Dot?"

"Do you have a weekly alarm set to ask me that question or is your internal clock just *impeccable*?"

Milton narrows his eyes.

Marley throws up her hands. "No, Milton, I have not heard from my ex-boyfriend. Because he's my *ex. Boyfriend.*"

"I don't mean to make you upset by bringing him up—"

"I'm not upset!"

"I just worry," Milton says. "Because I love you."

"Don't pull the I-love-you card right now. I'm too soft for that."

"That's why I did it. Anyway, it's for the best. From the moment you two met, it was constant trouble."

"The last time was different," Marley mutters.

"You do understand the gravity of what you did, right?" Milton says. "Because you almost got our coven exiled. And, oh yeah, you almost died."

Marley presses her lips together and stares at the floor. "I think about it every day. Is that what you want to hear? Because it's true."

Milton frowns. His goal isn't to make Marley relive what happened, but there's danger in forgetting. If Marley makes another mistake of this magnitude, she won't be the only one in trouble. Milton will have to answer for it, too.

But this is still his sister. He doesn't want to see her life reduced to this store, even to this town. As she's worked her days away in Second World Emporium over the last few months, Milton has seen how closely she's teetered to depression.

Milton wants something better for her. And he believes she wants it, too, even if she's too proud to ask for a second chance.

"I believe you," Milton says. Marley continues

to stare at the floor, so he pushes to his feet and walks over to her. "Don't you want to know why I called you in here?"

"To remind me that I almost destroyed our family's reputation?"

"Nope." Milton leans down so they're eye level, just like he's done since they were little.

Marley avoids his eyes at first, but eventually she can't anymore. She looks like she hates him a little, but Milton knows she loves him more. "Nobody's minding the front of the store right now, so you better tell me quick—"

"I have a job for you."

Marley's expression falls. "Please don't make me sort any more bundles of horsehair."

"It's not a job in the store. It's a job in the field."

That gets Marley's attention. "The…the field?"

"You want a chance to redeem yourself to Park YeaLee and the Council?" Milton says. "This is it."

It was Park YeaLee—the head of the Council of Witches and the descendent of Park HaeJung, one of the most powerful witches in history— who decided to be lenient with Marley after the incident with her, Dot, and a very young witch from Brooklyn. But it was also Park YeaLee who decided Marley's innate talents were too dangerous for her to use anymore.

Marley's brows furrow. She's intrigued, but she's trying not to show it. "What's the job?"

"There's a missing spell from *The Blackfire Grimoire*. The group in Idlewood needs help finding it."

"That's it? Why can't the De Luca coven handle that?"

"Normally, they could."

"So things aren't normal?"

"There's something going on with the youngest member of their coven."

"Alonso, right?"

"Yeah." Milton thinks back to August. After Penny Emberly crossed the Veil, they all rushed to the hospital to make sure her mom was okay— only to find out that she'd been pronounced dead. But seconds later, she was back.

To Milton's eyes, nothing happened. The heart monitor could've been faulty. The doctors and nurses could've been exceptionally bad at their jobs. But Milton is a witch. A damn strong one at that. And he felt something in the room that day, like a whole new presence. Something malevolent.

Milton watched Alonso closely as he was swept up in the celebrations, but Alonso didn't seem to notice. He only had eyes for Penny.

What would Alonso have risked to save her mom?

"Last summer, I tried to help the De Lucas and the Barrions," Milton says. "I'm starting to think that was a mistake."

"Why?"

"We'll get to that. First, I want you to help Corey Barrion find that spell, but I also need you to keep an eye on Alonso."

"You want me to tattle on him? To *you*?"

"Not the words I'd use, but sure, let's go with that."

"You're not going to tell me what I'm looking for?"

Milton laughs under his breath. "I'm surprised you gotta ask me that. You and Dot got into a very particular kind of trouble. Why do you think I'm asking you?"

It clicks, and Marley narrows her eyes. "You think Alonso is possessed."

"Maybe. You know the signs better than anyone. I already got you a hotel room, so you should leave tonight."

"But your party! You just became a member of the Council today—"

"You can party with me when you get back. This is more important." Milton drops his voice lower, in case their grandma is around. "I'm trusting you, M. No more rescue missions this time. You do what is required under Council law—unless you want to be tied to Bloomington for the rest of your life."

Milton holds out his hand. In it is a key, but not one made out of metal. It's been painstakingly folded from paper.

Marley stares unblinking at it. Then she takes the key, which begins to unfold until it lays flat in her hand, a simple piece of paper with MARLEY PIERRE written across it.

Marley is already untying her apron with her other hand. "I guess I'm going to Idlewood," she says, the old glint of mischief in her eyes. She's not scared at the prospect of ghosts or anything else. That's her problem.

"Don't let me down," Milton says.

Marley's smile fades. "I won't. I promise."

Penny

"WHERE'S ALONSO BEEN?"

Penny looks up from the pastry case with bleary eyes. It's barely past seven in the morning, but she's insisted on helping out more at the café on weekdays.

Naomi's voice rings in her head: *Are you helping your mom or just avoiding college applications?*

Penny ignores the echoes of her best friend's question. She knows the early deadline is approaching for most schools, but she'll get the applications done before the regular deadline. She just doesn't want to think about it yet.

"What do you mean?" Penny says. "He's around."

Penny's mom, Anita, pours beans into the coffee grinder. "I haven't seen him in a while. Usually he comes over in the evenings. Everything okay?"

"Oh, he's fine! Lots of homework. And he's been having trouble with migraines."

"Migraines! That's a bummer."

Penny narrows her eyes at her mom's forced nonchalance. "Can you say whatever you're not saying out loud, please? I feel like I'm being judged for something."

Anita sighs and leans back against the counter. "Sly told me, Penny. About what happened at Boxer's?"

Penny's stomach drops. She thought she was in the clear by now, but her mom has probably known about the fight at Boxer's for days and was waiting for the "right moment" to bring it up. Anita Emberly is nothing if not tactful.

Penny sets down the tray of croissants, but she avoids looking at her mom. "I know how it sounds."

"It sounds like he hurt someone. If it hadn't been the town drunk, he might've sued the De Lucas—"

"You weren't there, Mom. The guy was threatening Corey."

Penny's mom watches her with soft eyes. "Alonso is a good guy."

It's not what Penny was expecting, and it

catches her so off guard that she loses whatever she was about to say next. "Do you actually believe that?"

"I do. My memories of last summer are fuzzy, but I know what he did for me." Penny's mom considers her. "I've just seen the bad things that magic can do. Up close and personal."

"He's not cursing people."

"I know. But that kind of power in someone so young…it's a big responsibility. Don't give me that look, Penny, all I'm saying is that Alonso might have some growing pains." She crosses her arms. "I want you to be careful. If he gets violent—"

"He won't," Penny says. "But if he does, I'm not just going to stand by and let it happen."

The bell over the door rings, cutting off their conversation. Her mom puts on one of her warm customer-service smiles as she takes Mr. Washington's order ("The usual, Anita, but less sugar this time unless you want my doctor to come for you"). Penny smiles, too, but when Mr. Washington goes to sit in one of the booths, her mom turns to her again and lowers her voice to a whisper.

"I know you wouldn't be okay with him abusing his magic, sweet pea." She cups Penny's face with one hand. "I'm sorry. I'm just fretting. I've never had a child date a witch before."

Penny almost smiles. "I know."

Anita kisses Penny's forehead, and then she starts making Mr. Washington's "low-sugar" caramel macchiato. Penny ducks into the back office, her phone pressed to her ear.

Alonso's voice comes through muffled on the other end. "Mrph. Hello?"

"Time to get up."

Alonso sighs. "I slept through my fucking alarm again. Ugh, my head…"

"Still hurting?"

"It's fine. I'll make it to school."

Penny pauses. "Want me to pick you up?"

Alonso laughs, and it sends a feeling stirring low in Penny's stomach. "I guess you're my girl-friend, right? So you don't mind picking me up?"

"That's how relationships work."

"Okay. But you should leave right now."

"You don't want more time to get ready?"

"No. I want you."

Desire snakes up her limbs. "I'm on my way," she whispers.

As soon as they're off the phone, Penny throws off her apron and puts on her plaid coat.

She peeks out into the front of the café. "Do you mind if I use the Prius? Alonso still has a headache so I told him I'd drive him to school."

"Sure thing, sweet pea." But her mom still looks worried.

Penny holds her gaze. "I heard you. I promise."

Anita winks, and then Penny is out the door and into the crisp air. She brushes a few leaves off the window. People say autumn is the season of change. So why does Penny feel so comforted by it? Its rhythms are familiar, from the smell of apple to the shock of the cold.

When Penny arrives at the De Luca home, Alonso is already waiting at the foot of the driveway. He runs to the car, opening the door before she's even fully stopped.

"What are you—" Penny says, but he pulls her into a kiss. She relaxes into it, threading her fingers into his hair.

"Mm," Alonso murmurs against her mouth. "I feel better already."

But when Penny gets them back on the road, they fall into silence. Penny tries to think of something to say, but all she can do is shift in her seat and glance over at him. Alonso alternates between staring out the window and scrolling through his phone, not even registering when Penny clears her throat.

"Want to come over for dinner tonight?" Penny asks.

"I can't. So much homework to catch up on." He doesn't even look at her as he says it. "How are your college applications?"

"I…I'm still finalizing my list."

Now Alonso looks at her. "So you haven't started?"

He probably doesn't mean to sound critical, but Penny shrinks from this like he's accused her of murder. "I didn't say that."

"I hope you're not holding yourself back because of me."

"No! I just have a hard time picturing myself anywhere but here." That's only partly a lie. She was also waiting for Alonso to share his list with her. Maybe they could apply to some of the same schools. That doesn't mean she's holding herself back, does it?

Alonso reaches over, grabbing her thigh. "You'll figure it out."

As they fall into silence again, Penny can't help but wonder if he doesn't want them to go to the same school at all.

10

Corey

THE LINEBACKER CRASHES INTO COREY AT THE twenty-yard line.

"Yeowch!" says Mr. Riley over the speaker. "Number three, Corey Barrion, is knocked down again! The Williams High School team has been targeting the quarterback all night, and they seem to be succeeding in slowing him down."

There's a chorus of boos from the Idlewood Central fans. The linebacker offers Corey a hand, and Corey takes it without looking his opponent in the eyes.

He's been distracted tonight. His team has been down six points since the first quarter, and they're coming up on halftime. Corey needs to get it together.

As they line up for the next play, Corey glances up at the stands. There's Penny, sitting on the righthand bleachers with Naomi on one side and Alonso on the other. Penny and Naomi are watching the field and whispering to each other, looking worried. Alonso must sense Corey's gaze, because he gives him two thumbs up.

Helpful.

Corey lets out a harsh breath through his teeth. Then he crouches down, preparing to shout out the play.

That's when a dark-haired figure moves in Corey's peripheral vision. When he glances at the stands again, there's a familiar face sitting in the front row.

Julian.

He drove Corey to school, but when they parked, he wouldn't get out of the car. Corey was half convinced his cousin was going to abandon him, that Corey would end up hitching a ride from one of his teammates.

But Julian didn't leave. Now he's glancing around rapidly as if he needs to keep an eye on everyone sitting near him. As if they might hurt him once his back is turned.

"Let's go, man," says one of Corey's teammates.

Corey grits his teeth and calls out the play.

Within four seconds, as Corey is about to throw the football, someone hits him from the side. The wind is forced from Corey's lungs as he crashes into the ground, and before he can blink, three Williams players pile on top of him. There might be more, but Corey is too busy struggling to breathe to count them.

"That's halftime!" Mr. Riley says. He doesn't sound as energetic as usual. Probably because Corey is making the Idlewood Central Tigers have their worst game of the season.

His teammates clap him on the shoulders, tell him that he's doing fine. Even Coach Amodeo tries to tell him it isn't his fault as they're strategizing for the next quarter. They all know it's a lie, but the team needs Corey to keep up his morale.

Maybe he'll feel better after he checks on Julian.

After he grabs a Gatorade, he heads out to the bleachers. Over the speakers, Mr. Riley says, "And a special thank-you to Barrion Heating & Cooling, Idlewood Central's athletic sponsors for twenty-five years and counting! Join the Barrions in December for the opening of the brand-new Charles Barrion Center for Community and Belonging, in memory of the late, great patriarch of the family."

Julian is leaning forward, one knee bouncing

wildly. Corey's shadow makes him flinch, but when his eyes find Corey's face, he relaxes a little. "Hey."

"You good?"

Julian glances around again, suspicion sharpening the already sharp angles of his face. "Grandpa's murderer could be here right now. They could be watching us. So no, Corey, I'm not good. I shouldn't be here to begin with."

Corey crouches down so he can look Julian in the eyes. "Your therapist said it was time. You have to practice going to places with crowds. That will train your brain not to panic."

"I'm not sure my brain is capable of that."

"It is. And when you get nervous, just remember I'm right here," Corey says, nodding toward the field.

"I'm distracting you," Julian says. "That's why you're playing like shit."

Corey works his jaw. "My head just isn't in it."

Julian gives him a look of mock pity. "What about your *heart*, Corey? If you're gonna play this in college, you have to care about it."

That comment sends a prickle of annoyance down Corey's spine. "I don't need that right now. I have a game to finish."

"Maybe what you need is to tell your dad you don't actually want to play football anymore."

"I do want to play."

Julian laughs and looks away. "Sure."

Corey wants to leave before the conversation gets worse, but he knows what that would do to Julian's anxiety. He'd never agree to come to a game again. It felt like a huge victory just getting him out of the house for a single night; Corey can't screw this up.

Julian must see Corey's annoyance, because he curls in on himself like an insect. "I need a higher dose of my medication. Forty milligrams isn't doing anything."

"At least now you know, right? You wouldn't know if you hadn't come out."

Someone clears their throat from behind Corey. "Hey, guys."

Penny stands a few feet away. She's wearing Alonso's big leather jacket, and it reaches halfway down her thighs. The floodlight behind her shines through her wild curls.

Corey stands up, trying to hide how relieved he is to not have to continue that conversation with Julian. "Hey. How's it going?"

"*I'm* fine. You?"

Corey laughs bitterly. "Getting through."

"It's not your fault. I'll tell Alonso he needs to scream louder."

"Perfect, thanks."

Penny's eyes move to Julian, and her smile grows softer. "It's good to see you, Julian."

"Doubt that," he mutters.

Penny doesn't even flinch. "We're a few rows up, if you want to come sit with us?"

Corey's chest feels like it's made of guitar strings, and someone is tightening them until there's no more slack to give. *Thank you*, he wants to say, but he can't. Not in front of his cousin, who's looking at Penny like she just suggested he take off his clothes and streak across the football field.

"I'm staying here," Julian snaps.

"Come up if you change your mind." She walks toward the stairs, waving at them. "Good luck, Corey!"

Corey waves back. When she's out of earshot, he clears his throat.

"I already know what you want to say. Don't lecture me," Julian says, shooting to his feet.

"Hey," Corey says, stepping in front of him. "Just listen—"

"Did you listen to me when I said I didn't want to come tonight?" Julian says, shoving past him and disappearing toward the concession stand.

"Julian!" Corey calls, but his cousin leaves him alone, helmet dangling from his fingers.

Alonso

IT'S HALFTIME, AND THE CHEERLEADERS ARE doing gymnastics to some soulless dance pop track. Even though Alonso's migraine is turning the stands into an impressionist painting of movement and color and bright lights, his eyes find Penny immediately as she walks up the stairs. She moves to step over him, but he lurches forward and pulls her into his lap, the thudding in his head already growing duller. The migraines have become more common, forcing Alonso to take medicine almost every day even though it barely helps. Being with Penny is the only thing that makes it easier to ignore the pain.

"No snacks?" Naomi asks, deflating.

"I went to the bathroom," Penny says as she slides from Alonso's lap to the seat.

"And to talk to Julian Chaudhary?" Naomi says. "You're lucky he didn't hit you with a rock."

Alonso flinches at the memory of Julian attacking him at Elkie Lake. He rubs his temples. "Maybe Julian triggered this headache shit. I think I need to take another pill."

"Here—oh." Penny gazes sadly into her empty water bottle.

"I'll refill it. And grab snacks," Alonso says, kissing her on the cheek before bounding down the steps.

"Twix!" Naomi calls after him.

Alonso joins the line. The smell of popcorn and hot dogs makes him feel sick, but he'll be fine once he takes his headache meds.

There's a sharp intake of breath behind him. Normally Alonso would ignore it, but the way it cuts through the chatter, he can't help but glance over his shoulder.

And behind him stands Julian.

Corey's cousin is looking at Alonso like he's a caged animal that's been set loose on the general public. Alonso's good mood turns, and his headache immediately gets worse.

Alonso and Julian don't have much history, but what they do share are bad memories. Even if Penny wants to make nice with him, Alonso wouldn't complain if he never had to see Julian again in his life. Sure, Julian has been through bad stuff, but that doesn't change the fact that he's sniveling and he's cruel.

And now he's staring at Alonso in a way that really annoys him.

"What?" Alonso snaps.

Julian looks away, and his face grows red—with what? Embarrassment? Anger? Whatever it is, Alonso doesn't care. He'll never speak to Julian again if he can help it.

Where's the fun in that? says a voice in Alonso's ear.

"What?" Alonso says, looking around, but there's nobody there. A light flickers above him, and Alonso's eye is drawn to it. It pulses like a heartbeat, the whine of the electricity growing louder every time the light goes bright. Alonso is seeing spots, and he should look away, but he can't. It's hypnotic.

If he stares at it long enough, he suddenly believes his headache will get better. Forget the prescription in his back pocket. There's something so soothing about the light…

Then the light bulb pops, and Alonso falls into darkness.

Giovanni

AS SHARDS OF THE LIGHT BULB RAIN DOWN AND the people around him gasp and jump back, Giovanni De Luca closes his grandson's eyes.

They don't feel like sombody else's eyes, though; they feel like they belong to him.

He relishes in the feeling of blood pumping under his skin. Of all the sensations he thought he would miss after death, he never would've guessed he'd miss this the most. He didn't even realize how strong a heartbeat is, how loud the rush of blood in your ears.

It's delicious, being alive again.

"The line's moving."

Giovanni opens his eyes. Behind him stands a surly young man, watching him with a mixture of nervousness and unadulterated hatred.

Giovanni searches Alonso's memories until he

finds the name: *Julian Chaudhary*. Charles Barrion's grandson.

"The *line*," Julian says again, his tone sharp. "Look in front of you."

Giovanni considers, then he steps back until he and Julian are shoulder to shoulder. Julian veers from angry to terrified.

Excellent.

Gio has been waiting for this opportunity, and he's not about to squander it. His grandson has subconsciously been keeping Gio locked away since that night in August when he paid Charles Barrion his last visit. Gio wasn't anticipating that Alonso would have such a strong will. The one upside is that this has allowed Gio to save up his energy. Now that he's free—for how long, he isn't sure—he can't waste time.

He has a family to destroy, after all. And something tells him this Julian Chaudhary could be very useful.

Gio clears his throat. "I was trying to find the right words to say sorry about your grandfather."

Julian's expression goes blank.

"What a shame," Gio says. "A real loss to the community."

Julian lets out a low, pained breath. "Don't talk about him. Ever."

Gio arranges his grandson's face into an expression of concerned confusion. "Why not?"

"Because," Julian spits, "your family made his life hell. He never got over the—" He cuts off, glancing around them. Then the line starts moving again, and Julian steps forward, deliberately facing away from Giovanni.

Gio moves so they're side by side again. "He never got over what?"

"Stop talking to me."

"After you answer my question."

Julian accesses some of his bravery at last. He leans in and whispers, "Never got over the murder of half his family. Including my grandma. You remember that?"

"No," Giovanni says. "I wasn't alive at the time."

Julian gives him an incredulous look. Before he can say anything else, Gio cuts in with, "Back to your grandfather. Have you found the person who did it?"

"I'm not talking about this with you."

Giovanni almost lets him go. He can venture into the night, find other Barrions to toy with.

Maybe he can even visit Barrion Heating & Cooling.

Then Gio remembers the girl. Penny Emberly.

She's always there. He can sense her at Alonso's side. Somehow, she's made it more difficult for Giovanni to take control. The boy is too attached to her.

Giovanni needs to change that. But that's a problem for another day. In the meantime, he'll keep working on Julian.

He shrugs, letting a smile play at his lips. "I understand."

Julian looks taken aback. "Really."

"Yes." He pauses. He needs to gain Julian's trust. Draw him in. "I was surprised how quickly Corey . . . well. Never mind."

Julian narrows his eyes. "What about Corey?"

Gio sighs, as if he's reluctant to share this thought out loud. "He just seemed to move on right away. He barely even took time off school."

This is a risk. Julian could get angry and march away. He could cause a scene.

But he doesn't. He stands stock still, eyes unreadable.

"You noticed that?" Julian says, his voice low.

Bingo.

Gio shrugs. He can't seem too eager to tear Corey down. "I thought it was weird. Everyone grieves differently, I guess."

"That's what they tell me," Julian mutters.

"And you…?"

Julian laughs under his breath, but he doesn't answer.

"I see."

Julian examines him. "Why are you talking like that? You sound like a different person."

"Migraine," Gio says, distantly registering the ache in his grandson's head. His body is under stress from holding two spirits, and its cracks are starting to show. But it's easy for Gio to ignore it.

"Oh." Julian pauses, and almost too quietly for Gio to hear, he says, "I get those, too. I can feel one coming on. I told Corey I shouldn't be here…"

Julian's breath smells painfully of mint. It's almost astringent, and the scent makes Giovanni woozy. Of course. Spirits like him—*poltergeists*, the living call them—don't react well to mint. It's a defensive herb.

If only they made toothpaste out of hemlock.

Giovanni has to work quickly. He steps closer to Julian. "That explains it."

Julian looks suspicious again. "Explains what?"

"Why you look a little pale…" Gio lets his fingers brush Julian's wrist, and then he whispers a spell under his breath:

"Projection, deception,
From my mind to your eye,
See what I see."

Julian gasps as his eyes go wide, staring several feet ahead of them at an empty stretch of cinderblock wall next to the concession stand.

"Julian?" Gio says, but he feels the smile playing at his lips. "What's wrong?"

"He's here," Julian says.

"Who?" Gio asks as if he doesn't know.

"Grandpa," Julian chokes out.

Then he tumbles to the ground.

Penny

PENNY CRANES HER NECK, LOOKING FOR ALON-so's messy red-and-blond hair. "The game is about to start. Where is he?"

Naomi shrugs. "Maybe he's punching someone."

"Naomi."

"I'm kidding! There's probably a line for concessions." She nods down at the field. "Go find him. I want my Twix."

Penny moves quickly down the bleachers. When she turns the corner to the concession stand, there's no line at all.

There's chaos.

The crowd shifts like an ocean, but everyone is looking in the same direction. Penny moves closer, trying to make out what people are saying.

"He fainted!"

"Someone get the EMTs!"

Fear unfurls in Penny's stomach. She pushes

to get to the middle of the crowd, eyes on the ground, already preparing herself to see Alonso unconscious—

But it isn't Alonso who's on the ground. It's Julian. Alonso is standing above him, arms crossed as he looks down with an unconcerned expression.

Penny gasps. And, even though there's no way he should be able to hear her over the noise of the crowd, he looks straight at her.

But his face is different. For a moment, it doesn't even look like him. The light is strange in his eyes. For a moment, they almost look—

Green.

It stops Penny in her tracks. They watch each other for a long moment. But Alonso shifts, and when the light hits his eyes again, they're gray like always.

And Julian is still lying crumpled on the ground.

Penny runs, falling to her knees next to Julian. He's dead weight, but Penny manages to lift his head onto her legs. His eyes are closed, but his face is screwed up, as if he's seeing a monster behind his eyelids.

"What happened?" Penny says, looking up at Alonso.

But he's staring down at Julian with wide, shocked eyes. "Huh? He…what do you mean?" He takes in their surroundings, blinking rapidly.

"Alonso," Penny says, her voice low. *Did you do this?* she wants to yell, but there are too many people around.

Julian is still out cold, but his face looks pained. A minute later, the crowd around them shifts and a voice shouts, "Make a path, please!" Two EMTs appear with a stretcher, and they lay it down on the ground next to Julian.

"Why did he pass out?" one of them asks.

"I…I don't know," Penny says. She can feel Alonso standing behind her, but he doesn't offer an explanation either.

In the same second, Julian's eyes shoot open, and he sits up with a half scream, half gasp.

Penny falls back, and the EMTs jump. Julian sucks in air, each breath sounding painful. Then he twists around, and when his eyes focus on Penny, his expression goes from shocked to murderous.

"Get *away* from me!" His vitriol is so palpable, Penny flinches. Julian glances behind her, and she knows he's looking at Alonso now. Something like horror passes over his face, but then he turns his attention to the EMTs, who are trying to get him onto the stretcher.

Penny makes it to her feet and backs up. That's when she feels his hand on her.

"Penny," Alonso says, his voice ragged.

Penny looks up into his guilt-ridden face. Then he's pulling her away and under the bleachers. Floodlights shine far above them, and strips of light paint the ground and their bodies as they move farther underneath.

"Alonso, *stop*," Penny says, but he doesn't. He keeps going until they've almost reached the other side. Every few seconds, the bleachers shake with heavy footsteps as people climb up and down. It brings Penny back to their night under the bridge a week ago, but somehow, things feel different now.

Because Penny can't stop seeing that blank expression that was on Alonso's face when she walked up.

"What was that?" she says.

Alonso's eyes are wide, and his shoulders heave as if he's just run a marathon. "Nothing! We were talking and then...and then I..." He squeezes his eyes shut.

"And then what?" Penny doesn't mean for the words to come out jagged. Mean. But something just happened to Corey's cousin, and instead of owning up to it, Alonso is stalling. Like he's not sure how to explain this when he might've been the only witness.

Alonso's eyes narrow. "Why do you sound angry?"

"Because it didn't look good!"

"It never looks good when it comes to me. Everyone always wants to assume the worst. I just thought that didn't include you anymore."

Penny doesn't have a response for that. Because he's right—she *did* assume he had something to do with it. But she needs him to prove her wrong.

Alonso rubs his temples again. "I didn't even see him faint. I honestly don't remember it happening. This headache...I can barely open my eyes."

Penny softens a little. She's seen the way migraines pull him out of the present, how they put him in a bad mood. Maybe he's telling the truth. Alonso might yell at Julian, but he wouldn't deliberately hurt him, would he?

"I swear, if I'd seen it I would've tried to catch

him or something, okay?" Alonso says. "Or do you not believe that either?"

"Of course I do," Penny says, her voice small.

They stand there as the football game continues around them, all happy cheers and laughter and screaming. But in Penny's chest there's a sense of dread. Of something being so very wrong—but she's not sure if she's the one who's wrong, or if it's Alonso.

She wants it to be her. She was jumping to conclusions after all. Why?

Because of the way Alonso just stood by. The detached look on his face. And that moment when his eyes...they looked different. They seemed almost green, but that can't be right. Penny was seeing things.

"Let's go," Penny says. "We'll get you some water."

Alonso gives her a long, dark look. Then he nods.

On the field, Mr. Riley's voice echoes over the speakers. "Welcome back to the third quarter, folks! Can the Tigers make a comeback after a painful first half, or are they too far gone? Only time will tell..."

Corey

THE FINAL SCORE IS FOURTEEN TO TWENTY. THE Tigers lose.

Nobody on the team is comforting Corey anymore. Everyone feels the weight of the loss like an anvil. They all move slowly as they take off their gear. Brandon Kroller throws his helmet against the wall and gets told off by Coach Amodeo.

Through it all, their eyes are on Corey.

He doesn't bother drying off before he puts his clothes on. Nobody even says "good game" as he walks out the door, but that's fine. He doesn't need them to lie, to remind him that he let down a team that always has his back on the field. The sooner Corey can escape the locker room, the better.

The problem isn't that Corey's upset. It's that he should be, but he can't find it in himself to care.

Ever since middle school, football has been a

huge part of his life. But lately, he's been dreading practices. Dreading games even more. Every minute he spends playing football feels like an hour—and it's all wasted.

But if he wasn't playing football or working at the company or going to school, what would Corey be doing? Nothing. Because those things are his entire personality, even though it all makes him feel insubstantial. Like a ghost.

When Corey rounds the corner, he bumps into someone.

"Oof!" the guy says. "Oh, Corey! I was just looking for you."

It's Arvin, one of the EMTs that works their games. "Sorry about that."

"Hey, it's okay. Everyone has off nights."

"I meant for bumping into— Never mind. I'll see you later?"

"One second! I told your cousin I'd find you."

"My cousin?" Corey's heart drops. "Why?"

Arvin holds up his hands. "Before I get into this, you should know he's okay…"

⎯⎯⎯⎯

Corey runs to the parking lot.

Half of the cars are already gone. They took

Julian's new Mercedes to the game, something Helen bought him to encourage him to go out more. It's easy to spot; even in the dark, it gleams silver as if it's lit from within. The driver's side door is open, and Julian sits half in, half out of the car, with his feet resting on the pavement. He has one hand on his face, and the other grips the door like it's the only thing holding him upright.

"Julian!" Corey says.

His cousin looks up. His eyes are bloodshot, and the grooves around his mouth make him look older than twenty. It's as though he hasn't slept in days.

Corey comes to a stop, breathing hard. "The EMT told me you fell?"

"I passed out," Julian says, his voice low. Suddenly he pushes to his feet. "But before that, I saw something back there. By the concession stand."

Corey waits, but Julian doesn't continue. "What was it?"

Julian works his jaw, like he's not sure if he can get the words out. But then he says, "Grandpa."

And Corey does the worst thing he could possibly do: He laughs.

It's a small laugh. A laugh of disbelief. Corey

can't stop it, and he watches as the sound wraps around Julian's throat like a vise, cutting off his words and his breath and making his eyes bulge in his head.

"Julian," Corey says, his smile fading. "I wasn't laughing *at* you, that just sounds . . ."

"Crazy?" Julian whispers.

"No! No. I just wasn't expecting it." And now that Julian's words are sinking in, Corey's disbelief turns to terror. "You . . . you really saw him?"

"You believe me now?"

"Of course I do."

Now it's Julian's turn to laugh. "No you don't. He *told* me you wouldn't."

"Who?" It's Corey's turn to stop breathing. "Grandpa?"

Julian nods.

Ghosts are real. Corey has known that since this past summer, when Penny started seeing the spirit of his grandmother, Ellie, and they learned about the Second World—the place beyond the Veil, where spirits go after death. So if Julian is telling the truth, and he saw their grandfather . . .

What else did he say to him?

"I do believe you," Corey says. His thoughts are racing. What if Charles Barrion told Julian the truth about the bargain? People must have regrets after they die. Maybe his grandfather wanted to come clean.

Corey lays a hand on Julian's shoulder. "What did he say?"

Julian gives Corey a long look. Then he brushes Corey's hand away and starts walking toward the passenger door. "You should drive."

"Julian—"

Julian whips around. He's so angry that his whole body is shaking. "Is there something you're not telling me?"

Corey draws in a breath. This is it. *The bargain.*

Would Grandpa really have told Julian that there was never a curse on their family like they thought? That all along, people were dying because of the bargain?

The way Julian is looking at him makes Corey stop while he's ahead. Because Julian doesn't just look angry. He looks angry at *Corey.*

"No," Corey manages to say. "Why? What did Grandpa say?"

Julian's face falls. Suddenly he can't meet Corey's eyes. "Nothing that would be interesting to you."

Corey's hope turns sour in his mouth. He

always has to be the one to have patience with Julian. To be understanding.

Sometimes he just can't find it in him.

"You don't want to tell me," Corey says. "Fine. Keep this to yourself if it makes you feel special."

Each word is meant to cut. Corey knows that when Julian loses control of his emotions, he yells. He's brutally honest. And he'll probably tell Corey what their grandfather said—if he saw him at all.

Julian is standing on the other side of the car now, one hand gripping the open passenger door. He looks like he wants to scream. Instead, he gets into the car and slams the door shut.

The drive home is completely silent. When they get to Meredith House, Julian locks himself in his room.

Aunt Helen appears in the hallway, staring at Julian's door with an exhausted expression. "I'm guessing it didn't go well."

"You could say that," Corey mutters before he shuts himself away, too.

Alonso

WHEN ALONSO GETS THE TEXT FROM COREY asking to meet at the lake, he sighs, but he doesn't say no. He throws on his jeans and leather jacket, and as he leaves, Nimble's glowing eyes stare at him from the dark living room. It makes him stop mid-stride. Normally her presence is comforting; today, it leaves him with the feeling of being on the outside. Like she knows something that he doesn't.

And that's exactly how he felt at the football game today, when he and Penny were talking under the bleachers. That, even though Alonso would never hurt Julian, Penny's suspicion meant he was wrong about himself.

Hesitantly, Alonso reaches out a hand to pet Nimble.

She hisses, every hair on her body standing on end until she looks almost twice her usual size.

"Fine," Alonso mutters, but his heart thuds against his ribs.

The nights are getting colder, but Alonso runs hot. He blows out clouds of warm air in front of his face as he skulks through the woods to Elkie Lake.

Corey is there, arms crossed, still as a statue. Alonso has learned that the more unshakable Corey looks from the outside, the closer he is to losing control of his emotions. As someone who can't ever hide how he's feeling, Alonso envies it. But tonight, after the way Penny looked at Alonso, Corey's stoic attitude also makes him nervous.

"Hey," Alonso says.

Corey nods at him. "Thanks for coming out."

"It's no problem," Alonso says, even though it's the middle of the night and it is kind of a problem.

"What happened with Julian?"

There it is again: that sick feeling in Alonso's stomach. No matter how hard he tries to remember, it's all fuzzy, like the football game happened years ago instead of hours.

"He passed out."

Corey whips around, his eyes alight with anger. "He says he saw our grandfather."

That's when Alonso realizes Corey isn't angry at *him*. He's angry at Julian.

"Your grandfather?" Alonso says. "Did he talk to Julian about the bargain or what?"

"Julian won't tell me any details, but I'm pretty sure they didn't talk about the bargain."

"If he won't tell you, then how do you know?"

Corey looks off into the trees, his expression distant. "Because. I haven't told him either."

The pieces click together. "So if Julian found out…"

"He would've said something. But Julian was angry with me. It's like Grandpa—"

"If he really saw him," Alonso says.

Corey nods. "I guess. I get the sense that my grandpa told him something bad about *me*. But I have no idea what it could be. Julian looked up to Grandpa. I don't know how to…" He trails off, and the pain on his face is palpable.

Alonso blows out air between his lips. "So we're finding the bargain spell tonight. That's what we can do."

Corey's face falls, all the anger draining from him like blood from a wound. He looks spent now. Almost sick. "Thank you."

Alonso knows he shouldn't say it, but he can't

help himself. "You shouldn't be taking this on by yourself. Your whole family needs to know."

Corey runs a hand over his hair. "Julian can't handle it. I'm afraid he…I don't know. I'm afraid this would break him."

Alonso wants to argue. But Corey looks desperate, and against Alonso's better judgment, he basically likes him these days. They're friends, or something approximating that. And Corey needs that spell more than he needs a fight. Alonso nods at the path that will lead them out of the woods. "Let's go, Barrion."

They take the long way around Meredith House and end up at a small, dark house at the back of the property. Corey unlocks the door. "Give me a second to turn on the lights," he says before he disappears inside.

Alonso is left staring at the entryway. There's no sign of life in the house; it's like the darkness swallowed Corey up. A shiver passes over Alonso's skin. "All good in there?"

No answer.

"Corey? Are you—ah!" A sudden pain behind his eyes make Alonso double over, clutching his head.

A light inside the house turns on, and Corey's

silhouette appears. "Sorry, there was an outage and I had to reset the fuse. You okay?"

"Just another stupid headache," Alonso grumbles. "Let's get this over with."

They stand in the dim living room. Alonso sucks in a breath, ignoring the pain as he speaks the finding spell:

"From mind to hand,
from wish to presence,
light the journey,
light the eyes."

Magic pulses through Alonso, and it's like the drop at the top of a roller coaster. He forgets about the headache, about the incident with Julian, about everything. Instead, it's him and his magic, which hears his call and obeys.

As the rush subsides, Alonso opens his eyes. "There will be a light from wherever the spell is hidden. We should look around the house."

They rush from room to room, opening closets and looking under and behind furniture. But as the seconds tick by, no light appears.

"Maybe it's taking longer than usual," Alonso says, but something gnaws at him.

"It has to be here. I'll look again." But when Corey's done with his search, his eyes are wide with dread.

"Is there anywhere else it could be?" Alonso asks.

"The police took his laptop. They returned everything else. And he wouldn't have kept it in Meredith House…"

Alonso rubs his chin as his legs carry him toward the door. He's about to say he can try again. Maybe these headaches are messing with his spell work. But when he turns around and looks into the foyer, it isn't Corey he sees standing there.

It's Charles Barrion.

He's wearing a V-neck sweater over a button-up. His hand clutches the top of that ugly cane. And he's staring at Alonso with a look of feral terror.

"You!" Charles Barrion says, and then he falls to the ground.

Alonso leaps forward on instinct, reaching out a hand to catch him. But he's too late, and the scene changes before his eyes.

It's sunny outside. Light falls onto a creeping puddle of blood.

Corey's grandfather lies unmoving on the ground, eyes open but blank, a small red hole in his temple.

Alonso screams.

"What? What is it?" There are hands on Alonso's shoulders. He realizes he's crouching on the floor, hands over his eyes.

"Did you see something?" Corey asks. "Was it—"

"I have to go," Alonso says, shoving Corey's hands away and ignoring his shouts as he runs out the door and into the trees.

But he can't stop seeing Corey's grandfather, dead. Where did that image come from?

And why did it feel like a memory?

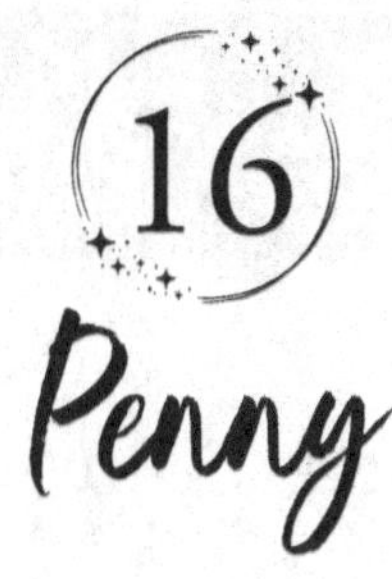

Penny

ALONSO HASN'T BEEN IN SCHOOL THE ENTIRE week.

Penny went to see him on Monday, but he could barely get out of bed. Instead she did homework in the solarium, Nimble curled around her feet. Tuesday and Wednesday evenings were taken up by a drag show and (reluctant) college application work with Naomi. Which mostly consisted of Penny looking at two college websites before scrolling through aesthetic pictures of Italian meals and open books lying on tastefully crumpled sheets. On Thursday, Alonso texts her:

"Penny?"

"Oh," Penny says, quickly dipping the measuring cup into the bag of flour and leveling off the top with the straight edge of a knife. "Here."

Penny's mom smiles as she takes the cup from her. In her way, she doesn't pry, but Penny feels her mom watching her, waiting for Penny to tell her what's wrong.

But that would mean admitting the truth: There's something going on with Alonso. He hasn't picked up her calls this week, claiming that he's been sleeping each time, but he never calls her back, either. Today she offered to bring him his homework, but he had Aidan Lostis bring it instead. Aidan lives closer to Alonso, but doesn't Alonso want to see Penny, even for a moment? She misses him so much that there's a constant ache in her chest and a knot in her stomach. They haven't gone this long without seeing each other since they started dating.

If Penny told her mom all of this, it would mean she'd have to acknowledge the reality that's staring her in the face:

Alonso is avoiding her.

17

Alonso

EVERY TIME ALONSO CLOSES HIS EYES, HE SEES Charles Barrion lying dead.

It was so real, down to the loose threads on the old man's sweater. Where did the vision come from? And why, when Charles Barrion said *You* in his weak, cracked voice, did it feel like Charles was speaking not to some unknown invader, but directly to Alonso?

When Penny calls, Alonso watches it ring. Every time the screen goes dark again, part of Alonso dies, like a plant deprived of light and water. He's never wanted to need somebody this much. But if he picks up, Penny will hear the terror in his voice. She'll know something is very wrong. And even though keeping his distance hurts, another, stronger, feeling grows in his chest: the desire to protect Penny from whatever is happening to him.

Because something *is* happening. He's not just being haunted by the vision of Corey's grandfather. He's sleeping longer. Harder. When he wakes up, he's still tired. It's like being sick but he has no symptoms. His mom took him to the doctor, but the blood tests came back normal. The doctor told him to take a multivitamin, which wasn't helpful, but Alonso did it anyway. If anything, the exhaustion and the headaches are getting worse.

And then there's Nimble. She's been avoiding him for months, but now she never leaves his room. She won't eat or use the litter box unless Alonso goes with her, but it's getting harder for him to get up.

He feels his coven's anxiety. Their fear. Their occasional attempts at magic that might unlock his situation. But the only real clue they've had is the tarot card Alonso pulls from Aunt Donna's deck every single day:

The Devil.

"Have you told Penny?" Aunt Emilia asks late Thursday night. Everyone else is asleep, but Emilia is staying up with him, knitting a cat sweater that Nimble will wear for probably ten seconds before ripping it to shreds.

Alonso is on his twin bed, back slumped against the wall. "No."

"She's your girlfriend. I'm sure she wants to help—"

"That's the problem," Alonso says. "She doesn't know when to back the fuck off."

It's harsh. Alonso clears his throat, trying to see through the anger that's suddenly clouding his vision.

"I see," Aunt Emilia says softly, and she leaves him and Nimble alone.

Alonso bangs his head against the wall, making his room shake. Why doesn't he just tell Penny? Is it such a bad thing that she'd want to be here for him?

Before he can find a good answer, sleep begins to pull him under again. And just on the edge of consciousness, a familiar voice speaks as if from a dream:

You're doing the right thing, Alonso. That girl would ruin all our plans.

18

Giovanni

WHEN ALONSO FALLS ASLEEP, GIOVANNI DOESN'T let him wake up. He keeps the boy subdued, in a dreamless, emotionless state. Gio didn't used to be strong enough for this, but now he is.

When the cat sees him, she hisses and runs from the room. Presumably to get the children. But when Vera, Donna, and Emilia poke their heads in, Gio pretends to be asleep.

"What do you think Nimble saw?" Donna asks.

"We can't know," Vera says. "Alonso is the only one who can communicate with her. But whatever it was, he seems peaceful enough now."

It's only Emilia who lingers. Emilia, who was an empath even as a little baby. She cried when her mother cried. Laughed when she laughed. To be so weak and easily swayed must be exhausting, but when Gio opens his eyes, Emilia doesn't look tired.

She looks angry. Because Gio himself is angry, as is his eternal right after everything he's been through.

"Hello," he says, smiling.

Emilia doesn't move.

Gio gets up and walks toward her. "I need the bathroom."

He hopes she doesn't hear the change in his voice. He sounds less like Alonso and more like his old self right now.

But if she hears it, she doesn't acknowledge it. Instead she flees the room, and Gio hears the click of a door closing and the turning of a lock.

He'll have to be more careful around his daughters.

Gio doesn't let Alonso's body sleep for the rest of the night or the day after. Instead he figures out how to use his portable telephone. It's not intuitive, but he manages to view messages sent back and forth between him and Penny. Alonso has grown weaker since they've been separated. It would be much easier if the boy would just give up and die, leaving his body to Giovanni. But his grandson is stubborn. Strong. Too strong for a witch of his age. So until Gio can get rid of him for good, he'll need to gain a stronger foothold in this body.

The true test will be taking Alonso around Penny. If Gio can maintain control, then he's golden.

Gio reads carefully through Penny's messages. Finally, she gives him something he can use.

"A bonfire," Gio says to himself. "Don't mind if I do."

19

Penny

"YOU'RE BEING PARANOID," NAOMI SAYS AS Penny drives them to Dylan's house on Friday.

"Probably," Penny says, glancing at her phone, which is angled toward her in the cupholder. The screen is dark. No new texts from Alonso. "He's just been so distant."

"He's having some health issues, but that boy looks at you like nobody else exists. I think you're fine."

But nothing about this situation feels *fine*.

Penny pulls into the field behind Dylan's house and puts the car in park. Usually they're too early to parties, but judging by the number of cars, they might be late. As they walk, Naomi slows for a moment, staring at something.

"What?" Penny says, and then she sees it.

Alonso's old blue Shelby is here.

"Guess he made it?" Naomi says.

Penny is filled with warmth at the sight of Alonso's car, but when she checks her phone, he still hasn't texted her. Why wouldn't he tell her he was here?

That nagging sense of unease is back, and it echoes inside her with every step: *Wrong, wrong, wrong. Something is* wrong.

The bonfire is visible long before Penny and Naomi join the crowd. Penny searches for Alonso, but she doesn't see him. They wave to a few people as they move through the crowd, and Penny hopes her smile is convincing.

"Wait here," Naomi says when they find a good spot. "I'll grab drinks."

Penny nods, adjusting her scarf. There's an edge to the air that feels almost wintery. She could get closer to the fire, but the bodies are dense, and she may not be able to see Alonso from there. When the wind blows harder, it reminds Penny of the way the Shadow's hands felt last summer. Cold as a void.

The fire reaches high into the night, smoke pluming from the top like the ghost of a river. It takes Penny's eyes a moment to adjust to the light, and that's when she notices the familiar figure watching her.

Corey.

Though he's backlit by the flames, Penny can just make out the warm smile Corey gives her. He's holding a beer, and he lifts two fingers in a wave. She waves back. He leans over to his group of friends and says something to them before walking her way.

"I was wondering if you'd be here," Corey says.

"Ditto."

"It was nice of Dylan to invite me. I haven't felt very social this week, but I think I needed this."

Penny considers him. "Is it because of the football game last week?"

Corey looks away. He's wearing a dark expression, and the self-loathing he must be feeling is suddenly palpable. Penny never noticed it before this summer, but it's always been there. It makes her want to help him. To protect him from himself.

Penny used to believe Corey was perfect. In middle school, she had the biggest crush on him, and even when those feelings faded, nobody in Idlewood could really compare. He was handsome and kind, an overachiever of the highest order. Once, Penny overheard Hannah Hartley reading aloud some fanfiction that had Corey as the love interest. The second Penny got out of school, she read it on her phone. Someone had posted it anonymously online, and it was pretty bad. But the takeaway was that Corey was everyone's dream. Their love interest of choice.

But after this past summer, Penny sees Corey up close. The way he has worked to keep people at a distance is obvious—even if it meant lying to everyone, including his ex-girlfriend.

So no, Corey isn't perfect. But Penny likes him better this way.

"What?" Corey says.

Penny blinks. "I was staring, wasn't I?"

"Yeah."

"Awkward."

Corey smiles, his eyes crinkling at the corners. "I'll let it slide if you tell me what you were thinking about."

The way Corey says that—with a warmth and something else Penny can't quite name—makes her blush. She changes the subject. "I was just wondering how it's going with Dylan."

Corey takes a sip of beer. "The breakup was good for both of us. I always thought ending things would hurt her too much, but I don't know. I underestimated her."

"She's a force of nature."

"Yeah. And she and I…we were draining each other. She seems different, doesn't she?"

"Less scary. I couldn't believe it when she invited me tonight. But to be fair, the entire school is here."

Someone clears his throat behind her, and Penny turns around. "Oh. Julian."

"Hi," he says, and it sounds reluctant. Like he would've preferred that they ignore each other.

Penny steps back, making space for Julian in the conversation. She tries to think of something to say, but she's got nothing.

Corey sips his beer. Julian stares at the grass.

Penny speaks out of desperation. "You want a drink? Naomi is getting one for me. I can text her if you—"

"No," Julian says. "My doctors say I can't drink right now because…" He trails off as his mouth flattens into a line, as if he regrets saying that out loud.

Penny gets it, though. She debates acknowledging it before finally saying, "I didn't drink while my doctor and I were figuring out my medication dosage."

Julian watches her warily. "You're on medication?"

"For anxiety."

Is it her imagination, or do Julian's shoulders relax ever so slightly? Then his eyes cut to Corey, and the tension between them becomes clear.

Penny thinks back to the football game. To Julian fainting, and Alonso's denial that he had anything to do with it.

Penny should talk to Julian. Get his side of the story.

But just as Penny is preparing herself to ask, she spots a head of red-and-blond hair in the distance.

"Oh, it's Alonso—" She cuts off. For a moment, despite the hair and the leather jacket and the long silver earring, it doesn't seem like Alonso at all. There's something about the way he moves that makes him look like a different person—someone arrogant and confident. Not like the boy Penny always thought Alonso was before she really knew him, but someone… older.

"Alonso!" Penny calls. But Alonso's head is bent low, and he moves as if he's deep in conversation with somoene.

Because he is. Standing next to him is Claire Polton, from bike polo. She's smiling, and when he says something, she giggles and hits his arm.

Penny sucks in a pained breath. As if he can feel her eyes on him, Alonso glances in her direction. Penny lifts her hand to wave—

And he looks away and starts talking with Claire again. As if he and Penny are nothing more than strangers.

The pain hits like cold water. The unease disappears and is replaced by ugly embarrassment and hurt—the kind that will etch this moment into memory for the rest of Penny's life.

"Great boyfriend," Julian mutters, and there's a mocking edge to the words.

Corey steps in front of Penny, blocking her view of Alonso. "Hey."

Penny can't even look at him, because the tone of his voice says he saw exactly what Penny saw. Is he pitying her? Judging her for not saying anything to Alonso?

Corey grabs her shoulder. The feeling sends

an electric shock through her entire system, and she can't help but look at him now.

He's close. His brown eyes are soft with concern. The light from the fire plays on his high cheekbones and full lips. "Is something going on with you two?"

Penny's throat goes tight. "We're fine."

Grass crunches underfoot as someone approaches them. "Hey!" Naomi says.

Corey turns around, but he stays close, his shoulder brushing Penny's. "Hey, Naomi."

Naomi's eyes linger for a second on Julian before she turns her attention to Penny, as if Corey's cousin hanging out with them is normal. "Penny, I got you hot cider with a little whiskey. I'll be the DD . . . hey, what's going on?"

"I need to find the bathroom." Penny takes the cider and weaves through the crowd.

She doesn't know which direction the house is in. She has to turn around multiple times, and the longer it takes, the harder it is to breathe.

Finally the house appears—it's a low, single-level home, with one window boarded up. Penny speedwalks toward it, but a hand reaches out and grabs her arm, stopping her in her tracks.

"I was calling for you," Alonso says. His eyes are bleary, as if he just woke up.

Claire stands a few feet behind him, wearing an unreadable expression. Penny doesn't want to know what Claire sees when she looks at her. She might actually be glaring.

"You already got a drink?" Alonso asks. "Where's Naomi?"

Penny yanks her arm out of Alonso's grip. His eyes go wide. "What's wrong?"

"You told me you wouldn't be here."

"Yeah, but…" Alonso squints. "I changed my mind. Didn't I text you earlier?"

"No, you didn't." Penny takes a few steps back, eyes cutting from him to Claire again. "Have a good night."

"Hey, Penny, wait!"

But Penny doesn't turn around again. She's already walking into the house, her breathing so loud in her own ears that she barely hears him calling after her. Penny makes her way through a dark hallway and locks herself in the bathroom. Then she downs her drink.

The whiskey hits quickly. Already her skin is warm like the sun is shining inside of her, and the bathroom has a hazy glow. The overhead light doesn't work when Penny flips the switch, so the only source of light is a string of orange bulbs that were probably left up after Halloween. There's a fake cornucopia with plastic squash and pumpkins inside it on the counter, and Penny's eyes anchor on to it like it's a life raft. She memorizes every detail, every nick in the paint on the vegetables, every speck of dust.

The safety Penny has felt with Alonso the past few months is real. She's not experienced with relationships, but thanks to her anxiety, she hardly ever feels safe with anyone. When she's with Alonso, there's no fight or flight. No alarms blaring in her head, telling her to protect herself from a threat.

Until today. Because suddenly, her nervous system is making her feel like a cornered animal, terrified and unable to think.

Penny sits on the edge of the tub. She wants to leave the party. She'd give anything to be home watching movies with her mom and her godfather, Ron. But Penny can't abandon Naomi like that. She'll just have to do her best to avoid Alonso.

From the way Claire was looking at him, it probably won't be difficult.

She pushes herself to her feet and is about to leave when movement catches her eye. It's the cornucopia. The air around it is almost…shifting. As if there's a gauzy curtain hanging in front of it.

Penny steps toward it. She doesn't feel light-headed, but there's no other explanation for what she's seeing. She squeezes her eyes shut and opens them again.

It's gone—for a second. Then the air almost splits in two, and a blast of cold hits Penny's entire body. It's so powerful that it shoves her back, knocking her off balance. Penny reaches out for something, *anything* to steady her, grabbing with all her might the moment her hand touches a solid surface.

Except it's not solid. It's the shower curtain.

Penny yelps as she falls back, taking the shower curtain with her. It makes a *pop pop pop* sound as it's ripped off every hook, and Penny tumbles into the tub.

For a minute, she doesn't move. She just sits there staring at the cornucopia, which now looks normal.

Someone knocks on the door. "Hey, there's a line out here."

"One second!" Penny pushes to her feet. She tries to hook the shower curtain up, but there's no saving it. She quickly shoves it into the tub and leaves the bathroom, avoiding eye contact as she walks past the line.

Until someone steps out of it.

From the corner of her eye, Penny sees long twists, a bright red athleisure jacket.

"Hey, you okay?"

A girl looks at her with large, concerned brown eyes. Penny doesn't recognize her, but she has the distinct sense that they've met before. Maybe the girl reminds her of someone, but Penny can't figure out who.

"Fine, thanks." Penny tries to smile at her before she continues walking to the door.

That same instinct tells her that the girl's eyes are on her back as she walks away.

20

Alonso

"WHAT'S UP WITH PENNY?"

Alonso doesn't turn back to Claire. He's still watching the spot where Penny disappeared into the crowd. He should follow her, but he can't make himself move.

Because there's a hole in his head.

He can't remember anything from before he saw Penny seconds ago. He doesn't know where he is. Why he's here. What he was doing before.

And Penny didn't even want to look at him.

"Alonso?" Claire Polton is still standing behind him. "What were you saying?"

"About what?"

"*The Day of the Locust.*"

Alonso's confusion turns to anger. "What are you talking about?"

"You said . . . isn't it one of your favorite books?" Claire blinks at him. "Hey, are you okay?"

Alonso is looking at his clothes now. He's wearing a black button-up...and it's *tucked into his jeans*.

The only time Alonso has ever willingly tucked in his shirt was when he snuck into the Barrions' gala last summer. And even that was painful.

So no. He's not okay.

Alonso turns to Claire, and whatever she sees in his face makes her flinch and take a step back. "What day is it?"

"Friday?"

Yesterday, Aunt Emilia in his room asking if he's told Penny the truth.

The day before, going to the doctor.

Two days before that—Penny coming over and doing homework downstairs while Alonso was in a fitful sleep.

And before that...

The weekend. Alonso at Charles Barrion's house. The sudden flash of memory that showed Corey's grandfather...

Dead.

Alonso suddenly can't breathe. He'd forgotten about last weekend. How is that possible? *Penny.* Seeing her brought him some clarity, and maybe it's wrong to need someone this much, but he can't help it.

He needs to find Penny first. Then he'll figure everything else out.

"I'll see you later," Alonso says, rushing off in the direction where she disappeared.

"Maybe at bike polo next week?" Claire calls after him, but he ignores her, unable to focus on anything but the memory of Penny's blue eyes staring at him like he was a stranger.

Alonso glimpses Dylan a few feet away. She's in the middle of a conversation, but Alonso pushes between her and some freshman girl and says, "You seen Penny?"

"Hello to you, too." Dylan looks him up and down. "Trouble in paradise?"

"I…" There's a flash of pain behind his eyes, and he screws them shut.

"What's wrong?" Dylan sounds almost concerned.

Before Alonso can answer, he gets the distinct feeling of breath on the back of his neck, like someone is standing right behind him. Alonso turns—

And there's nobody there.

Alonso stares into the empty space. He *felt*

someone behind him. Could it be another witch using an invisibility spell? But who? Dylan is right here with him, and Alonso's coven has no interest in attending a high school party in secret. There are no other witches living in Idlewood.

"Are you on drugs or something?" the freshman girl asks with a mean laugh.

Dylan turns to her with the energy of a guillotine falling onto its victim. "We don't say things like that to people, okay, sweetie?" she says, her voice dripping with condescension like she's a mom talking to a stupid child.

The girl flinches. "S-sorry."

Alonso doesn't even have it in him to react. He's too busy looking for the missing parts of himself, of his days.

The pain behind Alonso's eyes gets worse. All the breath leaves his lungs in a *whoosh*, and he tilts his head away from the bonfire's light. The talking, laughter, music around him—it's enough to split Alonso's head in half. This is a pain like he's never felt in his life, not even when his magic was sealed.

There's something wrong with me.

He has to get home. His coven will help him figure this out.

Dylan is saying something to him. "What?" he manages to ask.

"Do you need water?"

"I need to leave."

"Alonso!" Dylan calls, but he's already rushing away from her.

He has no idea where he parked, and there are rows of cars extending into the empty cornfields in every direction. Alonso runs his hands through his hair. Sweat is beading on his brow, and it immediately goes cold in the wind.

What if he didn't drive here? What if his family dropped him off? But why would his mom agree to that if he was sick?

A jeering laugh pulls Alonso from his thoughts. One row of cars over, Clay Thornberg—Idlewood's resident lowlife—is following some girl Alonso doesn't recognize.

"Hey, baby, where you going?" Clay calls. "I thought we were talking!'

The girl glances over her shoulder, her eyes narrowed in anger. She's wearing a bright red jacket, and her black hair is long down her back.

"I'd stop following me if I were you," she says, her voice steady.

"I saw you looking at me," Clay says. "I know you're just playing hard to get."

"If I wanted literally anything to do with you, you'd know."

Clay's smile disappears. "Where do you get off being so fucking superior? I find it hard to believe you have guys chasing after you all the time. You should be grateful that I even—"

"Hey," Alonso whispers, sending a small amount of magic into the word so that it echoes inside Clay's head.

Clay gasps, his bravado gone for a split second and replaced by a vacant, confused look. The girl doesn't hesitate; she glances at Alonso before she keeps walking, presumably to her car.

Clay whips around, finally spotting Alonso in the dark of the field. "Where the hell did you come from?"

"A social worker and an electrician. They're divorced now."

Clay gapes at him. "What are you talking about?"

Alonso steps between some cars, making his way closer. Already, he feels a little better. Putting Clay in his place is better than Advil any day.

Clay looks for the girl, and he scowls when he realizes she's disappeared. "Cockblocker."

"If you're the only one of us who couldn't see that she wasn't interested, you're stupider than I thought."

Clay laughs. "If *you* could get a hot little girlfriend, there's hope for all of us. No idea what Penny Emberly sees in you. The way you dress makes you look fucking gay."

Alonso's anger coalesces into something darker. It's almost as if a voice is whispering in Alonso's ear…

This guy doesn't deserve to laugh.

He barely deserves to breathe.

He certainly deserves to bleed.

For once, Alonso agrees. He closes his eyes, and the feeling of the cold air fades into warmth.

It's like being rocked to sleep.

21

Giovanni

GIOVANNI SUCKS IN A BREATH, RELISHING IN the feeling of brisk wind on his skin.

"Close call," he whispers to Alonso, who is now so far beneath consciousness that he'd never hear him.

Giovanni's test run in Alonso's body had been working without a hitch. He'd thought he'd go the whole night without even having to worry that his grandson might resurface.

It wasn't until Penny Emberly showed up that he felt his hold slipping. Her effect on his grandson seems to have only grown stronger in her absence.

No matter. There's one way he can guarantee Penny won't be around to distract Alonso anymore...

But that's on his to-do list for later.

For now, his focus is on Clay. When he

showed up and Alonso got agitated, it provided a brand-new opportunity for Gio to have some fun. It's easier to manipulate Alonso when he's overcome by negative emotions.

When Gio sucks in a breath, the world readies itself, as if it knows that he has the power to rearrange it at will. His grandson's magic is truly a marvel.

Clay is still talking, insult after insult, growing more agitated as Gio ignores him. But if Clay wants attention, Gio is more than happy to give it to him.

He whispers the spell:

> *"Scalp and toes and living skin,*
> *Feeling flays you from within."*

Gio repeats it three times under his breath until he feels the magic take hold.

Clay's laughter has faded. "What did you just say to me?"

Gio crosses his arms and waits.

Clay reaches up and scratches his stomach. "Hello?"

"I said you have a bug on your shirt."

Clay jumps. "Fuck, I can feel it!" He scratches his chest, his shoulders, his neck. "I...I think they're all over me!"

"Better take off your shirt," Gio says.

Clay doesn't even blink. He rips off his shirt, then his pants. "Why can't I see them?" he says, scratching every bare inch of skin that he can reach. "De Luca, grab some water or something! Help me out!"

"I would, but there's nothing on your chest, man. Maybe it's all in your head."

Clay gives him a deadly glare, teeth bared and all. But when he sees Giovanni's expression, his anger changes to panic. He stumbles back. "W-why are you smiling like that?"

Giovanni grins. "Me?"

Clay falls to the ground, rubbing his back against the dirt as he keeps scratching. His next words come out through gritted teeth: "You did something to me!"

"No idea what you're talking about."

There are bloodied scratches on his arms and one of his legs. As Gio watches, Clay's nails tear into the skin of his chest.

"Fuck you!" Clay screams.

There are hurried footsteps behind them. "Whoa, what's happening to him?!" someone says.

"I think he ate something," Gio says. "Allergic reaction."

"Clay?" A girl leans over him, but just as quickly, she jumps out of the way as his arm swipes at her.

"Do something!" Clay cries. Because yes, he's crying now. More people are coming over, and that means it's time for Giovanni to leave. He weaves between the cars as someone shouts that Clay needs medical help, they've got to call 911.

He finds the spot where he parked his grandson's decrepit car. He doesn't notice the tiny eyes underneath it until he gets closer.

The cat—the damned familiar—launches herself at Giovanni's legs.

Giovanni lets out a cry and falls back, banging his head on the next car over. Immediately, he starts to lose his grip on Alonso. Inside his grandson's head, he grapples for control, but the cat lands on his chest, hissing.

She's powerful. Much like Alonso, this cat is acquainted with what lurks in the Second World. This isn't the first time they've faced each other.

But this is the Primary World. The cat's realm. And here, she has dominion over the dead.

"Damn cat," Gio mutters. But he can't fight her any more than he could fight the gunshot that took his life. So Gio lets himself sink under . . .

Alonso

THERE'S A FEELING OF RAW EARTH AND FOLI-age digging into Alonso's back. And there's something painful digging into his chest, something like—

Claws.

"Ah!" Alonso yells, swiping wildly at whatever's sitting on him.

The animal leaps to avoid him, and then the claws slash at his face. The pain makes adrenaline spider through Alonso's veins, and his eyes shoot open.

"Nimble?" he breathes.

Nimble's ears are flat, and she's in a crouch as if she's ready to attack him. Because she *did* attack him.

"What the fuck?" Alonso sits up and wipes at his face. It comes away wet with trickles of blood. "Why did you . . . wait, where am I?"

Nimble blinks. He's always understood her on an innate level, but she's been silent for months.

Not tonight, though. The connection between them is suddenly so strong that Nimble's thoughts become words in Alonso's mind, as clear as if she'd spoken out loud:

On the earth.

She's right. He's in the field where the cars are parked. Alonso pushes to his feet and cranes his neck to see over the cars. The bonfire is still going on.

Go to sanctuary, Nimble thinks, the words ringing out clear in Alonso's head.

Alonso stares at her—his cat, his familiar, his magical companion.

"You know something is wrong with me," Alonso says. "That's why you've been such a bitch."

She narrows her eyes and crouches down again.

"Sorry." Alonso's eyes are drawn back to the blazing fire in the distance. "I should find Penny—"

Nimble hisses.

Alonso lets out a low breath. "Fine, I'll call her later. Let's go."

Alonso gets in the car. Nimble leaps over him and settles in the back seat, presumably where she can watch him. As Alonso turns the key in the ignition, a wave of nausea overcomes him. It's the feeling he gets during spell work, when the magic has drained too much of his energy.

Alonso gasps. "I cast a spell."

Now that he's realized it, he can feel that thread of magic still alive and working. There's a scream.

He puts the car in reverse and backs out of his spot. As he speeds out of the field, he rolls down his window, trying to figure out where his magic is flowing. What kind of spell it's powering.

Then he sees a figure squirming in the dirt.

Alonso hits the brakes. He lets his eyes lose focus, and there it is—the red light of his magic, like an aura around the person on the ground.

"Fucking De Luca!" the guy says, and the voice only makes Alonso more nauseous.

Clay Thornberg.

"*Enough*," Alonso says.

The command should cut his magic off at the source—but nothing changes. Alonso feels the spell holding on to Clay, digging its fingernails in and refusing to let go. His magic is *defying* him.

"I said *enough*!"

His muscles relax as the energy to the spell is finally cut off. The screaming in the distance subsides, but the crying doesn't. Somewhere in the night, sirens ring out.

Alonso puts the gas pedal to the floor. As he turns out of the lot, a figure in red appears out of the corner of his eye.

Someone watches him from the liminal space between the field and the party. Alonso squints. Then he sees the red jacket, the long hair.

It's that girl from earlier. The one Clay was harassing. And from the way she's watching him out in the open, it's like she *wants* Alonso to see her.

The single-minded focus that helped Alonso get in his car and out of this party shatters into pieces. This girl knows what he just did. Deep down, Alonso is sure of it.

Which means she knows he's a witch.

Mortals often don't know magic when they encounter it. And on the other hand, the things they think are supernatural can be tied back to concrete science. Which is why, even though Alonso uses his magic more freely, he doesn't worry about being discovered. Most people don't see the truth even when it's right under their noses.

But tonight, Alonso is worried. Because if that girl knows that Alonso used magic, it means she's probably a witch, too.

If there was another witch at the bonfire, that could mean a lot of things. But most likely, it means the Council sent someone to watch him.

"Why have you been keeping secrets from me?" Alonso says, throwing an angry glance over his shoulder at his familiar as he speeds down the road.

Nimble is silent, but Alonso feels her there. His sentry. She's the only thing giving him any comfort.

The ambulance appears over the hill, and Alonso's knuckles turn white on the steering wheel as it passes him by. The lights make him see spots, and he blinks them away.

When he closes his eyes, he sees something else. It's a flash of memory, much like when he was in Charles Barrion's house.

It's Clay Thornberg, nails digging into his own flesh as he writhes on the ground.

"Oh fuck," Alonso says. "What did I do?"

He speeds around a corner. Trees rise up on one side of the road, the forest growing thicker as he gets closer to home. Darkness gazes out from between the skinny birch trees. The sooner Alonso gets back and tells his coven about this, the better. He's suddenly burning hot. What if the witch is following him? Alonso reaches up to adjust his rearview mirror. There's nobody behind him.

Then he catches sight of his reflection.

Alonso squints. His hair looks different. It's—

Blond. There's no red in it anymore.

Alonso's hand shakes. Slowly he angles the mirror down.

It's not his face that's looking back. But it's a face Alonso recognizes.

A scar on the chin. Bright green eyes. Blond hair somehow even lighter than Alonso's.

A horn sounds, headlights coming straight at him. The yellow lines on the road are passing directly underneath Alonso's car—because he's drifting into the other lane. And barely twenty feet ahead is a truck.

Alonso screams. He jerks the steering wheel to the right, sending the Shelby skidding off the road and into the grass. It bounces violently as it heads for the trees. Alonso slams the brakes as the trees get closer, closer—

And the Shelby stops.

Alonso's breathing is ragged. In front of him, the trees hover like tall, quiet ghosts. It's as if they're mocking him. *We would've killed you tonight.*

"Nimble." Alonso turns around. Nimble is on the floor of the car, trembling. For the first time in months, she leaps into Alonso's lap, and he holds her to him, rocking her until her shaking subsides.

And then it's just them and the night, quiet and forboding.

Well, no. Not just them after all.

"Hello, grandson."

The voice is coming from right next to him. Alonso doesn't want to look.

He does it anyway.

His grandfather—looking no older than thirty, younger even than his mom and aunts—sits languidly in the seat. When he looks at Alonso, his eyes change from green to pure white.

And Alonso knows he's fucked.

23
Penny

PENNY WATCHES THE EMTS LOAD CLAY INTO THE ambulance. She catches sight of the blood smeared across his chest, the gash in his cheek.

It was Alonso.

Logically, Penny knows she's jumping to conclusions. But there's that same gut feeling she's been having all night—she just knows.

She looks for him everywhere, but there's no sign of him. She pulls out her phone.

Two minutes later, she gets a response:

Penny stares at the message, trying to process this.

He left without telling her. After he *hurt* someone.

Penny finds Naomi, who's on the other side of the fire. The crowd over here is still talking and laughing, as if nothing has happened. Maybe it's because the commotion is harder to hear over the roar of the flames—or maybe people just don't care.

"We have to go," Penny says.

"Ma'am, what? We haven't even been here an hour—whoa, are you crying?"

When she closes her eyes, she sees Clay's face, one cheek torn open. "I need you to take me to Alonso's."

Naomi doesn't react, not outwardly. She just takes in Penny's despair, does some Eldest Daughter calculations (*how close is Penny to a breakdown*, *how many questions should I ask before agreeing to this*, *who do I need to kill*), and nods. "I guess we're heading out."

" 'Kay," comes a familiar voice. When Penny looks up, Dylan is standing next to Naomi. She watches Penny with an unreadable expression.

"S-sorry, I didn't realize you were..." Penny trails off, looking back and forth between Dylan and Naomi. "You two talk?"

"I'm determined to make Naomi my friend." Dylan levels Penny with a judging stare. "You, I'm still debating."

"That makes two of us," Naomi says, glaring at Dylan.

Dylan's smile fades. "What was with the ambulance?"

"It's your house," Naomi mutters. "Your party. You didn't go see?"

Dylan shrugs. "I put the alcohol away. I did my duty." She turns back to Penny. "You're upset. Does that mean Alonso did something?"

"No," Penny says, but it's too quick.

Dylan cocks her head. "He was acting weird tonight. Good luck, I guess."

Penny is shocked that she noticed, but Naomi is already ushering her away before she can say anything else.

Once they're driving, Naomi asks, "What happened back there?"

"I'm not sure." Penny swallows. "Clay got hurt. Alonso went home. I don't know the details."

They turn into Alonso's driveway. Naomi is staring up at the house with a fierce expression. The De Lucas have left an open invitation for Naomi to be Penny's plus-one to their family dinners, but Naomi has never taken them up on it. She likes Alonso, but she's never liked that he's a witch. Alonso probably hasn't noticed, but Penny sees the wall this has built between them.

"I'll stay here," Naomi says, turning off the car. "Just...be careful."

Penny walks up the porch stairs to the heavy wooden door. Even though it's cold outside, the grass and plants in front of the old Victorian-style manor are thriving. The grass is uncut but vivid green, and there are new purple lilies and ranunculus blooming along the wraparound porch. There are a few candles lit in the stained-glass window, and figures move beyond the murky glass like shadow puppets.

Penny raises her hand to knock, but the door swings open before she can touch it.

Emilia De Luca stands inside. She's wearing a frilly bathrobe that brings to mind either a grandmother or an old-timey prostitute. Her dark brown hair reaches her waist, and it's tied into seven braids (a lucky number, according to the De Lucas).

"Penny! I didn't realize you were coming." Emilia's happy expression disappears, and she shivers. She looks stricken, as if Penny is visibly injured. "Something's happened, hasn't it?"

Since the De Lucas had their magic restored by the Council of Witches a couple months ago, their unique gifts have been slowly emerging. Alonso's mom, Vera, is good with plants, ergo the front yard. Aunt Donna gives eerily accurate and specific tarot card readings.

But the coven thinks Aunt Emilia showed signs of her gift even before her power was restored. She was always able to read people quickly, without them having to say a word. It's only natural that she would become an empath. These days, if you're within a ten-foot radius of Emilia, you might be in danger of an unsolicited mental health diagnosis.

"Come in," Aunt Emilia mumbles, stepping back from the door.

"Where is he?"

Before Penny can answer, Nimble appears at her feet, looking up with serious yellow eyes.

"Hi, baby," Penny whispers.

Emilia picks Nimble up and holds the cat close to her chest. "He's in his room."

"Thank you," Penny says, already walking to the stairs.

"Penny?" Emilia is still standing by the door, worry written in the fine lines of her face. "Please be careful. It's...it's like something has broken in him."

Penny grips the banister. Then she proceeds up, up, up, until she reaches the landing and Alonso's attic bedroom.

But it's the bathroom door next to it that opens. Alonso is shirtless, a towel slung over one shoulder. His necklaces dangle from his throat, trailing drops of water onto his chest and the floor. His eyes are downcast, and he's lost in thought. When he glances up, his expression doesn't change. It's like he's a million miles away.

"Penny," he says, his voice low and gravelly. When she doesn't respond, Alonso drops his gaze to the floor. "Come on," he says, and she follows him into his room.

His attic bedroom is so familiar now: the clothes on the floor, the orchid thriving in the window, the posters for Molchat Doma and Portishead on the walls. Penny faces Alonso, waiting for him to explain.

"I hurt Clay," Alonso says.

"With magic?"

Alonso nods. "Is he okay?"

Penny is supposed to be angry. But Alonso sounds so exhausted. She has the sudden urge to put her arms around him.

"I don't know," Penny says. "An ambulance took him."

Alonso's hands hang at his sides. He stares at nothing, but in the hollows under his eyes and the furrow between his brows, there's pain. Terror, even.

Penny steps closer, trying to get him to look at her. He won't.

"What did Clay do?" Penny asks.

"Does it matter?"

Penny swallows. Does it? Clay is a bully. He physically harassed Naomi last summer when they were at the old pharmacy. He's sexist. Hateful.

And now he's in the hospital. His face will probably be scarred for the rest of his life.

Alonso swallows, his Adam's apple bobbing. "Clay is a piece of shit, but I'm worse."

"No," Penny says, because it's still true, despite everything. "You care about people. You want to protect them. Clay just wants to belittle everyone, all the time. That isn't you, and it never will be. That's one of the reasons I love you so much."

Finally, Alonso looks at her, determination in the set of his jaw. Then he takes three strides over, grabs Penny's shoulders, and presses his lips to hers.

Sometimes kisses feel like kisses—bursts of happy chemicals in the brain, a way to say hello or goodbye, tiny reminders that you love and are loved. But this kiss feels like a *moment*. Like it's marking a shift in the earth, a date and time that will be remembered every year into the future until they're both dust.

It's terrifying. It's irresistible. It's all-consuming.

When they part, Alonso almost throws himself across the room. He's facing away from her, breathing heavily. Penny touches her swollen lips with a shaking hand.

But in the space where his body just was, Penny is cold. That feeling reaches deep into her, snaking into her throat. Her heart starts to pound.

The incident with Julian at the football game. The way Alonso looked right through her at the bonfire. Then Clay's bloodied body.

There's something Alonso isn't telling her.

"What's going on?" Penny whispers. When

Alonso still doesn't answer, she says, "*Please*. How am I your girlfriend if you can't even tell me the truth?"

The muscles in Alonso's back shift as he moves. When he turns to her, his face is different. Stony, uncaring. Just like it was at the bonfire. And when Alonso opens his mouth, he speaks the words she's dreaded hearing since the moment they started dating.

"Maybe you shouldn't be."

Penny lets that settle. She replays what she said—*how am I your girlfriend*—followed by the bright echo of Alonso's own words—*maybe you shouldn't be.*

You shouldn't be.

"You..." Penny trails off, blinking rapidly. When did her eyes fill with tears? "You're saying we..."

"Should break up."

"Oh," Penny says, but it doesn't sound the way she intended. It was supposed to be understanding. She's supposed to stay calm. But it sounds like a cry of pain instead. Suddenly she's clutching her chest, trying to breathe.

Alonso isn't even looking at her. "I've been

thinking about it, and we're too different. It's not really working for me."

"R-right," Penny says even as her brain fights against this. Alonso loves her. He's said it so many times. She *believes* him.

Except that isn't the full truth. There was always a tiny part of her that wondered. A part of her that listened to the whispers in the hallways at school that said the two of them made no sense together.

A part of her that knew it was only a matter of time before Alonso heard those whispers, too.

The disbelief leaves in a wave, and it's replaced by acceptance. This was inevitable, after all. Of course Alonso doesn't want to be with her. It was strange that he ever did. And tonight, when Penny saw Alonso with Claire, that fear grew.

She should've known this was coming. When did she become so wrapped up in this fairy tale— in this idea that she could love someone and they would actually want her back—that Penny failed to see what was right in front of her?

The near panic attack has faded, but the tears are still running down Penny's face. She looks up at Alonso, and he's watching her with some- thing that almost looks like concern—but no, of course it's not concern. It's pity.

"I totally understand," Penny manages to say. "I'll leave."

But Alonso blocks her way. His face has grown red, his eyes wide and bloodshot. He looks like he wants to say something, like he's barely holding back the words. But there's nothing he can tell her that will make this better.

"Alonso," Penny says, her voice small but even, "please let me go."

After a long, heavy moment, he steps aside and opens the door for her.

"See you later," Penny says, because she has no idea what else to say. He doesn't answer as she brushes by him.

Penny walks calmly down the stairs. Out the front door of the De Luca house for the final time. Into Naomi's car, where Naomi starts asking her questions until she realizes Penny isn't going to answer.

"Penz?" Naomi says as she pulls out onto the road. "What the fuck happened?"

"He broke up with me," Penny says.

Naomi slams the brakes. "He did *what*?!"

Penny listens calmly as Naomi goes off on him, alternating between asking questions and crowning him the worst human being to have ever walked the planet. She's being a good friend. Penny should be grateful.

But Penny can't feel gratitude. She can't feel anything.

Later that night, when she's lying in her bed at home, the shock gradually fades and is replaced by something much worse.

A realization.

Penny doesn't understand people. She doesn't understand herself. She is completely, utterly alone in a shattered world that doesn't care about anyone's pain.

And Alonso is gone from her life. Forever.

Alonso

THE COVEN FINDS OUT SOON ENOUGH.

Alonso's mom and Aunt Donna flutter around him like annoying birds, appalled that he would unceremoniously dump Penny, asking how he could be so cruel, what's gotten into him, why he can't just be *normal*.

Not Aunt Emilia, though. She just sits in the corner watching him, Nimble in her lap. When the fretting turns into screaming, Emilia says, "Let him talk."

Vera and Donna look at their little sister with a mixture of insult and shock. They make the rules; Emilia follows them. That's the natural order.

Not today, though. She's unwavering.

"Fine," Vera says, turning back to Alonso. "What the hell has gotten into that stubborn head of yours?"

Alonso starts laughing, because oh boy does he have an interesting answer to that question!

It was only hours before that Alonso's car was sitting on the side of the road with his dead grandfather in the passenger seat. Giovanni De Luca was in no rush to disappear. He enjoyed Alonso's meltdown, relishing in his screams. Then he grabbed the keys from the ignition and locked the door when Alonso tried to get out.

"This won't take long," Giovanni said. "I just want you to answer one question for me."

"Give me my keys, you undead piece of—"

"Oh, I'm quite dead. But lately, you've made me feel so…" Alonso's grandfather leaned forward, grinning with black teeth, "…alive."

Nimble screeched like a cat much larger than her size.

Giovanni leaned back against the door, but he wasn't panicked. And that's when Alonso realized why.

Giovanni wasn't really sitting in the passenger seat of the Shelby. He was in Alonso's head. How could Nimble defend him against what amounted to a really dangerous figment of Alonso's imagination?

Giovanni grinned again. "That's right. You're catching on."

Damn. The bastard could read his thoughts.

"As I was saying, I have a question," Giovanni said.

Alonso could barely keep the tremor out of his voice. "I don't care what you have to say—"

"Oh, but you will." His grandfather's white eyes didn't leave Alonso's face. He was waiting for Alonso's reaction. Aching for it.

Then he spoke the words that would change Alonso's life forever.

"If I kill Penny Emberly, will it become easier to kill you?"

Alonso launched himself at his grandfather, hands out, ready to do whatever damage he could to someone who's been six feet under for almost fifty years. It didn't matter if Giovanni De Luca was dead. After Alonso was done with him, he'd be wishing he was resting in peace.

But Giovanni disappeared. And Alonso was left all alone with a pit in his stomach. This thing—this poltergeist—was going to kill Penny.

Unless Alonso pushed Penny far away.

Alonso will never forget the look on Penny's face as he ended their relationship. The shocking part wasn't that she looked betrayed; it's that she was barely even surprised. Penny thinks so little of herself that when Alonso lied to her face about not loving her—and, in his opinion, did a pretty bad job of it—she nodded and left. When she walked by him, Alonso became terrified that he would never get her back again. He almost told her the truth.

But he didn't. Because what if the poltergeist gained control?

By the time Alonso is done telling his family the truth, there's no more yelling. Aunt Donna is leaning on Emilia for support; his mom is standing in the middle of the room, staring at the floor.

"He's here?" she says. "Right now?"

There's sweat on Alonso's brow. He wipes it away. "I guess so."

Vera is suddenly kneeling in front of Alonso, cupping his face in her hands.

"Dad?" she says. "Can you hear me?"

There's a low laugh in Alonso's ear, and Alonso has to look away from his mom's face. She's too hopeful. How does he tell her to stop without breaking her?

But he doesn't have to. It's Aunt Emilia who comes over and puts a hand on Vera's shoulder.

"It's not really him," Emilia says. "I feel this . . . *rage* inside Alonso. Different from the normal— no offense, Alonso, you know what I mean. This is . . ." She watches Alonso, and it's like she can see everything in his head, just like Grandpa De Luca could in the car. Unlike him, Aunt Emilia won't use what she sees against him. "This anger is truly dangerous. Cold."

"That card you kept pulling," Aunt Donna says.

Alonso nods. "The Devil."

"What were you thinking," Vera says, "crossing the Veil like that?"

Alonso looks out his window. The night is dark. He's never been scared of it until now.

"I was mostly thinking of Penny," he says.

They go quiet. Then his mom and aunts leave him alone. They need to "process," which means they'll be up all night drinking wine and crying.

Nimble stays.

"Will I keep hurting people forever?" Alonso asks.

Nimble doesn't meow. She doesn't telepathically comfort him or yell at him. She just goes to stand by the window. She looks at it, and then she looks at him.

With a pang, Alonso understands. He pushes to his feet and opens the window. The cold night air is vicious, and he sucks in a breath as it hits his face and bare arms.

Nimble blinks at him.

"It's okay," Alonso says. "Go be with Penny. If I can't stop the poltergeist, you can protect her."

Nimble considers him. Then she walks over, nudging his hand with her head. He scratches her behind the ears, and a purr rumbles deep within her.

Then she jumps through the window, running down the eaves and leaping to the ground and out of sight.

Alonso stands at the open window, even as the moths fly inside and flutter around the lampshades. His magic wells up like grief, and he's afraid of it. This is how he used to feel all the time, when he didn't know how to use it or control it—but now it's for a different reason.

It's not Alonso who might lose control. It's someone even more dangerous.

He has the sudden urge to get all this power out of him. To drain himself until there's nothing left for his grandfather to use against him and everyone he loves.

The power expands outside his body. He can feel every nook and cranny of his room, every iota of dust. He feels his mother, the way her heart is racing downstairs. He can hear Aunt Donna shuffling her tarot deck. Aunt Emilia writing furiously in her journal. Then Alonso's power expands beyond the house, up through his bedroom window and into the sky. He calls the clouds, and they gather above Idlewood. He sends his magic out, out, out until he collapses on the window seat, too weak to move.

It will rain for days.

Corey

ON MONDAY MORNING, SCHOOL IS DELAYED TWO hours due to the heavy rains, which have flooded some streets. Corey wonders if they'll cancel school, but Indiana weather can include three seasons in a day, and the principal's text message says *the show must go on!*

Corey's hair is already becoming frizzy as he walks into homeroom. He sits at his desk, takes out his tablet. But as the other students file in, he keeps looking up, waiting for Penny to walk into the room.

He hasn't spoken to her since the bonfire. He still doesn't understand what happened on Friday night. He didn't see Clay before he was taken to the hospital, but he saw the photos. The videos. Some people joked that it was all a stunt and he was using ketchup to freak people out, but Clay is too proud for that. If he wants to scare people, he has other ways to do it.

Penny doesn't show up to homeroom. Corey assumes she's home sick, but when he's on his way to lunch, he finds her. She's sitting in a deserted hallway on one of the benches.

"Hey, I was looking for you," Corey says, but then he freezes.

Her eyes are puffy. Her hair is usually wild, but it has an extra level of antigravity today.

The biggest tell, though, is the way she just keeps staring out the window. She doesn't smile. She doesn't even acknowledge Corey's presence

"Penny?"

She jumps. "Corey? Oh my god, sorry, I…" She laughs, but it sounds forced. "How long have you been standing there?"

She's smiling, but it looks like the effort is draining her. Her eyes are shining, and she flinches when a tear falls down her cheek.

Corey drops his backpack. He sits next to her and pulls her into his arms. She buries her face in his chest and starts sobbing.

"It was never going to work," Penny keeps saying, but she doesn't tell him *what* wouldn't work.

Corey doesn't tell her it's okay, because whatever happened has shaken her to a degree he's only seen once, last summer. Instead he sits there with her until her sobbing fades into hiccups. By the time she pulls away, her hair is matted, and her eyes are bleary and red.

Corey swallows. This isn't the Penny he knows—quiet but relentless, clear-eyed and honest. This is Penny at rock bottom. He should ask what's wrong. But he has a feeling that's not what she needs right now. So he reaches out and unsticks some hairs from her face, and then he tilts her chin up so she'll look at him.

"You eating lunch?" he asks.

Ten minutes later, they're back on that same bench in the hallway, this time with lunch trays. They're not supposed to eat here, but sneaking past the cafeteria monitors isn't hard. Now they eat silently while raindrops roll down foggy windows.

Penny half-heartedly bites a french fry, chewing slowly. The rest of the food on her tray remains untouched. She puts it down on the open seat next to her, and then she turns back to Corey.

"I don't know how to say this."

"You don't have to talk about it if you're not ready," Corey says.

"I do. Because pretty soon everyone in school is going to know." She looks out the window again. If anything, it's raining even harder than it was when Corey found her.

"Alonso," she says slowly, like she's not sure how to form the words, "broke up with me."

After school lets out, Corey speeds through the rain. There's almost nobody on the road, and Corey isn't even sure if he's staying in the lane.

But the car doesn't hydroplane. Corey doesn't crash. He makes it all the way to the street where his family lives. He doesn't turn into his driveway, though.

He turns into Alonso's.

Corey bangs on the De Lucas' door until Alonso's mom opens it.

"I need to see him," Corey says.

Vera De Luca narrows her eyes. Corey must look unhinged, the way he's standing there with his clothes soaking wet. But on top of that, Corey's entire family ostracized the De Lucas for years. The coven doesn't seem to hate Corey as much as they used to now that they have their magic back, but the Barrions and the De Lucas are *not* on good terms. And now Corey is showing up and making demands.

"He's not in a good place to see anyone right now," Alonso's mom says.

"This is about Penny."

"I figured."

"I'm not leaving until I see him."

Suddenly Ms. De Luca looks less angry and more nervous. As if on cue, Alonso's voice calls from inside.

"Let him in, Mom."

She sighs. Then she steps back and opens the door wider. "He's in the solarium."

When Corey steps into the glass-walled room at the back of the house, Alonso is sitting at a black wrought iron table. He's slumped in his seat, one hand covering his eyes. His family's menagerie of plants reaches up with giant leaves, dark green fronds, the occasional red flowers. Rain trails down the outside of the windows.

Corey isn't sure if Alonso knows he's there until the witch says, "You can sit down, I guess."

Corey doesn't sit down.

Alonso's hand drops, and he meets Corey's eyes. "You're mad."

Corey isn't just mad. He's ready for Alonso to be smug. He's barely holding himself back as it is, and all he needs is the weakest excuse to make Alonso hurt.

"If you'd seen Penny today," he says, "you'd understand why."

Corey isn't really an expert on anything, but he knows what it's like to fight with Alonso: about as easy as the final boss in a video game. And today, Corey wants Alonso to fight back. He wants to rage at him for what he's done.

But Alonso just sits there.

"Did you hear what I said?" Corey asks.

Alonso covers his eyes again, sinking even farther into his chair.

"I *said*—"

"I heard you." There's barely any fight in his tone, and that's more shocking than anything else.

Corey finally sits down across from him, but he's tense. "I'm not going to wait all day for you to explain what the fuck you were thinking."

"There are lighted paths to the exits. Please

put on your own oxygen mask before helping others."

"*You* look like you need an oxygen mask," Corey says.

Alonso laughs, but it's half-hearted. "Give me a second." Outside, thunder roars, and he flinches and rubs his temples. "My own magic is making my headache worse. How's that for divine justice?"

"Your own magic?"

"I might've made some rain."

Corey glances outside. "*You* started the storm?"

"How's that for emo?"

Corey grits his teeth. "Did you also hurt Clay Thornberg?"

"Sort of."

"It's a yes or no question."

The bags under Alonso's eyes look even darker next to his bloodshot eyes. "I didn't want to break up with Penny."

"Then fix it."

"Nope."

Corey's hands close into fists. "Alonso, she's in pain. I barely recognized her today. Meanwhile you're just sitting here being a stubborn—"

"I'm possessed."

"By self-loathing? Yeah, I can tell."

"No. By a poltergeist. Ergo, storm. And Clay's face."

Poltergeist. François from *Amityville High* is a poltergeist. Corey feels delirious, but that's his first thought.

Then it sinks in: This is real. He's sitting across from someone who's possessed.

Which means Corey is in danger.

He gets to his feet. "What the fuck, man?"

Alonso shrugs.

"You're saying the *poltergeist* did all this?"

The ghost of a smile plays at Alonso's lips. "The storm was technically me. I had a moment that's lasted for three days." His smile fades. "But my magic is becoming strange, Corey. I'm losing control of it. I thought it was my own fault, but it's the evil spirit that's squatting inside my body."

Corey tries to put the pieces together, but this isn't his world. "When did this happen?"

"When I brought Penny's mom back to life."

"You..." Corey is gaping at him now. "She was really dead?"

"Were you not in the same hospital room I was? She was completely dead."

Corey debates running. It's probably the safe choice. But he sits back down anyway.

Alonso almost smiles. "You're taking this well."

"It's all an act."

"You're good at that."

"I know." Corey works his jaw. Where do they go from here? In his mind, he sees Penny's tearstained face. "Penny doesn't know?"

"No."

"You can't keep this from her—"

"You don't understand." Alonso leans forward. "You saw what I did to Clay, right? Want that happening to Penny, too? You know her, she wouldn't even leave my side. She'd want to *help*." He spits out the last word like it tastes bad. "Fuckin' do-gooder."

Corey recoils. "You must be able to control this somehow—"

Alonso bangs a fist on the table. "You don't *understand*. When he takes over it's like I'm riding in the back seat. If I make him veer off the road, I'll die, and so will Penny. I'm going to figure this out, but I need you to keep Penny far away from me until I do."

"You need me to *lie* to her?" Corey says.

Alonso rubs his mouth. Then he leans forward, and interlaces his fingers like—

Like he's ready to beg.

"You're the only one I've told outside my family."

Corey waits for Alonso to laugh or crack a stupid joke to defuse the tension, but he just looks desperate.

Last summer, Alonso asked Corey to trust him. It was tough at first, but not anymore. Corey has already trusted Alonso with his life, even with the lives of his family. Alonso has sincerely tried to help all the Barrions.

So if Alonso needs Corey's help now, Corey wants to give that to him.

"How long would this take?" Corey asks.

"The coven is figuring out how to do an exorcism. It's pretty specialized magic, but we have to try it."

"An exorcism?" Corey says. "Will you be okay?"

Alonso shrugs.

Corey closes his eyes. He tries to think clearly. If Alonso really is possessed, that means Penny is in harm's way.

And no. Corey doesn't want that. He might do anything in his power to prevent that.

But Corey is the last person who should be spending time with Penny. He's been so good about keeping his distance. That warmth he feels whenever she's around has been stifled. He can't let it grow into something hotter. Something like need.

"Please, Corey," Alonso says.

Both Corey and Alonso could hurt Penny. But Alonso is more dangerous right now.

A few weeks. Corey can do a few weeks.

"Fine," Corey says. "I'll do what I can."

Penny

PENNY WAKES UP IN THE MIDDLE OF THE NIGHT covered in sweat.

"It's a fever," her mom says as she stares at the thermometer in her hand. "A high one. You'll need to stay home from school, okay sweet pea?"

As soon as her mom leaves the bedroom, Penny stares into the dark, hoping the rain will lull her to sleep.

That's when she first sees the Veil.

Except it's not really the Veil. Penny is lucid enough to realize that it's a dream, probably brought on by her fever. But for a dream, it's vivid. And she feels very awake.

It's in the corner of her bedroom, like a gauzy curtain billowing, visible one second and gone the next. As it moves, it lets out cold air that makes Penny shiver, but that's not the worst part.

The worst part is the distant shouts. Pained cries. The dead are *speaking*.

Penny wants to sit up and turn on the light, but the fever keeps her pinned to her bed like a sleep demon. All she can do is watch and listen.

"It's not real," she whispers to herself. But as the days blur together, the Veil keeps appearing.

Penny tries to sleep, but it's impossible, because during every waking moment she sees it. It's in front of her living room window. It's in the ceiling of the shower. And it's always in her bedroom.

The wailing grows louder. Penny squeezes the pillow around her head, humming to drown it out. When that doesn't work, she tries mantras: "It can't hurt you. None of this can hurt you. None of it can hurt…"

She wants to call Alonso so he can tell her why this is happening. He would explain it all to her, and he'd cast spells to protect her. But Alonso isn't her boyfriend anymore.

Every few hours sleep arrives, hesitating at the threshold. Penny begs for it until finally she drifts off, hoping her dreams will take her somewhere else.

But when she opens her eyes, the dreamworld in front of her is familiar.

She's sitting on the bench at the football field. It's completely abandoned, and instead of Idlewood Central High School's parking lot in the distance, it's just evenly cut grass as far as the eye can see.

It's all too perfect. Too still.

This is the Second World. Where her mom was trapped when she was in a coma. But something about it is different. Instead of a rolling purple sky above, the clouds and the light are a stark red that casts everything in a menacing glow.

Penny feels a presence above her. Slowly, she looks up.

Hanging upside down above her like a horrifying mirror image is a face Penny wishes she could forget.

"You'll be here before long," Charles Barrion says. His lips stretch into a painful-looking smile. "You have no idea what's coming for you and your witch."

"Is that a threat?" Penny says, her voice low.

To her surprise, Mr. Barrion hesitates. Then he points at her leg. "You're bleeding, I'm afraid."

Penny looks down. The cut—the one the Shadow gave her when she crossed the Veil to find her mom's spirit—has reopened. It's gushing blood, covering her leg in angry red.

There's a rumble, and the Second World is sucked away, leaving Penny in the dark. A weight lands on her chest, and her lungs seize. Penny gasps and opens her eyes.

And she stares into a pair of slitted pupils.

"Ah!" Penny sits up, and the weight falls off her chest and retreats to the foot of the bed. Penny blinks a few times, unsure if she's still dreaming—but no. The fluffy orange creature is still there, watching her.

"N-Nimble?" Penny says.

Nimble's tail swishes. She's purring, which explains the rumble.

"What are you doing here?" Penny gasps. There are bowls on her bedroom floor, one containing a small clump of wet cat food. "God, what day is it?"

She pushes to her knees, pulling aside the curtains. It's daytime. Rain is still coming down outside, but for the first time in days, Penny isn't shivering.

She grabs a cup of water from her nightstand, downing it in a few gulps. Her stomach responds with a loud growl.

"Meow," Nimble says.

Penny still isn't entirely convinced that she's real, but when she picks the cat up, she certainly feels like a living, breathing creature. Still holding Nimble, Penny pads out to the kitchen.

Her mom and Ron are at the old café booth that serves as their table. They're leaning close, talking in low voices.

"I don't remember much, but it's enough," Penny's mom says. "I don't think she's making this up."

"I know, I know. But that fever is nasty, Anita. We won't know anything until it breaks."

"Hi," Penny says.

They both look up. Penny's mom is immediately on her feet. "Oh my god." She grabs Penny's shoulders and looks her over. "You're okay?"

"I think so. But—"

Ron cuts Penny off as he pushes her hair back from her head and leans in as if he needs to examine every single one of Penny's pores. "Wow, you *smell*."

"Like cat?"

"Yes, but also body odor," her mom says.

"Mom." Penny looks down at Nimble, who blinks contentedly.

Anita sighs. "It's the funniest thing, sweet pea. She just … showed up here a few days ago. I found her in the bushes, terrorizing a whole family of mice. She looked absolutely ragged."

"You know this is Alonso's cat, right?"

"Of course, I met her when we went over for dinner. I called the De Lucas right away."

"And … ?"

Penny's mom crosses her arms, staring at the cat with a mixture of humor and suspicion. "Apparently she and Alonso are fighting."

"Some line," Ron mutters. "If they wanted to get rid of their cat, they should've brought her to the shelter like civilized people."

"But why is she *here*?" Penny asks.

Nimble starts to purr again, and Penny has no idea how to interpret that.

"They wondered if we wouldn't mind keeping her for a while. Apparently Nimble is quite attached to you." Penny's mom throws her hands in the air. "It's strange, but they *are* a strange family."

Penny swallows. Any reminder of Alonso is painful, but Nimble might be the worst of all. She's his familiar. Apart from his family, nobody is closer to Alonso than this cat.

Which makes it strange that she'd choose to come here.

As if sensing Penny's questions, Nimble leaps from Penny's arms to the counter, where she glares out at them.

"That's not sanitary," Ron says.

"Come on now," Penny's mom says, but instead of hopping to the floor, Nimble leaps to the top of the refrigerator. "That's . . . fine."

"I should shower." Penny's stomach growls, and she flinches and wraps her arms around herself.

"It's almost three o'clock," Ron says. "How about some breakfast for dinner? Oat cakes and bacon sound good?"

The thought of Ron's homemade oat cakes smothered in butter makes Penny ache. "Yes, please."

"I'll get some clothes for you," her mom says, putting an arm around her shoulders and leading her to the bathroom as Ron starts banging around in the kitchen.

Penny steps in front of the mirror and takes herself in. She looks like she was in some epic battle, and she definitely lost.

Alonso isn't my boyfriend, she thinks as she stares at herself. *I'm single. I'm not with him.*

Worst of all: *He'll be with someone who isn't me.*

By the time her mom comes back, Penny is crying again. Even though Penny smells like garbage, her mom holds her close, kissing her hair and rubbing her back like she's a baby.

"You're okay," Mrs. Emberly says. "Here, get in the shower."

Once Penny is under the hot water, she closes her eyes and holds her breath. Then she looks at the ceiling.

No sign of the Veil.

Penny rubs shampoo into her hair. On her leg, the cut from her fight with the Shadow is still scabbed over even though it's been more than two months since she crossed the Veil. Do wounds from supernatural creatures ever really heal? She tears her eyes away and grabs the body wash.

Later, Penny inhales her breakfast-slash-dinner as Nimble plays with a plant on the kitchen windowsill. Penny's phone sits on the table, but she's too afraid to look at it. When she finally does, it's as she expected: no texts from Alonso.

Then her eyes go to the date. It's Friday.

"I was sick for five days," she mutters to herself.

"The doctor said it's rare for fevers to be that stubborn, but it can happen," Penny's mom says.

Ron clucks his tongue. "You had us all real worried. We had to bar Naomi from coming over so she wouldn't catch whatever you had."

The doorbell rings.

"That might be her again," Ron says, standing up to get it. But when he says, "Look who's here!" it isn't Naomi who walks into the kitchen.

"Hey," Corey says. He's wearing a mask and holding a plastic tub of soup and a reusable grocery bag.

Penny feels warm at the sight of him. It's strange to see him in her house. He's almost as tall as Ron, and he looks around with curious eyes at all the photos and plants and tiny piles of flour on the counter from Ron's oat cakes and Anita's latest baking experiments.

"Is that tomato soup?" Penny's mom asks, looking with wide eyes at the tub.

"Homemade by Warren. I've got stuff for grilled cheese, too."

Warren is the Barrion family's all-purpose bodyguard, housekeeper, and—apparently—cook. Corey doesn't bring him up a lot, and even now he seems a little uncomfortable talking about this person who is paid to take care of his entire family.

But Ron has a singular focus right now. "Say *less*, baby doll," he says, swiping the food from Corey's hands.

In seconds, he and Anita are fixing second dinner. Mrs. Emberly ushers Corey to the table, and he looks around in either awe or horror as they become miniature tornados, kicking up silverware and clanking dishes.

"Don't be scared," Penny says. "They're just excited for soup."

Under his mask, Corey smiles. Then Nimble leaps onto the table.

"Whoa." Corey jumps. "Nimble? What is she doing here?"

"Honestly?" Penny sighs. "I don't know."

Corey and Nimble have never had the best relationship, probably because of Corey and Alonso's history. But now, she almost looks curious.

"I'm a dog person, but…" Corey holds out his hand, and Nimble sniffs it tentatively. "She *is* cute."

The soup and sandwiches are served. Nimble settles herself into loaf mode in the center of the table. Penny is still hungry enough that she eats everything, mopping up the last of her soup with the crust from her sandwich. When they're done, Penny's phone vibrates.

"You're *alive*," Naomi says as Penny answers the phone.

"Somehow."

"You up for *Amityville High* tonight?"

Penny gasps. "Oh my *god*, it's fight night."

"You watch boxing?" Corey says.

"Corey, *no*, it's François and Joey on *Amityville High*!"

Corey drops his spoon. "The duel."

"The duel?" Penny's mom says.

"The *duel*," Ron says, giddy. When Penny raises an eyebrow at him, he shrugs. "I started watching it, is that a crime? Come on, that episode has been streaming since midnight! I totally forgot!"

Naomi is there in ten minutes, and she pulls Penny into a long hug.

"Have you heard from him?" Naomi whispers.

"No, but his cat is here."

Naomi's face falls. "Come again?"

"Can we please not talk about it?"

"Copy that." When Naomi sees Corey, she squeals. "I *heard* you watched this show!" She grabs his arm and drags him to the couch. "You sit by me. We'll take the floor, okay, Ron?"

"You're too sweet," Ron says, one hand on his tailbone as he slowly lowers himself onto the couch. "I'm swearing off roller derby after this. I'm getting way too old to be walloped by twenty-year-olds."

Blankets are passed around and Penny's mom brings a bowl of popcorn topped with cayenne pepper. Nimble sits in front of the TV, staring at the screen. Penny looks around, waiting for everyone's presence to make her feel better. For a smile that doesn't feel forced.

But Alonso isn't there. In his place is a sinkhole in Penny's life, one that has changed all the scenery and destroyed every path she could've taken. Everywhere she looks, there are dead ends.

Naomi is sitting on the floor, and as if she can read Penny's mind, she reaches back. Penny grabs her hand. Onscreen, François the sexy poltergeist and Joey the werewolf are battered and bloody. They seem evenly matched. The full moon is about to come out, which means Joey will be able to transform, and he's trying to hold François off until that moment. The protagonist, Olivia, isn't even there; she's battling Joey's half sister in the gym at their school, unaware that the two boys are fighting over who gets to take her to prom.

"You forget," François says, "I'm not just a weak little ghost anymore."

Joey spits blood onto the ground. "Because you traded your soul for dark power."

"Yes. And now I can do this." François leaps across the room. Joey puts his fists up, but François doesn't punch him. Instead, he disappears *into* Joey.

"Oh my god, he's possessing Joey!" Naomi says.

"That little shit," Ron mutters through a mouthful of popcorn. "Was the writing better last season or is it just me?"

"Can someone explain what's going on?" Penny's mom asks.

Corey glances back at Penny with a strange expression. He almost looks sad. Penny tries to smile at him, but when she looks back to the screen, her smile fades as Joey's eyes change from brown to François's eerie yellow.

Nimble hisses and runs from the room.

"Boo," Ron mutters. "Wonder how long this storyline will last."

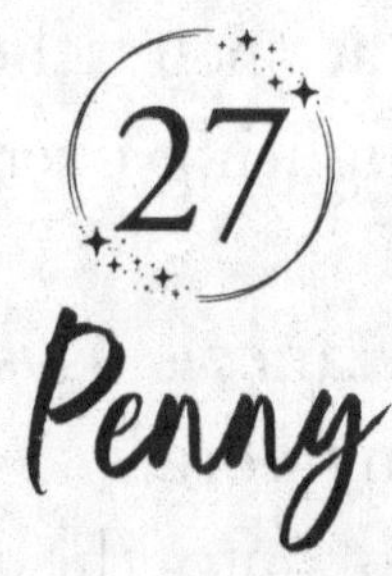

Penny

PENNY RETURNS TO SCHOOL THE FOLLOWING week.

The rain has washed all the leaves from the trees, turning late autumn in Idlewood as gray as winter. There are orange cones around new potholes on the streets that are full to the brim with water, and Penny learns when she gets back to school that the foreign languages hallway is closed because the roof has caved in.

For the first two days, Alonso isn't there. Penny can pretend everything is normal. When people ask why he hasn't been in school, she gives noncommittal answers.

"He's been sick, I think."

"Just a cold."

"He'll probably be back soon."

She wishes she knew the real answer. Because she can't keep from hoping that Alonso might be staying home because of her—to avoid her, maybe—and wouldn't that mean he still cares?

Then, on Wednesday, the rain stops. All of a sudden, when Penny is heading to AP calculus, she sees him.

Coming directly toward her is a mess of red and blond hair. A black flowing jacket. The glint of silver jewelry and gray eyes.

Alonso.

Penny jerks to a stop, and the person behind her steps on the back of her shoe, muttering, "Sorry," before he steps around her.

Penny barely registers it.

What did she expect? She can't avoid Alonso forever. But now that he's here, it's like someone is reaching into her chest and grabbing her lungs, squeezing all the air out of them. She shouldn't look at him, but she can't help it. And now he's close, so close he must see her too—

He brushes past. Not even a glance.

Penny's lungs refill with air, but she has to gasp for it. She hides in the bathroom, missing twenty minutes of calculus. It's like she's made of porcelain, but there's a crack in her somewhere, and she has to be careful how she moves to keep from falling apart.

Later, when Alonso sits on the opposite side of the history classroom and laughs at something Sango Rao says, Penny doesn't cry. But when the bell rings, she stays in her seat until the room is empty.

"Penny?" Mr. Abdi says when he notices she hasn't moved. "You should get to class, no?"

But Penny can't go to class. She wanders to her locker, gathers her books, and makes her way out to the Prius.

"They broke up," someone whispers as she walks by.

The news spreads quickly after that.

Thanksgiving comes and goes, but the grief stays. Every time Penny sees something that reminds her of Alonso, it brings on a pain that makes her sluggish. It takes her mind somewhere far, and it's like she can't recognize herself. Penny and Naomi start eating lunch in the library, because the less Penny has to see Alonso, the better. Not that anything helps, but it makes Penny feel like she's trying to move on.

"I can spit on him if you want," Naomi says from across the library table.

"I'm good."

"No, you're not. You're a shell of a human being."

Penny lays her head on the table. "It'll get better, right? That's what everyone says."

"Presumably." Naomi glances behind Penny and raises her eyebrows. "Oh, hey, Corey."

Corey stands behind them with his tray. He smiles at Naomi, and his eyes soften when they find Penny's face. "Can I sit with you?"

"No," Naomi says, smiling.

Corey rolls his eyes and puts down his tray. "The veggie burger tastes like nothing."

"They forgot the salt, I think," Naomi says.

"That's a crime against humanity."

"Agreed," Naomi says. She pushes Penny's tray a little closer. "You have to eat half of it."

"But you said it tastes like nothing," Penny says.

"You got the normal burger, not the veggie burger. This one will taste like chemicals."

Penny takes a bite, and Naomi claps like she just won an Olympic medal. "The hero we deserve."

Penny snorts. "Stop."

"Do you two want to come over for dinner tonight?" Corey says. "Warren is making a goose."

"A *goose*?" Penny and Naomi exclaim.

"He likes to experiment. I can promise it'll be good."

"I have to take my sisters to tutoring, so that's a no to the goose," Naomi says.

They both look at Penny.

"I . . . guess I can come?" Penny says.

"Okay. You have the car?"

"Not today."

"You can ride with me then." Corey takes another bite of his veggie burger and shivers.

That buoys Penny a little. She picks up her burger again, and when she takes another bite, it's not as difficult to get the food down. As she's eating, she looks up and catches Naomi's eye.

Her best friend quickly looks away, but not before Penny sees fear in her eyes.

And Penny knows why she's scared. Of course she does. If they were alone, Penny would tell Naomi she doesn't have to worry.

After all, Corey Barrion would never fall in love with someone like her.

Alonso

"WHY DID YOU DO IT?"

Alonso tears a bite from his disgusting veggie burger. "What?"

Kiki leans forward. Alonso doesn't let himself look at her face because she's probably giving him a withering glare, and he just can't handle that right now.

"Break up with Penny," she says.

Alonso shuts his eyes, suddenly consumed by the deep pain he feels when he hears her name.

"You've barely talked about it since it happened," Aidan says. "Did you really break up?"

The hamburger starts to taste like mud in his mouth. He forces himself to swallow.

"Alonso," Kiki says, a warning in her voice. "What's going on with you?"

"Nothing," Alonso says, swinging his legs over the cafeteria bench. "See you guys later."

He knows they'll be whispering about him. That's fine, as long as they leave him alone.

As Alonso moves between classes, his magic stirs under his skin like a hurricane waiting to unleash on unsuspecting citizens. It's been like this since the bonfire, and it got worse after the breakup. Thinking of Penny makes his magic burn like a hot branding iron against the inside of his chest. Alonso's power has become angry. Raw.

But it could also be the solution to all his problems. Because Alonso could dull this pain with a spell. He could forget her—temporarily. If he just allows the poltergeist to take over…

The thought emerges with such force that it shocks Alonso's system. This isn't him. It isn't what *he* wants. But the ghost is strong enough that Alonso almost believed it was his own idea.

How can Alonso trust himself anymore?

When Alonso passes Penny in the hallway for the second time, the temptation to numb his own pain is overwhelming. He has to throw himself into the nearest bathroom and splash cold water on his face. He stands there, staring at himself in the mirror, watching the water droplets make winding paths toward his chin and into the sink.

"I'm gonna send you back to the Second World where you belong," he mutters, hoping his grandfather can hear him.

The bell rings. Alonso is tardy, but he doesn't care. He saunters out of the restroom, heading to his locker.

But there's already someone there.

It's a girl in a red jacket. Long twists hang down her back.

Shock pulses through him. Because this is the girl from Dylan's bonfire—the one who was being harassed by Clay. Who may or may not know that Alonso is a witch.

The girl glances over her shoulder at him and raises an eyebrow. "You need something?"

That's when Alonso realizes she's not at *his* locker. She's at the one next to it, one hand grabbing a geology textbook.

"Who are you?" Alonso says, because he's never been good at subtlety.

The girl snorts. "Damn, okay. This is an interrogation, huh?" She slams the door closed and whips around, holding out a hand. "Name's Marley. I'm new here."

"Huh," Alonso says, brushing past her to get to his own locker.

"Excuse me?" Marley moves, leaning on her own locker so Alonso is forced to look at her. "You're supposed to tell me your name. Unless I don't know how this whole meeting-new-people thing works?"

"You don't know how meeting *me* works," Alonso says, grabbing his tablet before he closes his locker.

"I'd like to," Marley says.

Alonso feels himself blush. "Sorry, I'm—"

Taken. That's what he was about to say. Except he's not anymore.

It's temporary. Once his coven exorcises this poltergeist, he'll tell Penny the truth. He'll say sorry. He'll beg her to take him back.

The last thing Alonso needs right now is a distraction.

"You're what?" Marley says.

Alonso shakes his head. "Not dating right now."

"That's a shame."

"Sorry to disappoint."

"I'll survive."

"Anyway," Alonso says, walking backward. "See you, Marley."

"Bye, Alonso."

When Alonso gets to his next class, he remembers one very important detail that makes dread creep through him:

He never gave Marley his name.

Alonso goes to find Marley after the last bell. He speedwalks through the hallways, keeping an eye out for her red jacket. But she's not by their lockers. She could be long gone already. But Alonso has to get answers from her—particularly about why she knows him. It could be that she learned his name from somebody else, but Alonso has that same feeling he got when he saw her at Dylan's bonfire.

Marley knows more about Alonso than she's letting on.

He's about to race out to the parking lot. But as he nears the doors, he sees something else that makes him stop cold.

It's Corey and Penny. They're walking together, backpacks on, shoulders close. They're talking, and Penny smiles up at Corey…the exact same way she used to smile at Alonso.

Alonso stops breathing.

Corey is doing exactly what Alonso asked him

to do. He's looking out for Penny, keeping her distracted from the pain Alonso is causing her. This should make him happy.

Instead, a darkness takes hold inside his chest, wrapping tendrils around his heart. Alonso wants to scream. To throw something. To throw *himself* against something.

Now, now, Alonso. You're upset. Let me have a turn…

Alonso is about to say yes to the voice in his ear. He wants to be numb. He wants to forget.

No.

Alonso's eyes shoot open. He falls against the lockers, hand gripping the fabric of his T-shirt desperately, like he can claw his skin open and pry his grandfather's malevolent spirit out.

"Alonso?"

Naomi stands a few feet away. She looks like she doesn't want to talk to him, but apparently he's making such a scene that she's decided she can't in good conscience just walk by.

Alonso will take any help he can get right now. He nods toward the foreign languages hallway. "Can you help me?"

Naomi hesitates for a moment, but she gets close, letting Alonso lean on her as he struggles to breathe. They walk into the dark hall. The ceiling caved in during the rain, so it's been under construction, and no classes are being held here. Which means it's the best place to have a meltdown.

"Shit," Alonso says, placing both hands against the wall to hold himself up. His grandfather is so close to surfacing. He's fighting Alonso, sending jabs at all his weak spots, and suddenly the image of Corey and Penny fills his head again.

"I know what you're trying to do," Alonso says, "but it won't work."

"Why are you talking to yourself?" Naomi says.

Alonso's grandfather recedes. "Keep talking. I need a distraction."

"Um, okay…" Naomi pauses, and Alonso closes his eyes as he tries to stay in control of his body. Alonso throws a fist against the lockers, and Naomi mutters some choice words under her breath before she says, "Expensive foundations can sometimes be worthwhile, but not all the time. For example, L'Oréal owns Lancôme, and the formulations of their foundations are really similar—"

"Boring," Alonso mutters with relief as he

falls against the lockers. His grandfather sinks beneath his skin until Alonso can't feel him anymore.

"Thanks, asshole. You got a preview of the script for my next video." Naomi crosses her arms. "You want to tell me why you're having a panic attack in the middle of the hallway?"

Alonso cracks his eyes open. "It wasn't a panic attack."

"Then what?"

"Why do you care? Don't you hate me now?"

Naomi's face shutters. "Oh, you're right. See you later."

Alonso sighs. "Nay."

She whips around. "Excuse me? You don't get to use my nickname."

But Alonso needs her to stay. It's pathetic that he's so starved for contact with Penny that even talking with her best friend feels like a connection to her. And Alonso really does consider Naomi a friend. The way she's looking at him now is painful.

The truth comes out before he can stop it: "I didn't want to break up with her."

Naomi narrows her eyes. "Be more specific."

"You can't tell her."

"Why not?"

"Because I did this for her."

"Wow. Keep telling yourself that."

Alonso swallows. "I'm possessed."

When Alonso told Corey, it took him a full minute to really understand what that meant. But Naomi steps back as if she's been shoved, and Alonso knows she gets it.

"How?" Naomi says.

"The hospital back in August. I helped Penny's mom, but it required me to cross the Veil."

The hallway grows darker, shadows shifting around them like they're alive. The crevices in front of every locked doorway look haunted.

"You helped Anita?" Naomi's hand falls slowly to her side. "Never thought I'd say this, but I'm glad you're a witch. If I could've done the same thing, I would've."

"You're not scared of me?"

"Of course I am. My abuela gave me a healthy fear of the supernatural." Naomi lowers her voice. "So you're possessed. By a ghost?"

"A poltergeist, technically. Much worse."

"Excellent. You've got your own François."

"Don't think I'll be bingeing *Amityville High* anytime soon."

"Can't blame you."

Alonso crosses his arms. "He threatened Penny."

Naomi lets out a breath. "Oh. So that's why you cut her off."

"Yeah."

"That," Naomi says, "makes *so* much sense."

"It does?"

"Yes! I knew you still loved her! And you were acting like such a moody weirdo—no, wait, that was *before* you got possessed."

"You're hilarious."

Naomi taps her chin. "So what do we do?"

Alonso pushes off the lockers. "We?"

"Isn't that why you're telling me? You need help."

"I…" Why *did* Alonso tell her? Because he didn't want her to hate him. He didn't want her to judge.

And he doesn't just want Corey keeping Penny occupied. Seeing them together today shouldn't have ignited that jealousy in him, but it did, and Giovanni almost took control. What if that happens again, and in public? Alonso can't risk it.

He's about to tell Naomi as much when a voice comes from one of the shadowed alcoves in front of the classrooms. "No disrespect, Naomi, but you're not a witch. What can you really do? Provide moral support?"

Alonso's heart pounds against his chest as Dylan slinks into the hallway from the dark.

She waggles her fingers at him. "Sorry to hear about your little health problem. I thought my STI was bad, but some antibiotics cleared that right up. Guessing that won't be the case for you."

Shit.

"You can't know this," Alonso growls.

"Too late," Dylan says. "Unless you want to use a spell on me?"

"Stop giving me ideas."

Dylan waves him off. "I only followed you here because I thought maybe you and Naomi were a thing. It was too juicy to resist."

"You do know I'm a lesbian, right?" Naomi says, her tone flat.

"Oh yeah." Dylan shrugs. "Anyway. Now that I'm here, you should take advantage. Put me in, coach."

"What?" Alonso says.

"You're possessed," Dylan says. "I've seen enough movies to know that you probably need an exorcism."

"I'm not letting your magic anywhere near me," Alonso says. "You'll probably flirt with the poltergeist."

"I prefer a pulse in the men I date. And some of those books your mom lent me say the more witches you have, the safer the spell. This is a big one, right? Can we use Naomi's energy, too, even though she's a boring mortal?"

"Please fuck off," Naomi says.

Dylan is right, though. Naomi has some familiarity with magic, and the coven could siphon her energy for the spell.

"Wait," Alonso says, "my mom lent you spell books?"

"I paid her a visit and asked nicely." Dylan's smug smile wavers. "I don't have a coven like you do. The only way I can learn about magic is from your family."

Alonso feels a little bad, but his hackles are up. Dylan has betrayed them and helped them at different times. Trusting her is a gamble. But if it means they can perform this exorcism sooner, is it worth it?

"I won't tell Penny, if that's what you're worried about," Dylan says.

"I'm worried about a lot of things," Alonso

mutters. He steps closer, towering over Dylan. She doesn't even flinch. "Come over later tonight. Let's say seven."

"This almost feels like a date," Dylan says.

"I promise," Alonso says, "it'll be the opposite."

29

Penny

DINNER IS, INDEED, A GOOSE.

"Wow," Penny says as Warren lays out the silver platter in the center of the massive dining table. The cooked bird is surrounded by tomatoes, leafy greens, and rosemary. The smell almost makes Penny float out of her chair, but the expression on the goose's still-attached face keeps her feet on the ground.

"He can cut off the head if you want," Corey says.

"No, it's fine. This is just…different. From what I'm used to."

"Us too," Sofía says from across the table. She's Corey's first cousin once removed, a former pop musician who grew up in South America before moving to the United States after the death of her tech mogul husband. Her glossy dark hair hangs over her shoulder in a Rapunzel-like braid, and she's so dazzlingly beautiful that she can probably see the stars in Penny's eyes. But if she does, she doesn't show it. Sofía is warm—most of the Barrions are, actually. Penny expected to feel more uncomfortable than she does.

"Believe it or not," Sofía continues, "Warren doesn't cook like this all the time. His usual is fried chicken or tacos."

Warren is setting out carrots, but Sofía's comment makes him pause. His expression doesn't change—from what Corey has said about him, it rarely does—but something about the stiff set of his shoulders comes off as agitated.

"I would make other dishes," Warren says, "if this family was more adventurous."

Sofía's daughter, Camila, raises her small hand. "I'm adventurous!"

"Yes you are," Warren says, patting her on the head, "so please work on your mother."

Sofía gasps. "Just because I'm not a fan of garlic!"

"You say that as if it's not, like, the most common ingredient in all food," Corey says.

"I can take criticism from Warren, but you, too, Corey? Ouch."

"He has a point, Sof," Helen chimes in. She's

not saying much, just watching the conversation unfold from her seat at the head of the table. Corey's dad is working and Helen's son, Julian, is nowhere to be found. Julian seemed like he was doing better in large crowds when Penny saw him at Dylan's bonfire, but the way Corey sends a worried glance at the empty seat next to him makes Penny think she shouldn't ask about him.

Sofía turns her attention back to Penny. "What's your favorite food? Corey should've had Warren make that."

"Ramen," Penny says, "but that seems complicated."

"There's nothing he can't make," Corey says.

Warren's face shows the ghost of a smile before he disappears out of the dining room again.

"He's the only person in Idlewood taller than my godfather," Penny says once she's sure he's out of earshot.

"How is Ron?" Helen says. "Haven't seen him in a while."

"He's good. Mostly he just bothers me about college applications these days."

"Oh, that's right! The early deadline is coming up," Sofía says. "Corey just finished all his applications. Ivys, mostly, right?"

"Yeah," Corey says, as if it's completely normal to apply only to reach schools.

"How about you, Penny?" Helen says. "What's your top choice?"

Penny shifts uncomfortably in her seat. "I don't know. I might just do online school for freshman year."

"Oh, that's convenient," Sofía says, but it's obvious she's confused. Helen gives Penny an encouraging smile, but it comes off as pitying.

Penny hates herself for bringing up college. What she doesn't say is that she was waiting to see where Alonso applied. That the only way she would go far from home is if he was there, too. Penny's mom discouraged it with the typical you're-too-young, don't-base-life-decisions-on-your-boyfriend arguments, but she's been completely silent on the topic since the breakup.

Because now, Penny has no plan at all. Even community college feels impossible.

"We're actually the biggest graduating class in Idlewood Central's history," Corey says, and Penny silently thanks him for changing the subject.

"Which means what, two hundred kids?" Helen laughs.

"Three hundred," Corey says.

"Wow!" Sofía says. "I can't believe you're all graduating. I remember when Corey was a tiny boy. All he wanted to do was play piano."

"Piano?" Penny looks at Corey. "I didn't know you played music."

"Used to," Corey says.

"He was fantastic," Helen says. "He was winning competitions at age five."

Corey shrugs. "Against other five-year-olds."

"Be proud of it, Corey!" Camila says, rolling her eyes, which sends the whole table into a fit of laughter.

"I thought he'd become a professional musician," Sofía says. "He just has that ear, you know? He heard a song once and he could play a simple version of it right away. I wanted him to try other instruments. I even bought him that little guitar, remember?"

Corey is smiling, but there's something pained in it. "I still have it somewhere."

"Wait, so you loved music?" Penny says. "Then why didn't you keep playing?"

A new voice joins them: "Corey's mother and I had to pull him out of lessons. It was a distraction."

James Barrion, Corey's dad and the CEO of their family's company, stands at the entrance of the dining room. Penny unconsciously sits a little taller, then feels silly for it.

"I guess," Corey says, avoiding looking at his dad.

Mr. Barrion gives a small huff. "He still hasn't forgiven me for it." When his eyes land on Penny, he gives her a stiff smile, but it's not unfriendly. It's more like his facial muscles have forgotten how to do it. "Good to see you, Penny. Your mom is doing well?"

In the corner of Penny's eye, Helen stops eating, the fork halfway to her mouth. She dated Penny's mom in secret last summer—a fact Penny only discovered when her mom got into an accident. The bargain created by Charles Barrion almost killed her, and it would've made the Barrions richer and more successful in exchange.

None of the living Barrions knows about the bargain except Corey. Penny is uncomfortable holding this knowledge when they're all completely unaware of the truth. Helen has refused to go near Penny's mom again, even though Penny is certain they still have feelings for each other. They're both too afraid.

Penny can't blame them.

"She's great," she says, not looking at Helen.

"Thanks to you and Corey," Sofía says.

"And Alonso," James adds.

"Dad," Corey says, a warning.

The table goes quiet, and Sofía glances at Penny. So Corey told them about the breakup, probably to keep them from bringing it up. Penny would've done the same thing, but it hurts.

"Right," Penny says, and she wishes her voice didn't come out so soft.

"You joining us, James?" Helen says quickly.

"Not tonight," James says. "Have Warren save me some … what is that?"

"Goose!" Camila says, shoving a piece into her mouth.

"Of course it is," Mr. Barrion says, but it doesn't sound malicious. He turns to leave, but before he walks away, his eyes linger on Corey.

"You know," Mr. Barrion says, "you could play one of your old songs at the opening."

This *opening* must be the holiday party that's happening in December. After Corey's grandpa died, the Barrions gave a large donation to renovate and rename the community center. The newly named Charles Barrion Center for

Community and Belonging will reopen during the holidays, and in typical Barrion fashion, they're throwing a big party for everyone in Idlewood.

Corey's brow furrows. "You're serious?"

His dad shrugs, but he doesn't leave. Penny can't read him, but he seems to be waiting for Corey's answer. Is he hoping for something? Or does he just not want to look rude in front of a guest?

"No," Corey says. "I can't play anymore."

Mr. Barrion nods. "Suit yourself."

After he leaves, the conversation moves on. When Penny glances at Corey, he remains lost in thought, staring into his plate.

Penny leans over and whispers, "If you don't eat that goose, Camila might go feral and steal it from you."

Corey laughs, tapping her shoulder with his knuckles. "Save room for dessert. Warren made apple pie."

"I'm so full! But I'll never forgive myself if I don't try some." Penny rubs her stomach. "Remind me to prepare myself before I eat dinner here again. I mean—wait. Not that you need to invite me. Sorry, that was—ugh! I shouldn't talk."

Corey smiles. The light catches in his brown eyes, and Penny is so dazzled she has to blink a few times. "You're brave enough to try Warren's food experiments. You have no choice, you're coming over again."

Penny smiles. "Okay."

As she finishes dinner with the Barrions, she knows the warmth she feels isn't just from the food. Being with Corey is easy. It makes her feel like she belongs somewhere. That feeling of worthlessness that's haunted her for the last few weeks is easier to ignore, and she can almost believe she'll be okay.

Almost.

After dinner, Corey and Penny go out to his car. It's getting dark early, so it feels like the middle of the night even though it's only eight. Penny leans back against the Audi and squints up at Corey.

"What?" Corey asks, a smile creeping across his face.

"You played *piano*? When were you going to mention that?"

Corey's smile is suddenly gone. "It was a long time ago."

"Yeah, but you were obsessed!"

"I was." Corey sighs. "My dad wasn't totally wrong. Piano was a distraction, but there's more to it."

Penny waits for him to go on.

"I actually did play the guitar Sofía got me," Corey says. "I wanted to take lessons, but my dad was only okay with piano. I was a kid. I threw a fit."

"So he punished you by taking you out of piano, too?"

Corey shrugs. "I have to work at the company. I can't spend hours every day playing music. Don't look so concerned, Penny, I'm fine."

Penny pictures Corey holding a guitar. She pictures him onstage at Boxer's or another, larger venue. She never would've thought of Corey as a musician, but now that she knows this part of his past, it makes sense. Corey has the charisma, the focus, the celebrity-level good looks.

Wind whistles through the empty branches of the trees, kicking up faded leaves. It will probably snow soon. For now Idlewood exists in that liminal space between seasons, a time that feels charged and alive.

It makes Penny braver.

"Can I say something?"

Corey nods, but there's a note of concern in the way he looks at her.

"You always want to make everyone else happy. You brush things off, you laugh, you do what everyone asks. But what do *you* want?"

Corey watches her for a long moment. Then he sighs, looking up at the sky. The stars are bright in Idlewood, and Orion hangs above them, bow and arrow in hand.

"I don't know anymore," Corey mutters.

"You've got time to figure it out."

Corey looks down at her, his smile fading. What's left on his face is something much more overwhelming.

Vulnerability.

The sound of a car breaks the moment. Someone is pulling into the De Lucas' driveway.

And Penny recognizes that truck.

She ducks behind Corey's Audi. "What—" Corey starts to say, but she pulls him down with her. He follows her gaze just in time to see Dylan Mayberry walk up to the De Lucas' house. Donna answers the door and lets her inside.

Penny and Corey stay frozen for a while. Then they slowly stand up.

"That was weird," Corey says, but he doesn't sound as concerned as Penny feels. "Are you..."

"I'm fine," Penny says, walking to the other side of Corey's car. Corey follows her and opens the door, but Penny pauses before she gets in.

"Do you think they're..."

"No," Corey says immediately.

Penny looks over at Alonso's house again. She wants to believe Corey, but what if he's wrong?

"I really need to get over him," Penny whispers, "but I don't know how."

And then she's crying, because of course she is.

"S-sorry," Penny hiccups, but there's a hand on her shoulder, and then Corey pulls her against his chest. Penny wraps her arms around him.

"I can't tell you how to get through this," Corey says. "But I'll be here with you. And so will Naomi and your family."

"Right," Penny says, even though the words ring hollow. Because the emptiness inside her is always gnawing away, and soon there might not be anything left other than pain.

30

Alonso

IT TAKES FIVE MINUTES FOR ALONSO TO REGRET inviting Dylan Mayberry into his house.

As soon as she walks in, Dylan flops into one of the De Lucas' living room chairs and puts her feet up like she owns the place. "So when are we doing this?"

Irritation spikes, and Alonso is suddenly working to stave off another headache. "If you were in a rush, you shouldn't have offered to help."

"I'm not in a rush. Just bored." Dylan grabs a magical history book from the end table and starts leafing through it. "What are 'bindings'? Is that a BDSM thing?"

"We walked in at the wrong time," Aunt Donna mutters as she places a few bowls and vials on the coffee table, which they've pushed to the side of the room.

Naomi follows with a bowl full of petals in

rich red liquid. She's been visibly tense since Alonso drove her here, looking all around as if she expects the coven to have set magical booby traps at every doorway. When she sees Dylan, she stops cold.

"Oh right," Naomi says. "You're here."

Dylan blows a bubble with her gum.

"I guess we know why the cards told us we would have visitors today," Aunt Emilia says, smiling warmly at Dylan and Naomi. She's so excited to have guests. Alonso doesn't have it in him to tell her Naomi would rather be anywhere else and that Dylan is the worst person he's ever met.

Since she did volunteer to help with the exorcism, maybe Alonso will upgrade her to second-worst person. It's only fair.

"Cards?" Dylan's eyes find the tarot deck across the room.

"Don't," Alonso says, but she's already across the room, pulling a card from the deck. She stares at it and then shows the group. "What does this mean?"

"The Moon?" Alonso says.

Aunt Donna plucks the card from Dylan's hand. "It can mean a lot of things depending on the person who pulls the card. And I don't know you, my dear."

"Sad for you," Dylan says.

"Not from what I hear," Aunt Donna shoots back, and Alonso has to muffle his laugh. He didn't expect to be entertained by Aunt Donna and Dylan in the same room, but he's glad for it.

Because he's terrified of what's happening next.

"Alonso," his mom says, nodding to the salt circle that's on the old purple-and-navy rug in the middle of the room.

Alonso blows out a breath. Giovanni is quiet underneath his skin. Hopefully he stays that way.

"What are we doing?" Naomi asks, her voice quivering.

"What you came here for," Alonso's mom says. "Everyone link hands. Stay outside the circle, and make sure not to break it."

Alonso lays down in the circle as the coven, Naomi, and Dylan all position themselves around the outer edge and grab each other's hands. Even Dylan is subdued as her gaze darts from Alonso's mom to his aunts.

Alonso's heart is beating hard. He closes his eyes and grabs the protection signet he wears around his neck. "If he gains control, do what you have to do."

"What does that mean?" Dylan asks. "Wait… have *any* of you performed an exorcism before?"

Silence is her answer.

"Wait!" Naomi says. "I thought you knew what you were doing. That's the only reason I agreed to do this."

"Same," Dylan says, glaring at the De Lucas. "Whatever happens to him will be our fault, right? So what if it goes wrong?"

Leave it to Dylan to think of herself right now. Not that Alonso can disagree with her. It'd be hard to explain away a corpse.

"Even if we were experienced," Alonso's mom says, "that doesn't mean this would work."

"That's even worse!" Naomi says.

"Why don't you call Milton?" Dylan says.

"Because," Alonso says, "we heard through the grapevine that he's on the Council."

"So?" Naomi says.

No getting around this now. Alonso sits up, draping his arms over his knees. "The Council can't know."

Naomi and Dylan look at each other. Slowly, as if they share a brain, they turn back to him.

"What did you do?" Naomi says.

"Out with it," Dylan says, smirking.

Alonso works his jaw. "Necromancy."

"Yes, I know," Naomi says. "But why can't you tell Milton?"

"Necromancy?" Dylan repeats. "Like…you used magic on the dead? Wait, I read about this in one of the books you lent me. Isn't that…" Her eyes go wide. "Oh, Alonso. You're a bad boy."

Naomi glares at him. "Explain."

"If the Council finds out about this, they'll kill me," Alonso mutters. "They won't even attempt an exorcism until I'm already dead, and then they'll send dear Paw Paw back across the Veil along with me."

Naomi sinks to the chair, looking a little gray. "They would actually kill you?"

"With smiles on their faces."

"We just got our magic back," Alonso's mom says. "We may not have the training some witches do, but we're powerful together. And with both of you helping us, we can perform this exorcism and make sure the Council never finds out."

Dylan is still watching Alonso, though. Alonso

meets her gaze, trying to pretend that her having any kind of dirt on him isn't bone-chilling.

"Fine," she says, stepping back into the circle and grabbing Aunt Emilia's hand.

"Fine?" Alonso repeats.

"I'll try it."

"Dylan, seriously?" Naomi says. "We could become murderers! Or the ghost could use Alonso to murder *us*!"

"He's in the salt circle," Aunt Donna says, "so if the poltergeist causes a scene, we'll be protected. We'll just have to keep him in there until Alonso gets control again."

Naomi swallows. Her eyes are huge and terrified.

"Naomi," Alonso says. "Please."

She sucks in a breath. "Dammit. Fine. For Penny." She grabs Dylan's and Donna's hands again.

Alonso lies down. "Let's banish this bitch."

Everyone closes their eyes. Alonso feels the hum as their magic syncs up, and Naomi gasps as they tap into her energy.

"It's okay," Alonso says to her. "Just breathe through it."

Naomi's breathing evens out, though she's still wincing and shifting on her feet.

The De Lucas recite the spell:

> *"Life of the mind,*
> *Unite behind us as we call forth this*
> *spirit,*
> *Open the Veil for him*
> *And guide him back home."*

Aunt Emilia dips her hand into the dark red liquid and sprinkles it on Alonso. He flinches as the drops hit his skin, but nothing happens.

Aunt Donna takes the shredded mint and blows it over Alonso. He opens his mouth, and a few pieces land on his tongue.

One second later, there's a feeling like someone wrapping a hand around Alonso's heart.

He gasps. The pain is immense. He presses his hands against his chest, and there's too much heat radiating from his skin.

You didn't think I would let this happen, did you? Shameful, how weak this protective circle is . . .

"Run," Alonso gasps. "All of you, run!"

His grandfather's poltergeist is almost to the surface of his consciousness. Alonso has a premonition of what could happen. How much bloodshed he could cause. How much he wants to hurt everyone in this room—even his own daughters.

"Girls!" Alonso's mom shouts. "Behind us!"

Alonso screws his eyes shut. The muscles in his neck are straining, and the floor peels away from his back.

Because Alonso is floating. He's hovering off the ground because of his own magic.

But he's not the one using it.

"What in the horror movie *bullshit*!" Naomi yells.

Three things happen at once.

The De Luca sisters lock hands, prepared to use their magic.

Naomi accidentally touches the salt circle, breaking it.

And there's a crash as the front door flies open.

"Sorry!" someone yells from the foyer. "Don't know my own strength sometimes."

Alonso manages to open his eyes. He's barely fighting his grandfather off, but when he sees who walks into the living room, that struggle fades to the background.

Because Marley is standing at the threshold.

And she smiles at him like seeing someone floating several feet off the ground is just another
Tuesday.

"Oh good," Marley says, "you got the party
started."

31

Marley

ALONSO DE LUCA'S EYES ARE SHIFTING FROM gray to green. When Marley talked to him at school today, she took note of the stormy gray color. If his eyes stay green, she'll be in real danger, but Alonso isn't that far gone yet. So she works quickly.

Step one: Show the poltergeist you mean business.

Marley brings up one hand in a defensive position. The juice from the juniper berries drips onto the carpet, and the feel of the pulp between her fingers grounds her.

Alonso's body rights itself. He's still floating, but he's facing her now.

Marley spots the salt circle—they made a *circle*, the idiots—and the tiny gap in the line. It's already broken.

Marley has to work hard not to roll her eyes.

Step two: Subdue.

Marley takes a running jump. Since Alonso is still at least partly in control, his face shows shock, but she's seen this trick before. Sometimes poltergeists won't take full control so their adversaries will get confused about who they're really hurting.

Marley isn't confused.

Alonso barely has time to raise his hands before Marley hits him, forcing him to the ground. His head narrowly misses the coffee table—phew!—but he cracks his skull pretty good on the floor. They'll worry about that later.

"The fuck!" Alonso yells, his voice wavering between the one Marley heard in school today and another deeper, more menacing one.

Marley uses one hand to force his mouth open, and the other hand to shove the juniper berries inside. Then she closes his mouth and plugs his nose until he swallows.

It takes longer than it should. Marley sighs and glances over at the De Luca coven and the two girls she recognizes from school, who are staring at her open-mouthed. She tries to give them a smile. "I'll be with you in a moment!"

she says, using what she thinks of as her friendly flight attendant voice.

Alonso swallows. Marley releases his nose and mouth, and he sucks in a breath.

"What—" Alonso tries to say between gasps, but Marley shushes him and grabs his chin. She turns on her phone flashlight and shines the light directly at his eyes.

"Color is stabilizing," she says, "and pupils are reacting as they should." She turns off the light and dismounts, dusting the salt off her clothes as she stands up.

All told, that took about twenty seconds. Not Marley's best, but pretty good.

She catches the words of a spell—probably one meant to stun her—and she quickly holds up her hands. "Whoa, De Lucas! I'm on your side, if you couldn't tell."

The girls from school are still gaping at her. The De Lucas, though, have finally regained their composure. They've linked hands and are whispering under their breath. When Marley holds up her hands, only one of them stops speaking— a woman with brown hair and a poofy bathrobe hanging off her shoulders. Not Marley's style, but it's definitely a look.

"Wait," the woman says, her eyes trained on Marley's face like she can see into her brain. "We should listen."

The other witches hesitate before dropping their hands. "You'd better give us a good reason for barging into our home uninvited," the tallest one says.

"I have one." Marley clears her throat. "I'm Marley Pierre. And if you mess with me, you'll hear from the Council of Witches."

Twenty minutes later, they're all sitting in the plant room. The De Lucas used another word for it, but Marley didn't catch it and she doesn't care enough to ask. It's beautiful, though, with tall glass windows and plants that look like they might eat someone.

Alonso is sitting in a chair across from Marley. He's wrapped in a blanket, his hair sticking up in every direction and his eyes wide. He looks like a traumatized Chihuahua.

"So you've known since you got to Idlewood," Alonso says. "About me."

"Yeah."

"Which means Milton knows."

"He suspects."

The De Lucas look at each other. "You didn't tell him?" Emilia De Luca asks, her voice quivering.

Marley softens. "No. But I'm supposed to."

One second later, Alonso is on his knees in front of her, hands held together in a prayer position.

"Normally I don't have guys on their knees until date three," Marley says. Dylan snorts, and Marley decides she likes her.

"Don't tell Milton," Alonso says, his voice like sandpaper. "I'm literally begging you."

Alonso doesn't need to beg. Marley already decided before she arrived at the De Luca home that she wouldn't tell Milton what was going on.

The last thing Marley expected after the events of the last year was to get another chance to prove herself to the Council of Witches. They're not big on mercy, especially where Park YeaLee is concerned. She doesn't deal in hypotheticals. Thanks to YeaLee's very unique magic, she deals in probabilities.

That's what happens when you're born with the ability to see all possible futures at once.

Sometimes witches have innate abilities that

don't need to be taught. Alonso is one of these rare cases. According to Milton, Alonso has exceptional magical strength and, apparently, a talent for necromancy.

Park YeaLee is another one of those people.

After Marley and Dot were blamed for the disastrous exorcism of Lewis Karrington over in Brooklyn, the Council flew in for the hearings. As Marley and Dot begged for forgiveness, for the Council to consider that maybe their anti-quated rules weren't always good for witches and mortals alike, Park YeaLee read their futures. Statistically, she decided neither of them was worth a second chance. But it was only Dot who got exiled. Since the Pierres sit on the Council, Marley kept her magic, but she was basically under house arrest, never able to leave Bloomington. Just like that, her future went down the drain. All her dreams, destroyed.

Milton saw how miserable Marley was. That's why he assigned her to this case: because it's so similar to the one that got Marley and Dot into trouble in the first place. It's quite literally a do-over.

Marley's heart squeezes. She loves her brother more than anyone on the planet, except for their grandma. Milton deserves to be on the Council. He's worked harder than anyone she's ever met to prove himself to them. But if Marley's fatal flaw is a problem with authority, Milton's is that he sees a person's heart and thinks he understands them. That everyone is a science experiment, and given certain conditions, Milton can predict exactly how they'll react. Given a few more years, the Council of Witches is going to either turn Milton into a robot who spouts only their very narrow ideals—or they'll eat him alive.

Which is exactly why Marley has to take this situation into her own hands. If she can prove Milton and the entire Council wrong about necromancy, Milton will realize that the Council needs to change.

And Dot's exile will be revoked.

"I don't plan on telling my brother anything as long as you're all honest with me." Marley leans back. "Why were you attempting an exorcism when you had no way to ensure that you didn't send *Alonso* across the Veil?"

The De Lucas are silent. Alonso looks at them, eyes wide. "What is she talking about?"

Vera De Luca looks away from her son. "We were going to figure that out as we went along."

Naomi gasps. "You didn't think about this?"

"Sure we did," Donna De Luca snaps as she finishes one cigarette and takes out another from a slim silver case. "We just weren't sure of the mechanics of the spell—"

"No, no," Marley says, wagging a finger. "That spell isn't like surgery. You can't pick and choose which spirit stays in the body and which one goes. Alonso and his poltergeist both would've been banished."

Alonso is shaking now. At first it looks like fear, but when he pushes to his feet and throws the blanket across the room, it becomes clear.

This is rage.

"When were you going to tell me?" Alonso yells.

"After it was over," his mother says.

"We didn't want to give you another reason to worry," Emilia says.

Donna just puffs on her cigarette.

"We altered the spell a little," Vera says. "We thought it would work—"

"It wouldn't have," Marley says. "I know because I tried it."

The whole room turns to her. The silence is heavy, and Marley sucks in a breath. "If I'm expecting you to be transparent with me, then I guess I should be transparent with you."

"Yes," Naomi says, "you should."

A leaf taps the window outside. Marley is suddenly cold, but she tries not to show it.

"My coven, the Pierres…our specialty is ward magic. The Barrions' ward—that crescent moon necklace their partners wear—it was made by my grandmother. But I was born a little different." She looks out the window, to the dark treeline at the edge of the De Lucas' backyard. "The dead always called to me."

"What does that mean?" Alonso says.

"It means that I have crossed the Veil more times than any witch that I've ever met. I've also devoted my life to studying necromancy. Exorcisms, in particular."

"But that's illegal," Donna De Luca says.

"I know." Marley shrugs. "The heart wants what it wants." Dot's face flashes in her mind, and Marley pushes that image away.

Dylan huffs a laugh. "How's it going for you?"

Marley seesaws her hand. "So-so."

"Great," Alonso mutters, falling into his chair again.

"You didn't let me finish. The Council

recognized my skills when I was pretty young. I've performed twelve exorcisms for the Council. Eight mortals, four witches."

"Mortals can be possessed?" Naomi asks.

"Sure can. Sometimes poltergeists get so strong they can manage to cross and inhabit a body on their own. But Alonso here basically laid out a red carpet for his poltergeist."

Alonso grumbles something inaudible, and Marley decides she's fine with not knowing what he said.

"So, exorcisms," Dylan says.

"Right. The thing about exorcisms is that after you do a few, you start to wonder if people really have to die."

"What do you mean?" Alonso says. "I thought the Council kills people for necromancy and then performs the exorcism?"

"The exorcism *is* the thing that kills people," Marley says.

The De Lucas exclaim in protest—"That can't be right!" "Those poor people!"—and Marley waits for them to calm down before she continues.

Alonso is just staring at her. "So you've killed twelve people."

Marley interlaces her fingers on her lap.

"The Council had you doing this when you were a kid," Alonso says.

For the first time, Marley's composure cracks. Most witches just praise her, but judging by Alonso's face, he feels sorry for her.

Which only makes Marley more determined to fix this.

"My friend and I tried to exorcise a little boy while keeping him alive. He was just a kid. He hadn't done anything wrong." Marley swallows the lump in her throat. "It didn't work. The poltergeist got aggressive, which led to the collapse of a building, and a bunch of people ended up in the hospital. The Council found out we'd used a new, untested spell, and... well. Let's just say they don't use me for much of anything anymore."

"But the Council sent you here," Dylan says.

"My brother sent me here. The Council wasn't going to know until I figured out whether or not you were actually possessed."

Alonso glares at her. "Well, now you know. Shouldn't you be calling them?"

Marley pushes up from her chair and walks over to Alonso. She uses one of her power poses—arms crossed, stance wide.

"I want to make a deal," Marley says.

Alonso watches her evenly. "What kind of deal?"

"You let me work on a new spell that might save your life," Marley says. "If you agree to let me try it on you, I won't tell the Council."

"You want me to be a guinea pig."

Marley doesn't deny it.

Alonso looks to his mom, then to Dylan and Naomi. They're all uncertain. Afraid. But when Alonso turns back to Marley, he's wearing a lazy grin.

"Easy choice," he says. "What do you got for me, Pierre?"

32

Penny

THE CLOUD LAYER IN IDLEWOOD GROWS GLOOM-
ier by the day. The people who come into Horizon Café talk about an early snow this year,
and with the way the temperature is dropping,
it seems likely. It's staying darker later in the
morning, and it makes getting out of bed for
early shifts at the café almost impossible.

And yet, Penny does it over and over again.

When you're heartbroken, people like to
give you advice. Time, they say, makes the pain
more bearable. One day you wake up and realize you've moved on. After all, Penny and Alonso
were only together for two months. It will soon
feel like ancient history.

But Alonso isn't in the past. His face is in Penny's mind every second of every day, and every
time she catches sight of messy blond hair or

even someone around his height, Penny's brain stops functioning.

Time doesn't stop, though. The world keeps moving, and you can only pine for an ex for so long before people get tired of you. She sees it in the way Naomi tries to make her laugh and sighs when it doesn't work, or Ron asks for the hundredth time if Penny wants to watch *Howl's Moving Castle*.

To spare them, Penny has been spending more time alone. She goes to school. She works. She goes to the library to do homework until it closes. She goes to bed.

Every day Penny waits for the pain to stop, but it doesn't. It's worse now, because sometimes she sees Alonso and Dylan together, and she can't stop thinking about that night Dylan walked into the De Luca home—as if she belonged there.

"Penny? Did you hear me?"

She looks up from the empty cup she's been staring at for who knows how long. Ron is slowly disemboweling the tiny printer they use for receipts. "Can you find me some more paper?"

"Sure! I just need to make this..." Penny glances at the receipt. "Peppermint bark latte.

Coming right up," she says to the man waiting on the other side of the counter.

"I thought I had it down here," Ron says, looking in a cabinet. "We've been so busy that I'm losin' my damn mind."

"Definitely losing your hair," Penny's mom says as she puts more pastries in the bakery case.

"I bought that Rogaine like you told me, so no more negging today."

Anita laughs, but then she catches Penny's eye. "Penny, that's going to—"

Foam overflows from the frothing pitcher. "Ah!" Penny jumps back as milk spills onto the floor. "Oh my god. Sorry, I…" She trails off, all her excuses running dry. The customer blinks at her, clearly not amused.

"Here." Ron tosses her a rag.

"Found it!" Penny's mom says, holding up a roll of receipt paper.

Penny wipes up the milk, trying to ignore her embarassment. "You should take your break, Ron! We got through the rush."

Ron raises an eyebrow. "You sure?"

"I'm *fine.*"

Ron looks like he wants to argue, but he must

really want his break, because he leaves for the back office.

After Penny hands over the latte, her mom follows Ron into the back to work on finances, leaving Penny alone up front. There's that late afternoon lull in the quiet conversations and occasional clink of coffee mugs against laminate tables.

Penny takes out her phone. There's one text from Corey, sent over an hour ago:

> Still want to study at the café tonight?

Penny smiles to herself. She and Corey agreed that they'd help each other survive their physics final with a few study sessions. She texts back a quick yes and puts her phone away.

The clock ticks. Penny yawns. There's movement in the corner of her eye, and Penny looks, wondering if there's a customer sitting in the farthest booth.

But no. There's nobody.

"You didn't see the Veil," she whispers to herself. "It was the fever."

"Excuse me?"

Penny jumps. There's a customer standing at the counter. "Oh, I'm sorry, I didn't hear the bell—"

She cuts off.

Standing at the cash register is a girl in a red athletic jacket. Her long twists fall over her shoulder as she examines the pastry case.

"I know you," Penny says. "Don't I?"

The girl straightens up, smiling. She exudes the kind of confidence that Penny can only dream of having, and Penny is suddenly self-conscious. All at once, she remembers where they met. "You were at Dylan's party, weren't you? I saw you in line for the bathroom."

"Good memory," the girl says, and she holds out her hand. "Marley Pierre. Nice to meet you, Penny Emberly."

Penny shakes her hand. "Nice to—wait, how do you know my name?" She gasps. "Marley *Pierre*? As in Milton?"

"Guilty. I'm the baby of the family." Marley points at the almond croissant. "I'll have one of those."

Penny stumbles over herself as she puts the croissant in a paper bag. "A-anything to drink?"

"Nope." Marley slaps five dollars on the

counter and takes a bite of her croissant, little flakes falling to the floor. "So how are things?"

Penny starts in surprise as she holds out Marley's change. "Oh, uh. Good."

"Really?"

Penny is usually able to push through her depression when she's at work, but something about Marley is disarming. She feels her cheerful customer-service facade fall by the wayside. "No. Not really."

"Mm," Marley says. "Well, I can at least help with the grimoire."

That gives Penny a hopeful jolt. "*The Blackfire Grimoire*? You have a copy?"

"Nope. But I know somewhere we can look. Can you and Corey come to Chicago on Saturday?"

"*Chicago?*" Penny hasn't been there since a middle school field trip to the big art museum.

"We need to go to the Chicago Public Library," Marley says. "It's pretty cool, if you've never been there."

"Oh…maybe? I can take the day off work, but I'll have to see if Corey is free."

"'Kay. Where's your phone?"

They exchange numbers. "Great! Oh, and I

have something for you," Marley says, sliding a fabric-wrapped bundle over the counter. Penny unrolls it and gasps.

It's an intricate silver knife. The handle is carved with a pentagram, and the blade is smooth and gleaming.

"It's silver," Marley says. "Won't be much help in a swordfight since a steel blade would cut right through it, but it's an ideal defensive weapon across the Veil."

"Why would I need this?" Penny says, looking from the knife to Marley.

"It's a precaution. Also…" Marley raises a finger and taps Penny in the middle of the head. "Your third eye is wide open, girl. Guessing you've been to the Second World?"

"Third eye?!" Penny touches her forehead, terrified that she might feel a slimy new eyeball.

Marley snorts. "It's not *visible*."

"Then how can you tell?"

"You smell like the Veil."

"I…I crossed the Veil once. And I got injured."

"Whoa. Is it healing?"

"Not fully."

"Makes sense. The injury was to your spirit,

not your physical body. It'll heal at a glacial pace, but it's definitely what opened your third eye."

"That's why I've been seeing the Veil?" Penny whispers.

"Not a lot of mortals have that ability. Pay close attention to your instincts, because they'll usually be right."

As Marley is leaving, the door opens from the outside, and Corey walks in. "Hey, Penny. Sorry I'm here early—oh." He smiles at Marley and holds the door open for her.

"See you Saturday, Corey," Marley says, beaming as she brushes past him.

Corey blinks. "Who was that? And what's happening Saturday?"

"I'll explain," Penny says, "but first—strawberry milkshake?"

Corey smiles, and the fog that Penny has been living in recedes just a little. "You know my order? Damn. What service."

Penny laughs, looking quickly away from him to hide her blush. "I try."

Alonso

ALONSO IS AT WALMART SHOPPING FOR RAW spearmint. Except he has no idea where to find spearmint or basically anything except books, jewelry, and candy, which are the only things he ever shops for.

According to Marley, spearmint is the best tool for keeping Alonso's evil grandfather at bay. Apparently malevolent spirits hate it. But Alonso spends five minutes in the vegetable section before giving up and going to the candy aisle.

Alonso grabs caramels. The little red-and-blue candies that look like old-fashioned Coca-Cola bottles. Then—yes!—sour worms. If his grandfather knows what's good for him, the worms will do spearmint's job. They're atrocious, but in a way Alonso loves. Especially when you put them in the freezer.

Arms loaded with seven bags of candy, Alonso

is about to go find the spearmint for real. That's when he spots the Reese's.

Penny's favorite.

He remembers shopping these very same aisles with her. They got a bunch of Reese's and then picked out colored pencils and coloring books before they went back to her house to watch movies and (after her mom went to bed) make out on the couch until midnight.

The thought makes Alonso's mouth go dry.

He manages to find the spearmint. He goes to the checkout counter, where a sad millennial rings him up and makes him pay twenty-seven dollars. Later, when he's in the car, he misses his turn to go home.

Because he's going to Horizon Café instead.

He'll just drive by. Slowly. He won't park, he won't get out. He just needs to see Penny for a few seconds.

Just a glimpse. That's all.

When Alonso drives by the large front windows with their painted Horizon Café logo, his eyes find Penny behind the counter. She's talking. Smiling. The sight makes Alonso's heart feel constricted, like a bird in a too-small cage.

Then he realizes she's not alone. Corey is there, too.

He's sitting at the counter, sipping a milkshake as Penny talks animatedly about something. Her expression turns from serious to excited to uncertain within seconds.

And Corey never looks away. His eyes are locked on Penny.

Alonso is stopped in the middle of the street, his foot pressed on the brake. A car honks and goes around him, but he can't move.

Corey is doing exactly what Alonso asked him to do. No, Alonso didn't ask—he *begged*. He's been doing a lot of that lately. But the way Corey is looking at Penny right now makes Alonso want to do something violent. Something he would regret.

"Fuck this," Alonso mutters, and he's about to put his foot on the gas again.

But his foot stays where it is.

Alonso blinks. He tells his foot to move to the gas pedal.

And it won't.

Alonso gulps. When he looks in the mirror, green eyes stare back at him.

You only have yourself to blame for this one. Your jealousy makes you weak.

Panic floods him. "No," he says, "don't do this." He reaches for the spearmint, opens the plastic box…he's about to put a leaf into his mouth—

But he's not quick enough to beat the ghost inside of him.

34

Giovanni

GIOVANNI PRESSES HIS FOOT TO THE GAS.

As he speeds away from downtown Idlewood, he opens the window and throws the spearmint onto someone's lawn. "Won't be needing that, thank you."

It was the Pierre girl's influence, he knows. Katherine Pierre's granddaughter. In life, Giovanni respected the Pierres. But after he's done with the Barrions, he might need to end them.

Giovanni gets back to the De Lucas' old Victorian house. He parks the car and takes the path through the woods—the same one he walked before he took care of Chuck Barrion. This time, he stops at a small clearing near the Barrions' backyard, ducking behind a few trees.

Far away, in the middle of the yard, is a gazebo. And in the middle of the gazebo is a thin figure dressed all in black.

Julian Chaudhary. Exactly who Giovanni was hoping to see.

Julian is lounging in a chair, ankle on top of his knee, like he doesn't have a care in the world. Until a few seconds later, when he shifts forward, burying his face in his hands.

"A low moment, hm?" Giovanni whispers. "Or is every moment a low moment for you?"

As if in response, Julian's shoulders begin to shake. The boy is crying.

"Pathetic," Giovanni says, grinning. Then he whispers the spell.

> *"Projection, deception,*
> *From my mind to your eye,*
> *See what I see…"*

Julian

THE NIGHTMARES JUST WON'T STOP.

Every night, Julian wakes up screaming. The dreams are all the same: Julian is standing in Grandpa's house. He can see Grandpa, but Grandpa can't see him. The doorbell rings, and Grandpa goes to answer it.

A figure cloaked in shadow stands at the threshold. It doesn't have a face. It barely has limbs, and yet it's able to raise a gun and point it directly at Charles Barrion's head. Julian screams for Grandpa, but he's always too late.

Over the last week, the dreams have changed. It's no longer some horror video game trope that's on the other side of the door.

It's Corey.

Julian's therapist says his subconscious is focused on Corey because of all his unresolved feelings about his family's company. Because

Julian—and of course this is Julian's fault, isn't everything—still hasn't let go of the way Charles Barrion chose Corey as Barrion Heating & Cooling's eventual CEO. Even though Julian is older and has been preparing for that role his entire useless life.

Julian loves Corey. But it doesn't matter how much therapy he does. When the entire trajectory of your life changes because of one person, and that person goes on getting praised and loved by everyone around them, where's the closure? It doesn't exist.

And then there was the incident at the football game.

Seeing Grandpa's ghost was probably a result of dehydration, like the EMTs said. But everything about it felt real.

It terrified Julian on an atomic level. The EMTs must not have noticed, because they gave him electrolytes and a cookie and sent him stumbling on his way. They had football players to watch over. Julian wasn't a priority.

Except, if his grandpa really appeared to him, that has to mean something.

I trust you, Grandpa said that night. *Protect*

the family. Don't let Corey fool them the way he fooled me.

Julian moans, pressing the heels of his hands into his eyes as they start to water. "That wasn't real. You were sick. You don't see dead people."

"Well, that's good."

Julian jumps. Corey is standing just outside the gazebo, hands in his pockets.

"Shit," Julian says. "Say hello next time."

"You were somewhere far away."

Julian blinks. " 'Somewhere far away?' Why are you talking like that?"

"Like what?"

"Are you, like, upset or something?"

"I guess so." Corey pauses. "Thinking about Grandpa."

Julian softens. Moments ago he was dwelling on how unfair it is that Corey has everything Julian wants—including the ability to move on from grief. But that isn't fair. Maybe it's not even true. Corey has always kept things inside, so maybe he has a different way of showing his pain. "Me too. I miss him."

"Really?"

Julian nods, but something strange happens.

His vision flickers, and for a second, the grass in front of the gazebo is empty. In his gut, Julian feels alone, like Corey isn't standing in front of him at all.

But when he blinks, Corey is back. Julian shakes his head a few times, but this time his vision doesn't change.

Fear bubbles up inside him. Did he imagine that? Or was it something worse than a shadow of his imagination?

Julian's mind sometimes feels like an alien planet, one that nobody will ever reach or understand—even him. Human brains are supposed to keep people safe, but Julian's doesn't do that. He always says the wrong thing or feels the wrong emotion. It makes him panic and want to run from situations that don't scare anybody else.

His worst fear is that his mind will lie to him. That it will completely disconnect from reality and destroy his relationships and his life.

What Julian just saw—was that his mind altering what's right in front of him?

Julian realizes Corey is talking, and he manages to say, "W-what?"

Corey looks away. "I want to ask you something."

Julian swallows, trying to chase away the image of Corey flaring out of existence. "Sure."

"It's going to sound bad."

Julian wipes his sweaty palms on his pants. "Just ask me."

Corey looks toward Grandpa's house. He's not wearing a jacket, just a T-shirt, as if it's summertime. But he's not shivering, even though the temperature dropped to the forties when the sun went down. Julian is about to bring it up, but what Corey says next makes him forget about everything else.

"Are you ever...relieved?"

"Relieved?" Julian laughs, because he always laughs when he doesn't know what to say. When Corey doesn't fill the silence, Julian goes still. He has an urge to pick the hangnail at his thumb, but he rubs his nail instead, so hard that it starts to feel hot. "About what?"

"That he's gone."

Julian has to be imagining this again. There's no way Corey is telling him that he *wanted* Grandpa to die.

"It was so much pressure," Corey says, and then an ugly expression twists his features. "You could never relax when he was around."

"You weren't supposed to," Julian snaps. "He had high expectations for us. He was worried about the company. About our family!"

Corey lets out a huff of disbelief. His shoulders are curved, his head cocked. Julian is spiraling now, and his mind catches on Corey's posture. Usually he stands straight up, hands at his sides, a soft smile on his face. But this…this barely looks like him.

There's his mind playing dark tricks on him again. Julian tears his eyes away, pressing at his temples.

"Why are you yelling?" Corey asks, condescension dripping from every word.

Julian stands up and walks down the gazebo, getting into Corey's face. "So you wanted him gone? That's what you're telling me?"

Corey shakes his head. "Julian…"

"Did you?!" His voice echoes across the lawn, getting tangled in the trees, but his pain doesn't get carried away with it.

The sky grows darker, and the shadows from the gazebo stretch onto the grass.

To Julian's horror, Corey doesn't deny it. Instead, he smiles, and it's cold. Mean.

"Grandpa was right about you," Corey says.

"You really aren't normal." And then he walks away.

Julian listens as Corey's footsteps fade to nothing. He stays outside even when he can see the clouds of his breath.

"Please let this be another nightmare," Julian says, but he never wakes up. Because this is real life. Either he accepts his reality or he stays hidden away like a scared little kid.

And Julian is tired of being scared.

Later, when he goes upstairs, Corey's door opens. He's in an undershirt and boxers, a towel hanging around his shoulders.

"Where've you been?" Corey asks, as if they didn't just have a fight in the backyard.

You really aren't normal.

For the first time, Julian wants to hurt Corey. Badly. It's terrifying, but it's also freeing. Maybe now, Julian will be brave enough to do what he has to do, without worrying about Corey's feelings or his well-being.

From now on, Julian will only think of their grandfather.

"Where you left me," Julian says.

Corey blinks. "Huh?"

"Fuck off, Corey." Julian wants it to sound

cool, detached. But he can't control himself, and the words come out sharp, spittle flying from his mouth like he's a wild animal.

Corey flinches, but it's not enough. When Julian sequesters himself in his room, he thinks about his next steps.

Protect the family, Grandpa said. But how?

When Julian finally falls asleep, the nightmare returns. Except when Grandpa opens the door to his house, Corey doesn't point the gun at him.

He points it at Julian.

Corey

WHEN COREY ARRIVES AT PENNY'S HOUSE ON Saturday morning, he figures her mom will be at Horizon Café. Instead, she's sitting on the porch. Behind her, Nimble is perched in the Emberlys' front window. Her intelligent eyes lock on Corey, and he shivers. She might be cute, but she's still creepy.

"Road trip, huh?" Mrs. Emberly says when she walks up to the car.

Corey tries not to cringe. He and Penny should've coordinated their stories. "We both, uh. Really wanted to see the Art Institute of Chicago. Again, because we went in middle school, but, uh…"

Penny appears in time to save him from himself. She's wearing a red winter coat with a white scarf. She looks like she should be going on some cliche winter date and sipping hot chocolate or ice skating, not meeting a witch to talk about dangerous spells. Mrs. Emberly kisses Penny on the forehead, and when Corey looks in the rearview mirror as they drive away, Penny's mom is still standing outside, watching them.

"She okay?" Corey asks.

"She's fine," Penny says, but it's too quick.

"She doesn't like you hanging out with me?"

Penny sighs. "Barrions make her...a little nervous."

Corey's hands tighten on the steering wheel.

"Not that she thinks—I mean, she knows you and I are just friends."

"I get it. I'd probably feel the same way if I was her."

Penny pauses. "Hey, is everything okay with Julian?"

Corey doesn't know how to answer that. He's barely seen his cousin in days—not since that night Julian came in from the cold, practically radiating with anger at Corey even though they hadn't seen each other all day. Then Julian stormed off and slammed his door. Maybe Corey should've followed him, but he can only take so many of his cousin's mood swings. "He and I...

we have a complicated relationship. Especially after this summer."

"Makes sense," Penny says, her voice low. She doesn't press him on it, and Corey should feel relieved.

Instead, he keeps going.

"He was really attached to Grandpa," Corey says. "His death … it's made him paranoid."

"Paranoid? How so?"

Corey clears his throat. "He's gotten it into his head that … I don't know. That our grandpa is talking to him."

"Oh," Penny breathes. "About what?"

"I'm not sure," Corey says. "But it's making Julian resent me. It's like he thinks I wanted Grandpa to die."

"But you didn't."

Corey is glad he doesn't have to look at her. "I didn't. But sometimes it feels like it's my fault anyway."

"Corey—"

He doesn't let her finish that thought. "You told us about the bargain, Penny, and I didn't know what to think anymore. Grandpa wanted me to lead the company. He also respected me less and expected more of me because I'm Black. And…" Corey shakes his head. "I always thought he built up the company himself. Even if he was a difficult person, he had done something great—but no. He was a mediocre white person who cheated his way to the top and left people dead in his wake."

"You don't have to like him or forgive him," Penny says. "Ever. But don't be mad at yourself for having love for him."

The darkness that's been threatening to overtake his mood finally does. "He didn't deserve any love."

Penny pauses. "Maybe not. But if he had yours, he was really lucky."

Corey looks over at her. Her blue eyes meet his in an unflinching gaze, and she smiles. The darkness Corey felt recedes, and something else takes its place.

His heart. It's beating faster.

Corey clears his throat and looks straight ahead again. "I don't know. Maybe." He tries to ignore the way his thoughts are suddenly scrambled. Since when is he nervous talking to Penny? The silence becomes almost painful, so Corey turns on the music.

You don't feel anything, Corey tells himself. *It's a crush. That's it. The bargain doesn't care about crushes.*

But there's another side to this, too. Even if this is a crush, Penny isn't just his friend. She's his friend's girlfriend. Didn't Corey promise Alonso he would keep her away? Keep her *safe*? He can't turn around and make a move on her behind Alonso's back.

They barely talk after that, except to adjust the temperature or change the playlist. By the time they reach Chicago, the sky is heavy with unfallen snow. They're only a few blocks away from the Chicago Public Library, but traffic is so bad that they've been sitting at the same light for ten minutes.

The skyscrapers reach up around them like long gray arms. Penny is leaning forward in her seat, staring out at the city. Her lips are slightly parted, and her eyes are even brighter against the wintery gray of Chicago.

He clears his throat and looks away. "Have you heard from Alonso?"

Why did he say that? His face heats up. He knows Alonso is the last person Penny wants to talk about.

Penny's voice sounds far away when she answers him. "I don't think I will."

"Why not?"

"He's over me, Corey. He doesn't even notice me when we're in the same room."

How can Penny actually believe that? Does she really think she's so easy to forget? "Maybe he's going through some stuff."

"He is. But I don't get to be a part of that." She pauses. "Has he talked to you at all?"

"I don't hear from him," he mutters, which at least feels half-true. Their last conversation was at Alonso's house, when he begged Corey to keep Penny away. Alonso avoids him at school.

Maybe Corey has imagined it, but he's pretty sure he's caught Alonso looking at Corey and Penny in the cafeteria, or when they're walking down the halls. *You did this*, Corey wants to say. *Don't get mad at me for doing what you asked me to do.*

It wasn't so long ago that it was Penny, Corey, and Alonso taking road trips together, meeting up behind their families' backs, trying to put aside their bad blood. Now that time feels far away.

And Penny feels closer than ever.

Corey watches the stoplight go from green to yellow to red for the sixth time. The line of cars doesn't move. People mill about on the sidewalks, shopping bags in hand. Store windows are draped with holiday lights.

A sad smile spreads across Penny's face. "I thought tragedy was supposed to make me wise, but I feel like I don't know anything."

"I think the only thing tragedy teaches us is how to move on. Sometimes we don't even get that far."

"Have you?"

"Not yet. But I'm working on it." Corey pauses. "My brain is soup from football, so that helps."

That earns Corey a laugh. Relief floods through him at the sound. *Finally*, he thinks.

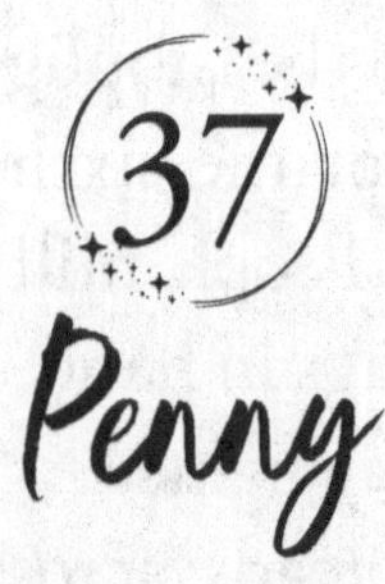

Penny

THE CHICAGO PUBLIC LIBRARY IS MORE GRAND than any building in Idlewood, even Meredith House. Marley told them to go to the ninth floor, and Penny's mouth falls open as she and Corey walk into a bright terrace. Above them, the ceiling is glass, and the afternoon light casts clean shadows on the limestone walls. Trees grow in square planters inside, and tidy hedges line the room.

What would it be like to grow up coming to a library like this? Penny pictures coming here every weekend and spending hours in the reading rooms or searching through the endless stacks of books.

Is this how it would feel to go to college somewhere far away? Would it be full of unknowns, but also possibility?

The thought startles her. When was the last

time she thought about living anywhere but Idle-wood? That's her home. She wants to stay there forever.

Doesn't she?

Corey elbows her. "You like it?"

"That's an understatement. You've been here before?"

"A few times. My dad used to drop me off here when he had meetings in Chicago." Corey is looking around, too, but his expression is guarded. He really is the definition of *inscrutable*. He's equally kind to everyone. Equally polite. But there's a wall between him and the world. Penny feels it when they sit on the couch watching television. She felt it during the drive to Chicago, after she made the mistake of asking questions about Corey's family.

The only thing that gets through the wall is anger. When Corey used to fight with Alonso, or when he stood up to his grandfather when they got caught doing magic in the woods, or when Dylan bullied Penny at a party, Corey seemed to say exactly what he was thinking.

Penny doesn't want to make him angry. But she wishes he was easier to read.

"Hey!" comes Marley's voice. She hops up

from one of the couches, waving at them. She's dressed like a yellow highlighter in a matching jacket and cargo pants. A black fanny pack hangs from her waist. "Thanks for meeting me up here! The Winter Garden is my favorite room."

"You're Milton's sister?" Corey says.

Marley holds out a hand. "And you're Corey. Nice to officially meet you. Sorry about the bargain."

"Uh…thanks?"

Marley waves them on. "Come on, it's this way."

"What is?" Penny asks as they follow her.

"You'll see."

Marley leads them down a few floors. It's quieter here, with the occasional library patron appearing around a corner before they disappear again a few moments later, leaving only the sound of their footsteps echoing against the tall ceilings.

Marley stops in front of a door with a stately plaque mounted to the front: STAFF ONLY.

"Are you staff?" Corey asks.

"Nope." Marley grabs a tiny drawstring pouch from her fanny pack. "Give me your hands."

Neither Penny nor Corey holds out their hands.

Marley sighs. "We're just going to another library, okay? For witches."

"We're not witches," Corey says.

"Obviously! That's why you're going to take *these*." Marley opens the little bag and dumps two gray feathers into her palm. But when Penny leans closer, they look more like leaves.

"Petrified belladonna," Marley says.

The word *belladonna* makes Penny catch her breath. "Belladonna as in . . . poison?"

"You might feel nauseous, but you'll be fine." Marley hands one to Penny and one to Corey. "After you put this on your tongue, it'll dissolve and hit your bloodstream instantly. Once we go inside, you'll have to lie and say you're witches. They'll test your magic, but the belladonna will make them think you're just like us. And then we're in!"

Corey looks a little squeamish as he stares at the gray leaf. Penny holds up her own to the light. It's delicate, as if one misplaced breath will make it disintegrate.

It reminds her of last summer. When every day held magic and wonder and, yes, fear. When Alonso was by her side—when Penny thought he loved her.

This isn't the same, but it gives Penny that familiar thrill. "I'll go first," she says, and she puts the belladonna on her tongue.

"Penny, wait a second!" Corey says, but the leaf is already touching Penny's tongue, and it immediately explodes into dust. Penny gasps as her mouth goes numb, and a shock of electricity travels through every limb of her body.

"Your turn," Marley says, smirking at Corey.

Penny gives him a weak thumbs-up. "Great," Corey mutters, but he puts the leaf on his own tongue. He flinches, and his pupils dilate. "Refreshing?"

Marley makes a spinning motion with one finger. "Let's move out, team." She turns around and knocks on the door one single time.

The knock is both loud and quiet, distant and heavy. It makes Penny dizzy. She stumbles back, and she thinks she's going to fall until she feels a hand resting low on her back, holding her up.

"You okay?" Corey asks, concern written on his brow.

"I think so," Penny says. Her mouth is still numb, and the words come out jumbled. But she's distracted by Corey's proximity. By his warmth.

In front of them, there's a click. The door shudders, and then it swings wide open.

Beyond it is darkness. And not the kind of darkness that lives in a room; it's the darkness of nothing. No floor, no walls, no people or living things.

Marley throws a grin over her shoulder. "Each of you should grab a shoulder. Don't want you getting lost in there."

Penny and Corey exchange a glance before they follow her advice. At the last second before they cross the threshold, Penny feels Corey's warm hand brush her own.

Without thinking, she grabs that, too.

———

The space beyond the door is exactly what it looks like: empty. It's absent of noise and any sense of time or place. Its only distinguishing feature is the freezing air. It might be colder than the Second World—or it might feel cold because of the warmth of Corey's hand.

After what could've been seconds or minutes, the darkness disappears. They're in some sort of entry hall made of stone. Sconces line the windowless walls, and a small flame glows in each one, tossing shadows all around them...

That's when Penny realizes Corey is still holding her hand.

He's gazing around the room, his brow furrowed. Despite his broad shoulders and muscled arms, this lighting makes his face look so young. Like the boy Penny used to watch from afar in middle school.

Corey notices her watching him, and his eyes go wide when he sees their interlaced fingers. "Sorry," he mutters, smiling awkwardly as he pulls his hand from hers.

"I'm the one who held your hand like a little baby," Penny says.

Corey smiles. "Pretty sure I was the one shaking."

Marley is already walking ahead of them. There's another door at the far end of the room. In front of it is a black card table, and a guy with messy dark hair sits hunched over, texting.

"Hey, Alec," Marley says.

Alec looks up and blinks slowly. " 'Sup."

Marley gives him a look. "Want to let us in?"

Alec's expression doesn't change, but he nods at Corey and Penny. "Who are they?" His voice is deep and monotone, like a late night jazz radio host.

Marley doesn't miss a beat. "Donaldson coven and Martin coven."

Alec blinks again, and Penny gives him a small wave. It's impossible to tell if he's suspicious or just bored.

"Come on through," Alec says, holding up a red crystal as he turns his eyes back to his phone.

Penny watches closely as Marley walks past him. She doesn't touch him, but there's an audible *snap* as Marley passes the crystal.

Penny is about to go next, but Corey grabs her arm and moves ahead of her. It's subtle enough that Alec wouldn't have noticed, but now Penny has to hold her breath as Corey walks through.

There's that same *snap* in the air. It worked.

Penny gathers her courage and walks by Alec's hand. *Snap.*

"Have fun," Alec mutters without looking up, and the door to the library swings open on its own.

When they walk in, Penny's eyes have to adjust to the dim lighting. Once they do, she gasps.

They're standing in the most bedraggled library Penny has ever seen.

There are stacks of books on shelves, on tables, and on the floor. Loose pages are piled here and there, with a few scattered across the stones under their feet. There are more sconces hanging from the ceiling. Half-burned candles sit inches away from books, which seems like a serious hazard, but maybe witches don't care.

"Whoa," Corey says when he nearly walks into a tilting stack of leatherbound volumes. His footsteps kick up dust, and a second later, he has a coughing fit.

"There's for *sure* mold in here somewhere," Marley says as Penny pats Corey's back.

"You don't have a spell for that?" Penny asks.

Marley shrugs. "Not my library, not my problem."

"Whose library is it?" Penny asks.

"This is 'an archive run by the Council of Witches for the benefit of all covens across the world.'" Marley rolls her eyes. "But they're stingy about who gets in, of course. Since Milton is on the Council, I get to do whatever I want. Gotta love being a nepo baby."

"Right," Penny whispers, but she gets the chills just being in here. "And this is in the Chicago Public Library?"

"Nope. The Chicago library is just the nearest door. Didn't you notice the portal we walked through?"

"Then the library is in another location?" Corey says. "Where are we?"

"I have no idea. The Council keeps it a secret. My guesses are either Sweden or Oklahoma. Sierra Leone is also a possibility—here, let's go this way." Marley leads them down an aisle with bookshelves on either side. They look like brown wood, but from the way they're sagging in the middle, Penny is guessing they're particleboard shelves from IKEA.

"How did *we* travel through a portal?" Penny asks. "Did you do some sort of spell?"

"Nope. The energy of the Second World can be manipulated in a lot of different ways."

Penny takes this in. "You mean you can use the Second World to travel to different places in the Primary World?"

"Basically." Marley nods toward the back of the room. "Corey, go check 'fraught with danger.' Everything should be alphabetized."

"Are you sure?" Corey asks, pointing at a pile of books on the floor.

"Only one way to find out."

Corey gives in. "I'll find you when I'm done," he says, his eyes lingering on Penny's face before he disappears into the shelves.

"Penny, you come with me," Marley says, and she walks to the lefthand wall. They stop in front of what looks like a prison cell with an old-fashioned padlock. Marley grabs the lock and glares at it. "This didn't used to be here."

"Do locks keep witches out?" Penny asks.

"It wouldn't if it was a regular lock." Marley sighs. "I'll have to stay out here and pour magic into this thing to keep the door open."

"What?" The lock looks normal at first glance, but Penny realizes for the first time that the keyhole has been filled in with silver. "B-but I need your help."

"You'll be fine! I won't be able to use a finding spell to help you, though, so you'll have to work quickly."

Penny peers through the bars of the door. "Are you sure it's in here?"

"This room is full of confiscated spell books, so yes, pretty sure." Marley pats Penny on the shoulder. "I believe in you."

Before Penny can argue, Marley is already

whispering to the lock in low, melodic words. There's a sigh, and the lock falls open.

Marley is still speaking, but she gestures for Penny to go inside. Gulping, Penny pulls open the iron gate. It makes a loud *creak*, as if nobody has moved it in years. The room is tiny, but it'll still take a while to look through all these books.

So Penny gets started.

She turns on her phone flashlight to help her see. Some of the books seem normal, but others send a shiver over her skin the moment she touches them. Ten minutes into her search, she opens one book to see pages stained in blood.

She quickly closes that one and throws it across the room.

Marley continues giving her magic to the lock. But after an hour, she starts to look a little gray, as if the life is being sucked out of her. Penny pushes herself as she reaches the last corner of the room. She remembers what *The Blackfire Grimoire* looks like: The cover is black fabric, and the animal-hide pages are thick and deckle-edged.

Which is why, when she reaches the final stack, she's positive the book isn't here.

Penny is about to leave the room when she

steps on a piece of paper and nearly slips. She manages to catch herself on the wall.

The paper is yellowed, and the title reads *Botanic Vivification*. Penny picks it up and reads through it. It seems to be a spell for bringing plants back to life. She moves to put it back, but something stops her. There's a twinge in her gut.

Marley said her third eye is open. Maybe Penny should listen to this feeling, whatever it means.

Marley can't see Penny from where she's standing. So Penny clears her throat, and she very slowly folds up the spell and tucks it into her pocket. Then she walks out of the room.

Marley lets her arms drop as she sucks in a breath. As soon as she finishes her spellwork, the door swings closed with a *bang*, as if someone angrily pulled it shut.

"Whew," Marley says, blinking a few times. "I need a nap."

"Here." Penny reaches out, and Marley leans on her.

"Your hands are empty."

"Yeah."

Marley closes her eyes. "Dammit."

"Is there anywhere else we can look?"

Marley's usual breezy attitude is gone. She grits her teeth. "We're done here. Let's talk after we get back to Chicago."

They find Corey, who is also empty-handed. Dejected, Marley leads them out of the dusty library. Alec doesn't look up from his phone as they stroll by. Once they're back in Chicago, they congregate on the steps outside the library.

"Are there any other copies of the grimoire?" Corey asks.

Marley doesn't answer. She's lost in thought, watching a group of tourists as they take videos of the library.

"Marley?" Penny says. "Are you okay?"

"Yeah." Marley sighs, letting her head fall back. "I know where we can find a copy."

"You don't sound excited about it," Corey says.

"The book is at my ex-boyfriend's house."

Penny grimaces. "Yikes."

Corey rubs his forehead. "We could reach out to him ourselves?"

"No way he'll show it to you if I'm not there," Marley says. "He's up in Wisconsin, so we'll have to figure this out later. I'm already running late, but I'll text you?" She hops down the stairs, stopping at the bottom to wave at them.

"What are you thinking?" Corey asks, his eyes roving Penny's face.

"There's something she's not telling us, right?" Penny says. "Otherwise, why would she be helping us like this?"

Corey looks toward the direction where Marley disappeared. "I don't know. She's Milton's sister, so I want to trust her."

Penny does, too. But there's that same pang in her gut—and it's telling her that something in Idlewood is very wrong. But what?

Penny

"A THIRD EYE," COREY SAYS. "WHAT'S THAT like?"

They're walking back to the parking garage in Chicago, weaving among the people on the side-walk. The wind hits like frozen knives. Penny shoves her hands into her pockets. Corey moves closer, and then they're huddling together against the cold.

"I thought I was seeing things," Penny says. "I wasn't sure I could trust myself, but Marley knew right away. She said it's because I've been to the Second World."

"So you can…tell the future?"

"No. It's more like an awareness of the Veil. It's visible to me sometimes, but it also gives me good instincts? Which should be useful, but so far…I don't know."

"What is it telling you about Marley?"

"That she wants to help us."

"And . . . ?"

Penny sighs. "That there's more to the story."

"I really don't need to meet any more witches after we deal with the bargain," Corey mutters. Penny tries to stifle her laugh, and he smiles down at her.

"You two are cute!" a girl says as she walks by.

"Oh, we're not—" Penny says, but she's already gone. "Sorry, Corey."

"What are you sorry for?"

She laughs again, but this time it's awkward. "I don't want to embarrass you."

Corey looks down at her, and for a moment Penny can't break eye contact with him. "Why would I be embarrassed?"

He's really going to make her say it. "Because I'm not your girlfriend, and it's *me*."

Penny realizes immediately how pathetic she sounds. She doesn't want Corey to have to talk her up. She's been a burden to all her friends since the breakup, and that needs to end. But when she looks up at Corey to apologize, he speaks first.

"When are you going to realize you're actually beautiful?"

Penny catches her breath.

They've stopped walking. Penny doesn't even feel the cold anymore; all she feels are Corey's eyes on her face.

A car honks its horn from the street, and they both jump, whatever spell they were under fully broken. Penny scrambles for something to say that can ease the tension. "Please ignore me, I don't know why these words come out of my mouth." She starts walking again. After a breath, she hears him following behind her, and eventually he falls into step with her.

They stay silent as they keep walking. It's only 4:30, but the sun is already down by the time they turn the corner to the parking garage. When they're half a block away, a sound makes Corey stop in his tracks.

"What is it?" Penny says. Her ears are officially numb, and her reaction time is slower than usual.

Corey doesn't answer, so Penny steps closer to listen. It's music—drums, a guitar, and a voice shouting just loud enough to be heard over the wind. It's coming from a bar on the garden level of a tall brick building. The first floor has a vintage clothing store, and the upper floors look like apartments with wrought iron balconies. But the basement bar's door is wide open, and red light is coming from inside.

A few feet away, there's a small chalkboard on the sidewalk:

STRANGE MEADOWS
w/ opener JANIE MAY

"It's a concert," Penny says. "Want to check it out?"

"I don't have a fake ID. They probably won't let us in," Corey says, but he's still staring at that red light.

Penny thinks back to that dinner at Corey's house. Corey is stressed about the bargain. She sees it in the slight curve of his shoulders; they were both hoping they'd be going back to Idlewood with a copy of *The Blackfire Grimoire*, but they're empty-handed.

A distraction is in order.

Penny walks down the steps. "Maybe it's all ages."

"Penny—" Corey says, but she's already poking her head inside.

"There's no bouncer," Penny says, beaming at him before she ducks into the bar.

This place is even tinier than Boxer's Irish Pub, and unlike Boxer's, it's almost empty. A young woman behind the bar smiles at Penny as she walks in. "Can I get you anything?"

Penny pauses. Doesn't she look too young? "Um…"

"One beer," Corey says. "An IPA, if you have it?"

He appeared beside Penny without her even noticing. The bartender's expression goes blank like she's been dazzled, but she recovers quickly. "Got it."

Penny glances up at Corey, but he doesn't seem to notice the way the bartender is staring at him. Of course.

Once they have the beer (which Corey insists on paying for even though he immediately gives it to Penny), they meander over to watch the band. There's a crowd of about seven people, most of whom appear to be friends with the musicians.

Penny elbows Corey. "Must be nice."

"Huh?"

"You know. Pretty privilege." Penny takes an exaggerated sip of her beer.

Corey laughs. "What are you talking about?"

"Um, that bartender? She couldn't stop staring at you."

Corey flinches, rubbing his neck. "I don't think so."

"I know so! You should go talk to her."

Corey doesn't reply to that, and when Penny looks at him, he's staring at her with that inscrutable expression again.

"What?" she says.

"I'd rather stay here," Corey says.

Penny stops breathing. Earlier, she convinced herself that she was imagining the longing in Corey's expression. Now it's undeniable. And what does Corey see in Penny's face? She should look away, but she can't. Maybe it's because of the beer. It's making her flirty, and she's saying too much. She can almost hear Naomi laughing and calling her a lightweight.

Penny shouldn't want this. But underneath her anxiety, there's a quiet desire she can't ignore. Her eyes rove his face, and there's something almost familiar in this feeling. It's like the beginning of … of what? She isn't sure.

But the last time Penny felt this, she was looking into a pair of gray eyes.

No. This can't be the start of anything between them. Corey doesn't want her. And even if he did, Corey has sworn off relationships until the bargain is gone. And Penny saw firsthand what her mom went through; developing feelings for Corey would literally be tempting the Shadow— which is the same as tempting death.

The band starts back up again, and Penny tears her eyes away from Corey. He shifts beside her, and when she dares a glance up at him, he's no longer looking at her.

Corey is completely focused on the band.

The lead singer is a girl with ghostly skin, bleached-blond hair, and more tiny tattoos than Penny can count. Her voice is rich and deep, but it's the guitar player who draws Penny's attention. He's got long brown hair in braids over either shoulder, and unlike the rest of the band, who are definitely performing for an audience, the guitarist seems to be in his own world. Half the time his eyes aren't even open, but his fingers move across the strings like it's the most natural thing in the world. When it's time for his solo, the other concertgoers scream louder than before. The guitarist's hands are a blur, and Penny finds herself holding her breath.

When the song is over, Penny claps and

whoops. She looks up at Corey, intending to say something about how amazing that was. But when she sees his face, she stops.

Because the wall has come down.

Corey is completely still, a small smile playing at his lips. He doesn't clap, but it's clear that it's out of awe, not apathy.

The band leaves the stage to go to the bar. The guitarist brushes past Corey, who moves quickly to let him through. But Corey glances at him again once his back is turned.

"Do you want to talk to him?" Penny asks.

"No. We should leave." Corey is already walking toward the door. Penny runs to catch up with him.

"Have you ever thought about playing again?" Penny asks when they're out on the sidewalk.

"Playing what?"

"Guitar."

Corey shakes his head. "I don't have time."

Penny doesn't want to be annoying, but it feels important to press him on this. "Corey—"

"I don't want to talk about it."

It's the closest Corey has ever come to snapping at Penny, and she hates that she's immediately so close to crying. She hides it, walking a pace behind him. For once she's grateful for this cold, which is so intense that her eyes dry up before tears can fall.

It takes them an hour just to get out of Chicago. Corey is still quiet, so Penny leans back and watches the city go by. But when they're on the highway that leads to Idlewood, Corey hands Penny his phone. "Why don't you put on some Quicklime?"

Penny looks from Corey to his phone. "Really?"

"Yeah. I've never listened to their stuff." His voice is soft. In it, Penny hears his apology. But it's like he's saying something else, too. Something like: *Tell me about your dad.*

Penny takes his phone and types the band name into the search engine. "This is my favorite album," she says as she taps on the first song.

Corey isn't quiet after that. He asks about Quicklime, about when Penny's dad started playing the guitar. About what it was like for her mom when her dad was out touring. About why Quicklime never moved to a city and tried to make it big.

"They were happy in Idlewood," Penny says. "Two of them moved away after my dad died, but Sly is still there. They had a huge following, though. They toured all over the country."

Corey shifts in his seat. "That life is so different."

"From what?"

"From everything I know. I was always taught you had to follow this very specific path to make a living, but I guess there are other ways to do it."

"Yeah," Penny says. "There are."

They fall into a more comfortable silence this time, but an idea has bloomed. When they're an hour away from home, Penny sends her mom a text:

Corey

COREY PULLS INTO PENNY'S DRIVEWAY JUST before nine PM. It isn't snowing in Idlewood, but the chill has followed them from Chicago. Penny is fast asleep in the passenger seat, leaning her head against the cold window.

"Hey, Penny," Corey says, shaking her shoulder gently. "We're back."

Penny sits up with a start. "Oh." She blinks the sleep out of her eyes. "I fell asleep."

"It must've been the dulcet tones of 'War Is an Art Form.'"

Penny laughs as she rubs her eyes. It puts Corey's stomach in knots, but he ignores that. *Just a crush. You're allowed to have a crush.*

"Hey, don't go yet. I have something for you." Penny opens the car door and runs into the house. The porch light is still on, and when Penny gets inside, the front windows of the house light up with a warm glow. When Penny reappears, Corey stops breathing.

She's holding a guitar case.

It's almost impossible to make himself move. Even looking at that case feels wrong, like Corey is acknowledging that he wants something he can't have. But he can't just drive off without saying anything, so he steps out, looking between her and the guitar-shaped black case. It has a few stickers on it, some of them torn and all of them faded.

"What's that?" Corey asks.

"A flute."

"Penny…"

"You're not allowed to argue with me." She pushes the case in his direction. "Take it. It's a gift from us."

But even if Corey accepts it, it won't be real. His entire life is already defined for him, and taking this guitar feels like the perfect way to hurt himself. Because he wouldn't just be taking the guitar—he would be admitting that maybe, all along, he's wanted to do a job that his family would never accept.

Penny gives him an encouraging smile. She thinks his silence is politeness. She doesn't realize he's having a full-blown crisis. "It's okay," she says. "It was my dad's, and obviously he's not using it anymore."

Corey's nose is stinging. He's about to fucking cry. He clears his throat, hoping she doesn't notice. "I can't accept that."

"It's been sitting in our house for a decade. My mom didn't want to get rid of it at first, but as the years go by...I don't know. It's not comforting anymore, having it around. We want to see it in the world, being played."

Penny is still holding out the case. There are a million things Corey wants to say to her. He wants to act like he doesn't want it and tell her to go back inside. He wants to tell her to never get rid of the guitar, ever, to hold on to every memory of her dad for as long as she can.

But Corey also wants to say yes.

"We have one condition," Penny says. "You have to learn one of Quicklime's songs for my mom. 'Battle Bouquet.'"

Corey laughs under his breath. "Is it difficult?"

"It's *easy*, Corey. My mom isn't evil."

Corey swallows. Slowly, he reaches out and takes the guitar. Penny beams, as if he just gave *her* a present.

He wants to pull her against him.

The urge is so sudden and so powerful that Corey almost can't fight it. He pictures digging a hole deep in himself and putting everything that happened with Penny today—the long car rides and the concert and this present—at the bottom. Then he covers it up.

"Thank you," Corey says. It doesn't feel like enough, but no words would be.

As he drives away, those memories and feelings deep inside of him shift. Already they're resurfacing. Corey needs some space from Penny.

If he starves these feelings, they'll die out like a flame.

40

Alonso

ALONSO IS SUPPOSED TO BE HEADED TO HIS locker before lunch. But as he passes the library door, someone whispers his name.

"Whoa," Alonso says as Naomi steps into the hall, looking around them as if they might get caught. "We have to stop meeting like this."

"Shut up and follow me," Naomi says, unamused.

She leads him into the library. "We need to make this quick. Penny will be here soon."

Alonso's heart constricts. "So this is where you guys have been eating."

"Not many other options. It was library or car, and car will get us detention."

Alonso looks at the books on the nearest shelf. Shakespeare's tragedies, because of course.

"Have you heard any updates from Marley?" asks Naomi.

"She went MIA this weekend. I was blowing up her phone, but she never responded."

Naomi drums her fingers against her bottom lip. "Are you sure we can trust her?"

Alonso thinks back to what Marley shared with them—that, because of her failed spell, a possessed boy died. The Council would've killed him anyway, but they punished Marley for trying to save him. She didn't care about the Council's stupid rules; she just wanted to do what was right.

"Yeah. We can trust her."

Alonso wants to look toward the tables, which are on the other side of the library, but he stops himself. Is Penny already there waiting for Naomi? It's been so long since Alonso has been close to her, since they've uttered a single word to each other. In the few classes they have together, Alonso can barely concentrate. Even if he can't see her, he can always feel her. Last week it was so distracting that he slammed his tablet on the desk and got the hall pass so he could cool off.

"Why is your face all red?" Naomi asks.

"It's nothing." Alonso stretches out his neck, avoiding her eyes. "How is she?"

Naomi crosses her arms. She almost looks pissed.

"What?"

"Haven't you noticed Corey's spending a lot of time with her?"

Jealousy flares in Alonso's chest again, but he ignores it. There's spearmint in the back of his mouth, and he starts chewing it like gum. "Yeah. I asked him to."

"I'm sorry, *what*?"

"He agreed to distract her. To keep her away from me."

"And that doesn't sound like a terrible idea because…?"

"They're not dating, Naomi," Alonso says, but he's trying to convince himself as much as her. He remembers the way Corey looked at Penny that day at the café. How steady his eyes were on her face.

Corey knows better, though. He's so terrified of the dark magic that's plagued his family for decades that he literally dated someone he didn't even like for three years. If Corey had feelings for Penny, Alonso is positive he wouldn't be spending so much time with her.

"Glad you're confident," Naomi mutters. "You know, it's really not fun keeping this from her."

"You promised."

"I know, and I haven't broken that promise." Naomi rubs her temples. She suddenly looks tired. "I just keep thinking about how she'll feel when she finds out the truth. I'm betraying her."

"So am I. But I'd rather betray her than risk her life."

"Fair point," she mutters before she walks away.

When Alonso gets home, Marley is there poring over spell books with the De Lucas. Or that's what Alonso *thinks* they're doing, until Marley whispers something and they all start laughing.

"Are you working on the spell or talking shit?" Alonso asks.

"Why not both? I can multitask," Marley says.

"She's great at spell work," Alonso's mom says. "She has a good sense for what words fit."

"I used to do slam poetry," Marley says by way of explanation.

"She was showing us some of her YouTube videos," Emilia says.

"Cool," Alonso mutters. "Still possessed over here."

"He's normally more fun than this," Aunt

Donna says as she places a cup of tea in front of Alonso. "Unfortunately he's decided to break up with the girl he's in love with—"

"Penny!" Marley says. "I love her. *So* pretty."

Alonso almost falls off his chair. "W-why do you know Penny?"

"We go to the same school," Marley says, smirking.

"Fuck off," Alonso mutters, which earns him a smack on the back of the head from Aunt Donna. *"Ow!"*

"Don't talk to her like that! We need her to save your life!" Aunt Donna says.

"I can't really picture the two of you together, though," Marley continues as if she was never interrupted. "Is it one of those opposites attract situations?"

"They're not opposites," Aunt Emilia says, smiling. "They're quite similar! More than you'd imagine."

"Hm," Marley says. "And how does that play out now that you've got this…situation?" She waggles her fingers up and down, presumably to indicate "possession."

"How does *what* play out?"

"The you-and-Penny thing."

"It doesn't," Alonso says. "Like Aunt Donna said, I ended it."

"And do you feel better or worse now?"

Alonso pictures Penny with Corey in the hall-way at school. He sinks into his chair and leans his head on his fist. "Worse."

"That tracks," Marley says. "Strong emotional bonds usually make it more difficult for poltergeists to manifest their will."

"So he never should've broken up with her?" Aunt Emilia says, sounding hopeful.

"I never said that. Penny could definitely get hurt. But it's good for us to know, just in case."

"Just in case *what*?" Alonso says.

"In case we need her during the exorcism," Marley says. She's not nonchalant anymore; she's scrolling through notes on her tablet and chewing on her nail.

"She can't be there. She doesn't even know I'm possessed."

Marley considers him. "Here. Look at this." She lays the tablet down. There are Leonardo-esque drawings of a human form, bisected with lines and circles. Small, neat handwriting decorates the edges of the drawings. Marley points at the line that passes through the very center of the form. "We need a spell that splits your soul from his."

"But we're already separate," Alonso says.

"During possession, the souls become very intertwined. It's hard to tell where one person ends and the other begins."

Alonso doesn't like the sound of that.

"Having Penny nearby might help," Marley says. "She's a stabilizing force for your spirit, so maybe she'll help you keep a firmer grip on your body. In theory."

"I don't want her around for any of this," Alonso says.

"But—"

"I'm not debating it," Alonso says.

Marley sighs. "Did Giovanni tell you to break up with her?"

"What? No, he wanted to hurt her—" Alonso cuts off, because even as he's saying it, he realizes the truth. "Oh shit. He *wanted* this."

Marley points at him. "Exactly. Because she made him weaker."

Alonso runs a hand through his hair. "I still can't be around her, Marley."

"What does Penny think?"

"Like I said, she doesn't know—"

"She's a big girl. Maybe you let her make her own decisions."

"This is for her own good!" Alonso snaps.

Marley throws up her hands. "You win *for now*. But I set the terms of this new spell, remember? If I say we need Penny there, then you can't tell me no. That's part of our deal."

Alonso grumbles, but he's too tired to keep arguing. Marley might be the only person alive who's more stubborn than he is.

"I'm having a thought," Aunt Emilia says, her voice small.

They all turn to her.

"Maybe we're thinking about this the wrong way," Aunt Emilia says. "We could focus on keeping Alonso in his own body, but could we do something that would make the poltergeist leave on his own?"

"He'd never do that," Marley says.

"Not on purpose," Aunt Emilia says, "but what if we make him lose control emotionally? Would it be easier to split them apart?"

Marley purses her lips. "Theoretically."

"I thought poltergeists only feel anger or a desire to kill things," Alonso says.

"That's what we're all taught," Marley says, "but I've seen poltergeists display sadness and longing. They're driven by grudges, so in a way, they're still ruled by their emotions. But that makes them stronger. To make them weak, we'd have to scare them. Remind them what it feels like to be human."

Alonso rubs his lip. "Emotions are visible through auras, right?"

"Right," Marley says.

"Hang on." Alonso walks over to a pile of spell books in the far corner. Nimble's cat bowls are still on the floor next to them, gathering dust. His throat goes tight, and he tries not to look at them. Instead he grabs one thin volume called *Rainbow Theory*.

"There's a spell in here that makes a person's aura visible," Alonso says. "Why can't that work on the dead? And if you can see *him*—"

"We can aim the spell," Marley says. "But first we'd need to make sure his hold on you was loose enough that the exorcism would work."

"Then we shouldn't be looking at spell books," Alonso's mom says, nodding at her sisters. "We need to dig up more information about Dad."

"It'll have to be something earth-shattering," Marley says. "And you can't tell Alonso. The poltergeist can access his thoughts and memories."

"I'll grab his old journals from the attic," Aunt Emilia says.

"There's nothing in his journal that will shock him enough," Marley argues.

"It could give us some ideas," Aunt Donna points out.

In Alonso's head, Giovanni is silent, but his presence is heavy.

"In the meantime," Marley says, turning to Alonso, "how would you feel about crossing the Veil?"

"You're joking, right? Giovanni would go apeshit."

"Maybe," Marley says, smirking. "But I want to test my theory about Penny."

Penny

PENNY WEAVES THE PRIUS OVER THE CRACKED cement of the abandoned mall's parking lot. Marley texted her early this morning telling Penny to meet here after school—something about finally talking to her ex-boyfriend. If he's in Wisconsin, it doesn't make sense why they would meet here, but Marley didn't respond to Penny's question about it.

Her phone dings. Another text from Marley:

I'm inside by the chicken place.

Marley is *inside* the mall? Penny glances up at the wide, single-story structure. The mall has been out of use for almost five years, and the roof looks like it might collapse.

"Why did I agree to this again?" Penny mutters. She takes her time walking to what used to be the main entrance. The sign above the door reads NORTHVILLE MALL. It used to be cerulean blue, but now it's faded to a sun-bleached incarnation of its former glory.

Penny used to come here with her mom in elementary school. She bought new clothes for sixth grade at the Limited Too. Now it looks like a home for ghosts.

The door opens, and Marley appears with a backpack over her shoulder, looking way too cheerful for her surroundings. "You made it!"

A pane of glass falls from the door and shatters on the ground.

"Oops," Marley says before stepping back. "Come on in."

Penny follows the witch into the depths of the mall. In the center, the skylight above them is miraculously intact. Underneath it is the old carousel, paint chipped and wires exposed.

"Sorry we had to meet here," Marley says. "It just so happens the Veil is especially thin in places like this."

"It is? Why?"

"Lots of old energy and nostalgia are built up in abandoned places. That's truer where there used to be big crowds." Marley unsheathes a knife, but this one is bigger than the one she gave Penny at the café. Scarier, too. And instead of silver, the blade is made of obsidian.

"Whoa," Penny says.

"You like it?" Marley says, holding it up. "The Guayama coven makes them. Weapons are their family specialty."

"Oh, right. And you make wards?"

Marley's smile fades. "My family does. But my interests are a little different."

There's an echo from the direction where they entered. "What was that?" Penny asks.

"Not sure."

The carousel emits a creak. Penny shivers. Even if she didn't know ghosts existed, she'd think this place was haunted. "Marley?"

"Yeah?"

"Why isn't Milton here? Is he actually busy?"

Marley considers her. "There's that third eye again." She tosses the knife in the air, catching it easily. "Milton wants to do things by the book. That's the Council's influence. Their rules are old and their attitudes are even older, which is why they get nothing done."

"You...don't like them?"

"The Council should be more lenient. They

see magic that breaks their *extremely* old rules and they lose their minds."

"I'm not trying to break any rules, though," Penny says. "Neither is Corey."

"Right." Marley crosses her arms. "If Milton was here, he would be able to help you, too. But let's just say I'm more efficient."

"So you don't want to be on the Council like him?"

"Oh, I want to. But when I'm on the Council, I'm going to advocate for change. We have to get out of the seventeenth century."

"You were raised by a Council member, too, right?" Penny whispers. "So what made you change your mind about all this?"

Marley doesn't answer for a long moment, and Penny wonders if she crossed a line. Finally Marley says, "It's complicated."

Penny should be scared. There's so much Marley isn't telling her. But that gut instinct is still telling her to trust Marley.

It only takes thirty seconds to regret that.

"You're here!" Marley says, waving to someone behind Penny.

When Penny turns around, she forgets why

she's here. Where she is. Everything leaves her mind except what's right in front of her.

Because Alonso is here.

He's wearing torn black pants and his black leather jacket with a red scarf. His hair has grown out, but the ends are still scarlet. He wears the same necklaces, the same silver earring, but he's different now. Disheveled. Wild. But it's the familiarity of him that's the most jarring part.

Penny can't move. What can she do, or say? She just has to wait for him to acknowledge her.

"Scary as fuck in here," he mutters, glancing around them. When his eyes land on Penny, his expression doesn't change. "Hey."

He's not surprised. Not like Penny is. Marley must've told Alonso she would be here—even though she left Penny in the dark.

"What are you doing here?" Penny says. Suddenly she's aware of the fact that she didn't put makeup on today, and her hair is pulled into a wild bun on top of her head. If she'd known...

But no. Alonso made it clear he doesn't want her. Eyeliner wouldn't have changed that.

"I, uh." Alonso pauses.

"We're friends," Marley says, smiling. "He

and I are on the same page about the Council and everything. And I'm teaching him something today. I hope that's okay?"

No. It's not okay. Penny has desperately tried to claw back some self-worth since the breakup, and now it's crumbling just like the mall around them. And it gets worse as Alonso ignores her. Penny notices every time Alonso chooses to look at his phone, at the empty stores around them, at...

Marley.

Penny looks between them. Alonso whispers something to her, and Marley laughs, hitting him playfully on the arm.

Oh. That's what this is.

Nausea makes Penny turn away. She can't be mad at Marley. Maybe she doesn't know their history.

That doesn't change the fact that Penny is feeling all the cracks in her heart break open again. She's bleeding pain and betrayal and any ability to pretend she's okay. She needs to leave.

But she can't. She's here for Corey. She anchors onto the memory of him, trying to bring herself back from the brink of fight or flight.

"Are we ready?" Marley says, sounding entirely unconcerned.

"For what, exactly?" Alonso says, but when he spots the obsidian knife in her hand, his jaw drops and he takes a quick step back. "Whoa."

"Calm down," Marley says. "How else did you think we were getting there? A Greyhound? We have to cross the Veil."

Penny forgets her pain for a moment. "The *Veil*?"

Marley points to Penny with the knife. "Remember what I told you about that portal?"

"That…" Penny searches through her memory. "That you can use the Second World to travel in the Primary World."

"You're about to see that firsthand." Marley lifts the blade as if she's getting ready to slice through the air.

"Wait," Alonso says, stepping in front of Marley. "I don't know if this is a good idea."

Something passes silently between them. The moment feels almost intimate, and Penny can't look at them.

"It'll be fine," Marley says. "Trust me."

Is it Penny's imagination, or does Marley

glance her way? Alonso grits his teeth before standing back, silently giving in.

"Can't we get across the Veil another way?" Penny asks. "We did it in August."

"Not if we want our bodies to cross, too. We have to cut a hole."

"That sounds stupid," Alonso growls.

"I've done it a hundred times." Marley looks thoughtful. "Or, no. At least a dozen? Don't worry, it's only a *tiny* hole and I seal it back up afterward." She holds out her free hand and closes her eyes. Slowly she turns in a circle.

From somewhere deep in the abandoned mall—maybe a broken window, maybe a disintegrating wall—the wind blows. It curls around them, lifting tendrils of Penny's hair and Alonso's scarf before rising to echo through the empty space. The wind gets louder and louder, and suddenly it hits Penny so hard that she has to turn away.

When she manages to open her eyes, Alonso is standing still, watching her. His expression is intense. Maybe angry, though what right does he have to be angry? Rage wells up in Penny's chest—at Marley for deceiving her, but mostly at Alonso for having the nerve to be here with her after he tore her life to shreds.

The wind moves around Marley, who continues turning in a circle. Not for the first time, Penny notices how beautiful she is. Watching her like this, with her long twists moving around her and her trench coat flapping behind her in the wind, she really does look like a witch. The kind Penny would want to be if she was born into a coven.

Maybe this is the sort of girl Alonso wants. Penny can't blame him.

Suddenly Marley stops and, in one smooth motion, brings the knife down in an arc.

The light above them was shining through the skylight, but now it flickers, as if the sun is going out. Marley turns to Penny and Alonso and gestures for them to follow her. Then she disappears into thin air.

Penny sucks in a breath and walks to where Marley disappeared. But an arm shoots out in front of her, stopping her in her tracks.

Alonso is so near she can feel the heat of his body. It makes her step back. She forgot what it felt like, to be so hungry for him.

Alonso is looking down at her with a furrowed brow, tension in his jaw. "I'll go first in case something's waiting on the other side."

Penny grits her teeth. "Fine."

He levels her with that glare—the one that he used to give her in classes and in the cafeteria, the one she used to think was hate, but that he said was longing. Now Penny knows better.

It's indifference.

Alonso moves ahead of her, and in a blink, he disappears into another world.

Penny moves closer. If she lets her eyes unfocus, she can see it—the billowing weft of the Veil, and the gap.

Penny sucks in a breath. Then she goes through it.

That familiar cold envelops Penny again. This time, it hits so quickly that it makes her dizzy. A hand grabs her arm, and when Penny opens her eyes, Alonso is standing before her washed in red light.

"You okay?" he asks, his voice low.

Penny nods and quickly disentangles herself from him.

Marley whispers a few words and moves the knife in the opposite direction, sealing the hole in the Veil. Then she sheathes her knife. "Come on, it's this way. We'll be walking for a while, so keep your voices down so we don't attract the wrong kind of attention."

"Wait," Alonso says. His eyes are closed. "I don't know if I can do this."

"Sure you can," Marley says, and there it is again—she glances pointedly at Penny. Then she turns around and marches ahead.

Penny is still confused. Even more so when she realizes Alonso is watching her.

"What?" she snaps. She can't help it. Because when he watches her, it makes her hope, and she can't handle the pain that comes along with that.

"Nothing," Alonso says, and he nods at Marley. "Go ahead. I'll follow."

They walk in silence for a while. The ghosts of the Second World keep their distance, and thankfully no poltergeists appear. The scenery around them starts to change, blurring into somewhere less familiar. Instead of flat plains and forests, it becomes hilly and overgrown with skeletal trees and shrubs.

Marley stops. "We're here."

They're in another town, and the dilapidated buildings rest on hills near a central river with pitch-black water. This time, when Marley draws her knife down, the tear in the Veil is immediately visible.

Somewhere behind them, there's crying. Penny turns, but there's nobody there.

"Go," Marley says, "before the dead find us."

Penny steps forward, and Alonso falls into stride with her. Just before they duck through the Veil, Alonso puts an arm protectively around her shoulders.

There's no time to protest. They're already passing through the Veil, and Penny leans into him as the cold reaches so deep that it might freeze her blood.

They exit onto a sidewalk in the Primary World. The buildings are no longer falling apart, but they're still old. Faded. The ground is covered in snow. They're on the edge of a river, and gray water rushes by, the edges limned in jagged patches of ice and dark rocks.

Alonso can't get away from Penny fast enough. She blinks, and suddenly he's giving her a six-foot radius. "Wisconsin, huh?" he says. "Cold as fuck."

Marley appears behind them. She whispers the words to seal the hole in the Veil, and just like that, it's over. They've traveled two states north in less than an hour.

"Whew," Marley says, tucking the knife back

into her jacket and walking up the street. "You two feel okay?"

"Fine," Penny says, but when she tries to walk, the cut on her thigh—the gift from the Shadow—throbs with pain. She stumbles.

Alonso is there in a flash, holding her up.

"What happened?" Alonso asks. "Is it your leg?"

Penny can't take this. She pulls away, even though she can barely stand. "I'm fine."

Alonso watches her, and if she didn't know better, she'd be convinced he was worried. But his expression disappears, and he rolls out his neck. "Whatever," he says, following Marley.

They turn into the driveway of a white clapboard house with a peaked roof. There's a mixture of both Christmas lights and Halloween lights on the porch, and from the sounds inside, there might be a party happening.

Marley raises her hand to knock on the front door, but she hesitates.

"Want me to do it?" Penny asks.

Marley sucks in a breath. "I didn't break up with him just to be afraid of him."

And she knocks.

Alonso

"IS IT JUST ME," ALONSO SAYS, TRYING TO HIDE his grin, "or did the music inside get louder?"

Marley huffs and knocks again. They wait.

And wait.

"This mother*fucker*," Marley spits, and she bangs violently on the door.

A literal record scratch comes from inside the house. There are footsteps, and then the door opens.

A short Asian guy with huge muscles stands over the threshold. His head is shaved close to the scalp. It's the definition of winter outside, but he wears a tropical shirt that's completely unbuttoned. There's a litany of tattoos along his torso and arms all the way up his neck. Alonso's eyes get stuck on one that looks exactly like this guy, tropical shirt and all, but he's holding his own severed head. Next to that is an image that Alonso has seen in Aunt Donna's tarot deck.

The Magician.

"Well," the guy says, raising a cigarette to his lips and taking a puff. His eyes are locked on Marley. "Wasn't expecting this today."

"Merry Christmas, Dot," Marley says, already pushing past him into the house. A few seconds later, she starts yelling: "Everybody out! Now! Family emergency."

Dot laughs under his breath and gestures for Penny and Alonso to come in. A few people are by the door now, struggling to put on snow boots.

"Y'all don't *look* related," one of them mutters, but with how red all their eyes are, they probably won't be putting up much of a fight.

Alonso follows Penny into the living room, which smells like weed. There are ten times more string lights inside than there were on the porch. There's also a Green Bay Packers tapestry covering half of one wall, along with lanyards for Lawrence University and UW–Madison. There's a football game on the big-screen TV, but Marley is already pointing different remotes at it, trying to turn it off.

The front door slams, and Dot stands at the entrance to the living room. He's still smoking, and Alonso and Penny might as well not even be there, because he's staring at Marley like she's the only thing that exists.

"How do you turn this shit off?" Marley grumbles, and a second later, the TV goes dark. She whips around to see Dot holding a remote.

"I keep this in my pocket," he says. "Can't have anyone trying to change the channel during the game."

Marley glares at him. She drops her bag on the chair and walks over, grabbing his cigarette and putting it out in an ashtray. "I need you in your right mind for this conversation."

"You know that stuff helps me think." Dot is smiling, though. "You look good, Marley."

"Of course I do," she says, matter-of-fact. She gestures behind her. "This is Penny, and that's Alonso."

"Hey," Dot says, shaking their hands. "Welcome to my humble abode. Can I get you a beer?"

"We're here on a work trip," Marley says.

"I figured. Why else would the legendary Marley Pierre show up on my doorstep?" Dot walks over to a cooler and grabs a beer can.

There's one tattoo that stands out on the back of his neck. It's simpler than the rest of his tattoos, with clean lines and a little uninked skin around it. It's only two letters:

MP.

It takes a second, and then it clicks. Marley Pierre.

Alonso looks at Penny, and apparently she came to the same conclusion, because she's staring at Dot's neck with wide eyes.

Marley doesn't seem fazed. "Your little brother isn't here, is he?"

"He's at the community center getting ready for Noj Peb Caug."

"Good. We need your grimoire."

For the first time, Dot looks surprised. "*Blackfire?*"

"Yes."

"Why?"

"We've got a bargain," Marley says. "It's a nasty one. Almost fifty years old."

"Fifty exactly?"

Marley looks to Alonso. "Forty-six," he says.

"Good. There's power in fifty that would make it harder to get rid of." Dot nods at Alonso. "You're a witch?"

"De Luca coven."

"Oh *shit*, no way." Dot holds up his hand for a high five. "We're exile twins."

Alonso frowns. "Not anymore."

"Oh." Dot lowers his hand, but he's still grinning.

"What's your coven?" Alonso asks.

"Fang. But like I said, we're not officially recognized anymore."

"Sorry," Penny says.

He holds up his beer can as if to cheers her. "It's fine, babe. My life is easier this way."

Marley grabs the can from him before he can take a sip. "*Dot.* The book?"

Dot holds up his hands. "Yeah, okay. But first…" He raises an eyebrow. "Does Milton know you're here?"

"No, and if you tell him I'll lock you in the Second World."

Dot laughs. His cheeks are red, but Alonso is wondering now if it's actually from substances. The way his eyes rove over Marley's face makes Alonso want to look away, except he can't. Alonso knows what chemistry feels like from a first-person perspective, but watching it second hand is kind of humiliating.

"You still get things done, Marley. I respect it," Dot says.

Marley just glares at him until he bows to her and leaves the room.

Penny clears her throat. "So. How long since you two . . . ?"

Marley looks around the living room. She's annoyed, but she doesn't look uncomfortable here. If Alonso had to guess, she's probably spent a lot of time in this house.

"I don't know," Marley says. "Six months, I think."

"Six months, two weeks, one day," Dot says as he walks back into the room with a large, tattered volume tucked under his arm. He holds out the book to Marley, but when she moves to take it, he pulls it away from her. "Am I getting this back?"

"Yes."

"When."

"We don't know."

Dot looks from Marley to Penny and Alonso. "Tell me about this bargain."

"Their friend's grandfather created it," Marley says. "Using De Luca blood."

"He killed a member of your coven?" Dot asks.

Anger that isn't his own flares in Alonso's chest. "Yeah."

"Has it killed other people?"

"Twelve," Penny whispers.

Dot's easy smile disappears. "God. That's a lot of blood."

Penny's eyes are on the floor. Alonso can't look away from her. Her mom was so close to joining them. Even though she's safe, the bargain has changed all their lives forever.

And it isn't over yet.

"So you need the bargain spell," Dot says.

"About that," Penny says. "Milton told us we need to make another bargain, and our friend has to follow the exact same steps as his grandfather. But that can't be right."

"What do you mean, Penny?" Marley says.

"His grandfather killed someone, but why should he have to do the same thing?" Penny says. "It's not what he wants, or what anyone in his family wants."

Dot nods at Marley. "You want to explain or should I?"

"He should be able to," Marley says, pointing at Alonso.

Alonso grits his teeth. "Magic has a cost."

"And to escape something like this..." Dot says. "You need to pay a high price. Your friend doesn't just have to kill someone. It has to be someone he loves."

Penny's breath catches.

"Sorry," Dot says. "Wish we had better news for you."

"I need a minute," Penny says, walking out of the living room. The front door slams again, and Alonso can see her through the front window, standing in the snow. Her shoulders rise and fall quickly, and when she looks up at the sky, her face isn't just red from the cold. She's crying for Corey. For everything he still has to go through.

Penny cares deeply. It's what made Alonso fall in love with her in the first place. But this feels different.

Alonso knew ending things with Penny would hurt her. But in his mind, this was going to be temporary. When they exorcised this demon from him, he and Penny would go back to the way things used to be. She would understand why he distanced himself.

But what if Alonso got it all wrong? What if pushing Penny away to protect her means he's going to lose her forever...

To Corey?

Something like fire ignites in Alonso's core, and there's a chuckle in his ear. *Giovanni.* Alonso turns away, already grabbing the spearmint out of his pocket and shoving a few leaves into his mouth. The taste is bitter and jolting, like caffeine without any of the brightness.

Dot sidles up to him. "So Penny. She's your ex?"

"How could you tell?" Alonso says, staring at the carpet.

"Because I get it." Dot nods at Marley, who isn't even paying attention. She's flipping through the grimoire, muttering to herself about how some of those spells shouldn't exist.

"How do you deal with it?" Alonso says.

Dot shrugs. "She didn't give me a choice. And I can't hold her back. I'm exiled, she's from a Council family. We're in different worlds now."

"Different worlds," Alonso repeats, his gaze moving to the window again. Penny is still outside, wiping furiously at her eyes and trying to compose herself. "No."

"No?"

"I won't accept that," Alonso says.

"Uh-huh. What's your story, man? Wait..."

Dot narrows his eyes. He steps back and looks Alonso up and down. "Hey, Marl."

"What, Dot?"

"You wanna tell me why you brought a possessed witch into my house—"

Marley smacks a hand over Dot's mouth, looking over her shoulder.

"Not in front of Penny!" Alonso whispers sharply.

Dot gently removes her hand. "*Now* I get it. She doesn't know." His smile fades. "Marley. What are you doing, babe?"

"My best," Marley growls.

"You know what I mean."

Marley throws up her hands. "Trying again."

Since they arrived, Dot has come across as confident, easygoing, uncaring. But this revelation turns him serious, and he suddenly seems older. Like the kind of person you call when you're afraid and need to be reassured—or protected.

Dot moves closer to Marley, forcing her to look at him. "Why?"

Her eyes soften. "Because we were so close, Dot. I know we were."

"I think we were, too." Dot glances at Alonso. "If Milton and the Council find out…"

"I know," Marley says. "I've got this."

Dot lets out a breathy laugh. "If anyone can do it, it's you."

Alonso looks back and forth between them. "You two want a minute?"

Marley tears her eyes away from Dot's face. "Nope."

Dot points to the grimoire. "I want this back. Hand-delivered."

"I'll hand-deliver something," Marley growls.

"Are you hitting on me?" Dot whispers. "I'll take it."

"Time to leave." Marley sweeps out of the room.

As they're putting their shoes on, Alonso glances up at Marley. "Why'd you bring me here?"

Marley cocks her head at him, and Alonso can't tell if she tries to make people feel stupid on purpose, but she's good at it. "Did you feel him while we were across the Veil?"

"Uh . . . no. Not really."

Marley nods at Dot's front door. "You got Penny to thank for that. Being around her makes you stronger, remember?"

"Because I love her?" Alonso says, the words low.

"Yes, but also because her third eye is open."

Alonso knows that should mean something to him, but it doesn't. "Her third eye? What are you talking about?"

"She's got a connection to the Veil. Her instincts are sharp, and it makes her a magical good luck charm, too, especially for complex spells."

Alonso tries to think back. His magic was always easy to access around her, but he thought he was just getting stronger. But that wasn't the whole story—Penny was making him a better witch all along.

But knowing that Giovanni wanted to separate them doesn't change the fact that the poltergeist threatened Penny's life. Part of Alonso wants to pull Penny aside and take it all back, right now—and then what? He just has to hope, the next time Giovanni gains control, the poltergeist won't hurt her?

"I'm not changing my mind," Alonso says. "About the breakup."

"I know you're stubborn. But this is a good data point for you to have. If you feel him taking control while she's around…" Marley links her arm through Alonso's. "You find her, and you do this, and I guarantee that bitch will sit his ass down."

The door opens, and then Penny is there. "Oh," she says, her eyes dropping to their linked arms. Her expression goes blank. "Are we leaving?"

Alonso steps away from Marley. "Yeah." He tries to catch Penny's eye again, but she won't look at him. It sends a stab of pain through his chest.

Having Penny close keeps Alonso's demons at bay. But what if she won't come near him again after this?

Alonso has to accept that risk. He's taking Giovanni down, and if Alonso has to go down with him, so be it. But he'll make sure Penny is safe.

Even if it's the last thing he ever does.

43

Corey

"COREY? WHAT DO YOU THINK?"

Corey looks up from his tablet, bleary-eyed. His dad sits across the conference table, waiting for Corey's response to a question he only half heard. Corey is in one of the uncomfortable but sleek chairs his dad chose to decorate the corporate offices at Barrion Heating & Cooling. It's early in the morning before school, but Corey's dad has started scheduling meetings with East Coast staff at this time so Corey can't escape them.

Not that Corey wants to escape.

On the projector screen next to the conference table, three vice presidents of sales sit quietly, waiting for his answer.

"I don't think investing in social media makes sense for a company like ours," Corey says. "You're not going to go viral with content about HVAC units. And even if you did, would that make a difference in sales? If people in high school or college see it, they're not going to have money or a need for our products."

There are murmurs of agreement among the VPs. James gives Corey an even look that says he's proud of him. Corey waits for that to buoy him. Even if he doesn't like this work, at least he can do it well.

But Corey just feels exhausted.

When they log off, Corey's dad starts swiping through his iPad. "I'll send you an AI-generated summary of the meeting later. But you did well."

"Thanks. I should probably get going." Corey starts putting his water bottle and his own tablet into his backpack.

Through the glass wall of the conference room, Corey can just see Julian. He's sitting at a desk, doing data entry. His eyes are open painfully wide, like he's exhausted but doesn't want to show it. He insisted on coming along this morning, which Corey should've been happy about—except Julian is barely acknowledging him now outside of one-word answers and cryptic looks.

If Julian wants to create a one-sided fight with

Corey, fine. Corey hates it, but he has to focus on the bargain right now.

Corey's phone buzzes, and he grabs for it immediately. There's a text from Penny. Corey was up half the night hoping she would send him good news, but there was nothing.

Now, Corey sucks in a breath, steeling himself before he opens her message.

We got the spell.

Corey shoots to his feet, the chair falling to the floor behind him. "Holy shit." Then he remembers who's sitting across from him.

Corey's dad taps his stylus against the table. "Something you'd like to share with the group?" It's meant to be a joke, but he's never been very funny.

"Nothing," Corey says, shoving his phone into his bag.

His dad sighs. "That came out wrong."

"Like everything else you say to me?"

The words leave Corey's mouth before he can really consider what he's saying. Corey freezes, one hand still in his backpack.

"I see," his dad mutters, his expression distant.

Corey can't remember ever hurting his dad's feelings. It's basically impossible. So why does his dad look *almost* upset?

Corey should apologize. His dad is only human. He lost Corey's mom, and he's doing his best. But when *sorry* is on the tip of Corey's tongue, his dad stands up. "I'm going to need you to cut out whatever is distracting you."

"Distracting me from...?"

"This." His dad gestures around at the room. "Your future."

"I'm not distracted."

"Please, Corey. I know you've been spending a lot of time with Penny Emberly. That would be inappropriate even if you weren't interning here at the company—"

Corey cuts him off. "And why do you think that?"

"Because of our history with her mother."

"And what *else*?" Corey snaps, because there's something his dad isn't saying. Deep down, Corey already knows what it is, but he still has a trickle of hope that maybe, just maybe, his dad isn't a classist piece of shit.

But his dad proves him wrong.

"She's not the kind of person who will be a

good match for you. You need someone more like your mother—ambitious and driven and with bigger ideas." His dad pauses. "I don't mean this as an insult to Penny. You know that."

The edges of Corey's vision fill with red. Since this past summer, Corey has been protective of Penny. Maybe *too* protective. But now, hearing his father tear her down, talk about her like she's worthless instead of one of the best people Corey knows . . .

Corey can't hold himself back. He opens his mouth expecting to scream, but he laughs. It's loud and bitter, and it makes his dad go perfectly still.

"Corey," James says, a warning in his voice.

"I'm sorry, I can't help it," Corey says. "You were already winning worst father in the world for ten years in a row, but somehow you manage to get worse every fucking day."

"Do *not* use that kind of language with me—"

"Then don't insult one of my best friends to my face and expect me to just stand here!"

"You cannot let the people you surround yourself with hold you back!" James is yelling now. "I see how your *friendship* is already making you deprioritize this job! Do you know how many people would kill to be in your position?

To have a C-level job and lifelong financial security waiting for them on a silver platter?"

Corey can name at least one person who would kill for all that and more.

They're both on their feet, the table still between them, and Corey is this close to launching himself over it.

"Financial security?" Corey says. "You want to know why we *really* have money, Dad? Why you have this fancy job and billions of dollars and endless success that you don't deserve?"

His dad's mouth falls open. "Corey—"

"Because it's the exact same reason I'm spending so much time with someone you have no respect for! Someone with no *ambition*. Someone who cares more about our family than Grandpa ever did." Corey leans over the table, aware that he can't take back what he's about to say. But he's so sick of watching his words. Of making sure his family doesn't carry this burden.

Maybe they all should.

"We have everything because of this fucking curse!"

His dad goes silent. He doesn't look distant anymore. His eyes are wide, almost vulnerable.

Good. Corey wants him to be scared. He wants

to hurt his dad the way his dad has hurt him time and time again since a train hit his mom's SUV ten years ago. All the times Corey needed a father and he didn't have one. All the times he just wanted his dad to acknowledge that being depressed, being hurt, was okay. That it didn't make Corey weak; it just made him human.

"Your dad did this to us!" Corey screams. "It wasn't a curse. It was a *trade-off*. Death for money. Death for his success, and yours. But not mine, Dad. Never mine. Penny and I are going to make sure of that."

James's fingers are splayed on the conference table, and he hangs his head. "Dear god. You're trying to stop it?"

The question makes Corey come up short. His dad's voice is low. Uncertain.

But he doesn't sound surprised.

"You knew," Corey breathes.

His dad looks at him, eyes wide with panic. "Corey…"

"How?" Corey says, his voice fragile now.

"His journals. He wrote about it, back when…when he…"

"Murdered Giovanni De Luca? I really hope that's what you're going to say."

His dad swallows. Nods.

His dad is quiet when it suits him. His silence is a business strategy. But he's never lost for words the way he is right now.

"How long have you known?" Corey demands.

"Since a few weeks after his death."

"Right," Corey growls. "And what were you going to do about it?"

His dad stands tall. "I hadn't gotten that far yet."

Corey's heart sinks. For one bright, brief moment, he thought his dad might save him from this. That he would offer to make a new bargain in Corey's place.

That was never going to happen, though. Because Corey's dad is just like his own father: selfish and greedy and concerned more about the bottom line than about their actual family.

"You were going to keep things exactly the same," Corey says.

"The only reason this town still exists is because of the company, Corey!" his dad says. "What will happen to your classmates, your friends, if it goes away? We'll be fine, but they'll be destitute! Idlewood will go the way of so many former industry towns in Indiana. It will be a *ghost town*. We have a responsibility to—"

"To sacrifice the people we love for a cause they never chose?"

"We have to think of Idlewood!" James yells.

Corey leans in. Every bit of resentment for his dad that has built up over the years is about to explode from him, and nobody will be left standing.

"I would trade it all to have Mom back," Corey says. "Looks like I can't say the same for you. You really are Grandpa's son, huh?"

His dad's face twists with rage. But there's movement at the door.

Julian is standing there, clenched fists at his sides. And it's clear from the intense hatred in his expression that he heard everything.

Corey isn't relieved, though. Because Julian is shaking so badly that he looks like he's going to break into a million pieces.

"Grandpa was right about you," Julian says, his voice cracking. "He said you hated him! That you would lie to make him look like he deserved to die!"

Corey grits his teeth. "Grandpa is dead, Julian—"

"He talked to me!" Julian screams, jabbing a finger into his own chest. "He knew he could trust me! He told me you . . . that *you* had something to do with his death!"

Corey's dad inhales sharply. Corey almost laughs again, because there's no way Julian believes that. They're cousins. Brothers, almost. Corey would never have hurt Grandpa, and Julian knows it.

But the longer the silence stretches, filled only with Julian's ragged breathing, Corey realizes that's no longer true. Something has broken in Julian. Not only is he convinced their grandfather's ghost is talking to him—the ghost is telling him things to drive him and Corey apart. It's clear as day.

But is the ghost real? Or is Julian's grief causing him to detach from reality?

"You can't even deny it," Julian spits.

Corey steps toward him. "Of course I deny it. Julian . . . come on. You know me."

"I guess I don't," Julian says. "I've heard the words from Grandpa's mouth, Corey! You can't manipulate me anymore! I *know* the truth! Even Alonso could see it—you barely mourned Grandpa! Not like I did!"

"Alonso?" Corey repeats. "What are you talking about?"

"The football game!" Julian says. "I've known since the football game!"

That's when Julian passed out. When Alonso did something to him . . .

Except it wasn't Alonso.

Everything clicks into place. That must've been the poltergeist messing with Julian. And maybe whatever Julian is thinking now is also because of the poltergeist.

Did Giovanni De Luca's ghost make Julian see something that wasn't there?

But there's one more piece of this puzzle that hasn't made sense. The way Corey's grandpa died felt like revenge. No money was stolen. His house wasn't even vandalized. The killer was there with one motive.

And Corey's grandpa died a few days after Alonso brought Mrs. Emberly back to life. When he was already possessed by Giovanni—Charles Barrion's original victim.

"Oh my god," Corey says.

"Corey?" His dad takes a step closer. "What's wrong?"

Corey ignores him. There's only one person he needs to talk to right now—because he has to know if his grandfather died by Alonso's hand.

"I'm going to school," Corey says, grabbing his bag.

"You can't even face me!" Julian says as Corey pushes past him. Julian tries to grab his shirt, keeping him there.

"Get *off*!" Corey screams, shoving Julian.

His cousin falls to the floor, crumpling like paper. Corey's dad tries to catch him, but he's too far and too late.

Nausea roils Corey's stomach. When Julian pushes himself onto his elbows and looks up at Corey, his anger is gone. He just looks afraid.

"If you're so ready to believe I'm a murderer," Corey says, "then it should be easy to stay the hell away from me."

He leaves before Julian can respond.

Alonso

ALONSO HAS RESORTED TO WEARING NOISE-
canceling headphones in the hallways at school.
It signals two things: One, that he doesn't care
if people are still gossiping about his breakup
with Penny. And two, that he doesn't want anyone to say a fucking word to him.

The one contingency he didn't plan for was
someone grabbing him out of the middle of the
hallway and dragging him into the empty biology classroom during passing period.

"What the—" Alonso cuts off. Because it's
Corey who dragged him in here, and now Corey
is pacing, his fists clenched at his sides. Alonso
pulls his headphones down around his neck.
"Corey? What's wrong? Is it…" His heart
squeezes. "Is it Penny?"

"No." Corey stops. He turns to Alonso, slowly,

as if moving faster means he won't be able to control his anger.

Because Corey is angry. Having been on the other side of more than a few fights with him, Alonso knows when to be afraid. Not that he ever runs away or gives in, but still.

Corey lifts his chin. "What do you know about how my grandfather died?"

Alonso flinches. "W-what?"

"You heard the question."

"Corey." Alonso gulps. "I don't know anything—"

Corey grabs Alonso by the shirt collar. "Then what do you *think* happened to him? How do you think he died?"

Alonso shoves him away. Now his own anger is stirring like an untamed animal. How dare Corey push him around? How *dare* he assume that Alonso knows a damn thing about what happened to Corey's malicious, racist, greedy grandfather?

Except Alonso does know something.

That image he saw at Corey's grandfather's house hasn't left his nightmares. It was Charles Barrion, eyes wide with terror—then, moments later, lying dead in a pool of his own blood.

Alonso might've had a vision. But, given who exactly is possessing him, he has another idea, too. And this one is so much worse that Alonso buried it deep down inside of him, never letting even the prospect of it into his conscious mind since that night.

But now, Alonso digs it up. He lets all that fear rise to the surface. And Corey must see it in his face, because he lets out a sound halfway between a laugh and some sort of animal keening.

"How did he get the gun?" Corey spits. "Was it yours? Or did he steal it from my grandfather? Did he wait inside his fucking house and jump out at him from the dark, or did he knock at the door?"

"I . . ." Alonso gasps for air. Suddenly, breathing is difficult. Is this what it's like for Penny when she has a panic attack? "I don't know if he did it. I don't know the details. I don't *know*."

"Then answer my first question," Corey says, his voice low. "What *do* you know?"

Alonso squeezes his eyes shut. The room is silent other than the muffled sound of students talking as they walk by the closed door.

"Answer me!" Corey yells.

"Shut up!" Alonso says, throwing his hands up

to hide his face. Because, goddammit, he's close to crying. "I already told you, I don't know!" He pushes past Corey and throws the door open, joining the throng of students.

"Alonso!" Corey yells.

The commotion in the hallway fades as people turn their attention to Alonso and Corey. Alonso stops walking. He can't escape this, just like he can't escape his poltergeist.

The anger inside Alonso becomes an untethered, wild thing. Nothing he can do about it. From here on out, Alonso is just along for the ride.

If Corey wants to give everyone a show, fine.

Slowly, Alonso turns around. "I'll tell you the truth if you want to tell me why you're stealing my fucking girlfriend."

The people around them gasp. From the corner of his eye, Alonso sees Marley. She's moving closer, trying to get his attention, shaking her head.

She doesn't realize it's too late to stop him.

"You mean ex-girlfriend," Corey says.

"You know exactly what I'm talking about," Alonso says. "You promised to help me. You *promised*. But I've seen you together, and—"

"And what?" Corey yells. "You didn't have to

break up with her! You could've just told her the truth!"

They're dancing around reality. Everyone here thinks this is just some simple love triangle, but it's so much more than that. This is a matter of life and death on both sides.

Corey must've forgotten that part.

"If you hurt her," Alonso says through gritted teeth, "I don't know what I'll do."

"The same thing *he* did?" Corey is pushing him. He wants him to say it. To confirm what Corey is already certain of.

He doesn't understand that Alonso can't say it. He can't admit that his own two hands were used to take a life. Alonso spent years trying to be a better person, and in one fell swoop, his grandfather destroyed that for him.

And Alonso had no idea for months.

During arguments or when Alonso was being especially difficult, his mom would tell him how much he was like his grandfather—the bitter, angry former patriarch of the De Luca coven. For the last few months, Alonso thought he'd finally outgrown that part of himself. But family is family, and no matter how hard you run, you can't escape them.

Maybe it's time that Alonso stopped fighting.

"I don't know," Alonso finally says. "Try me."

Corey's expression turns murderous. And he breaks into a full-on run, heading directly for Alonso.

Alonso wants to stop this. He wants to beg Corey to listen to him. But it's too late for listening, so he closes his eyes as Corey sends a fist directly at his face.

The pain is an explosion of light, an electric shock to all the senses. The impact makes him bite the inside of his cheek, and he tastes blood.

Alonso stumbles back, but he doesn't fall. His reflexes take over, and he sends a punch right back.

Corey dodges this one. He's fast, and Alonso is disoriented from the first punch, which is slowing him down. So Alonso decides to throw his entire body at Corey instead.

They tumble to the dirty floor, each of them fighting to land the next punch. Alonso's fist connects with Corey's nose, and Corey yells. Corey somehow manages to twist his leg so that he can send a thrust kick at Alonso's stomach, and Alonso falls back, clutching his middle as he gasps for air.

"Break it up!" someone yells.

Hands pull Alonso to his feet, dragging him away from Corey. By the time he can focus his eyes, Corey is on the other side of the hallway, being held back by his football teammates.

Alonso glances behind him. Aidan is holding him under the arms with a surprising amount of strength, but his eyes are pleading.

"You have to stop," Aidan says. "Okay? Just calm down."

Unfortunately, nothing pisses Alonso off more than someone telling him to calm down. He struggles against Aidan's hold and yells, "You'd better stay far away from her, Barrion! Or you'll see what happens!"

"Alonso!" Aidan pulls him backward again, Alonso's feet sliding on the linoleum. "Don't look at him, just look at..." He trails off, his face going a shade paler. Alonso follows his gaze.

Penny has appeared at the far end of the hallway.

Time stops, but only for Alonso. Around him, the crowd grows louder, phones are still out filming, and some people even laugh. But it all fades into the background.

"Penny," Alonso says. "Penny, I...I didn't mean..."

But Penny has already turned away from him. She's walking up to Corey. When he sees her, he seems to forget Alonso is even there. His face softens, and Penny raises a hand to his cheek.

It's a perfect scene straight out of a bad romantic movie. And Alonso is the fucking villain.

"Let's go, De Luca." The school security guard has arrived, and he has one hand on Alonso's arm. Alonso is about to shake him off, but there's a murmur in the crowd.

Because Penny is walking toward him.

Alonso stops breathing. This is his chance to explain everything. To finally tell Penny the truth about the possession, about why he had to end things with her. If he doesn't do it now, he may never get another chance—but Penny will listen. She's always understood that he was good at his core.

He takes a step toward her. "Penny."

"No," Penny says, her voice strained and low. She's shaking, but it's not out of fear.

Penny is the angry one now.

"I just have one thing to say." She blinks rapidly a few times, and then her bright blue eyes focus on his face. "I'm done trying to understand and justify every horrible thing you do."

"Penny," Alonso says, his voice cracking. He's grappling for a foothold in this conversation, for a way to make this okay again.

She doesn't give him the chance. She steps closer, getting in his face. There are no signs of fear anymore.

"Stay away from Corey," Penny says, "and stay far, *far* away from me."

"Penny!" Alonso calls, but the security officer and Aidan are both dragging him away now. "Wait, I can explain! Penny, *please*!"

She doesn't look back.

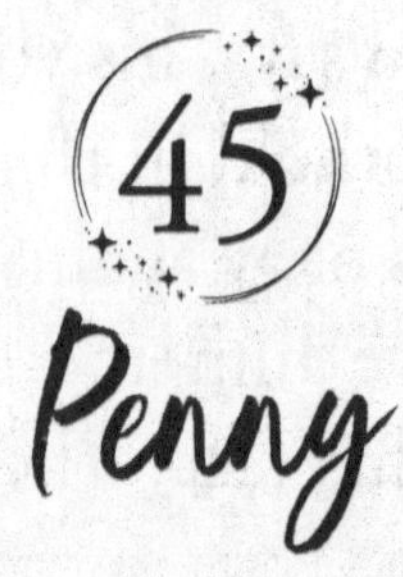

Penny

COMPARED TO THE CHAOS IN THE HALLWAY, THE nurse's office is peaceful. Penny sits next to the bed while the nurse bandages Corey's nose.

"You're lucky it's not broken," the nurse says, shaking his head. "Slight change to the angle and you'd be on your way to the hospital right now."

"Just lucky I guess," Corey says, and Penny doesn't miss the note of irony in his words.

"Rest up," the nurse says, looking from Corey to Penny. "I'll give you a few minutes."

When the nurse is gone, Penny waits on the edge of her seat, hoping Corey will say something. But he just sits there, staring off into nothing. He hasn't looked this defeated since his family's charity gala last summer, when they cast a cursebreaker spell and realized they'd failed to save his family.

But Penny has to know.

"What happened?" Penny says.

"It's a long story."

"You're just not going to tell me?"

Corey leans his elbows on his knees. "As much as I hate Alonso right now, I...I can't."

There's that wall again. He's not going to let her in, and Penny won't push him. She stands up. "I know you need space. I'll go."

But as Penny makes to leave, a hand wraps around her wrist.

"Wait."

Corey is standing now. He towers over her, and Penny's breath catches as he comes closer.

She's still holding her breath as he wraps his arms around her and pulls her against his chest.

It's like Penny has forgotten how to hug. She doesn't know what to do with her hands. All she can think about is the feel of Corey's muscles against her body, his chest against her face.

Penny had no idea if she would ever feel safe with anyone again. But here she is with Corey, and she knows with certainty that he wouldn't let anyone hurt her.

Even himself.

Penny raises a hand and places it on Corey's chest. His heart is beating rapidly.

"Corey," Penny says, "should we talk about this? About . . . about us?"

"No," Corey says, his voice muffled in her hair.

"But—"

"I can't, Penny."

Penny pulls back. She looks up at him and moves her hand from his chest to his cheek. His soft brown eyes move down her face, settling on her lips. He gets closer, and Penny lets her eyes drift shut.

She wants him. Maybe a part of her always has since all those years ago, when she watched him from afar and wondered if he would ever acknowledge her existence.

Now, Corey has done more than that. He's become one of her closest friends. Someone who understands her innately, who she can sit in silence with, who makes her blush with a well-placed smile . . .

Because Penny's feelings have grown beyond friendship. She's tried to deny it, but here, alone with him, she can't anymore.

Corey's lips brush hers.

Penny gasps, leaning in before she can stop herself. But before their lips can truly touch, she feels Corey pull away.

"No," Corey says again, stepping back and turning away from her. "We can't."

"I want to," she breathes.

Corey turns around, his eyes alight. "Are you insane? You saw what your mom went through! Why would you ever want to be close to me? I'm a fucking poison and there's no cure!"

"Because I…" Everything Penny wants to say is too much. *I care about you. I want you to have everything you want. And if that includes me, I want you to have me.* Instead she says, "We have the spell. We're going to create a new bargain—"

"*I'm* going to create a new bargain. *I'm* going to have to kill someone." His voice is a whisper, but every word is sharp and clear. "I don't know how to do that, Penny. And until I do…you should keep your distance."

The rejection hits directly in Penny's core like an arrow. She might stand here in the nurse's office forever. She might throw up. Hard to tell.

"Penny," Corey says, grabbing her face. "This isn't me saying I don't want you."

Penny gently grabs his wrists and lowers his hands. "I'm going to . . . to get back to class."

She wants him to stop her. To prove he wants her after all.

But he doesn't.

46

Corey

COREY SKIPS THE REST OF HIS CLASSES. Instead he goes home, locks himself in his room, and plays guitar until his fingers are sore.

"*Ouch,*" he mutters. He lays the guitar on his lap and looks at the indentations in his thumb and index finger. He can barely touch anything without his hands throbbing.

There's a knock at his door.

"Come in."

At first, there's no response. Corey's heart drops. What if it's the Shadow? He flashes back to the nurse's office. To Penny's lips, so close to his…

He wanted Penny so badly today that it terrified him. How could he let himself be so irresponsible?

Still. He's not in love. If he was, he would know it without a doubt. Falling in love isn't the kind of thing that can happen in the background. Every time he's seen it happen to his friends, his Aunt Helen, even Alonso and Penny, it changed them. They were the same people, but bigger somehow. More open.

Corey is the same as he ever was.

"Come in!" he says again, louder. To his relief, the door creaks open.

Then he sees who's on the other side.

"Dad?" Corey says. "Why aren't you at work?"

His dad crosses his arms. "Warren told me you were here. We need to talk about this morning."

But that's the last thing Corey needs. "I'm busy," he says, picking up the guitar again.

"Where did you get that thing? And..." Corey's dad steps closer. "Your nose?"

"It was a gift. The guitar, I mean. This..." He touches the bridge of his nose and winces. "...wasn't a gift."

"Hm." Corey's dad closes the door behind him. "I wanted to apologize. About our fight."

Corey stops playing. His dad doesn't apologize, at least never to Corey.

"I was shocked," his dad says. "That you knew the truth about the...about my dad. I didn't react well."

Corey softens a little. His dad is trying. He can see it. But that doesn't mean Corey should go easy on him. "So what are you going to do about it?"

"I told you, Corey, I came here to talk about the fight."

The words land like a physical blow. His dad is deflecting again.

"Get out," Corey says.

"Corey, we need to talk—"

Corey stands, throwing the guitar onto the bed. "I don't care about our fight! I care about the magic your dad used to make us rich! The magic that killed Mom!"

His dad's face falls. Rearranges. Suddenly he's pissed, and Corey is glad. He wants his dad to be angry. He wants his dad to feel *something* about Corey other than indifference.

"Don't act like I'm the bad guy here," his dad says, pointing a finger at Corey's chest. "You're being childish! Get yourself together."

Get.

Yourself.

Together.

These three words could be the theme of Corey's entire life. He's always been expected to be more mature than the other kids. Smarter. More polite. More focused. And when he wasn't?

He was judged. By his dad, yes, but mostly by his grandfather. The man who saw him as less than just because he was Black. The man who cast a spell on their family that would kill all the outsiders and make them that much richer for it.

Corey is sick of holding himself to the expectations of his family. Because they don't deserve all that effort and pain.

"Guess what, Dad?" Corey says, stepping closer. "If you're not going to undo this bargain, that means you *are* the bad guy. I don't care what stories you're telling yourself about *saving Idlewood* and *protecting people's jobs*. If you're willing to let people die, then you need to stop lying to yourself about what you are."

"And what's that?" his dad says.

"Exactly like your dad," Corey says. "The man that would've given this company to a white grandchild if he had any. The man that took Julian's future from him instead of believing in him and training him!"

"So now you're on Julian's side?" Corey's dad says.

"That's not the point!" Corey says. No, he

yells it. He's yelling again. His throat is tight, voice going hoarse. "The point is that someone needs to do the right thing, and it isn't going to be you!"

Corey is already grabbing his coat. He needs to get out of here. But his dad isn't done.

"And what are you going to do about it?" he says. "You're a kid, Corey!"

"Not anymore," Corey says, "but I guess you missed the part where I grew up without any help from you."

Corey tries to leave, but his dad blocks the door.

"I would give everything to have her back!" his dad says. *"Everything!"*

Corey is suddenly exhausted. "So you'd do what you had to for Mom, but not for me. Am I understanding everything, Dad? Or do you want to send me an AI-generated summary of this conversation later?"

The muscles in his dad's jaw tense, but he doesn't say another word. And when Corey moves around him to leave, his dad lets him.

Corey has to get out of this house.

Dylan

"IF I HAVE TO LOOK THROUGH ONE MORE BOX OF clothes that smell like the 1970s, I'm done," Dylan says, shoving the cardboard box aside. It falls over, and the clothes spill out, but that isn't her problem. This possession isn't hers to solve; she's just here to be nice.

And, as usual, Dylan regrets being nice.

Naomi sits across from her on the living room floor of the De Lucas' house. Or manor. Whatever they call this creepy place. If it were Dylan's home, she'd make it a year-round haunted house and charge thirty bucks per person for admission. Not monetizing this shit is a missed opportunity.

"If we're trying to make the poltergeist remember his own humanity, dressing Alonso in his old clothes seems like a good start," Naomi says. "You heard Alonso's mom! Our belongings hold memories."

"I believe in capitalism," Dylan says, "which is to say, I want to buy a ten dollar piece of clothing, wear it three times until it starts to pill, then donate it. I promise, none of my clothes hold any significant memories."

"You're soulless," Naomi says, but there's less venom in her voice than there used to be.

They've been coming to the De Lucas' home regularly to help the coven come up with strategies to loosen Giovanni's hold on Alonso's body. They've tested a few things to see how the poltergeist reacts, which seems like tempting death to Dylan, but apparently she's the only one who thinks so.

Not that it matters, because nothing has worked. They've played the poltergeist's favorite records, showed him photos of his former lover Ellie Barrion, and now they're going to have Alonso play dress-up.

"This all feels like a massive waste of time," Dylan says, sitting back against the wall. She pauses, cocking her head at Naomi. "I have another idea."

"Hm?"

"What if we talk to someone who actually knew Giovanni? All his secrets?"

"None of those people are alive anymore."

"Exactly."

Naomi drops a vintage polo shirt. "Like…we summon the dead?"

"We're doing an exorcism. Might as well add séance to our resumés."

But Naomi is already shaking her head. "Nope. Absolutely not. Literally never suggest that to me again."

Dylan sighs and grabs a box of old papers instead of clothes. "Whatever. You're boring."

"And I plan on staying that way."

Dylan starts sorting through the box, which has old receipts, recipes, even grocery lists. These people really don't throw anything away. "So did you see the fight?"

"What fight?"

"The Corey and Alonso fight, obviously. Everyone was talking about it at school."

Naomi sighs. "Trying to block it out, but yes."

Dylan tries to sound nonchalant. "Were they fighting over Penny?"

"Shh!" Naomi glances behind her, but Alonso is in the back of the house with his family.

"Fine. We'll whisper."

Naomi glares at her. "I think it was about more than just Penny."

"But you *know* she was a factor." When Naomi doesn't respond, Dylan snorts. "It's fine, Salazar. Corey and I are over. I accepted that a long time ago."

"No offense, but I don't care if you have unresolved feelings."

"So you're thinking about the curse?"

"It's not technically a curse, remember? But yes." Naomi pushes some baby hairs out of her face. She's always put together, but today she does look messier than usual. "I don't know what Penny is thinking."

Dylan swallows. She turns back to the box she's digging through. Thankfully she has a black belt in projecting nonchalance. "So she and Corey are…?"

"Not that she's told me. But there's something there. It's pretty obvious. And Penny changes the subject every time I bring it up, or she tells me there's nothing to worry about."

"She's an idiot," Dylan mutters.

"No," Naomi says, whispering again. "She's heartbroken. She doesn't think anyone could possibly love her again."

Dylan pulls a few notebooks out of the box, barely holding back a sneeze as a plume of dust envelops her entire face. She'll be taking a one-hour shower when she gets home. "Never thought I'd say this, but I understand where Penny's coming from. I thought I'd never want love again after Corey and I…you know." She clears her throat and starts flipping through the notebooks. "But what you don't realize is that you're more likely to fall in love again than you were before, because now you know what it's like. You're never going to stop wanting it, no matter how badly you got hurt."

"Sounds fun."

"It probably is, when the person you love actually wants you back."

Naomi lets out a low laugh. "For once, I don't know what to say."

"Silence is always a good decision. Especially because it makes most people uncomfortable."

"So diabolical!"

"That's my brand." Dylan opens an old leather-bound book. "Whoa. This is the grandpa's journal."

Naomi scoots over. "Really? Salacious."

"I think it's his last one. He died in 1979, right?"

There are footsteps, and then Alonso walks

into the living room. "Don't bother. We've already read it cover to cover."

Dylan keeps looking through the pages anyway. Her eyes land on a name. "Was Allison your grandmother?"

"Yep." Alonso plops down on the couch. His black eye shines in the low light of the living room. "She died a few years back. Alzheimer's."

"Sorry," Naomi says.

"She wouldn't have wanted to be alive for this," Alonso says. "She loved my grandpa a lot. Talked about him almost every day, even after she got sick. If she could see this whole situation, it would fuck her up."

Dylan files that away for later. "Any updates from Marley?"

Alonso's eyes grow distant. He might actually be nervous. "She's got the spell figured out, or so she thinks."

"Oh!" Naomi says, but when she sees the dark look on Alonso's face, her excitement disappears. "I mean…*oh*."

It's almost time to do the exorcism. And even with Marley's help, there's a good chance that Alonso won't make it.

"You think wearing his clothes is going to work?" Dylan asks.

"Nope. So I'm not doing it."

"Why not?" Naomi says. "It can't hurt."

Alonso shrugs. "Marley is going to try to separate our auras. That'll have to be enough."

"And if it isn't?" Dylan asks.

Alonso smirks. "You almost look upset."

"I don't exactly want you dead."

"That's the nicest thing anyone has ever said to me."

Dylan snorts.

"Both of you should go," Alonso says. "You probably have something better to do, like college applications or whatever."

"I've been done for weeks," Naomi says, as if this should be obvious.

"How about you, Dylan?" Alonso asks. "I picture you at a big state school. Evil sorority president. You'll run that place and terrorize anyone who gets in your way."

Alonso couldn't possibly know this is the last thing Dylan wants to talk about. She gets angry anyway. "I'm not going to college." She deliberately looks at her phone so she doesn't have to see their faces as she says it.

"Oh," Naomi says. "That's fine, if it's what you want."

"Why wouldn't it be what I want?" Dylan snaps.

"I don't know, because you're like tenth in our class?"

Despite the fire burning in the fireplace, Dylan feels suddenly cold. Damn, Naomi is good. "How do you know that?"

"Kelly's mom works in the admin office. She always posts the rankings online. You didn't know?"

"No. And just because I'm good at school doesn't mean I like it."

Naomi and Alonso go silent. Dylan tries to ignore it, but there's nothing she hates more than looking stupid, and admitting out loud that she's not going to college while acting like a toddler having a fit makes her look *very* stupid. She's never been good at hiding what she wants, but in the past, that mostly applied to Corey.

That was until her family went broke, and college was suddenly no longer an option. And by the time it is, most of the people Dylan's age will have graduated already.

Even this past summer, Dylan's future looked

bright. She was only considering schools in Los Angeles—USC, UCLA, Pomona, Pepperdine. She imagined waking up every day in a dorm room with an ocean view. She had good enough grades to get scholarships, and the money her grandmother left for Dylan would get her the rest of the way through the nauseating tuition.

Until Dylan's dad spent it all. Gambling addictions are a bitch like that.

"Anyway," Naomi says, "are there any more boxes you want us to search through?"

But Dylan is done here. "I'm out," she says, grabbing her backpack.

"Dylan, we didn't mean to make you upset," Naomi says.

"I'm not! I'm so happy that I spent an entire evening with the two of you. You make living fun."

"Remind me never to bring up anything serious with you again," Alonso mutters.

"Good plan," Dylan says.

Alonso moves to get up, and he's immediately wobbly on his feet.

"Whoa," Naomi says, reaching out to steady him.

"It's the parasite," Alonso growls. "I just need to rest."

Dylan should offer to help him to his room or something. She could at least get him to the stairs. But she doesn't.

"Sweet dreams," Dylan says, turning on her heel and heading for the front door.

But as she opens it, there's movement across the street at Meredith House. It's hard to see in the dark, but someone is running out the front door. The Audi's lights turn on as it's unlocked.

It's Corey. As he gets closer to the car, he drops his keys, and he yells. Actually *yells*.

Dylan waits until the Audi is speeding down the road. Then she runs to her own car and pulls out onto the street. When she's supposed to turn left to go home, she turns right, her eyes on Corey's taillights in the distance.

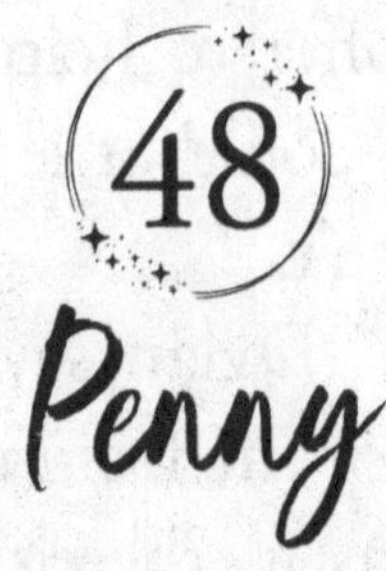

Penny

"I NEED TO ASK YOU SOMETHING," PENNY'S mom says.

Penny pauses in the middle of hanging up garland. They're at the newly renovated Charles Barrion Center for Community and Belonging, which is a day away from reopening with a holiday party for all the residents of Idlewood. It used to be a grimy building with chipped paint on the walls and old card tables in every room. Now it's full of modern furniture and tasteful wallpaper—and, as of today, a photo of Charles Barrion hanging in the entryway.

Penny can't look at it without feeling sick.

"What's up?" Penny says.

"What's going on with you and Corey?"

Penny was trying so hard to keep her mind off what happened today: the fight between Corey and Alonso, and Corey rejecting her in the nurse's office. But now it all comes rushing back, and it sends a stab of pain through her stomach.

She shouldn't have tried to kiss Corey. He's going through so much with his family and the bargain. What was she thinking?

"Nothing," Penny says, refusing to look at her mom.

"Penny." Her mom's voice cracks, and Penny has to look at her now.

Her mom's eyebrows are drawn together, her face twisted with worry. Penny is immediately overcome with guilt. She lets the garland fall. "Mom, I swear. Nothing is going on." And isn't it the truth? Corey will probably want nothing to do with her after today.

Penny's mom must hear the honesty in her words, because she relaxes. "You're sure?"

"Yes."

Penny's mom sighs, turning back to the decorations. "Okay. I won't bring it up again."

"You can. I get why you're worried." What Penny doesn't say out loud is that she's lost her sense of self-preservation. She thinks of Corey, and she doesn't think about the fact that being with him might kill her. She just thinks about what it would be like—to take more road trips and watch bad TV and cheer him on at his football games or concerts or whatever he does next. Corey makes everything look easy, but it's not. He works hard. He's determined. And Penny wants to witness it. To soak it up so that maybe, just maybe, she can figure out what's important to her, and she can make it happen.

Penny thought the heartbreak from Alonso would keep her far away from relationships, but clearly she hasn't learned her lesson.

She realizes her mom is talking. "Sorry, what?"

There's a rustle as Penny's mom digs through a box. "Where did all the string lights go?"

"Why don't you ask your landlord? Since he's the one who made us help."

"He's sponsoring the holiday party, and we have to keep him happy so he doesn't raise the café's rent. Our lease renewal is coming up." Mrs. Emberly sighs, hands on her hips. "Can you check the meeting room on the second floor? That's where they're keeping everything."

"Sure." Penny tapes up the end of the garland. "Ron is okay working the café by himself?"

"No SOS texts yet. We need to get back before the open mic, though."

"Okay." Penny hops over the boxes.

"Hey, sweet pea?"

"Hm?" Penny whirls around, but she's not prepared for the expression on her mom's face. She looks pained. Terrified.

"Tell me you're okay."

Penny swallows. "I'm okay."

Her mom nods, once. Then she gets back to decorating.

Penny hates the guilt she feels as she goes upstairs to the meeting room. She doesn't want to lie, but really, what is there to say? Yes, she tried to kiss Corey Barrion against her better judgment. No, he's not in love with her. Penny isn't in danger of anything other than more heartache. But how much more can she realistically take? The pain of losing Alonso has already changed her forever.

It's good that Corey pulled back. At least one of them is being rational.

Penny opens the door to the second floor, and she gasps.

Instead of overhead lights, the entire room is lit by dozens of plugged-in holiday lights. Realistically this must be so the volunteers who are decorating know which colors and style they're grabbing, but for a moment it takes Penny's breath away.

A voice comes from the far end of the room. "Who's there?"

Penny's heart gives a stutter. "Corey?"

He stands up from the table. The lights cast his face in reds and blues and greens and golds, and for a moment, Penny can't look away from him.

He's beautiful.

"What are you doing here?" Corey says. His voice is tight. Fragile.

"I-I'm helping decorate. Our landlord, he... um..." She laughs nervously. "Sorry, I'm just so surprised! I didn't think anyone would be up here."

I didn't think you would be here. I wasn't ready to see you again.

"I had to get out of my house, and I...I knew this place was open, so..." He trails off, leaving the rest unsaid. He's a Barrion. This place was funded by his family. Nobody would question him being here, locking himself in a room alone.

"I just need some of these," Penny says, moving quickly toward the red-and-green string lights on the opposite wall.

Corey is silent as Penny unplugs a strand of lights and winds it around her arm. By the time she straightens up, her heart is racing, and she's ready to run for the door.

But Corey has moved. He's standing between her and the door, and the expression on his face is impossible to read.

That's when Penny notices his eyes. They're puffy. "Were you crying?"

Corey doesn't answer. He just takes a step closer to her, and then another.

"Corey…" Penny begins, but what does she want to say? Not *don't come closer*. In truth, she wants the opposite of that.

"I'm so sick," Corey says, his voice low, "of holding back from everything I want." He lifts a hand and strokes Penny's cheek, and the touch sends a shock through her. He leans closer until his lips are only inches away from hers. "Where has that ever gotten me?"

"I don't know if you want this," Penny whispers.

"I do," Corey says, and he sounds so certain that it's all Penny can do to stay standing. She drops the lights and leans into him.

He's about to kiss her, and she wants it. But at the last moment, he moves his lips to her neck instead, and Penny gasps as he runs his open mouth along the place where her neck meets her jaw.

The last thread of Penny's self-control snaps. She grabs fistfuls of his shirt and presses her lips to his.

Corey tangles his hands in her hair, deepening the kiss. Electricity shoots through her, and she opens her mouth.

And then Penny's thighs hit the back of the table in the middle of the room. Corey lifts her onto it, and the feeling of his hands on the backs of her thighs makes Penny arch into him, pressing every inch of her body against his.

Corey groans into her mouth. "Don't hate me for this," he says against her lips before he kisses her again.

Except how could she ever hate him for this when she wants it just as badly? This is Corey, who's always understood her on a level that's almost innate. They've both grieved. They've both faced this bargain. They've both been desperate to do the right thing.

Penny feels something grow within her. Something that could become love, if they do this right.

And she wants to do it right this time. She

wants to give it her all. She wants to be the kind of person Corey wants…

And then Corey breaks the kiss.

They stare at each other for a long moment. Then it sinks in.

"I…" He stumbles back, running a hand over his hair. "I'm sorry."

"Don't be," Penny says, her voice ragged.

"Not me. I'm not the one you want. I *can't* be, Penny."

"But you *are*—"

"No!" Corey is yelling now. He sounds frantic. He backs up, and when he looks at her again, his eyes are wild. "I have to go."

"Corey!" she says, but he's already running out into the hallway. She follows him, but he's disappearing down the stairs, to where the rest of the volunteers are. And Penny can't let her mom see them together.

There's a sound behind Penny, like the squeaking of shoes against the floor. Penny gasps, turning around.

There's nobody. Nothing but shadows.

49

Corey

COREY DELETES PENNY'S NUMBER FROM HIS phone. He deletes their texts. He'll never speak to her again, no matter how much it hurts to stay away from her.

When he gets home, he doesn't turn on the light in his room. He gets in bed and closes his eyes. Tries to sleep. Tries to forget the feeling of Penny's lips on his.

But minutes pass like hours, and he doesn't forget a thing.

Corey gets out of bed, goes to the bathroom. He splashes water on his face. When he looks up into the mirror, he's overcome with hate. "You know better. You fucking *know* better."

But then he sees it. The change.

Maybe it's been slow. So slow that he hasn't even noticed it. But the Corey in the mirror isn't the Corey he's used to seeing.

His fingers are covered in bandages to protect the calluses that are forming from guitar. His hair is a little longer. His eyes are softer—less serious. This isn't the Corey he's been for years. This is the Corey he wants to be.

"Oh my god," Corey says, his words choked.

As if on cue, his phone vibrates. It's the family group chat.

S Sofía

> I saw the Shadow outside Camila's window.

AH Aunt Helen

> It was in the next booth over at the restaurant.

D Dad

> Family meeting. Now.

"No," Corey says, watching helplessly as the messages roll in. "No, no, no…"

Then he freezes. The air behind him has shifted, as if there's someone in the bathroom with him. Slowly, he brings his eyes up to the mirror.

The Shadow is standing behind him.

Even though it has no features, Corey feels it watching him. It's almost smug, as if it's saying *got you*.

Corey turns, already raising his fist. Rationally, he knows he can't hurt the Shadow. It's a creature of the Second World. But nothing can stop Corey's rage, and he puts all his weight behind the throw—

And his fist meets empty air. The Shadow is gone.

Corey sucks in rapid breaths, falling back against the bathroom counter. He doesn't feel relief; if anything, he's more trapped than ever.

His phone vibrates with a call from his dad, but Corey ignores it. All his thoughts are on the person who's now in the greatest danger.

"Penny," Corey says, and he runs from the bathroom.

Alonso

ALONSO CAN'T SLEEP.

His head is killing him, but now it's not just the poltergeist's fault. His black eye is throbbing, too. And every single time Alonso closes his eyes, he flashes back to his fight with Corey.

Specifically, to the moment when Penny put her hand on Corey's cheek.

"Don't think about it," Alonso mutters, putting the pillow over his face. He's so weak right now that he can barely walk in a straight line. But sitting here stewing isn't going to help him. It's just going to make it easier for Giovanni to take control.

Alonso sits up and grabs his phone. It's still open to the text Marley sent him an hour ago. She sent only one word:

Tomorrow.

They're going to attempt the exorcism in less than twenty-four hours.

Alonso needs a distraction. His eyes linger on Marley's name. Alonso met Dot; he could see that they were still in love. Marley would understand how Alonso feels.

But he can't text a girl he doesn't know that well and ask if she wants to hang out this late in the day. Not that she'd say no—probably the opposite. And then certain expectations might be placed on the evening.

Would it make Penny jealous?

"Shut *up*," Alonso says, throwing his phone onto the bed and burying his hands in his hair.

The worst part about having his grandfather— no, this *poltergeist*—in his head is that sometimes he plays on Alonso's worst instincts. His fears. His desire to hurt people after they've hurt him. And Alonso can't tell if Giovanni is coming up with this stuff on his own, or if he's seeing it within Alonso and then using it to manipulate him.

Alonso's phone buzzes, and his mind immediately goes to Penny. But when he picks it up, he sees a text from Aidan.

Come to my place! I'm having
people over.

Alonso sighs, typing out a response.

i got in a fight today

Aidan replies immediately:

So what? You're Alonso, it happens.

Alonso smirks. Maybe this is the distraction
he needs. He knows Penny and Corey won't be
there; Aidan and Kiki run in different circles
from them. Which means Alonso will be safe.

He throws on some clothes and grabs the keys
to the Shelby. For a second he waits for Nimble
to try to block the door or attack his calf.

Then he remembers. She's with Penny now.

That puts a damper on Alonso's mood. He
pulls up his collar against the wind outside, and
not for the first time, he wishes it was this past
July. That the weather was warm and his familiar
was still by his side.

That he and Penny could start over.

A *caw* draws his attention. Sitting on a tree branch nearby is a huge crow. It watches Alonso with beady black eyes, as if it's waiting for something.

A pit forms in Alonso's stomach. The crow's gaze is too steady. Almost knowing. It brings him back to the night the four crows flew into the De Lucas' home—and to the large crow who watched Alonso burn their small bodies from this same tree.

Could this be the same bird?

"Go away!" Alonso yells.

The crow doesn't move.

"Animals have no respect for witches anymore," Alonso grumbles as he gets into his car.

Music is blasting from Aidan's house when Alonso pulls up. His dad must be out of town for work again. Alonso swings his car keys around his index finger, saying hello to a few people as he walks up. "I was rooting for you today!" someone yells, and Alonso ignores them.

Before he can find Aidan or Kiki, Dylan appears in front of him like a banshee.

"Whoa," Alonso says. "Hello."

But Dylan doesn't say hello back. In fact, she looks like a wreck. Her eyes are red and watery, her hair is messy, and her hands are clenched into fists at her sides. "I need to talk to you."

Alonso sighs, but he follows her down the hallway. "Dylan, what is this about?"

She doesn't say another word until they're in a bedroom. She closes the door behind him and crosses her arms, sniffling. "Do you want to know what I saw tonight?"

"Judging by how rough you look, probably not—"

"Penny and Corey. At the community center."

Alonso suddenly can't breathe. "So what, Dylan?"

"They were together, Alonso," Dylan sneers. *"Kissing."*

Alonso's vision goes blurry around the edges. There's a roar like the rush of water in his ears.

"It wasn't supposed to go like this, was it?" Dylan says, each word pained and desperate. "I thought you didn't *want* Penny to get hurt, but now—"

Alonso doesn't hear the rest of what Dylan says. He's already gone.

And this time, he's thankful for the darkness.

51

Giovanni

"YOU CAN STOP TALKING NOW."

The girl stops. Dylan. Giovanni would be thrilled that she's here if his head wasn't pounding something fierce.

"Give me a moment," Giovanni says, tapping his temple.

"Why do you sound like that?"

Giovanni sighs. "Because I'm not your friend."

His hand is around Dylan's throat before she has the opportunity to scream. He lifts her off her feet until she begins to flail just a little, gasping for air, and then he lets her go. She falls to the floor in a heap, and it takes only a millisecond for her to scurry away like the little rat she is.

Or the rat Giovanni hopes she will be.

"Don't be afraid," Giovanni says, crouching down. "I've wanted to meet you for a while."

"Get the fuck away from me, you freak!" Dylan screams.

Giovanni cocks his head, waiting to see if anyone comes to her rescue. When there's no knock at the door, he shrugs. "Guess the music's too loud. I don't even understand music these days. I suppose I could request Billy Joel or Lou Rawls…"

"If you're going to hurt me, don't make me listen to you talk," Dylan says. "I can only take one kind of torture at a time."

Giovanni grins. "This is exactly why I wanted to talk to you. Now tell me…what's the real reason you can't go to college?"

Dylan's eyes go wide and afraid. This isn't what she was expecting, apparently. "How do you know about that?"

"I heard you talking about it. I understand it's a sensitive topic—"

"It's not," Dylan snaps.

"But I think we can help each other."

"I highly doubt that."

Giovanni pushes on. "There are only so many reasons someone wouldn't go to college if they want to. And the main one is money. Am I getting warmer?"

"Why are you asking me about this? Why should you care? You're fucking *dead*!"

"That's true," Giovanni says. "But money never dies. And I might be willing to give you the money you need if you help me with one tiny thing."

"You're a poltergeist," Dylan says. "What's the median salary for that job these days?"

Giovanni is losing his patience. This girl thinks she's smarter than everyone, but he could kill her with a flick of his wrist.

He won't. The Barrions are more important than she is, and he can't lose sight of that.

The muscles in Dylan's jaw strain, but she doesn't yell at him, which means he's getting somewhere. Giovanni knew as soon as she pulled Alonso aside at the party that this was his night to act. She's visibly angry, maybe even feeling a little betrayed by Corey and Penny. Which means it's the perfect time to ask her to betray *them*.

"According to Alonso's memories . . ." Giovanni closes his eyes. "You have a brother who works at Barrion Heating & Cooling."

"So what?"

"I want the code to get into the building."

Dylan's mouth falls open. "W-why?"

"You don't get to know that. But you do get to know about the money I buried." He leans closer. "Money my coven has never found."

"That sounds like such a lie."

"Like I said, we have something to offer each other. You give me the code, you get the location of the money."

"Or maybe, now that I know there's money, I'll find it by myself."

"You won't. I promise you that."

Dylan laughs. "And you'd just give it to me?"

Giovanni shrugs. "The dead have no use for mortal money. Everything I want is free."

Dylan's smile wavers. "There's no way it would be enough. You died like fifty years ago. What did you hide, a thousand dollars? College costs a little more than that these days. If you want to kill me, then try it."

Giovanni's smile fades. "You're no use to me dead. And fine. I can tell you how much it is."

After she hears the amount, Dylan's expression changes. She sits up a little taller, and now he really has her attention.

"I ran a very successful pharmacy," Giovanni says. "I saved money from the day I started work at thirteen years old. Just a little bit at a time. But it added up. It's amazing what some people were willing to pay for our medicines."

Dylan wets her lips. "Are you going to hurt Corey?"

"The Barrions will be—"

"I'm not asking about the Barrions. I don't care about them. I care about *Corey*."

"Corey will be unharmed."

"And my brother?"

"Just make sure he stays home from work tonight."

Dylan grits her teeth. "He won't just give the code to me, you know."

"I trust that you can make it happen if you put your mind to it. You're resourceful."

Giovanni can see his arguments working on her. He wasn't sure they would; after all, she's been helping the coven in their flimsy attempts to get rid of him. But Alonso never has fully trusted her. Gio saw some of what Dylan has done in the past—truly atrocious behavior. He was impressed.

Dylan watches him cautiously. "Back up."

Giovanni grins. He lifts his hands and takes a few steps back. Dylan gets to her feet and walks around him, never turning her back to him.

"I'll be waiting for your message on the little phone," Giovanni says, holding his grandson's telephone up.

Dylan gives a low, mean laugh. "God, you are so *old*." And she leaves.

52

Alonso

ALONSO WAKES UP TO THE SOUND OF A DOOR opening.

"Whoa!" someone says, laughing.

Alonso sits up, blinking rapidly. He was asleep, but apparently not in his own bed.

"Hey man, would you mind?" says a guy Alonso vaguely recognizes from freshman year biology. A girl hangs around his neck, giggling.

Alonso gets to his feet, grabbing the bed when his vision goes black. When it's back, he straightens up. "Have fun," he mutters, slamming the door behind him.

What just happened? Why was he passed out in a bedroom in Aidan's house? He leans against the wall, trying to think, but the pounding bass in the other room makes it hard. Wasn't he with someone?

Blond hair. Permanent frown lines. Wearing a tank top in winter.

Dylan.

Alonso pushes off the wall and heads into the party. He stands on his toes to see over the heads of everyone in the room. "Dylan?" he calls. A few people turn his way, but none of them is Dylan.

"If you hurt her . . ." Alonso mutters.

Giovanni's laughter cuts through the music. *Don't worry. She's doing just fine. Penny, though . . . you might want to check up on her.*

Alonso's eyes go wide.

Penny. Corey. *Together.* That's what Dylan said.

Alonso is already pushing through the party, ignoring Aidan as he shouts for him, asking where he's been.

Run, little Alonso. You might already be too late.

"I'm not!" Alonso yells, drawing more eyes as he talks to himself.

When he's outside, he checks his phone. He still remembers Penny's work schedule. Tonight is the open mic, which means Penny should be at the café.

The terror has curdled inside him, and it's

almost impossible to concentrate as he's driving. He nearly runs a red light, slamming on the brakes just in time. He sits there staring into the stoplight, willing it to change.

"Please be okay, Penny," he says, his voice cracking.

The light shifts from red to green, and Alonso presses the gas pedal to the floor.

Penny

"WELL, THE STOVE IS MISBEHAVING AGAIN," Penny's mom says. "I need to fix this tonight."

"Your tools are at home," Penny says. The open mic at the café was packed, and between that and decorating the community center, Penny can barely keep her eyes open. She probably deserves some kind of award for even being awake, especially after . . .

Corey standing close. His mouth on hers. His breath on her neck.

"Penny? Did you hear me?"

Penny straightens up. "S-sorry, what?"

"I said I can drop you off, grab the tools, and come back. Ron will just have to take the early shift tomorrow."

"I'll stay while you run home. I can finish cleaning the tables."

Penny's mom gives her a grateful smile. "Okay, sweet pea. I'll be back in ten."

Penny starts wiping down the booths one by one. It's already almost ten thirty, and she has her world history final tomorrow morning. She hasn't studied at all, so she should try to fit in at least an hour of reading before she goes to sleep. Maybe she should make herself some coffee...

The bell hanging over the front door jingles.

"I'm sorry, we're closed," Penny says, turning around, but her heart almost stops in her chest when she sees who's standing at the door.

It's Alonso. He's breathing hard, and his eyes are bright. When he speaks, it's through a sneer. "Is it true?"

Penny's grip tightens on the washcloth. Alonso hasn't been here in weeks, and his presence puts fissures in Penny's reality. Stringing even a sentence together suddenly seems impossible.

"What are you doing here?" Penny manages to say.

"I said," Alonso spits, his voice shaking, "is it true about you and Corey?"

Penny's jaw drops. He couldn't possibly know about today. Nobody does. "What do you mean?"

"I mean," Alonso says, "did he put his fucking hands on you?"

He's yelling now. And suddenly Penny forgets that he's not supposed to be here.

Because he's not the only one who gets to be angry.

Penny marches up to him, gets in his face. "Why do you care? I'm not your girlfriend. I didn't *understand* what you were going through, and you threw our relationship away. So why does it matter if he and I—"

"Because it's *Corey*!" Alonso says. "Did you already forget about this summer? About the hell we went through? That's what hooking up with a Barrion does to a person, and I won't just stand by while you and he—"

"He doesn't love me!" Penny says.

Alonso leans in a little closer. His breath is warm on her cheeks, her mouth. When he speaks again, his voice is low. Dangerous.

"Are you sure?"

Penny can't take this. Alonso already broke her—now she wants to break *him*.

"You don't get to do this!" Penny says, each word leaving her with force. "You don't get to interrogate me about my life, no matter how good your reasons are!" The tears are finally brimming over, but Penny doesn't even care. "I'll be lucky if I can ever love someone the right way again after what you did to me! You looked me in the eyes and you told me…" She screws her eyes shut. "You told me you'd loved me for years. But you changed your mind after *two months*. All it took was knowing the real me, I guess."

Alonso shrinks back. His expression is no longer angry; instead, he looks like he's wavering between shock and pain. "Penny—"

"No!" Penny yells. "Leave, Alonso. Now."

Alonso doesn't move, though. His gaze is liquid fire, and she hates how much it makes her want him.

"I do love you."

He's not yelling anymore. His words are quiet. Pained. A sob escapes Penny's throat like it's tied to a string and someone is pulling it out of her.

"Don't say that," Penny says, pressing her hands to her eyes. "Don't lie to me. Please just go."

"It's the truth," Alonso says, and suddenly he's close to her again. He grabs her shoulders, and she makes the mistake of looking at him.

His gray eyes are intense, boring into hers,

trying to communicate something. He opens his mouth, but no words come out. He swallows and tries again.

And when that still doesn't work, he leans in and presses his mouth to hers.

The second Alonso kisses Penny, he swallows the rest of her words along with the little bit of willpower she could've used to push him away. Penny grabs the front of his jacket, and Alonso lets out a low moan before pushing her against the counter. He's all over her, and the feel of him, the smell of him, the weight of him against her is too much.

He grips her waist.

She grabs his hair in a fist.

He groans into her mouth.

Time loses meaning. Someone could've told Penny they were there for hours or for minutes and she would've believed them either way. Alonso moves to take off his coat and Penny helps him. It falls to the floor, already forgotten. Alonso slides his hands up the front of Penny's shirt, running his fingers along her bare torso, slipping them under the bottom edge of her bra.

That's when the pain—all the sleepless nights,

the way he looked past her in the hallway, how thoroughly he broke her heart back in November—it all comes back.

Penny breaks the kiss and pushes Alonso away. He stumbles back, catching himself on one of the booths. His lips are swollen, and he looks at her with a mixture of longing and shock.

Penny can't become one of those people. The ones who let their exes touch them even when they'd just as soon touch someone else. The ones who spend months or even years wanting people who don't want them back unless it's convenient—or to prove a point.

"Get out," Penny says, and she almost doesn't recognize her own voice.

The sound of their ragged breathing fills the empty café. But Alonso doesn't leave; instead he steps toward her. "Please don't."

His words are like an electric shock that sends Penny barrelling toward him. She shoves his shoulders. "I said get *out*!"

"Penny, just listen to me!" Alonso yells, raising his hands. "I don't have a right to be here, or to pass any judgment, ever. But I need you to know why I did it."

"Did what?"

"Ended things," Alonso says, "with you. I never wanted to."

"Wow," Penny laughs bitterly. "All I needed to do to get you back was start to fall for somebody else?"

Alonso's face drains of all color. "You're falling for him?"

Penny didn't think about the words before she spoke them. But now that they're out, the truth of them sends a shiver through her. Yes, she is falling for Corey. Part of it happened years ago. Most of it, though? It's happened in the last month. When he was there for her in all her lowest moments. When he sat on the couch and debated the merits of François vs. Joey on *Amityville High*. When he ate lunch with her and Naomi, or drove her to Chicago or his house.

Penny never thought she could have feelings like that for anyone again. And here it started to happen, without her even knowing it at first. She was so mired in pain that she didn't realize love was growing over the wreckage of her heart. And if she lets it continue…

"So I'm too late," Alonso says.

Is he? If Penny continued to be with Corey, would their relationship become Penny's whole heart? Or would Alonso always have a piece of it?

He would. She knows he would, and the realization makes her ache.

Penny moves away from him. She doesn't want him or Corey or anyone else here with her; she just needs to be alone to sort through the mess in her head. "My mom is going to be back any minute, Alonso. Please just go."

But Alonso steps forward again, grabbing Penny by the shoulders. "Penny. I broke up with you because I'm possessed."

Possessed. The word doesn't mean anything at first. Possessed by what? Boredom with their relationship? Temporary insanity? The urge to date other people?

"It's my grandfather's poltergeist," Alonso says through gritted teeth. "I just wanted to keep you safe, but with him…he's so angry and violent and I couldn't risk your life, Penny. If anything happened to you…" His eyes rove her face. "I couldn't live with myself."

Poltergeist. Possession. *Alonso is possessed.*

Alonso at the football game. He was acting so strange, possibly using magic on Julian Chaudhary.

Alonso at the bonfire. The way he was flirting with Claire Polton. How Penny's eyes almost missed him because he looked like someone else. It was in his stance, in his smile . . . in his eyes.

"The headaches?" Penny breathes.

Alonso nods.

"Then you never wanted us to . . ."

"Being apart from you," Alonso says, "is the hardest thing I've ever done. And I brought your mom back from the dead."

Penny's eyes go wide. "That's when it happened. That day in August."

Alonso opens his mouth to respond, but there's a sound from somewhere behind them. Alonso lifts his head. "That smell . . ." He gasps. "Penny—"

Then an explosion tears through the back of the café.

Penny's feet are off the ground. It's as though somebody picked her up and threw her. Her body hits the wall—*above the booth*, she vaguely realizes—but her head is where she feels it the most. She falls onto the table and rolls to the floor, pain shooting up her side.

She's dizzy. Her body is wracked with deep coughs, and there's an ashy taste in her mouth . . .

Smoke.

Penny manages to open her eyes for a split second, long enough to see bright orange and yellow flames everywhere.

The café is on fire.

"Alonso!" she screams, looking around frantically.

He's lying a few feet away. His eyes are closed, his mouth hanging open. Blood trickles from a cut on the side of his head.

Penny drags herself over to him. "Alonso," she says, turning his face toward her. But he's out cold. She puts a hand near his mouth, and—

There. He's breathing.

"Help!" Penny screams.

There's movement from the front of the café, and Penny turns, hoping to see her mom or Ron, or maybe someone called the firefighters and they're already here—

But it's not a person. It's a tall spot of darkness.

Penny recognizes it. She's seen it so many times. She's spoken to it. She's fought tooth and nail against it.

The Shadow.

The smoke forces Penny into unconsciousness before she has a chance to scream.

"ALONSO!"

Someone is calling for him, but it sounds far away. Muffled.

Alonso opens his eyes. The air is so thick with smoke that he can barely see.

"Help!"

Penny...

It comes back to him: their argument, his confessions, the explosion.

Alonso sucks in a breath, trying to sit up. But there's a familiar weight on his chest. Penny is on top of him, eyes closed and head lolling back.

"Penny!" He pats her face. She doesn't respond. He presses two fingers to her neck—and *there*. A pulse.

Alonso lets out something halfway between a sob and a sigh of relief. He scoops her up in his arms. He doesn't want to risk going back through the office; she's inhaled too much smoke, and the fire is concentrated back there.

He has to get them out through the front.

The flames have spread fast. Even if he runs, the fire will get them.

Penny coughs, her body working to get the smoke out even though she isn't conscious.

Air. That's what they need.

Alonso turns to the front door. All the sound around him fades to a high-pitched buzz as he sucks in his breath.

His magic is ready.

> *"Currents through me, around me,*
> *Tempest at my beck and call.*
> *Gasp for me, earth and sky,*
> *Send your zephyrs as protection."*

He doesn't hold back, and he feels the spell working before he finishes the incantation. A cone of air forms around them, pushing back the flames even as it helps feed the fire. Alonso carries Penny through the café, dodging toppled chairs and the tattered remains of the booths. He tries to grab the door's metal handle using the sleeve of his jacket as a makeshift glove, but he hears a sizzle, and there's a burning smell as the leather scorches.

The window at the front of the café is still intact. Alonso steps into a booth, and he whispers a spell that shatters glass. As he watches, the window—with its familiar painted *Horizon Café* logo—breaks into thousands of pieces.

Alonso launches both of them through.

They land on the sidewalk, Alonso's shoes crunching on shards of glass. He stumbles, almost dropping Penny, who is still unconscious in his arms.

"Oh my god!" Mrs. Emberly runs up to them and grabs Penny's face. "Oh my god, *Penny*! Sweet pea! Wake up, baby, wake up!"

The ambulance and fire truck pull up, and the EMTs insist that Alonso put Penny onto the gurney. He's terrified to let her go, but he does it.

"Is she okay?" he asks.

"Let us do our jobs, son," the EMT says, but it isn't unkind. It's understanding. Gentle.

That's almost worse. Because just under Alonso's shock is a rage unlike any he's ever known.

As if Alonso summoned him, a familiar Audi pulls up. Corey jumps out of the driver's seat, terror etched into his face. He stops next to Alonso, watching as Mrs. Emberly climbs into the ambulance and it drives away.

"Is she okay?" Corey says, his voice ragged.

Alonso can't answer. All he can do is watch Corey, waiting for him to feel all the anger and fear and disbelief that's turning Alonso's vision neon red.

Corey finally looks at him, and his face goes blank. They stare at each other, waiting to see who will strike first, even though the injuries from their last fight are still fresh.

"Was this your fault?" Alonso says, his voice low.

Corey looks from him to the café. His last fragment of composure crumbles.

"I'm sorry," Corey says. "I never wanted this, Alonso, I swear. I was just trying to be there for her, I didn't mean—"

Alonso sends his fist into Corey's mouth, cutting off whatever bullshit apology he was stringing together. Corey's teeth cut into Alonso's knuckles, and Alonso relishes in the agony of it.

Corey falls back to the pavement. Alonso climbs on top of him and punches him again. Again.

Then Corey gets his strength back, and he

grabs Alonso's shoulders and throws him to the side. By the time Alonso scrambles to his feet, the police are already holding Alonso back.

"Get him away from Corey!" Officer Erickson says, and suddenly Alonso is face down on a cop car. They're going to cuff him. They're going to take him in.

"Don't arrest him," Corey says, and even the sound of his voice makes Alonso want to scream. But he's getting weaker. His vision is dark around the edges.

His grandfather is getting ready.

55

Corey

"I SAID LET HIM GO!" COREY SAYS.

"Lower the volume, Corey," says Officer Erickson. "We're just doing our jobs." He's still holding Alonso down, but Alonso has his face turned away, and he's shaking. Corey wishes Alonso would look at him, but of course he doesn't. It's like they're back to where they used to be when all they felt toward each other was hatred. Bitterness.

But Alonso is still his friend, and for once, Corey wants to use whatever privilege he has to fix this. Corey can guarantee that however much Alonso hates him right now, Corey hates himself more. He needs to fix *something* today instead of destroying everything.

"I don't want to press charges," Corey says. "It was a misunderstanding—"

Officer Erickson looks up at the sky, like

Corey is trying his patience. "I won't discuss this with you. Take it up with our—" The officer's voice abruptly cuts off. His eyes grow wide and vacant, like Corey isn't even there.

"What…" Corey begins, and then the two police officers step back from Alonso.

The witch straightens up and rolls out his neck. He seems leisurely, as if he wasn't about to be arrested. When he turns around, Corey realizes why.

Alonso's eyes aren't his usual gray. They're an eerie, almost glowing green.

Corey sucks in a breath. The cops are still frozen in place, like toys that have been shut off.

"Whew," Alonso says—but his voice is pitched lower, like he's aged a decade. He looks at his hands, waggling his fingers as if to test them out. "He almost died tonight…oh well. I guess things don't always work in our favor, do they, Corey?"

Corey wants to run. To scream. Everyone around him is in some sort of waking sleep: eyes open, unmoving. The lights of the fire truck are still flashing, and one of the firefighters is holding a dripping hose in limp hands.

"Finally," says Giovanni De Luca, "we get a chance to talk. I've wanted to meet you."

Corey grits his teeth. "It's not mutual."

"Can't blame you." Giovanni moves closer, and Corey backs away. "Isn't it funny how humans keep making the same mistakes, generation after generation? We never learn."

"I don't think that's true," Corey says, trying to keep his voice from shaking.

Giovanni cocks his head. "You don't seem much like your grandfather. It was obvious to anyone who paid attention that Chuck was a manipulative, thieving coward."

"Are you trying to give me a compliment?"

"No. Just expressing regret for what I'm about to do next." He lifts a hand.

A small figure jumps in front of Giovanni, knocking into his arm. Giovanni screams as Nimble dangles from his forearm by her teeth. He sends a fist into her stomach and Nimble drops. She lands on her feet and darts over to Corey, standing in front of him protectively.

"Little shit," Giovanni mutters, holding his arm to his chest. His leather jacket should've protected him from Nimble's teeth, but there's blood gushing down his arm, dripping to the pavement.

"Remind me never to mess with you," Corey says to the cat.

Nimble gives him an even look. Then she starts to hack up a hairball.

"Really? *Now?*" Corey mutters, and he leans down to pick her up before Giovanni can compose himself. But the hairball is already coming, and with one final hack, Nimble throws up a clump of congealed blood.

Except it's not just blood. From the middle of the mess, an eye stares up at Corey.

Corey's stomach roils. He wants to look away, but he can't. The eyeball is yellow with a pitch black, perfectly round iris.

An owl's eye.

Nimble pushes it toward him. She looks from Corey to the eyeball, clearly trying to tell him something.

"I...okay, fine," Corey says quickly, reaching out a shaking hand and picking it up.

Giovanni is glaring at them. "Hollow!"

The call echoes into the night. Through the flames of the café, a black bird flies down, eyes reflecting the fire. It lands on Giovanni's outstretched arm and lets out an earsplitting, "*Caw!*"

Nimble hisses.

"What do I do with this?" Corey mutters as he holds up the eyeball, but Nimble doesn't answer, because she's a cat who can't speak.

Giovanni is already whispering another spell, his eyes ablaze with Alonso's power. So Corey does the only thing that seems like it could work.

He holds out the eye.

Giovanni finishes the spell—

Corey gasps. There's heat and pain and something sharp at his shoulders, like claws digging in. But he keeps the eye facing the poltergeist until he feels nothing but the cold night air again.

Giovanni scowls. "Clever beast!"

Corey glances at Nimble, whose tail is swishing in a way that almost looks like gloating. Because, Corey realizes, the eye protected him from Giovanni's magic.

The crow flies from Giovanni's arm and heads straight for Nimble. Corey jumps in front of her, grabbing for the bird. It's impossibly strong and heavy for a crow, but Corey manages to get a hold of its wings. It screeches and lunges for Corey's face, its sharp beak ready to slice his skin wide open. Corey grits his teeth as he squeezes the crow's wings—until he feels a sickening *crack*. Then he throws the bird to the ground.

"Hollow!" Giovanni says.

Corey is already running. He scoops Nimble into his arms and tosses her into his car, where she lands on the passenger seat. The engine is still on, and he puts it in drive, barely avoiding Giovanni and Hollow as he goes. In the rearview mirror, the crow tries to take flight, but one of its wings is bent. Broken.

"What do we do?" Corey says, looking over to Nimble.

The cat just stares at him, bloodied fur around her mouth growing matted. So Corey takes a left, heading for the hospital—and for Penny.

Giovanni

GIOVANNI LETS COREY BARRION GO. HE'S FEEL-ing especially generous tonight—and he has other plans that need to see the light of day.

"There are so many ways to hurt someone," Gio says to Hollow, who once again flies alongside him. Gio set the bone in his wing, and already it's healed. Like witch, like familiar. The stronger Giovanni gets, the stronger Hollow becomes.

Unfortunately, since this is still Alonso's magic, that's also true for his mangy feline.

"You'll get a chance to get back at her, Hollow," Giovanni says.

Hollow's wings flutter in anticipation.

After an hour of walking along streets, then through forests and empty fields, Barrion Heating & Cooling appears in the distance. It's no longer a faded warehouse like it was during the seventies; instead, it's a large white structure that Gio can only describe as pretentious.

As he suspected, the manufacturing floor runs twenty-four hours a day. There are dozens of cars in the parking lot, and he picks up a sharp rock and scrapes lines along car doors as he walks by.

There's a vibration from Alonso's pocket. Giovanni takes out his phone. "There she is," he whispers, and he opens the text from Dylan Mayberry.

It's a series of six numbers.

Giovanni grins. She was an easy target. One thing about being a poltergeist is that you can sense the darkness in other people. Dylan was fighting it, but her greed was stronger.

The phone buzzes again as another message comes through from Dylan.

> Send the location.

Giovanni slides the phone into his pocket. He will keep his word, but not until he knows the girl wasn't lying to him.

The keypad is by the first door. Giovanni types in the code, and the screen turns green as the door unlocks. He grins to himself as he opens it, already taking out the phone again. The place where the money is buried has no address, but Gio memorized the coordinates. He sends them to her without explanation. Let her figure it out. Dylan seems to like a challenge.

Giovanni follows the signs to the manufacturing floor, but he's not expecting what's waiting for him: another locked door. And next to this one is a security guard sitting in a tiny room behind a thick glass window.

Giovanni clears his throat and waves to the figure beyond the tinted glass as if he's supposed to be there. But the security guard narrows her eyes, and she doesn't unlock the door. She presses a button, and her voice echoes through a mic. "Can I help you, kid?"

This isn't going to work. Giovanni closes his eyes.

Hollow . . . let's put on a show.

"Caw!" his familiar screeches as he appears from around the corner.

"Oh my god!" Giovanni says, ducking as he dives for him.

"What is that?" comes the security guard's voice, but Giovanni stays low to the ground as

Hollow flaps around. Finally the guard opens the door to the security office.

Hollow changes direction immediately, heading straight for her.

The guard screams and falls to the ground. Hollow pecks at her face, aiming for her eyes. When she tries to reach for her gun, Giovanni stomps on her foot.

The sound the guard lets out is delicious. Giovanni dodges her weak attempt at a kick, and then he brings the butt of the gun down onto her head.

Once the security guard is unconscious, Giovanni finds the button inside the security office that opens the door. He could disable the cameras like he did when he murdered Chuck, but this time he doesn't bother. He wants the Barrions to know he's coming for them.

Giovanni finds the stairs, and they lead him to a platform over the manufacturing floor. Below him are hundreds of people running assembly lines, performing quality control checks, barking out orders. A well-oiled machine that has made the Barrions money for decades.

And it's all about to come crashing down.

Giovanni will have to be more subtle about

this. Shouting a spell at them will be too quick—and it may not reach all their ears. He sucks in a breath, his skin buzzing as Alonso's magic builds. Then he speaks the spell:

> *"Petals from my lips*
> *Become artful in their ears,*
> *Lend me their attention,*
> *Lend me their fears."*

Giovanni grabs the railing. "Good evening, folks!"

His voice echoes over the hall. The people closest to him look up first, and then their whispers spread.

"My name is Gio, and tonight I have a question for you." He leans over, eyes boring into one face and then another and another. He wants each of them to feel his gaze. "Why do you worship Charles Barrion when he was a murderer?"

There are gasps in the crowd. "The hell are you talking about?" one man cries.

"Oh, you didn't know? He killed his wife."

The man clearly wants to argue with him, but something stops him. He blinks a few times, as if he's trying to understand what he's hearing and seeing.

The spell is doing its job. To everyone here, Gio's words sound persuasive. He continues, "He killed someone else, too. In cold blood. A bullet to the head. And he lived out his life in the lap of luxury, never having to pay for the pain he caused. For the lives he took!"

There are cries of shock. With how quickly everyone is growing agitated, that means they likely had their suspicions about Charles Barrion long before today. Certain stories must've gotten around over the years—like when they were in their mid-twenties and Chuck berated a group of employees to the point that they attacked him, and he had them all imprisoned. Or the many times he coerced farmers into selling their land so he could expand the company's operations.

Coming here and bringing this up was a risk. Perhaps Idlewood had forgotten all about Chuck's bad behavior. But if Gio is confident in one thing, it's that his former friend wouldn't have become a better person as he lived out his life. From the way people are whispering to each other, their faces growing ruddy and their shoulders tensing up, he was right.

"Charles Barrion might be gone—" Gio says.

"Good riddance!" one of the employees shouts.

"But his family is still here. And every day you work, you make them richer. So let me ask…" Gio shrugs. "Why do it?"

The room is silent now.

"Do they show you the respect you deserve? Do they let you have a part in their decision-making? Do they make sure your working conditions are safe? Do you ever get invited to their parties?" Gio is yelling now. "No! Because you're beneath them, and no matter how long you work here, you will never earn their respect…unless you get their attention."

"He's right!" someone shouts.

"I still can't afford a bigger home for my family!"

"They've stolen from the farmers! Got their acres for dirt cheap!"

"They think they're gods!"

"So!" Gio claps his hands together. "What are you going to do about it?"

They fall silent again. Did Gio lose them? He doesn't let his smile waver, but he looks desperately around the room, urging someone to make the first move.

Then, the man who first questioned Gio grabs a wrench from a nearby toolbox. He walks over to someone's tablet, lifts the wrench, and brings it down on the screen. The person holding it screams and jumps back, and the tablet crashes to the floor.

"Phil!"

"Someone stop him!"

But Phil is going to town on one of the conveyer belts, tearing it apart with his bare hands.

A woman joins in. She goes to the large air conditioners and starts pushing them to the floor, one by one, the crashes echoing through the room. But she isn't paying attention to who is on the other side, and one machine lands on someone's leg.

There's screaming. Someone grabs the woman and throws her to the floor.

The delirium spreads. As Gio watches, the entire factory floor descends into violence. Destruction.

"Finally, your family is going to get what they deserve, old friend," Gio says.

He leaves before the police show up, a smile on his face.

Corey

WHEN COREY ARRIVES AT THE HOSPITAL, NIM-ble runs off into the night, leaving him to face this alone. Instead of asking someone where Penny's room is, he sits in the farthest corner of the waiting room and tries to gather the last shreds of his courage.

Hours pass. Corey still doesn't get up.

How can he face her? Penny's mom will be there, and she'll know the truth if she doesn't already. She must hate him.

Maybe Penny hates him, too.

The television plays reruns of soap operas. Every time Corey comes back to himself, someone is screaming or crying, or they're attending a funeral.

Penny could've died tonight. And it's because of him.

"Corey?"

He pushes immediately to his feet. Penny's mom is standing across the waiting room. She looks so small, her suede jacket clamped tightly around her and her face in an expression of shock that could be permanent. She and Penny have never looked much alike, but right now, Corey sees the resemblance. This is exactly how Penny looked the night her mom fell into a coma this past July.

"Ron said he saw you down here," Mrs. Emberly says.

Corey nods. Then the words pour out of him: "I'm sorry. I'm so sorry. I tried to . . . I didn't mean to . . ."

Mrs. Emberly holds up a hand. Then she gestures for Corey to follow her.

They take a silent elevator ride to the fifth floor. Mrs. Emberly leads the way to a darkened hospital room, but she doesn't go inside.

"Do you have it?" Mrs. Emberly asks, the words strained.

Corey puts a hand into his jacket pocket, wrapping it around the necklace. The crescent moon charm digs into his skin. "Yes."

"Go on then," Mrs. Emberly says, gesturing to the door. She leaves him, heading for the coffee machine.

If Corey were a normal person, he would've been able to choose when he told someone he loved them. He would've set up a date, maybe, or had them over for a movie. He could've whispered the words in the car, or during lunch period, or on the couch late on a Saturday night.

But Corey has never had a normal life. So he steels himself and walks into Penny's hospital room.

Penny

PENNY'S THROAT IS AS ROUGH AS SANDPAPER.
She can *feel* the smoke in her lungs, in her veins—like she'll never be able to get it out.

That's what her anxiety is choosing to focus on right now. Because thinking about smoke inhalation is easier than thinking about what actually happened tonight.

The café has been destroyed. This place where Penny grew up, where she learned to live with her anxiety by taking orders, where she has so many memories of drag shows and quiet moments with her mom and evenings with Naomi and Alonso and Corey—it's gone forever.

"We'll rebuild, sweet pea," her mom kept saying. "I promise."

But Penny could see it in her mom's face: She's terrified that the results of the fire inspection will somehow show that *they* were at fault, not the landlord. If that's the case, Penny's mom and Ron will have to pay for repairs, and their savings are already nonexistent.

When her mom finally started crying, somehow that made it easier to ignore what Penny was feeling. She grabbed her mom's hand, and this time it was her turn to say, "You're right. We're going to figure it out."

But when her mom left to get coffee, the emotions rushed back in a tidal wave. Penny sank deeper into the bed, squeezing her eyes shut.

Now, when she opens them, Corey is standing at the door.

He's got a hand on the doorframe, and his eyes are searching her with quiet desperation. "You're…"

"I'm okay. They say I'll be able to go home tomorrow."

Corey nods, but he doesn't move.

"Please come here," Penny says, her voice cracking.

That's all it takes. He's a blur of motion, and then she's in his arms. She pulls him tight against her, and they stay that way until the pain of the day begins to ebb just a little.

"Did you see the Shadow?" Corey asks.

Penny nods against his chest, and he lets out a low, painful sound. Slowly he moves away from her, grabbing her face in his hands.

"I didn't know, otherwise I would've warned you or…" Corey trails off. He lowers one hand, and there's a rustling as he digs around in his jacket pocket. Penny can't breathe as he removes a long gold chain with a charm at the end. An obsidian crescent moon.

The ward. The necklace that protects people from the dark magic that's killed so many members of Corey's family—the very same necklace Penny's mom wore this past summer.

Penny's breathing comes quicker now. Another panic attack. She's always more vulnerable to them after she's already had one.

Corey unclasps the ward and puts it around Penny's neck, even as Penny grabs both of his arms and tries to breathe evenly. But it's no use.

He stays with her until the panic attack subsides, holding her to him. As soon as Penny can see straight again, she pulls away from him, looking up into his face.

"I'm going to get rid of this bargain as soon as possible," Corey says. "I promise."

"But—but the sacrifice" is all Penny can say.

"I'll figure it out." He stands up. "I'll be staying at Carlos's place."

"Carlos Flores? From the football team?"

Corey nods. "I can't be at home right now. If you need me, his house is on Marrietta Street."

"Okay." Penny fiddles with the hem of the thin hospital blanket. "Have you…did you see Alonso?"

"Yeah." Corey pauses. "Was he with you when the explosion happened?"

Penny nods.

"Why was he there?" There's something in Corey's voice. Suspicion, maybe? Worry? Which means…

Corey already knows about what's going on with Alonso. He has to.

"He told me the truth. About the poltergeist."

Penny watches his reaction, and when guilt flickers across his features, she knows she was right.

"I was supposed to help him," Corey says. "He was worried about you, and I told him I'd…distract you."

Silence grows between them. The anger she felt when Alonso showed up at the café is back, but for an entirely different reason. "So everyone was lying to me."

"Not everyone."

Penny presses the heels of her hands against her eyes. "Just the most important people in my life."

"I'm sorry," Corey says. "We were both trying to do the right thing, but we both fucked up."

"Yeah. You did."

Corey stiffens. "I should leave."

Penny presses her lips together to keep from crying.

"If Alonso shows up, you should know," Corey says, "the poltergeist is in control. Or he was, last time I saw him."

Penny's heart lurches. "Was he okay?"

"I think he was fine, physically. I don't think he's coming here, either. I got the sense that he has other priorities. But if he does, you call me immediately." Corey takes out his phone and holds it out to her sheepishly. "Also…I need your number."

"You…don't have it?"

Corey works his jaw. "I deleted it after…"

Penny hears the words he doesn't say: *After our kiss.*

Her face is burning with embarrassment as she puts her number in his phone and hands it back to him. Corey sucks in a breath, and she thinks he's going to leave. But suddenly he kneels down and grabs Penny's face, eyes boring into hers.

"I love you," he breathes.

The words wash over Penny like warm water. She forgets to be angry, but she has no idea what she's feeling in its place.

Does she love Corey? She's starting to. But everything feels different than it did a day ago. Alonso reentered her life with all the grace of a monster truck, and she found out they were both lying to her for weeks.

"I care about you," Penny says. "So much."

She means it, but she still flinches when Corey's face closes up. The wall is there again, but Penny knows what's behind it.

Pain.

Corey is already backing up toward the door. "Get some sleep. I'll call you."

But Penny can't sleep. Because whenever she closes her eyes, she sees one of them: Corey, with his warm eyes and steady presence—or Alonso, frantic as he told her the truth at the café.

Penny's doesn't know what she wants. She just knows that her heart hurts.

Soon after the sun comes up, Naomi runs into the room, and she convinces Penny's mom to go home for a shower and a change of clothes.

"It's always exciting with you, huh?" Naomi says as she grabs Penny's hand. She's trying to make a joke out of it, but her eyes are heavy with worry. "What happened?"

Penny fills her in on the most dramatic twenty-four hours of her life. When Penny shows her the ward, Naomi bites her lip, as if she's afraid of what she might say and she's trying to keep the words inside. But she has the opposite reaction to the news about Alonso. Naomi slumps back in her chair, almost as if she's . . . relieved.

"Finally," Naomi says.

"Finally . . . ?"

Naomi looks uncertain, but she barrels on. "I . . . might've known about the possession part."

"God. Not you, too. Who didn't know? Dylan?"

"Nope. She knew. And while we're being honest, so does Marley."

Penny gapes at her.

"Don't be so shocked, Penz. It's not as though

you've never lied to me before." Naomi's words
are sharp, but she shakes her head and immediately softens. "We were trying to help him ... get
rid of it. With the exorcism and all."

Exorcism. The word is violent. Severe.

She's about to tell Naomi she can't handle any
of this right now, that she needs some time alone,
when both of their phones buzz. It's a text from
Corey:

> Riot at Barrion Heating & Cooling
> last night. People were hurt.

> It was Giovanni.

Cozy Mystery Book Club

DECEMBER 13, 7:15 AM

PENNY EMBERLY removed ALONSO DE LUCA from the group chat.

PENNY EMBERLY added MARLEY PIERRE to the group chat.

Penny Emberly

Has anyone heard from Alonso?

 Marley Pierre

I just talked to the De Lucas. He's missing after the riot.

Penny I'm just going to assume you're caught up.

Naomi Salazar
I'm at the hospital with her. She is.

Marley Pierre
The exorcism was supposed to be today. I'm sure that's why Giovanni is going apeshit.

Corey Barrion
Can you do it if we find him?

Marley Pierre
We don't have a choice.

Corey Barrion
The holiday party is tonight.

Naomi Salazar
Still? They're not canceling it?

CB Corey Barrion

I'm sure my dad will use it as an opportunity to make a statement.

Or at least to make the family look less bad.

MP Marley Pierre

Classic politician move.

What are the odds that Alonso/Giovanni will show up tonight?

If he was behind the riot, then probably good.

CB Corey Barrion

Agreed.

MP Marley Pierre

Then I guess that's where we need to be.

I helped set up. I know the layout of the community center. If we position two people on the first floor in the main hall and two other people near the front and back entrances, we'll see him when he gets there.

NS Naomi Salazar

But where should we do the exorcism?

The roof is off-limits but they keep the door unlocked.

NS Naomi Salazar

Great.

How scared should we be?

CB Corey Barrion

Not scared of Alonso.

You'll know if it's Giovanni by the eyes. They turn green.

As soon as you see him, text the group. Once he knows we're trying to stop him, he'll probably fight us, right?

MP Marley Pierre

He'll do everything in his power to keep his hold on Alonso.

NS Naomi Salazar

So as soon as we get that text, run to the roof.

Marley

Can this actually work?

MP Marley Pierre

I would have already called the Council if I didn't think it could.

DM Dylan Mayberry

I can't make it.

MP Marley Pierre

> What??? Why?

NS Naomi Salazar

> Seriously? After all the work we did?

> You can always trust Dylan to be noncommittal.

DM Dylan Mayberry

> I've had enough of this witchcraft shit.

MP Marley Pierre

> You're a witch too. You can't escape it.

DM Dylan Mayberry

> That won't stop me from trying.

> Good luck I guess. You'll need it.

Marley

MARLEY TOSSES THE PHONE ONTO HER BED. THE day has finally come. This is her moment to prove the Council was wrong about necromancy—to convince them that they need to change their rules.

She wishes she could text Dot. Talk through her plans with him. But she left him out of this for a reason—if Marley defies the Council, her coven will make sure she survives their punishment. But what would they do to Dot? The Pierres couldn't save him.

Her phone buzzes, making her heart skip a beat. But she already knows it isn't Dot. He's too respectful of her bounderies to call her out of the blue. Marley grabs her phone, and the name on the screen makes her nerves flare.

Marley swallows her fear and answers it. "Milton! Hey."

There's no smile in Milton's voice when he says, "Why are you ignoring my calls?"

"Huh? Oh, I meant to call you back but it slipped my mind—"

"For a week?"

Marley is suddenly questioning her choice to put his calls on mute. "It's been busy."

"How are you busy, Marley? You don't live there. You don't have a job."

"You know me. I make friends everywhere."

"So you've had a good vacation. Nothing to tell me?"

Marley laughs. "No, Milton, if I had something to tell you, I would've told you! I know what my job is."

Milton goes silent. Marley checks her phone, wondering if she lost him. "Hello?"

Milton's next words send Marley's heart to the floor.

"The Council received a phone call this morning. From the Barrions."

Marley closes her eyes. The riot. She should've known the Barrions would do this after seeing Alonso on the security footage.

"Why are two very expensive knives missing from inventory?" Milton asks.

"I . . . I don't know."

"I gave you a chance, Marley. Grandma didn't want me to, but I did it anyway. And you've made me look like a fool."

"That's not what I was trying to do!" Marley changes her tactic. "Milton, please. You can help me!" She's pacing the room now, so full of energy and fear and hope. "You believe in me, don't you? You know I can do this. I'm so close!"

There's barely any fight in his voice as he says, "I did believe in you."

Marley stops pacing.

"I'll see you soon," Milton says.

"Why?"

"Because the Council is on their way to Idlewood."

The call disconnects.

Corey

THE CHARLES BARRION CENTER FOR COMMU-
nity and Belonging is bright with holiday
lights. There are two Christmas trees out front,
and many more inside. A menorah sits on a table
in the lobby, empty of candles in anticipation of
the first day of Hanukkah tomorrow. Hot chocolate and eggnog are being served to everyone who
walks through the door. The people of Idlewood
are all smiles—or that's true for the ones who
showed up. It's not as crowded as they'd planned,
but there are a lot of people here who are pretending that everything is okay.

Sometimes Corey wonders if Idlewood is rot-
ten from the inside out.

He spots Aunt Helen right away when he
arrives. She's standing by herself, staring at the
photo of Grandpa that's hanging on the wall.

"They told me," she says when Corey walks

over to her. "When I asked why you'd left home. I *made* your dad tell me. Everyone knows now."

"You mean..."

"The bargain," Aunt Helen says.

Corey wants to feel relief, but after the revelation that his dad has known for weeks, he can't. Not yet. "And?"

Aunt Helen turns sharply to him. "What kind of question is that?"

"I need to know where you stand. I thought our entire family would be on the same page, but..." Corey lets out a bitter laugh. "I was wrong. I feel alone in this."

Aunt Helen's face softens. "You're not alone, Corey."

Something unfurls in Corey's chest. He didn't know how badly he needed to hear that. She must see it in his face, because she grabs his arm and says, "Sofía and I were heartbroken when we found out. She's so disgusted with your father that she didn't even come tonight."

"Did you talk to Julian?"

Aunt Helen's face softens. "Yes. You told him."

"Yesterday." Corey looks away. "He didn't believe me. He still doesn't."

"He's sick, Corey," Aunt Helen says. "I've

barely been a mother to that boy. He only looks up to your grandfather and to you."

"*Looked* up to. Past tense."

"Relationships are fluid. They can change. I can still show up for Julian despite the tragedies in our lives. I can do better." Aunt Helen squeezes Corey's shoulder. "I want you to remember this, too. Because one day, I think he'll ask for your forgiveness."

Maybe Aunt Helen is right, but Corey can't imagine Julian wanting anything from him again.

The holiday music fades, and a familiar voice comes on over the sound system. "Good evening, everyone!"

It's Corey's dad. His mood sours instantly.

"Let's go," Aunt Helen says, her own expression dark. They walk into the main hall, which is aglow with red and green and blue and gold decorations.

James Barrion is standing at the podium, an evergreen sprig peeking out from the pocket of his suit jacket. He smiles as he looks out over the crowd, exuding warmth and confidence.

Marley walks by, heading for her post at the front door, where she'll look out for Alonso.

Corey tries to catch her eye, but she's staring into the crowd, chewing on her lip. She seemed a lot more confident over text. Corey tries not to think about what that might mean.

Then the crowd shifts, and Corey catches a glimpse of familiar curly hair across the room.

Penny is there with her mom and her godfather. She's already looking at Corey, and when he makes eye contact, she doesn't smile, but she doesn't look away from him, either.

Corey's heart pounds painfully in his chest. Penny knows the truth about his feelings. He dropped them on her in the form of a burden and a necklace, and then he left her to deal with it by herself.

He wants her to know he'd be a better boyfriend than this—but would he?

"Thank you for coming to the grand opening of the Charles Barrion Center for Community and Belonging," Corey's dad says. "It's fitting that this would be a holiday party, because this was my dad's favorite time of year. I know if he were here, he'd be drinking more eggnog than any of you."

He's humanizing him. Making jokes. Corey will have to steel himself to get through this.

"I'm so glad our Idlewood community could come together tonight," he continues, looking out over the gathered crowd. "As you all know, yesterday's tragedy at Barrion Heating & Cooling has left many of us reeling. The company has been a beacon of hope and stability for Idlewood residents since my great-grandfather founded it in the 1950s. As we've grown, so has Idlewood—from a town of three thousand in 1957 to a town of almost twenty thousand today. We're still small, and we like it that way. But to see our community thrive requires taking chances. Welcoming people from other cities, states, or countries, in the case of my late wife, Tanya."

Corey's dad pauses. To the rest of the room, it's probably barely noticeable. But to Corey it's as loud as an alarm. James's eyes find Corey in the crowd, and all Corey can do is project his disgust. His disappointment. Just when Corey thinks his dad can't stoop any lower, he brings up Corey's mom for sympathy points. As the crowd glances at Corey with sad smiles, he wishes he could cut off his dad's mic.

James clears his throat and pastes the smile back on his face. "The tragedy at Barrion Heating & Cooling was avoidable, and I take full responsibility for it. And I'm thrilled to unveil our strategy to rebuild trust within the company, starting with a listening tour and the convening of a council of staff to ..."

"I can't listen to this," Corey says, turning to leave. But as he does, someone bumps roughly into his shoulder, knocking him into Aunt Helen. The smell of alcohol is so strong, Corey can almost see it wafting through the air.

"Outta my way," the guy mutters, and Corey recognizes the fresh scar on his cheek. It's Clay Thornberg.

Clay keeps walking, bumping into other people and throwing insults at everyone.

"That boy..." Aunt Helen says. "Should I get security?"

But Clay seems to settle into the crowd, even though a group makes space around him so they don't have to stand too close.

"Once the speech is over," Corey says, unable to hide his bitterness. "I'm sure the last thing my dad wants is another scene."

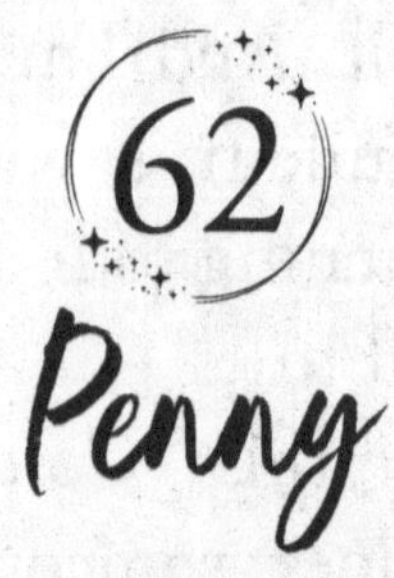

62

Penny

"WE ARE PROUD TO BE THE BACKBONE OF IDLE-wood," Mr. Barrion says. "And while none of us—including my late father—has been perfect, we want to grow with you. We hope you'll let us. And with that, I'm proud to officially open the Charles Barrion Center for Community and Belonging!"

Penny doesn't realize she's gaping at Corey's dad until the crowd bursts into applause. They're inspired. They're in love. Corey's dad soaks it up, smiling and waving before he walks down the stairs and is escorted away by Warren.

"I'll tell you what," Ron mutters, "those two could've fooled me while Charles Barrion was alive. Never seen James smile around him, not once."

Anita glances at Penny. "It's...definitely a complicated family."

Penny can't respond. Hearing Charles Barrion talked about with such love when the man embodied racism and prejudice and *evil* makes it feel like the world Penny sees isn't the real world at all. Like she's making it all up, and Corey's grandfather really is the hero who made Idlewood prosper.

But these people don't know the truth. They were never intimidated and threatened by the Barrion patriarch. They didn't witness him kill somebody in cold blood.

If Penny is feeling this gross after Mr. Barrion's speech, Corey must be doing much worse. The ward is heavy around Penny's neck, and she can't stop herself from scanning the crowd . . .

Corey is gone. But he's not the one Penny should be looking for.

"You haven't seen Alonso, have you?" Penny says.

"No," her mom says, frowning. "Not since the fire."

"I don't see Alonso, but someone is checking one of us out. Can't tell who because of those sunglasses," Ron says.

"Sunglasses?" Penny follows Ron's gaze.

A woman stands in the middle of the crowd,

a spot of stillness in the merriment. She has long, straight black hair that matches her long, heavy black coat—and she's wearing sunglasses indoors. At night.

"She's pulling it off," Penny's mom says, but Penny doesn't laugh. She can't help but feel that the woman's eyes are trained on her, and her skin crawls. She's considering walking up to her when the woman turns and disappears into the party.

Penny shakes her head, and it feels like waking up from a strange dream.

"Penny," her mom says, nodding at the crowd again.

Penny follows her mom's gaze. A flash of red-and-blond hair appears across the room, and she gasps.

"I'll be right back," Penny says, leaving her mom and Ron behind.

She pushes through the crowd in the direction where she thought she saw Alonso, already grabbing her phone from her purse to text the group—

But he's gone. All Penny sees now are people laughing and chatting. Maybe he just left the room—or maybe he was never there at all.

There's a warm presence at her shoulder.

Penny looks up to see Corey gazing down at her, eyes serious. "Did you see him?"

"I think so. He must've snuck in."

"I'll tell everyone he's here. Let's see if we can get him up to the roof."

Penny nods. Shoulder to shoulder, they set off to find Alonso.

Giovanni

IT WAS EASIER TO GET INTO THE HOLIDAY PARTY than Giovanni expected. There's security at every door, but he hid his grandson's stupid hairstyle under a Santa hat and walked in alongside a big crowd. That was all it took. It was barely satisfying.

As he watches James Barrion pontificate on the greatness of his dead dad, Giovanni gets the sudden urge to fall asleep. Hearing people lie about Chuck doesn't even bother him anymore. Since he watched the employees of Barrion Heating & Cooling beat each other with thermal expansion valves last night, nothing else has lived up. It doesn't help that Giovanni has spent the last day in the woods—just him and Hollow, sleeping fitfully in the leaves and using magic to stay warm. He'd forgotten that being alive has its downsides, namely a finite limit of energy before your body forces you to sleep. So much time is wasted resting.

Once the speech is over, Giovanni watches James leave the stage. As the lights dim and the music returns, Gio's mood begins to sour. They're all having fun because Gio suffered. Because *Ellie* suffered. Their deaths allowed the residents of Idlewood to live in comfort, but it's the Barrions who get the credit.

Gio's eyes find James again. He's talking with some people off-stage. They're fawning over him, and he looks away in fake humility.

Anger turns Gio's skin hot. Maybe it's James's turn to hurt. Gio starts to walk over, but he stops when a figure appears in the crowd, eyes boring into him.

It's a boy around Alonso's age, but he carries the resentment of an old man who believes the world owes him everything he never had. Everything he never worked for.

"I need to talk to you," says the boy. His speech is heavy with alcohol, and his movements are slow and clumsy.

Then Gio recognizes him. It's the boy from the bonfire. *Clay.*

Gio is about to say they can chat later and brush past him, but Clay blocks his path.

Fine. If this is the game he wants to play, Gio is more than happy to go along with it.

He follows him out into the lobby. There are fewer people here now that the party has started in earnest.

"If you have something to say, then talk," Gio says.

Clay grins. When he shifts his stance, there's the glimmer of something in his hand.

"What—" Pain shoots through his body, cutting off Gio's words. His vision goes white. He can't think. He's conscious but unable to move, and he can't form the words to any sort of spell.

Then Clay is dragging him up a set of stairs. There's the sound of a door being pushed open, and cold air makes the hair on Gio's arms stand up. Clay drops him, and Gio's head smacks against concrete. Slowly he manages to lift his head and look around.

They're on the roof. The night is bleak and cold. The holiday lights decorating homes in the distance are blurry.

"Get up," Clay says, holding up a taser, "unless you want some more juice."

468

Then Gio realizes something. Now that his vision is less blurry, the electricity in his veins makes him feel more alive. Magic buzzes at the tips of his fingers, on the insides of his mouth.

So he stays on the ground.

"Fucker," Clay says, and he kneels down and presses the taser to Giovanni's torso.

This time, Gio closes his eyes and lets the electricity in. It powers him like a battery, and he breathes in as a smile stretches across his face.

The taser stops, and Clay sucks in a breath. "Why are you smiling?"

Giovanni raises an eyebrow. "What? No more?"

Clay lets out a shaky breath. He stumbles to his feet and backs away.

Giovanni gets up, too, brushing the dust from his shoulders. "You had something to say to me, didn't you?"

Clay glances behind Gio—at the door. The boy is shaking like a rabbit cornered by a fox. He only likes prey that's weaker than him. To his credit, he says, "Y-you never apologized."

Gio pretends to think about it. "For . . . ?"

Clay grits his teeth and points to his face. "This." He tugs down the neck of his shirt. There are more scars along his chest in the shape of scratch marks. "And *this*."

"I would apologize," Gio says, "but my philosophy on this is different. If someone deserved what they got—"

"Don't *fucking* say that!" Clay howls. "You ruined me! And you need to pay!"

He takes something out of his pocket. A switchblade.

Don't hurt him!

The voice comes as a surprise.

"Why, Alonso," Giovanni mutters, "you're awake. That's inconvenient."

Go fuck yourself.

A hint of annoyance prickles at Giovanni. It's so distracting that he almost doesn't realize Clay is lunging at him.

He leaps out of the way, just missing being hit by Clay's blade. Giovanni kicks out, his foot connecting with Clay's arm. The blade skitters across the roof and out of reach. Giovanni laughs, his voice ringing out into the night.

"It's been fun, but I think I'm done playing with you," Gio says. He moves toward Clay slowly, deliberately.

Clay backs up, his sense of superiority changing quickly to fear. "D-don't come any closer!"

Giovanni stops.

Clay looks surprised that he actually listened.
He starts to move around him, heading for the
door.

Gio lets him think he might get away for
about five seconds. Then he raises his hand.

*"Push of the earth, wuthering forces,
gather behind me in submission."*

"What the fuck did you just say?" Clay asks,
but a distant whistling sound distracts him. He
looks up, far behind Gio, and whatever he sees
makes his eyes go wide. "Holy shit. Holy—"

Three things happen at the same time.

A huge gust of wind blows across the roof,
lifting Clay off his feet and carrying him over the
edge.

Behind Gio, the door to the roof opens.

And Alonso screams in Gio's head, the sound
dragging Gio down, down, down . . .

Alonso

ALONSO DID IT. HE TOOK HIS BODY BACK FOR the first time.

And he's still too late.

"No!" Alonso runs for the edge of the roof as Clay disappears over it.

Alonso will catch him. He has to.

"Clay—" Alonso says as he reaches the edge, reaching over as far as he can—

Just as Clay hits the sidewalk.

The sound is wet. Final.

Alonso lets out a cry that's halfway between a scream and a sob. He's choking on it.

But Clay doesn't hear him. He doesn't hear anything.

People start appearing on the sidewalk below. Alonso stumbles back from the edge of the roof, turns around—

Penny is standing there watching him. Her

eyes are wide, and she's clutching the front of her jacket. She's shivering.

Corey is behind her. He's turned away, one hand covering his mouth. The door flies open, and Marley and Naomi run onto the roof.

"You've got him!" Marley says, but when nobody reacts, she looks from Alonso to Penny. "What is it?"

"He went over," Corey manages to say.

Marley looks among all of them rapidly, trying to understand. Down on the sidewalk, someone screams. Naomi is looking at Alonso like she doesn't know who he is anymore. "It was *you*?"

Shame coats Alonso, muffling the world, blurring his sight. This is his final evolution into the person he never wanted to be. The fate he worked so hard to avoid.

It's too late to go back now.

"He fell from the roof!" another voice yells from the street below.

Penny is suddenly in front of Alonso. She grabs his shoulders. "It's you now? You're back?"

Alonso wants to touch her, but he can't move his arms. He can't feel anything, physical or otherwise.

"I killed him," Alonso says.

Penny shakes her head vigorously. "It wasn't you."

"He used my hands. My magic." Alonso starts crying.

"Alonso, listen to me," Penny says. "You need to run."

Marley walks up beside her. "She's right. The Council is here; they'll know you had something to do with it."

The Council.

"How?" Alonso says. "They're here for me?"

"No questions now. Just get the hell out."

Penny is pulling him to the door, pushing him through it. And because it's the only thing to do, Alonso throws himself down the stairs, out the back door, into the night.

"Hey, you!" someone yells. "Stop!"

Alonso's feet only carry him away faster. He inhales the cold air until his lungs hurt—until the night consumes him.

Penny

PENNY RUNS DOWN THE STAIRS AFTER ALONSO,
the rest of their group following close on her
heels, their shoes almost impossibly loud. The
whole time, her heart is pounding in her chest,
threatening to break through her ribs. There's a
panic attack waiting in the wings of her mind,
but it never arrives—because the moment she
saw Alonso's gray eyes, she had to focus on getting him out.

Clay is dead. Clay is dead. Clay is…

Penny pushes through the door and into the
panic that has engulfed the holiday party. People
are no longer drinking and laughing. Some are
shouting, others are crying, and a few are standing stock still and staring into nothing.

"I saw him," someone whispers as Penny walks
by. "His head was all…"

"Did anyone see who did it?"

"Penny!"

A familiar figure runs to her. He's tall and thin, with locs and large brown eyes.

Penny gasps. "Milton?" She looks behind her, but Marley has disappeared.

Milton takes in the group, his brow set in determination. "What just happened?"

"I—I don't know," Penny says.

Milton narrows his eyes. "I heard about the riot. I'm assuming this is Alonso's doing, too?"

Penny should be scared. But she has to hold Milton off from searching for him for as long as she can. "So what? Is the Council going to punish him?"

"Not just punish," Naomi says, moving up to stand beside Penny. "They're going to kill him."

Penny can't speak. She looks to Milton, hoping he'll deny it, but his expression doesn't change.

"Milton," Penny says, "please, you have to understand, it wasn't him—"

"He's dangerous, Penny," Milton says, sounding like a reasonable adult talking to a little kid. "Look what just happened. If you weren't convinced before, you should be convinced now."

"*Giovanni* is dangerous," Penny says. "Alonso isn't."

"Alonso is the reason this is happening. He broke Council law—"

"He saved my mom!" Penny says. "You were fine with him breaking rules then. What happened was an accident, but you're okay with Alonso dying because of it?"

Milton's expression shifts, and for a moment he's uncertain. Penny is getting through to him after all. But he shakes his head. "You all need to stay inside."

"Milton," Penny says, letting the panic into her voice. But he leaves without another word.

Milton can't find Alonso first. Penny won't let him.

Penny runs out to Main Street, ignoring Naomi and Corey as they call after her. There are police lights flashing, and people are placing a blanket over Clay's body. But one of his hands is visible, and Penny can't look away from it. There's dirt under his fingernails. His skin is still pink.

Penny loses all momentum. Instead, she turns and vomits into a trash can. When the second wave comes on, someone grabs her hair and holds it back.

When she finally looks up, Corey is standing there with her. Embarrassed, she looks away and wipes her mouth.

"We have to find Alonso," Corey says, grabbing her arm. "Where should we look?"

"I don't know," Penny says, looking around desperately. "I don't know where he'd be. I don't know anything."

So they stand there, letting the chaos of the night fill their ears and then their veins until it erases who they were and leaves them as something entirely new.

This is a night they will never come back from.

"Keep running, Alonso," Penny whispers.

Alonso

ALONSO LOOKS FOR HIS CAR, BUT IT'S NOWHERE near the community center. From the way his feet and back hurt, he figures Giovanni has been walking everywhere. He doesn't even have his phone anymore; Giovanni probably fed it to his stupid crow.

Alonso doesn't know where he's supposed to go. Home? Penny's house? She's not there. He could go to Meredith House, but what would Corey's family say when they saw him? There's no way they'd allow him inside, especially with the cuts and scrapes all over his body and dried blood on his hands. He might've helped save Mrs. Emberly, but now that he's a murderer, nobody will remember the good he did. Or tried to do.

So Alonso runs. He cuts through parks and across residential streets. He runs past Neon

Lanes Bowling, the Walmart, IHOP. He runs until the big box stores turn into empty fields.

When his feet start throbbing with pain, he slows to a stop, hands on his knees as he tries to catch his breath. But that allows the truth to catch up to him.

Clay is dead because of him.

The sound of sirens breaks through the night, and Alonso forces himself to keep running. But the sirens get louder. Alonso needs to hide, but he's surrounded by open fields. His only hope is to make it to a stand of trees a quarter mile down the road.

Alonso pushes harder, but it feels like he's slowing down. He tries to think of a spell that can help him, but even the thought of doing magic makes him sick. All he sees is Clay's surprise, his outstretched arm as he fell...

Alonso is almost to the trees. He's ten seconds away—

And that's when the police cars come into view. A voice echoes over the car speakers:

"Stop right there!"

All his motivation vanishes. Alonso slows to a stop, and he puts his hands up as five police cars surround him in the middle of the street.

He doesn't know what comes next, but if he's in police custody, he won't be able to hurt anyone. At least until his grandfather finds a way to break them out.

"Walk forward slowly," one of the police officers says.

Alonso takes a few steps. He expects someone to come forward and put handcuffs on him, but it never happens. Alonso dares a glance up.

And the police cars have vanished. There's a brand-new scene in front of him.

There are still five cars, but they're strange. One is a rusty Ford pickup truck. One is a black Lamborghini. Another is a compact car, like the kind you'd see in Italy. Another has "COVEN KREWE" painted on the side, and the last one is a huge old SUV.

Alonso lowers his hands, looking from unfamiliar face to unfamiliar face. "Who...who are you?"

The woman who was driving the Lamborghini steps forward. She has long black hair and a black coat. She's wearing sunglasses at night, which makes Alonso want to throw up on her.

"Hello, Alonso," she says. "I'm Park YeaLee. I've been wondering when we'd finally meet."

Alonso's bravado disappears. It sinks in: This is the Council of Witches.

"Park YeaLee," Alonso says. "As in, the Park coven? Park HaeJung was your ancestor?"

She gives him an unfriendly smile. "Our coven was disgraced once, like yours. Unfortunately, it looks like that's still going to be your fate."

Alonso looks around. "The police cars were an illusion? How did you do that?"

"You're not in the position to ask questions, I'm afraid."

Someone gets out of the SUV. Alonso sucks in a breath when he recognizes the lanky figure. "Milton! You've got to help me. You know that wasn't—"

Milton throws something at him. Alonso gasps and ducks, but the object finds his wrists like a magnet, clamping on and weighing him down.

Handcuffs. But not the normal kind. These are medieval, heavy as hell, and Alonso can barely lift his arms.

Alonso is ready to beg. To plead. To ask what they're going to do to him—but the Council all raise their hands, their mouths moving quickly and silently.

Alonso can't move. But he can feel his feet as they're lifted from the ground, and he's suddenly floating like a piece of paper on the air.

"Light as a feather, stiff as a board," Milton says as he places a cloth soaked in some foul-smelling liquid underneath Alonso's nose. Alonso tries not to inhale, but Milton presses it harder to his face, and Alonso can only hold his breath for so long.

The last thing Alonso sees is Park YeaLee opening the back door of her car.

67
Cozy Mystery Book Club

DECEMBER 14, 6:58 AM

Naomi Salazar

Any sign of Alonso?

Penny Emberly

We were out all night looking for him. He's nowhere.

Naomi Salazar

Did the police get him??

Corey Barrion

No. My family would've heard something

Marley have you heard from Milton??

Marley Pierre

Yes.

And??

Marley Pierre

The Council has Alonso.

Naomi Salazar

omg

Where are they?

Marley Pierre

No idea.

We have to find him Marley.

 **Marley Pierre**

That's going to be difficult. Milton is officially not speaking to me anymore. He only told me about Alonso because he thought it would convince me to give up.

Please don't give up

Please

 **Marley Pierre**

Oh don't worry. I will go down fighting.

I'm going to call the De Lucas to see if they have any idea where the Council might be keeping him.

Marley Pierre

I know it's in Idlewood. They called the entire Council here.

The De Lucas aren't picking up.

MP Marley Pierre

They hold all their meetings at night so that buys us today at the very least. His trial will probably be tonight.

NS Naomi Salazar

Marley

We weren't even sure the exorcism was going to work. We had zero dirt on Giovanni.

Maybe we use today to fix that?

Dylan suggested a séance.

MP Marley Pierre

Whoa.

CB Corey Barrion

Oh no.

Dylan Mayberry
Stealing my ideas?

Naomi Salazar
And she reappears!

Dylan Mayberry
I don't wake up this early if I don't have to. But my phone has been vibrating for ten minutes straight. Thanks for that.

Why do we need to know more about Giovanni? What difference will that make?

Marley Pierre
If we can remind him of his humanity, it might be easier to send him packing.

Is that even possible with a poltergeist?

Marley Pierre
In theory.

CB **Corey Barrion**

In theory?

MP **Marley Pierre**

It's all a theory. I'm trying to change the world here.

The witching world.

So who would we talk to if we did a séance?

DM **Dylan Mayberry**

I was thinking his grandma.

Allison.

CB **Corey Barrion**

Wasn't she mortal?

She was. Alonso also told me she was really in love with Giovanni.

She probably knew more about him than almost anyone.

Marley Pierre

Let's do it. Where is she buried?

Naomi Salazar

Wait

Why

Marley Pierre

That's where we'll do the séance? Obvi

Naomi Salazar

we have to do the séance in a CEMETERY??

Please please please no no no nooooo

She's in the same cemetery as my dad. I'll send along the address.

Naomi Salazar
PENNY. Some support here please.
Anyone?
Fine. I'll pack my holy water.

Penny

THE CLOUDS ARE SLATE GRAY AND HEAVY, making the middle of the day feel like evening. It's entirely appropriate for a séance. Penny winds her scarf tighter around her neck to keep the chill out, but the wind is sharp and intimate, finding its way beneath her coat and making her wonder if her shivering is because of the weather or the thought of what they're about to do.

"What if she's moved on to whatever is after the Second World?" Penny asks Marley as they search for Allison De Luca's headstone. "Don't they leave at some point?"

"Sure do," Marley says. "If she's moved on, she won't come. Simple as that."

"Where do they go?" Dylan asks. She's been oddly quiet since she arrived. It isn't like her, but

Dylan doesn't like questions, so Penny is just letting her exist.

"Depends on who you ask. Maybe they're reincarnated, maybe they go to heaven, maybe they rejoin the great energy stream of life."

"That's not a thing," Naomi mutters.

"It might be," Corey says, shrugging.

Penny stops walking. "She's here."

The headstone is flush with the grass. It's modest, with a small tree next to her name:

ALLISON DE LUCA

FEBRUARY 16, 1952—DECEMBER 8, 2022

LOVING MOTHER, WIFE, AND GRANDMOTHER

They all sit in a circle on the grave. Marley sent them a list of items to bring, and Penny pulls a pomegranate out of her bag and splits it in half. Naomi brings out salt. Corey holds a bouquet of lilies, and Dylan has a cheap bottle of whiskey.

"What's that for?" Naomi asks.

"Me," Marley says, opening the bottle and taking a swig. Dylan rolls her eyes, but she grabs it from her and does the same. Soon they're passing it around as Marley assures them it will be helpful and make them more "open to the spirits."

"I feel more open to sheer terror," Naomi mutters, but she's wearing a dreamy smile, so that's progress.

"Join hands," Marley says as she lights a few mismatched, half-burned candles that look like they were picked up at Goodwill.

When they're holding hands, Marley sucks in a breath. "Okay everyone. We don't break this circle. If we do, we'll lose contact with whoever we're talking to."

"*Whoever?* It's going to be Alonso's grandmother, right?" Naomi says.

Marley shrugs. "Just because we call her doesn't mean she'll be the one who answers."

Corey squeezes Penny's hand. His eyes are already closed, so Penny uses the opportunity to watch him breathe. Since their conversation at the hospital, her anger has already started to fade. Maybe it's the life-and-death stakes, or maybe it's because she knows Corey meant it when he said this isn't how it was supposed to happen.

But then, her mind goes to Alonso. To the terror he must be feeling now, wherever he is.

The anger returns, but this time it's with

herself. The only thing that saves her from it is Marley's voice.

"Repeat after me . . ." she begins.

> *"Spirit, we come to you with offerings.*
> *We call to you,*
> *We lend your spirit our roar.*
> *Allison De Luca, cross the Veil.*
> *Join the land of the living once more."*

"Why are we asking?" Dylan mutters. "Shouldn't we demand that she cross?"

"Shut up," Naomi whispers sharply.

The wind gets colder. Penny feels something like a finger travel up the back of her neck, and she gasps, opening her eyes.

"What?" Corey says.

"I thought I felt something," Penny says.

"Don't break the circle," Marley says.

Naomi has gone completely still. She's staring directly behind Penny with wide, terrified eyes.

"Nay?" Penny says. She begins to turn around, but Marley stops her.

"Nobody move," she whispers.

Slowly, everyone but Penny turns to look. Corey's eyes find hers.

"What is it?" Penny whispers.

Corey swallows, but he doesn't say anything.

Cold hits Penny's cheek, but it's not a breeze. It's something else. Something static.

"Penny," a voice whispers. And even though she's only heard that voice on videos and albums for the last ten years, Penny recognizes it immediately.

Her heart becomes light. She lets her eyes drift closed again.

"Dad?" Penny says.

"Penny," Marley whispers, "we can't hear him. You have to do the talking."

Penny nods, but she feels like she might break into a million pieces.

"Look at you," he says. "The most beautiful girl I ever saw, besides your mother."

His voice is so soft, and the cold turns to warmth. This is her father. He loved her mother. He loved *Penny*.

"Can I look at you?" Penny says, her voice cracking.

"I wouldn't. It might break the connection, and I can't stay long. I know you didn't call for me, but I heard your voice. It was so clear."

Maybe that's because of Penny's third eye.

She's never been more grateful for it. "Is Alonso's grandma…"

"She's traveled beyond."

"But you haven't?"

"I was just about ready to, but I had a feeling I should stay. Especially after what happened to your mother."

"You knew about the bargain?"

"Yes. I did what I could to protect her."

Penny's face is wet. Tears are running down her cheeks, and she wavers from being hardly able to breathe to wanting to ask him a million questions. Instead she says nothing.

"Quickly, babe," her dad says. "I'm not sure how long I can manage this."

"We…we need information about Giovanni De Luca, but you didn't know him."

"No, I didn't. But I heard a lot of rumors."

"What kinds of rumors?"

"About him being a witch."

"That's true," Penny says, almost smiling.

Her dad laughs, and it's warm as honey. "I know that now. But how do *you* know that?"

"Long story."

"And we don't have much time."

"Right," Penny says, her voice shaking.

"There were a lot of rumors about Ellie Barrion and their affair."

"Right, everyone knows those stories." Penny pauses, her thoughts snagging on one word. "Wait. An affair?"

"After she married Charles."

"What affair? What is he saying?" Corey asks, but Penny doesn't have time to answer. Maybe it's her imagination or maybe it's her third eye, but it feels like her dad's voice is getting softer. As if he's being pulled away from them.

And then she processes what her dad just said. An *affair*. Between Giovanni and Ellie. This is brand-new information, isn't it? Charles Barrion blackmailed Giovanni De Luca into using his magic to help the company years after Gio's relationship with Ellie ended, but Penny has never heard anything about an affair.

Decades *can* kill rumors, apparently.

"I have to go, Penny," her dad says.

"Wait," she says, scrabbling for more questions. For a reason to keep him here. All she comes up with is, "I don't want you to go."

"Hey, it's okay. Don't you know I love you?"

Now Penny is laughing and crying. It's something Penny's dad always used to say out of the blue. Even though he died when she was young, she remembers it: *Hey. Don't you know I love you?* Penny wishes her mom could be here. That they could all be together before this moment is over.

But that's not an option. All she can do is lean into that coldness near her cheek and say, "I know. I love you, too."

There's a heavy silence, and the patch of cold is gone.

When Penny opens her eyes, they're all staring at her.

"He looks like the guy version of you," Naomi says. Her eyes are puffy, and she sniffles.

Penny closes her eyes again, trying to remember everything about his voice. About this moment.

"Penny," Corey says, "look."

In the middle of their circle, the pomegranate has been picked clean of its ruby-red seeds.

Penny

PENNY TELLS EVERYONE THAT SHE NEEDS TO investigate before she shares what her dad told her about Giovanni De Luca. It takes some convincing, but eventually they agree. Mostly, Penny just doesn't want to tell Corey that his grandmother might have been having an affair. Not until she knows for sure.

Which is why, one hour later, she's knocking on the door to Meredith House.

When Warren opens it, Penny tries to act nonchalant. "Hi."

"Hi, Penny." Warren doesn't smile, but his presence is warm anyway. Penny feels herself relax. "Corey isn't here right now."

"I'm actually here to talk to Helen. Is she home?"

"Afraid not."

"Oh." Penny grasps for a backup plan. They

don't have much time before they try to find Alonso. "Do you know when she'll be back?"

"I don't."

"Okay." Penny is already backing up, her mind racing. She'll have to find another way to contact Helen. "Thanks anyway."

But Warren doesn't close the door. "James is home."

James Barrion. Corey's dad.

He would've been a baby when Ellie and Giovanni had their affair, so there's probably nothing he could tell her. And how would he feel about Penny digging into his family's sordid history?

Then again, Penny is on a tight schedule.

"If he doesn't mind," she says.

Warren leaves her waiting in the foyer. She remembers this past summer, when Meredith House was packed with guests who were there to enjoy the Barrions' annual charity gala. Now it echoes with emptiness, and despite the warm touches—the golden light fixtures, the thoughtful stacks of coffee table books, the unusual and intriguing art hanging on the walls—Penny doesn't know if she could ever live in a place like this and be able to call it home.

"Penny," Warren calls from the first door off the foyer. "You can come in."

When Penny enters the library, James Barrion is across the room, sitting behind a stately wooden desk. He's shuffling through papers, and he glances up at her. "Hi, Penny. Have a seat."

The door shuts behind her, and Warren's footsteps fade out in the hall.

Penny sits on the edge of a gleaming leather armchair. Mr. Barrion sighs and puts the papers aside, giving Penny a formal smile.

"How are you?" Mr. Barrion finally asks.

Penny swallows. Corey's dad still doesn't know she's wearing the ward, but she's not about to tell him. "Fine."

"And your mom?'

Penny pauses. "She misses your sister. Talks about her a lot."

Mr. Barrion appears to soften. "I think it's mutual."

The moment the silence settles, Penny's control of the situation goes out the window. How does she even approach this topic with him?

"I know you wanted to talk with Helen," Mr. Barrion says. "If you're here to beg us not to press charges against Alonso for his actions at the company, I'm afraid I can't promise that. I know he's young and impressionable, but clearly he still holds a lot of hatred for my family. Surely you understand—"

"I understand what you believe happened. You already called the Council, and they have him, Mr. Barrion. But I'm here to tell you that it wasn't Alonso."

Mr. Barrion raises an eyebrow. "We have him on camera. He's using his magic irresponsibly, Penny, and you can't convince me otherwise. He's dangerous."

"If you hear me out, it'll all make sense. Or if it doesn't make sense, it'll at least assure you that I have a good reason for coming here."

Mr. Barrion laughs under his breath. It's so condescending that Penny's skin crawls. She decides to be direct: "I want to talk about your mom."

That gets his attention. His smile fades, and he sits up a little taller, as if he's on guard. "I see."

James Barrion still doesn't know that Penny spoke to his mom not once but multiple times last summer. Her spirit is trapped by the Shadow, but she managed to break free long enough to show Penny glimpses of the past—glimpses that painted Charles Barrion as a very different man than Penny had always imagined him to be.

"I know you didn't have much time with her—"

"*Any* time," Mr. Barrion says. "She died before I was one."

Penny flinches. "Of course. Sorry."

Mr. Barrion sighs, falling back into his chair. "You don't need to apologize, Penny. You're catching me at a bad time."

Penny has always thought of James Barrion as strictly business all the time, more CEO than human being. But he's not trying to scare her away right now. Actually, he looks exhausted. His hazel eyes are alert, but his dark circles hint at a lack of sleep.

Do you miss Corey? she wants to ask. *Don't you want him home again? Why aren't you doing everything in your power to bring him back? Don't you know how much he needs you?*

Instead she says, "This is a really inappropriate question, but I have a good reason for asking you."

"You don't have to preface everything you say with a disclaimer, Penny." Mr. Barrion picks up a glass from his desk and swirls the amber liquid around a large piece of ice. "You saved your mother from our family's curse. I have a lot of respect for that, and for you."

"Really? Because you were just laughing at me."

Penny sounds older when she says it. She *feels* older. She's the definition of a pleasure to have in class under normal circumstances, but today she doesn't have the patience. Not when Alonso is about to be put on trial before the Council of Witches.

Mr. Barrion nods. "Then I guess it's my turn to apologize."

"Thank you." Penny swallows. "I want to know if your mom had an affair with Giovanni De Luca just before she died."

Mr. Barrion pauses with his glass a few inches from his lips. "Excuse me?"

Penny doesn't say it again. She just waits.

Mr. Barrion throws back the rest of his drink and puts the glass aside. "I'll be direct, too. Why do you want to know?"

"Because Alonso is in danger."

"What does this have to do with him? Giovanni and my mother are long dead. What difference would it make if they had a relationship?"

"So it's true," Penny breathes. "They did have an affair."

Mr. Barrion is perfectly still. This must be how he wins negotiations, because it's terrifying. But finally he says, "Yes. They did."

Penny's dad was right. Giovanni had never gotten over Ellie Barrion, but she always thought Ellie had hated Giovanni for using a love spell on her when they were teenagers. Maybe she did for a while—but not forever.

"Now you need to tell me why you're asking," Mr. Barrion says.

Penny isn't sure she can trust James Barrion. Corey certainly doesn't. But doesn't trusting someone always involve risk? Even if this won't convince the Barrions not to press charges against Alonso, it's worth a shot.

"Giovanni has kind of . . . come back."

Mr. Barrion's face goes completely blank. Not poker-face blank, but shocked blank. "How?"

"Alonso is possessed by him. Or what used to be him. His grandfather . . . he's become a poltergeist. A very malevolent spirit. That's why he did what he did at your company. He holds a grudge against your family because—" Penny cuts off. She can't finish that sentence. If she tells Mr.

Barrion that his dad is actually a murderer, how will he react?

But when Mr. Barrion speaks, it's Penny's turn to be stunned.

"Because my father killed him."

Penny sits up in her chair. "You knew that?" Her words come out breathy, almost insubstantial.

"Why else do you think Corey left home? He's disgusted by me." His knuckles turn white. "I can't blame him."

"But why would that make Corey leave?" As soon as the question is out of her mouth, Penny figures out the answer. "You know about the bargain?"

"Yes."

It all clicks together. *This* must be why Corey actually left home.

Mr. Barrion taps the empty whiskey glass with his nail. "He can't stand me, can he?"

"He loves you."

"It's not me he loves," Mr. Barrion says, "is it?"

The ward is cold against Penny's chest, pulsing with magic. She can't answer him.

"I suspected it was you. So did Helen. That's why she's visiting your mom right now."

Maybe Penny should feel shocked by that. Instead, she just feels immense relief that her mom isn't dealing with this on her own.

"Penny," Mr. Barrion says, "you need to tell me where Corey is. I know he wants to save you, but we can't let this turn him into a murderer."

"So you'll do it instead?"

Mr. Barrion says nothing. Now he's not even looking at her; he's staring at the stack of papers on his desk. On top of the stack is a yellowed page that looks eerily familiar.

"That…" Penny sits up. "Is that the bargain spell?"

"I found it in my dad's house. I didn't know what it was at first." He turns a cold stare on her. "I won't let you have it."

The words are bitter and resolute.

But Penny is focused on the irony of all this. They traveled through the Veil to find a copy of the spell, but the whole time it was hidden away in here, where Corey wouldn't think to look for it.

Rage overwhelms her. She pushes to her feet. "We don't need it. We have our own copy. Have a good day, Mr. Barrion." She turns on her heel to leave, and already she can hear Corey's dad getting up.

"Wait! What did my mother's affair have to do with any of this?"

Penny whirls around again. "Because tonight I have to help Alonso. We're sending Giovanni back across the Veil."

"Is Corey involved?"

"Of course he is."

Mr. Barrion shakes his head. "Then I'll send Warren out for him. I can't control what you do, Penny. You're not my kid. But Corey is not going anywhere near Giovanni De Luca."

"You're too late. Months late, actually—"

"I don't care!" Mr. Barrion raises his voice, and Penny fights the urge to curl in on herself. "You'll tell me where he is right now."

But Penny grits her teeth. "I won't!" She's yelling, too, and she doesn't even care. Distantly, Penny wonders if this is how Alonso feels when he gives in to his anger—terrified and euphoric at the same time.

"Penny, I'm sorry to do this, but I swear I'll make your life very difficult if you do not take me to my son."

"He's not a child anymore, Mr. Barrion. He's been making his own decisions for a long time." Penny heads for the door.

But Mr. Barrion's footsteps ring out, and then he's between her and her way out.

"Think about this from my perspective," Mr. Barrion says, a note of pleading in his voice now. "Please. I'm his father. I can't let him march into whatever it is you're planning."

Penny is going to argue again. The words are on the tip of her tongue.

That's when Penny really looks at Mr. Barrion's eyes.

Before, they looked hazel. Now, in the light, she realizes she was wrong.

"Your eyes," Penny says. "They're green."

Mr. Barrion goes silent. Penny looks from him to the family photos on the wall. There are quite a few of him as a young man—he's lanky, wiry, with messy blond hair.

There are also photos of his parents—Ellie with her familiar dark bob, and Charles. With his thick brown hair.

Penny lifts a hand to her mouth. How has she never noticed it before—how little Mr. Barrion looks like his dad?

When Penny found the love letters between Charles and Ellie Barrion all those weeks ago, she noticed the latest one was written in 1975—four

510

years before Corey's dad was born. She never considered what that might mean about Ellie's feelings for Charles Barrion.

"The affair," Penny says. "Why do you know about it?"

Mr. Barrion presses his lips together. He's breathing heavily through his nose, like a bull about to charge.

But Penny doesn't care if he's angry. Because she finally has her ace.

As she steps around him, she half-expects Corey's dad to try and stop her. But for once, all the fight has gone out of him—because Penny knows the truth.

James is a Barrion in name. But he's not a Barrion in blood.

70

Alonso

CONSCIOUSNESS COMES BACK SLOWLY, LIKE the drip of syrup, sticky and too sweet. When Alonso opens his eyes, he first notices the pain in his neck. He can barely lift his head. Then he realizes he's already sitting up, and there are pins and needles in his arms—because they're chained above him.

"The fuck is this?" he mutters.

There's a rustling sound a few feet away. In the dark, a shape that's distinctly Milton-like grabs a Styrofoam cup from a desk.

"Here," he says, kneeling down in front of Alonso. "Water."

Alonso drinks from the straw without thinking, and the water brings him back to life. Then he remembers why he's here, and he spits out the straw and uses his head to knock the cup away.

Unfortunately, the liquid spills all over his pants, and he's immediately freezing.

Milton sighs. "You really make your life harder than it has to be."

"Where are we?" Alonso says, looking around. He answers his own question. This is a motel room. Cheap blinds are drawn over the windows. A faded painting of Indianapolis in the 1920s hangs over the narrow, dusty bed.

"Are we in Idlewood?" Alonso asks, trying to keep the fear out of his voice.

Milton lowers himself into a chair. The way he's hesitating makes Alonso's heart pound.

"Milton," Alonso pleads. "Tell me what's happening."

Milton looks away. "The Council is putting you on trial tonight."

"Trial," he repeats, suddenly numb. "For..."

"Necromancy."

Alonso's ears start to buzz. Because the Council knows everything about what he's done. And the punishment for necromancy is...

Death.

Alonso has done a lot of scary things in his life. He's crossed the Veil multiple times. He's cast dangerous spells. He's played bike polo without a helmet. But the thought of going on trial in front of the Council of Witches sends a chill through Alonso like he's never felt before.

He has to get out of here.

Alonso thrashes against the wall, trying to loosen the restraints. But the chains are tight, and they dig painfully into his wrists. He doesn't stop until he's bleeding, but his blood doesn't fall to the carpet. Instead the restraints grow hot, and when Alonso looks up, the blood is drifting *upward*—because it's being absorbed by the restraints.

"These chains are enchanted," Alonso says, his voice hoarse.

"They're soaking up any energy you put out there, magical or otherwise." Milton pauses. "You probably won't believe me, but I really wish it didn't have to be this way."

"It *doesn't*. Marley sees things differently from you. She actually tried to help me—"

"Marley is an idealist. I see things as they really are. That's why she'll never be on the Council."

"Or maybe she's exactly what the Council needs. Do you really think we should be following rules set down by witches who died hundreds of years ago? The world has changed, Milton. Shouldn't we evolve, too?"

"You really have been spending time with my baby sister." Milton rubs his brow. "I'm not saying you're wrong, but, Alonso—I'm in trouble, too. Two people are dead, and it's because I chose to trust you and Marley."

Clay. Alonso sees his last moments when he closes his eyes. The terror on his face when he realized what was happening, that Alonso wouldn't get to the edge of the roof in time to grab him.

But Milton said two people are dead.

Alonso lets his head hang. "You know about Corey's grandpa."

"Why do you think I sent Marley here in the first place? I suspected something was up."

Alonso nods, once. Maybe he deserves what's coming.

Milton crosses his arms. "If my job is protecting mortals, I have to do this by the book. No more bending rules to give you another chance. I've done that too many times."

"Why is this a rule?"

"What do you mean?"

"The ban on necromancy. I know people are

dead. I deserve to fucking suffer for it. But I also saved Penny's mom's life. I'm not saying these things cancel each other out, but doesn't this mean necromancy *can* be used for good?"

There's a new edge to Milton's voice. "I'm not debating this."

"Why? Because you'll lose your precious Council seat and be a normal witch like the rest of us?"

Milton scoffs. "I'm done with you. You want water, you're going to have to drink the sweat from your upper lip."

Alonso is ready to argue—and that's when Milton puts on his noise-canceling headphones.

"Wow," Alonso says, but of course Milton doesn't react. Because whatever tenuous alliance Milton and Alonso had is long gone.

Alonso is now at the mercy of the Council of Witches. And he doubts they'll have much mercy to spare.

71

Cozy Mystery Book Club

DECEMBER 14, 5:47 PM

MP Marley Pierre

any news?

Penny Emberly

I just got a call from Alonso's mom. They have to attend his trial tonight.

CB Corey Barrion

So they know the location?

The CozyStay Motel.

NS Naomi Salazar

That place? Why? It's disgusting.

DM **Dylan Mayberry**

I doubt aesthetics were high on their list of priorities.

Marley, do you think they'll let you into the meeting?

MP **Marley Pierre**

My brother will sound the alarm if I'm anywhere NEAR that motel

NS **Naomi Salazar**

Soooo we have to face off against the Council? Because I don't think that will go well for us.

What if we make them panic? Like force them out of their meeting somehow?

MP **Marley Pierre**

How?

We could pull the fire alarm?

Dylan Mayberry

You're suggesting we commit a felony?
I'm impressed.

Marley Pierre

Don't get TOO excited, but that might
actually work.

The Council are great at being
witches but sometimes they're bad
at mortal shit.

Corey Barrion

Are you saying they don't have fire
drills over at the Council?

Marley Pierre

They spend their time thinking about
magical problems, not mortal ones.
They'll probably get scared.

In other words this is the perfect plan.

So we wait until the Council meeting starts, and then . . .

Naomi Salazar

Fire alarm time. We grab Alonso and get out.

Corey Barrion

So we're meeting at the motel. Is there anything we need to bring?

Marley Pierre

Thoughts and prayers, please. Thoughts and prayers.

Dylan Mayberry

Because those are ALWAYS helpful.

72

Corey

THE COZYSTAY MOTEL IS A LONELY PLACE JUST off the highway, with two weak lights in the parking lot making it barely visible in the dark. It's U-shaped, with a landing stretching around the second floor. Identical doors painted in faded red line each of the two levels. Corey has always been scared of places like this, where it's easy for anyone to walk up to your room and stand outside the door that separates your bed from the outside.

Naomi is the only one of them who's already eighteen, so she goes into the office to rent a motel room. The rest of them wait in Corey's Audi. Corey taps his fingers on the wheel, eyes on the other cars in the parking lot: a Ford truck, a Fiat, a Chrysler SUV, and an old purple Cadillac that looks like it belongs in a parade. There's one more black car that Corey is 99 percent sure is a Lambo.

"The Council's taste is eclectic," he mutters.

Marley unzips the duffel bag in her lap. "What's in here? It's so heavy."

"Stuff I thought might be helpful," Penny says from the passenger seat.

"A set of hand weights, a hammer, and pepper spray."

"I have a gun?" Corey says. "Warren taught me how to use it."

Marley raises her eyebrows. "That's intense, but I'll take it."

Corey's phone buzzes. It's Naomi:

> Room 204.

When they knock on the door a few moments later, Naomi swings it open and ushers everyone inside.

"You look stressed," Marley says.

"You should be *more* stressed." Naomi looks around. "Is Dylan still coming?"

"She said she was meeting us here," Penny says, but there's a thread of doubt in her voice.

Corey can't look away from her. He wants to

know what she's thinking. How she feels now that she knows the truth about Alonso...

Alonso. Whose life is on the line.

Corey has to focus. The priority is saving Alonso. He'll deal with the bargain and his feelings for Penny after that's done—if they manage to face off against the Council of Witches and make it out alive.

They fall into a tense silence for hours. Close to midnight, there's a frantic knock at the door.

Corey pushes off the wall. "I've got it." He looks through the peephole—and he lets out a surprised laugh. He unlocks the door and swings it open. "We weren't sure you were coming."

Dylan has her arms crossed, and she surveys them with her permanently narrowed eyes.

"You made it!" Penny says.

Dylan shrugs, as if that point is still up for debate. She comes in and drops her backpack on the floor.

"Um," Naomi says, "is that dirt under your gel extensions?"

"Yep."

"Why...?" Naomi says, drawing the end of the word out.

"Just burying bodies," Dylan says.

The scariest part is that she could be telling the truth.

"What?" Dylan snaps.

Corey realizes he's smirking. "I'm glad you're on our side."

Dylan's face goes red, and she looks away.

"Marley?" Penny says. "What's wrong?"

Marley has taken Corey's place at the window. She looks up at the moon, and her face is impossible to read.

"Well?" Naomi says.

"The moon is high." She walks over to the duffel bag and fishes out the hammer. "It's time to move."

73

Alonso

THE COUNCIL WOULD LOOK MORE INTIMIDATING if they hadn't squeezed themselves into a dingy motel room.

"Couldn't spring for a Hilton, huh?" Alonso says as Milton walks him into the room, which is a few doors down from where they were keeping him locked up. "Even a nice little conference room. Is that too much to ask?"

But it's *not* just a dingy motel room. Even though it's small, it fits a circle of thirteen chairs—and on these chairs sit the members of the Council of Witches. They must've enchanted the room to make more space. For some witches, that would be complicated magic.

For the Council of Witches, it's just another day.

The most powerful witches in the world watch Alonso with a mixture of judgment, curiosity, and disdain. He gulps.

"Everyone," says Park YeaLee, who's still wearing her stupid sunglasses, "this is Alonso De Luca. The subject of much speculation in our circles."

"The gang's all here, huh?" Alonso says. "You're bringing out the big guns to deal with a stupid kid from Indiana."

YeaLee frowns. "You forced our hand. Trust me, I'd rather be anywhere else."

"Alonso!"

Alonso's head snaps to the corner of the room. Crowded back by the window, partially blocked by the Council members, are the De Lucas. They watch him with weary, panicked expressions. Aunt Emilia is wringing her hands, and Aunt Donna is chain smoking, already lighting a new cigarette as her previous one burns out. He hates that his coven is here. He also wouldn't have it any other way.

"Isn't this a nonsmoking room?" Alonso asks, but his voice is soft.

Aunt Emilia dissolves. Aunt Donna won't look at him. But Alonso's mom is standing tall. She tries to smile at him, but it's clearly a struggle for her.

That's when Alonso feels himself break. His

shoulders are impossibly heavy, as if the weight of everything that's happened is finally settling on him, pulling him down to the earth—and, very soon, under it.

Because Alonso is going to die tonight.

"Alonso De Luca," says YeaLee. "You are charged with the use of necromancy resulting in your own possession. In turn, you have now murdered two mortals."

"I swear," Alonso says, his voice cracking, "I didn't kill anyone."

"We thought that's what you would say."

"So you don't believe me?"

YeaLee kneels before him. "The question isn't whether we believe you. Whether you committed murder or it was the work of the spirit you carry, people are dead. We hear you possess great magic. This means the poltergeist can cause large-scale damage." She looks to Milton. "His power is bound?"

"By the cuffs. He's broken a binding spell before so I took extra precautions."

"You're really going to stand there like a coward, huh?" Alonso growls at him.

Milton stiffens. "I'm doing my duty."

"Calling it your duty doesn't make it right."

A hand grabs Alonso's chin, and YeaLee wrenches his face toward hers.

Alonso gasps. For the first time, her sunglasses are gone. Her eyes . . .

They're a pale violet. And as she looks at Alonso, they begin to glow. She leans in, examining him.

Alonso loses himself in the color of her irises. Vaguely he wonders if he's being hypnotized, but he can't look away until she lets go.

"Hm," YeaLee says, putting black gloves onto her hands.

"What did you see?" Milton asks.

"What we expected," YeaLee says. "For the most part."

"W-what did you just do?" Alonos manages to say. There's a buzzing in his skull, as though he's just been through an X-ray machine.

"My mother," YeaLee says, "died in child-birth. Her death gave me an unusual gift. I can see the future—or futures, I should say. For you, there are many ways your path could unfold. All of them are disastrous."

"All of them?" he has to ask. "Are you sure?"

YeaLee's smile wavers. "Most. And that tells me enough."

528

Alonso's mouth goes dry. This is what he's always been afraid of: having no future at all.

YeaLee looks at one of the Council members, a girl who appears even younger than Milton. "Manuela, guard the doors. They'll be here."

"Who?" Alonso says, but nobody answers him. "Please, just hear me out!"

"Fine." YeaLee sits on a folding chair. "Tell us the details of how it happened. We need to know everything if we're going to consider your case fairly."

And because his family is here—and maybe because he still has some tiny shred of hope that they'll forgive him, that YeaLee saying "most" means there's a version of himself that convinces them of his innocence and survives—Alonso is honest with the Council. He tells them exactly how he brought Mrs. Emberly back to life, and how he came to be inhabited by the poltergeist of his grandfather.

When he finishes, the room is silent. Breaths are held.

"And you have control over this poltergeist?" YeaLee asks.

"I've been able to subdue him," Alonso says.

"I know some of his triggers. And I know what makes him more powerful."

There's a murmur throughout the room. The Council is interested—but YeaLee's expression is stony.

"I move to vote," she says.

Milton steps forward. For the first time, he looks almost afraid on Alonso's behalf. "Aren't we supposed to deliberate?"

A man with a long ponytail rubs his chin. "This is a unique case. Perhaps we should consider the circumstances."

"The details are clear as day," YeaLee snaps. "And I don't want him out of our sight. Not while his friends are waiting for him out there."

Friends? Alonso looks at the door. Is Penny here? Did she figure out where he was?

"Seconded," says a person with close-cropped hair and the tattoo of a skeletal hand wrapped around their throat.

"Vote on what?" Alonso's mom says, looking between the Council members. "What's happening?"

"All in favor of putting Alonso Pietro De Luca to death for breaking the Council's laws and posing great danger to the world of witches and mortals alike?" YeaLee says.

"Wait!" Alonso says. "Don't I get to argue for myself?"

The girl, Manuela, actually laughs at him. "The Council's rules are the rules that govern all witches. If you don't understand that, then I guess you were always going to end up here."

"Enough, Manuela," YeaLee snaps. "We do not taunt our prisoners. If you continue to act like these meetings are a fun extracurricular, I'll be forced to reconsider your appointment."

Manuela shrinks from her. "Yes. Sorry."

Alonso is almost grateful to YeaLee. But that goes away as soon as she says, "Now we vote."

As Alonso watches, every single Council member raises their hand—except one.

Milton stares at the floor, his jaw tense with whatever battle is going on inside his head.

"She said most of my paths are bad, but not all," Alonso says through his teeth. "Milton, believe in me. You did it once before, and we did something that you thought was impossible. Remember?"

Milton closes his eyes, and Alonso is buoyed.

He'll argue for him. He'll change the Council's minds—

And then Milton puts his hand in the air.

YeaLee nods. "Unanimous."

"He's a *child*," Alonso's mother shouts.

YeaLee nods in the De Lucas' direction. "Restrain them."

Spells are whispered, words weaving together into a hypnotic rhythm. Alonso's mom opens her mouth to shout, but a serene expression suddenly crosses her face. She sits down softly, like she's at afternoon tea, and stares off into space. Aunt Donna and Aunt Emilia do the same.

YeaLee kneels in front of Alonso one more time.

"If I didn't know better," Alonso growls, "I'd say you look disappointed."

"You're not wrong." YeaLee purses her lips. "This girl whose mother you saved. You love her?"

"Till I die and beyond," Alonso says.

"I thought so. Love makes us foolish, Alonso. I'm sorry you learned this too late." She stands up, nodding to the man with the long ponytail.

"My name is Nicholas Guayama," the man says, nodding at Alonso in greeting. "I will be the one to lead the exorcism."

This man is going to send both Alonso and his grandfather across the Veil. Alonso is about to die.

He starts shaking. The De Luca coven sits quiet and unaware while the Council looks on—except Milton, who is turned away.

Alonso stares at Milton. Then he looks back down at the chains around his wrists.

They're soaking up any energy you put out there, magical or otherwise.

As Nicholas raises a hand to Alonso's head, Alonso closes his eyes. Maybe love is foolish, like YeaLee said. But is being foolish always such a bad thing?

It's Giovanni who answers him: *Being foolish is never a bad thing when you have nothing left to lose.*

Alonso sucks in a breath. Then he begins whispering every spell he can think of.

He has so many memorized now—spells to enhance hearing, to cure skin rashes, to make people look at your face and see someone else's.

Nicholas's hand stops short. "What is he—"

"He has no power because of the restraints," YeaLee says. "Continue."

Alonso keeps whispering spells until one

finally takes hold: a spell to drop the temperature within roughly a ten-foot radius.

> *"High atmosphere descend,*
> *Make clouds of these currents…"*

Alonso speaks faster, putting all the magic he possesses into every word—until he can see his breath.

The restraints start to glow red.

Nicholas flinches, falling back. "YeaLee! We need to—"

The chains shatter into pieces. Alonso runs for the door, ignoring the aching pain in his wrists.

He only takes three steps before Giovanni's voice rings like a piercing alarm in his head.

Leaving already? But I haven't had a chance to introduce myself.

Pain thrums in Alonso's every limb. He drops to his knees, clutching his chest. He opens his mouth to tell the Council to run—

He's too late.

74

Giovanni

GIOVANNI'S SPIRIT REVS LIKE AN ENGINE.

"The next generation," Giovanni says, looking around the room at the assembled Council members. "Quite a party you've thrown for me."

"It's the poltergeist," YeaLee says, and the magic in the room grows loud in Gio's ears. So he decides to beat them to it.

He whispers, "*Tear the spider's web,*" and lifts his foot, bringing it down on the ground.

The entire room shakes. There's the sound of something cracking.

Giovanni is already running to the door, and before anyone can even draw a breath long enough to speak a spell, the floor falls out from underneath them. The Council disappears as they fall to the first floor of the motel.

"*Dad!*"

Giovanni grabs the doorframe, jerking himself to a stop. His daughters are still standing at the far end of the room. They're trapped against the wall, pushed up on tiptoes on a thin strip of intact floor—the only thing that's keeping them from falling to the hotel room below.

"Help us!" Vera yells.

Some distant part of Giovanni stirs. It's an old protective instinct, peeking out from the dust of his memory like a half-buried artifact. It pulls him to Vera, Donna, and Emilia, and he draws a quick, pained breath.

"Dad?" Emilia says, her voice quavering.

Giovanni screws his eyes shut. He's had decades of practice forgetting his humanity, and soon the desire to help his daughters is gone. He feels himself relax, and he smiles.

"Good luck, girls," Giovanni says, running from the room.

And Giovanni is free.

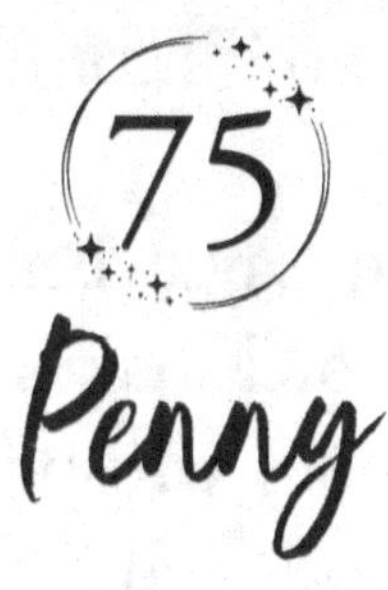

Penny

THE NIGHT IS TOO QUIET.

Penny, Corey, Marley, and Dylan are crouched down on the second floor of the motel. They're waiting on the landing across from room 211, where they saw Milton bring Alonso. Marley holds the hammer, Corey holds the salt and has the gun in his back pocket, and Penny has three different pepper sprays (courtesy of Ron).

Penny has never pepper-sprayed anyone before. "What if I point it the wrong way?" she whispers.

"Then we leave you behind," Dylan mutters. "Natural selection."

"When should we pull the alarm?" Corey asks.

Marley opens her mouth to answer, but she never gets the chance. Because there's a sound like someone yelling, and then—

An explosion. And it's coming from the direction of room 211.

"Whoa!" Dylan says. Penny grabs Corey's arm as the entire motel shakes.

"Get ready," Marley whispers.

The door opens, and Alonso appears in a cloud of smoke and screams. He runs at top speed toward the staircase.

"Alonso!" Penny says, already running after him down the open-air hallway.

Alonso stops at the sound of her voice, but he doesn't turn around.

"We have to go!" Penny says.

That's when she notices the strange way he's standing. And when he turns around, it's not Alonso's gray eyes that take her in.

His eyes are green.

"We finally meet, Miss Emberly," Giovanni says.

A hand grabs Penny's shoulder, pulling her back. "Run," Corey says, and they sprint down the hallway, away from Giovanni.

He's following them, though. His pace is leisurely compared to theirs.

As Penny and Corey turn the corner to the staircase, Marley is waiting there. "Dylan is downstairs," she says. "She'll give you cover."

Penny catches herself against the wall. "What are you doing?"

"I'll distract him." Marley grabs a water bottle from her jacket pocket and tosses the water over the floor. She whispers a few words, and the water turns to ice.

Giovanni doesn't stop in time. He loses his balance, sliding over the floor—but he's heading right for Marley. He grabs her shoulders and shoves her roughly back—and over the railing that acts as a barrier between the hallway and the cement ten feet below them.

"Marley!" Penny screams. Corey dashes for her. But Marley catches herself on the railing, hanging by her fingertips.

"Go!" Marley says through gritted teeth.

But Corey is already running to help her. Penny moves with him, stopping between Marley and Giovanni.

"Alonso wouldn't want me to hurt you," Giovanni says as he gets to his feet, "but that just makes me want to do it more."

A figure appears silently behind Giovanni. A woman with dark hair and haunting purple eyes.

Penny recognizes her. It's the woman from the holiday party, the one who was wearing sunglasses at night. This time, there are no sunglasses—but now she's holding a knife.

"NO!" Penny screams, but the woman throws it. Giovanni turns around at exactly the wrong time, and he jerks back on impact. He falls to his knees, gasping.

Penny runs to him. The knife is lodged in his shoulder, and from the little bit of metal she can see, this is another silver knife like the one Marley gave her.

"You bitch," Giovanni growls. He blinks a few times as if he's dizzy. "You've disabled my magic."

"That was the idea," the woman says. Her eyes cut to Penny and Corey. "You're Alonso's friends, I'm guessing."

"Yeah," Penny says. Then she takes two steps forward and pepper sprays the woman's beautiful eyes.

The witch screams, covering her face with her hands. Penny grabs Giovanni's arm and tries to pull him up. Even if he wants to fight her, she can't leave him behind. If Alonso's body dies, there's no hope of ever getting him back.

But it isn't green eyes she looks into.

"Penny," Alonso says, his voice weak. "My family...where are they?"

Penny shakes her head. "I don't know, but we need to get you out of here."

Alonso catches sight of the knife sticking out of his arm, and he loses whatever color was left in his face. "I'm going to pass out…"

"No you're not," Corey says, and he grabs Alonso's other arm and hauls him up. Alonso groans in pain. "We're getting you out of here."

76

Alonso

ALONSO THOUGHT HE KNEW WHAT PAIN FELT like. That was until he got stabbed. He can't tell for sure, but he might be crying.

Naomi pulls up in the Audi as Penny, Alonso, and Corey run down the stairs. Dylan meets them there. "Where's Marley?" she asks.

"Here!" Marley says, taking the stairs two at a time. "Go, go, go!"

Dylan opens the car door, and she and Marley dive into the back seat.

"*Stop!*" comes Manuela's voice from behind them. Alonso barely has any energy left to panic. He's drained, and his arm is throbbing with a pain that's like a lite version of the binding spell.

A scream comes from the second floor. Alonso stops, nearly stumbling to the ground and taking Penny and Corey with him. But he can't move— because he knows that voice.

It belongs to Aunt Emilia.

"Help them!" Alonso yells.

"Who?" Corey asks.

Alonso can't answer. His eyes search frantically for sight of his mom, his aunts, but all he sees is Manuela. She stops in her tracks at the top of the stairs, confused as she turns toward the scream. She doesn't know who it's coming from. In her mind, it could be a member of the Council.

That's when Alonso finally feels his coven's presence. There's no pain. Just a calculating, purposeful calm.

They're stalling so Alonso can get away.

"Alonso?" Penny says, her voice strained.

"They're okay!" Alonso says, nodding at the car. "Let's go!"

Penny and Corey help Alonso into the front seat, but when Alonso hears a string of words that are both whispered and echoing, he grabs Penny's hand. "Look out!"

Penny stumbles forward like someone hit her in the back.

"That's for the pepper spray," Manuela calls.

Alonso pulls Penny onto his lap. A muscle in Corey's jaw twitches, but he closes the door and jumps into the back seat.

"Go!" Dylan says, and Naomi takes off.

"Someone's following us," Naomi says, looking in the rearview mirror.

"It's Milton," Marley says, eyes narrowed as she eyes the SUV behind them. "Can you lose him?"

"I can try," Naomi says, speeding up.

"Head to my place," Corey says.

"We have an injury here," Marley says. "Shouldn't we go to the hospital?"

"Warren is a retired Navy doctor. He'll be able to help." Corey grabs Naomi's shoulder. "You should take the road by the river. It's faster."

"Copy that," Naomi says as she takes a tight turn, and they drive into the dark countryside.

Penny's mouth opens, but no words come out. "What?" Alonso says. "What's wrong?"

Penny sucks in a shaky breath and touches her fingers to her throat. Then she digs under her jacket and pulls out a necklace—the ward.

Except where there should be a charm, there's nothing but a tiny shard of obsidian.

Alonso's chest goes tight with panic. "Oh my god."

"What?" Naomi and Corey say at the same time.

"That Council witch," Alonso says. "The spell she used on Penny... it destroyed the ward."

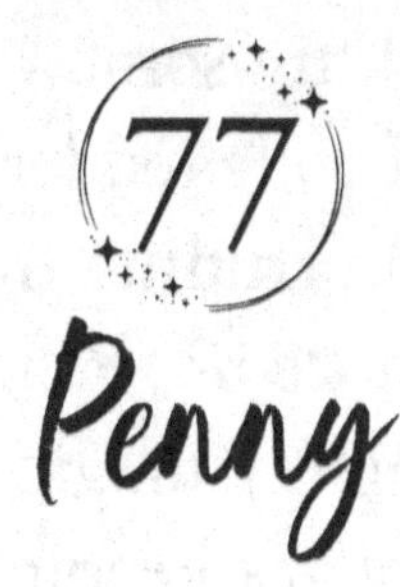

Penny

PENNY CLUTCHES THE CRESCENT MOON CHARM—
or what's left of it.

A tiny part of the onyx charm still dangles from the gold chain. She shakes out her sweater, and the rest of the shattered pieces come raining down.

"How did she know about it?" Penny says, looking from Alonso to Marley.

"Ward magic is strong," Marley says. "She must've been able to sense it, even if she didn't know what it was for."

Corey's gaze darkens. He turns away, shaking his head.

"I'm okay, Corey," Penny says, "but I need Naomi to stop the car and let me out. None of you are safe around me right now."

"You're not going anywhere," Corey snaps.

"I'm gonna fuck up some Council witches—*ouch*." Alonso shifts. He tenderly presses the skin around the knife protruding from his shoulder.

"Should we remove it?" Penny says.

"No. It's keeping my magic subdued," Alonso says, "which means it's keeping my grandfather quiet."

"Plus those wounds bleed a lot, so it's better to leave the knife where it is," Marley says.

"I hate magic," Naomi says, glancing nervously at Penny.

"Welcome to my life," Corey says. "There's the train bridge. We're only ten minutes away. Once we get to my house, we'll be safe. At least we lost Milton—"

Naomi screams, and Penny is jerked to the side as she turns the wheel. Penny's eyes fill with bright light . . .

Headlights. Coming straight for them.

There isn't time to scream.

Then there's an earsplitting *crash*—

It feels like the car is being torn in half. The glass cracks. There's a *pop*, and Penny's face hits something soft and hard at the same time, and it knocks the wind from her lungs.

When it all stops, the world goes silent as death.

Corey

IT HAPPENS SO FAST—THE HEADLIGHTS COM-ing straight toward them across the yellow line, the crash, the momentum stealing Corey's voice.

When Corey opens his eyes, all he sees is wreckage.

There's steam in the air. It takes him a second to realize it's from the car's engine.

"Penny," he croaks, leaning over the front seat.

Both airbags are deployed. Naomi is slumped in the seat, and Alonso is curled over Penny.

"Hey," Corey says, reaching out to touch Alonso's back. "Hey! Talk to me!"

This crash was Corey's fault. It was because of the bargain. If any of them die . . .

"Corey," Penny says.

The sound of her voice is like a splash of cold water. Suddenly Corey is moving fast—he checks on Dylan, who is dazed but seems unharmed, before he helps Marley as she's trying to sit up, and then he dives into the front seat and touches Naomi's shoulder. She's hunched over the airbag.

"Naomi?" Corey whispers.

No answer.

"Naomi!" Corey says.

Penny pulls herself up. Pieces of glass fall out of her hair. "Naomi? Please, please—"

Naomi's body jerks with a sudden coughing fit. Penny slumps in relief, and Corey presses a fist to his mouth as his hammering heartbeat slows.

"I'm okay," Naomi says. "I…I think." When she sits up, Corey gasps. There's blood gushing from her nose, making her face gleam red.

"Ow," Naomi says, touching her nose gingerly.

"You look like Carrie at prom," Dylan says, her voice hoarse.

"What the fuck," Alonso says, coughing. "*Agh,* my arm…"

Then Corey sees the other car. It looks just as wrecked, but Corey can still make out the Mercedes logo on the front.

Corey goes numb. Because he knows that car.

He opens the back door just as Julian stumbles

out of the Mercedes. He's coughing and sputtering, barely able to stand.

Corey closes the space between them before Julian even has a chance to look up. Corey grabs his shirt and shoves him against his ruined car.

"What did you do?!" Corey says. No, he's *screaming*. It's so loud it makes his throat raw.

Tears run down Julian's face, but he isn't sobbing. He shivers with adrenaline.

"You had to be stopped," Julian says. "I had to do this for . . . for Grandpa. He trusted me to take care . . . to take care of everyone . . ."

Corey doesn't have to ask how he found him. They've shared their locations for years. It never occurred to Corey that he should turn his off.

Turns out it might've been the greatest mistake of Corey's entire life.

"You tried to kill me!" Corey says. "After I've loved you like a brother my entire. Fucking. Life!" He shoves Julian against the car, and Julian crumples into a heap.

"No!" Julian's determination wavers. "He told me what you did, Corey, and I couldn't just let you hurt anyone else!"

"What did Grandpa tell you?" Corey says.

"Because I guarantee, no matter what he said about me, what he did was worse—"

"*You killed him!*"

Corey's next words get lodged in his throat. Julian can't believe he'd even be capable of that, right?

Julian keeps talking. "You barely mourned him! You just went back to your normal life, while I was *destroyed*. Even Alonso noticed—"

"Alonso." Corey's voice cuts through Julian's rambling. "You didn't see Grandpa."

"Yes I did—"

"That was *magic*, Julian! You were fooled!"

Julian's conviction wavers. "I…no…" His eyes move from Corey to the other car.

Then another voice makes Corey forget his anger.

"Corey…"

There's a figure in the driver's seat of the Mercedes, leaning over the steering wheel. The airbag didn't deploy, and his body is at a strange angle.

Corey's heart stutters. Julian got out of the passenger seat, not the driver's seat.

When he sees blond-and-gray hair, it's like a bomb goes off in his chest.

"Dad?" Corey says.

His dad coughs, and it sounds wet.

Corey is already leaping over the front of the car, opening the driver's-side door. His dad isn't moving, but his eyes are open. Blinking. Trying to focus.

Corey kneels. His hands hover over his dad's body, but he doesn't want to touch him. What if he makes it worse?

There's a sound behind him. The crunching of glass. When Corey turns around, Penny and Alonso are there, looking on in horror.

"What do I do?" Corey says, his voice cracking with desperation. He turns back to his dad. "Dad, stay awake!"

"We…" his dad says, struggling through every word. "We were coming to find you. The bargain, we…we were going to help…I'm sorry…"

"Julian grabbed the wheel?" Corey asks.

His dad attempts a nod and flinches, as if even that is painful.

When Corey closes his eyes, it's not his dad's face he sees. It's his mom's, just before the train hit her car ten years ago.

This can't be happening again.

"Someone has to call 911," he manages to say.

"Dylan is doing it now," Penny says.

There's a hand on Corey's shoulder. "Look at me," Alonso says.

Alonso's face is stricken. Almost gray. The wound at his shoulder is bleeding heavily.

"I heard Julian," Alonso says. "Giovanni did something to him?"

Corey grits his teeth and nods.

Alonso lets his hand fall. "You know the bargain spell?"

"I have it memorized," Corey says, his voice still shaking.

Alonso nods at Corey's back pocket. "Then let's do this."

"What?" Corey squints up at him. Then it all comes together: Alonso noticed the gun. And he wants Corey to use it. On him.

"No," Corey says. "No fucking way."

Alonso just stands there, like it's inevitable that Corey will change his mind.

"I can't escape this," Alonso says. "I've already hurt so many people. Clay, Julian…your grandfather. That woman, Park YeaLee…she saw my future and she said there was no hope for me."

"Alonso—" Penny starts.

"You almost died tonight, Penny!" Alonso

yells over her. "Everything I've done this year has been to protect you! And if I still lose you now..."

"This isn't over yet!" Penny says. "You can't give up."

Alonso looks down at the knife, at his blood-drenched shoulder. "I could only hold Giovanni off before because I was strong in my body and in my magic. Now my body...it's dying. And if it does, Giovanni will win. There will be no more switching back and forth, him and me playing a game of cat and mouse." Alonso is shivering violently, but he manages to nod at Corey. "You have to send us both across the Veil."

The gun is suddenly heavy in Corey's pocket. Growing up, Corey used to picture killing Alonso. He hated him so much. He was a murderer. He took Corey's mom away. Now, the thought of him dying makes Corey sick. Already nausea is roiling his stomach.

But he needs to save Penny's life. The lives of his family. Of everyone in Idlewood. And here's the path, laid out in front of him.

But Penny's life isn't worth more than Alonso's. Corey is in love with Penny, but Alonso is his friend.

Corey is about to say as much when Alonso ducks around him. He grabs the gun and shoves it into Corey's hand, forcing it up until the barrel of the gun is sitting in the center of Alonso's forehead.

"Get it over with," he growls.

THIS IS LIKE SOMETHING OUT OF PENNY'S DARK-est nightmares.

"No!" Penny screams.

"Alonso, stop!" Corey yells.

"No!" Alonso says, gritting his teeth. "Just do it before I change my mind."

Penny is aware of the people all around them, watching. Waiting. Dylan, her expression unreadable. Marley, looking on with tension as she holds Naomi up. Julian, peeking over his wrecked car with silent tears running down his face.

For their entire friendship, Penny has been the one to throw herself between Corey and Alonso. She's the peacemaker. Corey is the strong and silent type. Alonso is the hothead. They've fallen into these roles over and over again.

But this time is different. Because Alonso is

standing there, resigned to death. And seconds later, Corey wrenches the gun away and backs up, his shoulders rising and falling rapidly.

"Don't be an idiot," Corey says.

Penny breathes out, almost falling to her knees in relief.

"You're the idiot," Alonso says. His words are slurring now, and as he looks over at Penny, his eyes become strange.

The color is shifting.

"Penny," Alonso says, reaching for her. She grabs his arm, steadying him before he falls.

"Stay close to him!" Marley says. "It'll make him stronger!"

"It will?" Penny looks from Marley to Alonso.

"You're my good luck charm," he says, trying to smile.

And for a moment, Penny sees the green in his eyes recede. "I think it's working—"

And all at once, they change to solid green. And when Alonso smiles again, it doesn't look like him at all.

"That was close," Giovanni says, and he shoves Penny to the ground.

She gasps as she hits the dirt. When she

looks back up at him, he's shoving his uninjured shoulder into Corey's chest. The gun flies out of Corey's hand onto the ground.

Penny lunges for the gun, but Giovanni sends his other foot at Penny's face. She throws up her arms, and pain shoots through her wrist as Giovanni kicks her away.

"Everyone calm down," Giovanni says. With the gun tucked under his elbow, he pulls the silver knife out of his shoulder. Blood gushes down his arm, sprinkling onto the grass, but when he lifts his fingers and mutters a spell, fire appears at his fingertips, cauterizing the wound.

"I used to hate how difficult it was to manage Alonso when you were around," Giovanni says. "Luckily for me, he's on the brink of death. Even *you* can't save him from that."

Penny pushes to her feet. This is the moment they've been waiting for, but now that it's here, she's terrified.

There's no living in the past. No going back to how things were. There's only the unknown future, and Penny is as ready for it as she'll ever be.

"Are we doing this?" Marley shouts to her.

Penny looks at her. "Give me a minute."

Marley looks like she wants to fight her on that, but she nods.

Penny turns back to Giovanni, who is rolling out his shoulder. "Much better," he says. "Now let's have some fun."

And he runs directly at Penny.

80

Giovanni

THE GIRL TRIES TO RUN.

Hollow's cry rings through the night, and the crow dives for Penny. He pecks at her and flaps his wings, making her stumble.

Giovanni reaches her and wraps an arm around her neck, pointing the gun at her head. "Nobody move."

Corey and all his friends freeze. Naomi sobs, and she looks like a ghoul the way her tears mix with the blood on her face. It almost makes Giovanni laugh.

He backs up, the Emberly girl quivering with fear against him. They stop where the bridge meets the grass.

"Careful now," Giovanni says to her. "You don't die until I say you do." Then he throws the silver knife and the gun into the river below. "Mortal weapons are no fun. I prefer to improvise."

Corey is at the edge of the tracks, but he hasn't tried to move closer—yet. He's good and scared.

"The Barrions killed the woman I love!" Giovanni shouts. "Now I will kill *her*. You only have your grandfather to thank for this."

"You don't want to do this," Penny whispers.

"Why is that?" Giovanni asks, grinning.

"Because I know something about you that you don't." She speaks quickly. "You had an affair with Ellie right before you both died, didn't you?"

Giovanni's easy mood vanishes. He grips Penny's neck tighter, leaning into her ear to whisper, "That's not a revelation. Why else do you think Chuck chose to kill us as part of the bargain?"

"That wasn't why. Ellie kept something from you."

The urge Gio has to throw Penny off the train bridge ebbs for a moment. He feels her swallow against his arm. She's not taking in a lot of oxygen right now. If he holds her just a little tighter, she'll fall unconscious.

"There's a piece of paper in my pocket," Penny says. "Give it to Corey."

"You aren't in the position to play games, Penny Emberly."

"None of this is a game to any of us but you," Penny says, her voice sharp.

Poltergeists don't care for feelings. Sadness, grief, excitement—those are vestiges of an old life that Gio was happy to leave behind. He's had enough of these inconvenient emotions to last a dozen lifetimes.

But, Gio notes with clinical fascination, he *does* still enjoy a bit of gossip.

Before he can say as much, there's a rustle, and a paper bursts from Penny's jacket pocket and flies into the hands of Marley Pierre. "Here," she says, handing it to Corey.

There's a silence as Corey looks over the page. "Botanic Vivification? What is this?"

"A spell?" Giovanni says, looking down at Penny. "If this is indeed a game, you're losing."

"Read it, Corey!" Penny yells.

Corey looks at her. "Why?"

"Trust me," Penny says.

"I'm getting bored," Giovanni says. "And when I get bored, I do terrible things."

Marley is looking at Penny with wide, shocked eyes. She seems to understand something. "Corey, there," she says, pointing to a small patch of dead plants next to the railroad tracks.

Corey hesitates, but he finally kneels down. He reads the spell in a loud voice:

> *"Life is green and brown and yellow,*
> *Undo the rot and putrid sallow.*
> *Revive and relight and renourish*
> *Until this vein is new."*

"Again!" Penny says. "You have to do it again!"

So he does. And the words hypnotize Giovanni, because as Corey repeats the spell, Giovanni feels something tugging at him, as though a tiny insect has gotten into his heart and is pulling the tendons and muscles this way and that.

This was how it used to feel doing magic with his coven. They were all connected.

"I feel dizzy," Corey says.

"Again," Penny demands.

And this time, when Corey is halfway through, he stops.

"Penny," he breathes.

Marley's hands fly up to her mouth. Giovanni looks to the plant—

And where there was a pile of withered stems, there's now one small red flower. It stands out against the browned winter grasses and the dead foliage around it, impossible to miss.

"What is this?" Giovanni says. His heart is still doing that strange stutter.

There's movement out of the corner of his eye. James Barrion has dragged himself from the car. He looks up at Giovanni, and he points at his own eyes.

"Green," Penny says, "just like yours. Charles Barrion chose to kill you because he knew the baby wasn't his."

Baby.

"He's my…" There's a sharp pain in Gio's chest, but when he looks down, there's no wound. This isn't physical pain.

It's grief.

"My son," Gio says.

His and Ellie's. They had a *child*.

In the distance, a train whistle howls.

Their son lives. The proof that he and Ellie loved each other once, living and breathing in the Primary World—

"Now!" Penny yells.

Penny shoves backward, catching Giovanni off guard. Gio's head cracks against the train tracks. His vision doubles, and he's too dizzy to right himself. Hands grab his ankles and pull him onto the grass, and Marley moves quickly around him—with salt. She's making a pentagram.

Penny, Marley, Corey, and Dylan surround him. As Giovanni blinks, Hollow comes into view, heading for the group. Trying to save him. But there's a hiss, and Alonso's wretched familiar leaps into view. She sinks her claws into Hollow, intercepting him. The animals tumble to the grass at the end of the train bridge in a mess of screeches and snarls.

"Hollow!" Giovanni yells.

The cat—Nimble—is on top of Hollow. The crow is cawing, crying. Nimble leans down.

"No!" Giovanni cries as the cat sinks her teeth into Hollow's neck and pulls, coming up with blood and sinew and muscle.

Hollow's spirit flickers like a light. Then it goes out.

Giovanni screams. Whatever tenuous hold he has on Alonso's body is gone. His spirit is flying wildly around like a pinball, and he can't stop it.

"I can see his aura!" Marley grabs something from her pocket and holds it over him. Then she begins to recite another spell . . .

The exorcism.

> *"Hunger of the wolf, life of the mind
> and belief of the soul,
> Unite behind us as we call forth this
> spirit from his hold,
> Open the Veil for him and only him,
> Crack open this living body and guide
> him back home."*

They whisper the words over and over, the sounds clashing and overlapping, until Giovanni can't hear anything else. He opens his mouth to scream again just as Marley opens her fist, and tiny juniper berries fall from her hand. They stop before they hit the ground, floating on air.

One of the berries catches flame, and inside Alonso's skin, it's like an explosion. The bond Gio had with Alonso's body breaks, thread by thread, until Giovanni is floating.

And he's cold. So very cold.

Giovanni tries to hold on, but these witches—these children—are too strong. It isn't until the Veil becomes visible in front of him that his panic translates into power. The Second World is already pulling him in, condemning him to wander its lifeless paths with all his anger and grief and hurt.

Giovanni won't allow it.

He gathers all the energy he has left until his spirit becomes almost solid. And, as the Second World pulls him back again, Giovanni uses the last bit of his strength to reach for Alonso.

81

Penny

PENNY WATCHES THE JUNIPER BERRIES CATCH fire. Every time it happens, Alonso's body jerks to unnatural angles.

It's *working.*

The last berry burns. A ripple passes through the air, and Penny feels it deep in her gut. She looks up—

And Giovanni is hovering there, just above Alonso's body.

The Veil is open, waiting for him. But Giovanni doesn't cross right away. He lets out a cry, and then...

He grabs Alonso, pulling him off the ground.

In an instant, they're both gone.

There's an electric *snap* in the air. Then it's quiet.

"Where are they?" Penny breathes.

Marley is staring at the grass, her mouth open in horror.

"They crossed," Dylan says. "Didn't they? Both of them?"

They crossed the Veil. Alonso was taken from them.

Marley still hasn't said a word. Penny walks up to her and grabs her shoulders. "Marley, you have to open the Veil."

"What?" Marley asks, dazed.

"Cut a hole in the Veil!" Penny says. "I have to go after him!"

Marley breathes out. Penny doesn't understand what's going on. Why isn't she panicking?

"Penny," Marley says, "I'm sorry."

Penny stares at her. Then she looks from Marley to Dylan to Corey and Naomi. The wind whips around them, threatening to push them off into the river.

Marley is shaking her head. "I can't open the Veil. Giovanni could get through again."

"But Alonso is across—"

"I can't!" Marley's eyes are watering now. "I'm sorry! I just can't!"

These are the words that shatter Penny.

The train whistle is getting closer, and now it's joined by the sound of an ambulance. But none of it matters, because Alonso isn't here.

"Penny." Corey grabs her shoulders. "We have to move."

"Come on," Marley says, avoiding Penny's eyes as she walks away.

When Corey speaks again, his voice is softer this time. "Look at me."

But she can't. Because if Penny looks at him, Corey will see the truth in her face.

The truth is that Alonso is gone. And, after these weeks without him, Penny can't accept that. She would give everything to have him back.

Even a future with Corey.

"Tell me what you need," he whispers, the words urgent.

She sucks in a breath. Then she finally meets Corey's eyes. Despite everything, there's still part of her that doesn't want to lose Corey. But now that she knows how she feels, she can't lie to him.

She has to let him go.

"I need to find Alonso," Penny says, her voice cracking.

She's prepared for Corey's face to go blank.

For the wall to come up again. For him to walk away and leave her on this bridge by herself.

But that's not what happens. Instead, when Corey understands what Penny is really saying, he shatters. He takes a step back from her, but his eyes never leave Penny's face. Then he presses the heels of his hands to his eyes and lets out a deep, pained sound.

"Corey..." Penny begins, but she can't tell him she's sorry. All she can do is tell him the truth now that she knows what she wants.

"You guys!" Naomi yells. "Come on!"

The train whistle is getting closer. When they needed to save Penny's mom back in August, Alonso found his own way across.

So Penny will do the same.

She closes her eyes. She thinks back to that night with Alonso on this bridge. To the words they whispered in the dark.

No matter what city or country or realm you find yourself in, this spell will guide me to where you are.

If the spell would bring Alonso to Penny, would it also bring Penny to him?

The words come to her like she's known them all her life:

Penny is not a witch, but she prays that the words still have Alonso's magic woven into them. That this will be enough to open a doorway . . .

"Penny, what are you doing?" Marley says.

But Penny keeps repeating the words, over and over, just like Alonso always does when he's using magic. She puts every bit of love, every bit of pain, every memory good and bad of Alonso into these words.

A hand closes around hers.

Corey is standing beside her. There's still pain in his eyes, but his jaw is set with determination. "Keep going. I'll help you."

Penny squeezes his hand. "Okay."

She starts from the beginning, and as she repeats the spell over and over again, Corey joins in. Penny can feel his magic imbuing this spell with power, and soon, a blast of cold air hits her.

When Penny opens her eyes, the Veil is visible in the middle of the train bridge. Waiting for her.

571

When she was sick, seeing the Veil felt like a curse. Now it's a lifeline.

"Don't!" Marley shouts.

But Penny is already running toward that shimmer in the air, just visible in the nighttime. As she's about to cross, she feels a presence at her side.

Corey is running with her. And together, they cross into the Second World.

Corey

THE SKY IN THE SECOND WORLD IS RED. RED like blood. Red like love.

It's disorienting, and Corey stumbles onto his knees once they're across. There's a strange smell like rotting wood in the air, and he gags.

An arm settles around Corey's shoulders. "Are you okay?"

"I think so." Corey looks up at Penny. Her gaze is steady, and she's pressed close to him.

And god, it hurts.

Corey looks away from her. "You're not feeling sick?"

"No. Maybe it's the third eye." Penny looks out at the horizon. "The spell should've taken us to Alonso—"

A voice croaks behind them. "Penny?"

They whip around. Alonso is on the ground a few feet away, half-conscious. Blood is flowing out of the stab wound on his shoulder again, but now it rises into the air like mist.

Penny runs to him, lifting his head onto her knees, telling him it's going to be okay. But Corey follows the trail of the blood. It arches over their heads before dipping down to . . .

Corey gasps and pushes to his feet.

Giovanni is there, too. His head hangs low, and he's unmoving. Alonso's blood is being absorbed into him, melting through his skin.

"Penny," Corey says, his voice low.

"I see him."

But Giovanni doesn't attack them. He barely seems aware of anything. He's muttering to himself, and Corey takes a small step closer so he can hear.

"Why didn't she tell me?" Giovanni is saying.

Corey swallows. "Who?"

In a blink, Giovanni is in Corey's face. He grabs Corey's collar, hoisting him up. Alonso's blood has made Giovanni's eyes pure red. Corey grabs his forearms, and they're cold as marble.

"About your father," Giovanni says. Each word is leaden with pain and grief.

Corey tries to pry Giovanni's hands away, but

it's no use. In the Second World, Giovanni is even stronger than before.

But a figure in the distance makes Corey go cold. "Maybe you should ask her yourself."

The Shadow approaches, floating along the too-perfect grass under the nightmare red sky. Giovanni follows Corey's gaze, and when he sees the Shadow, he drops Corey to the ground.

"She's in there?" Giovanni whispers.

"She's trapped," Penny says. She's on her feet behind them, standing between Giovanni and Alonso.

"Trapped," Giovanni repeats. His eyes turn green again. Instead of being absorbed, Alonso's blood starts to run down his skin in small droplets. "I have to help her."

He suddenly looks less like a poltergeist and more like a regular man. Learning this secret about Corey's dad has changed him somehow.

Is it making him human again?

"We know how to help her," Penny says.

Corey looks at her. "We do?"

"What if you don't have to kill anyone to make this bargain? What if you can do it on your own terms?"

"How?"

"Maybe you can negotiate. Maybe there's something else the Shadow wants."

This sinks in, and Corey's mind begins to buzz. He steps forward to meet the Shadow.

It's bigger here. The darkness of it is all-consuming. It's the personification of grief, of lost love, of hopelessness.

"I want to make a new bargain," Corey says.

The Shadow rumbles with something that might be anger or might just be an acknowledgment. Corey doesn't wait to find out. Instead he speaks the bargain spell from memory:

> *"I open my heart to the Second World*
> *to offer an exchange.*
> *Deeper than an oath,*
> *undying as the ocean."*

The Shadow shudders, and suddenly it's not just one figure. It's twelve. They're all connected by ropes of blood and sinew. One extends to Corey, and another reaches behind him. He doesn't have to look to know that it leads to Penny.

Corey's eyes find his mom first.

She stands near the front, a ghostly version of

the woman she used to be. She shows no signs of recognizing him. Her eyes are blank, and her skin is threaded with black and purple veins.

Another woman with a black bob steps forward. Corey has never met her, but there are enough photos of her in their home that he would recognize her anywhere.

"Grandma," Corey says.

When his grandma opens her mouth, all the figures speak in unison:

"Name your terms."

Corey clenches his hands into fists. Marley warned him that this would be the hardest part, but he didn't have time to settle on the way he should word this. If he misspeaks, that could ruin the entire bargain.

A voice whispers in his ear: "Make it simple."

Corey steps quickly away from Giovanni, who hovers behind him. But the ghost's eyes are fixed on Corey's grandmother.

"Simple?" Corey says.

Giovanni's gaze cuts to Corey. "State what you want in the fewest words. Don't overcomplicate it."

Giovanni is actually helping him. And Corey is desperate enough to accept it.

Corey turns back to the Shadow. "I ask for the destruction of the bargain made by Charles Barrion in 1979. He exchanged the lives of people we loved for the success of his company."

"And what do you offer in exchange that could possibly be a worthy substitute for all these lives?"

"I offer that company," Corey says. "Its success. And its ownership. I will convince my family to sell it."

"This will leave your family with riches still," the Shadow says. "That is not sufficient. We want blood."

Red like blood. Red like love.

Corey looks back at Penny. She's holding Alonso, her eyes locked on his face as she pushes his hair out of his eyes.

For a moment, Corey imagines that she loves him. What would their lives have been like?

They would visit each other's colleges on the weekends. She would come to his first music gigs. During summers, they would spend late nights in the pool or have campfires in his backyard. She would make him memorize her favorite Taylor Swift songs, and he would make her angry with how closed off he can be.

And this, Corey knows deep in his heart, will have to be enough. This idea of what they could've been. Corey didn't know he could feel this kind of pain. It's like grief, but for a living person.

But if Corey still holds all this love for her, maybe he can use it.

"I give up my love for Penny Emberly," Corey says.

Behind him, Penny sucks in a breath. But Corey continues, facing the Shadow again. "This is what I offer in exchange for my family no longer having to sacrifice their own partners."

"Love?" says the Shadow, a hint of wonder in its voice. "You would give us love?"

"I won't be a murderer like my grandfather. I want to offer something different. But I swear, this is much more valuable to me than anything else I could give."

The figures disappear, and the Shadow is suddenly back. It approaches Corey and reaches out a hand.

"Stay strong," Giovanni says as the Shadow plunges its darkness into Corey's chest.

Corey screams as searing heat spreads through him. It doesn't feel like it's just reaching into

Corey's chest—it's in his mind. It's in something deeper . . .

His spirit.

It wants what he's offered. And Corey realizes too late that by giving up his love for Penny, he's giving up part of himself. As the Shadow wraps its hand around the love Corey has for Penny, he knows that after this, he'll never be the same again. He'll be a shell of a person.

But then, something changes. The Shadow shivers, and it's pushed away from Corey as if by some great wind he can't feel. Corey can breathe again, and he falls to his knees, clutching at his chest, trying to figure out what part of him has been taken.

But he feels . . . whole. How is that possible?

Before him, the Shadow shimmers as if it's become a mirage. Then, limb by limb, it begins to unravel like a ball of yarn.

"What's happening?" Corey says, but nobody answers him.

Suddenly there's a snap inside Corey's chest, and as he watches, the bloody rope connecting him to the Shadow shrivels and disappears.

Corey sucks in air as if for the first time. That pressure he felt fades, and with a certainty he can't explain, Corey knows he's free of the inheritance he never wanted. Of the burden his grandfather placed on their entire family out of jealousy and greed.

He's not making a new bargain. Instead, the bargain is disappearing completely.

"Corey."

Corey looks up into a familiar face. One that's so much like his own.

"Mom?" Corey whispers.

She leans down, helping him stand up. She's solid. Strong. Which is good, because seeing her is making his knees weak.

"Is the Shadow gone?" Corey whispers.

"Yes."

"But I thought bargains couldn't be destroyed?"

His mom puts a hand on Corey's cheek. "That bargain was created by a man who wanted to hurt the person he loved, but what you just offered was the opposite. That kind of selflessness can't sustain dark magic."

"You're saying I did that?"

Above them, the sky turns from red to dark blue. Corey's mom gives him a smile that makes the residual pain disappear. "You have your own magic, Corey. And you used it to create a new legacy. I couldn't be prouder."

They look out over the crowd of people who have appeared behind Corey's mom. There's Sofía's husband, Ramón, and her mother, Nina. Uncle Jason, Julian's dad. The partners of his dad's other cousins and his grandfather's cousins.

And, at the center, Ellie Barrion.

They all look dazed. But Ellie is already alert and focused.

"Gio?" she says.

Giovanni moves toward her. They clasp hands, and Giovanni brings her fingers to his mouth. He kisses each hand.

"Corey!"

He turns to see Alonso on his feet. Penny is tucked under his good shoulder, holding him up.

"Want to help me open up the Veil?" he calls.

"You're hurt."

He looks pale, but he manages a smirk. "My adrenaline is on its last legs. One more spell and then I'll probably faint, so we should hurry."

"Time to go," Corey's mom says. She leans in and places a kiss on Corey's forehead. "Your dad needs you. He's on his way to the hospital, along with Julian."

His dad. His cousin. Corey needs to get back to them.

He starts to walk toward his friends, but he hesitates, turning back to his mom one last time. "I love you."

She smiles. "I love you too, baby. Go live your beautiful life."

Alonso, Corey, and Penny join hands. Every time he's done magic, Corey has thought the pull he felt in his chest and the electricity in his veins was from Alonso's magic.

Now he knows better. He has power all his own.

"We can try that spell we used last summer at the football game," Alonso says.

"That sent my spirit across, not my body." Penny pulls something from her jacket. "Or we could use this? Marley gave it to me."

It's a silver knife. A pentagram is carved into the handle.

Alonso's eyes go wide. "That should work."

Corey and Penny put their hands on Alonso's shoulders to lend him their energy. When Alonso brings his arm down, it's like a lightning strike in Corey's chest.

And then they hear Marley's voice, calling for them.

As they pass through the Veil, Corey looks

back one last time. But by then, all the spirits that made up the Shadow are gone.

When they get back into the Primary World, they land on the railroad tracks. There are police lights flashing, and Corey immediately feels dizzy. Wind gusts around them, and they reach out, steadying each other.

"You did it!"

Marley stands at the edge of the tracks. She's smiling, and there are tears rolling down her face.

"Hey! There are kids on the tracks!" one of the cops calls.

Then a whistle sounds—and it's close.

"*Train!*" Penny yells as the light washes over them.

They run together, feet flying over the tracks. Marley, Naomi, and Dylan are screaming for them as the train gets closer.

"Jump!" Naomi yells.

Corey reaches out, grabbing Penny and Alonso. "Now!" he says, and they all leap at the same time.

They tumble into the dirt just as the train passes, kicking up a fierce wind.

"Thank god!" Naomi screams.

"Y'all were almost flat," Marley says through her tears, and Dylan bursts out laughing.

Corey is still lying on his back. He stares up at the night sky. There are stars far above them, gleaming in the darkness of Idlewood, a place light pollution can't touch. He flinches as something cold lands on his cheek.

It's snowing.

Go live your beautiful life, his mom said.

Corey silently promises her that he will. Every single day until he crosses the Veil for the last time, he will live for her. For his family. For his friends.

And now, for the first time, Corey will live for himself.

83
Alonso

WHEN ALONSO WAKES UP FROM SURGERY THE next afternoon, his family is there. They still have plaster dust in their hair, but they're fine otherwise. The Council saw no reason to hold them, but Alonso knows this isn't the last they'll hear from them.

They blamed the stab wound on the car accident. Actually, they blamed pretty much everything on the car accident. But knives and shards of glass leave different wounds, and Alonso could tell right away that the doctors and the police weren't buying it.

"We'll tell them you were playing with a knife in the car and you stabbed yourself during the collision," Aunt Donna says when they're eating dinner in his room that evening.

"Who would believe that?" Alonso mutters as he tries to adjust his own shoulder sling.

"I would. You look like you'd be that stupid."

"We could say the person who did it disappeared?" Emilia suggests.

"It might be the truth, but they'll still ask for details," Vera says. "Like a description, if they were involved in the accident…that's too much. We'll sound like we're lying."

"We could just use magic," Alonso says.

The coven goes silent.

"Alonso," his mom says, "you were sentenced to death by the Council yesterday."

"Oh, thanks for reminding me. Totally forgot."

"My point," his mom says, "is that we have to be ready to make some promises if there's any hope of them changing their minds."

"Like…?"

The coven stares at him, waiting for him to catch up.

"You want them to seal our magic again," Alonso says, his voice low.

"We don't *want* it. But if we have to choose between you and being witches—"

"We'll always choose you," Donna says. "We're a family first. Coven second."

Alonso nods, trying to hide how emotional that makes him. "Cool."

There's a knock at the door, and they all go silent. Alonso's mom stands up, straightening her long black dress. "Come in!" But when the door opens, it's not the doctor who stands there.

It's Park YeaLee. Sunglasses and everything.

Cold fear snakes through Alonso's veins. This is the woman who decided yesterday that he needed to die. There's only one reason she'd be here now.

The coven assembles themselves around Alonso's bed. Despite his terror, it makes Alonso feel warm. Protected. They would die for him, just like he would die for them.

But preferably not today.

"De Lucas," YeaLee says. "Lovely to see you again."

"Can't say it's mutual," grumbles Donna.

"I understand." YeaLee closes the door gently behind her. The way she turns her back on the De Lucas, it's clear she's not afraid of them. Maybe that's what happens when you're able to see the future—you know when to be scared. And YeaLee understands that the De Lucas won't hurt her.

"I'd like to examine Alonso," YeaLee says.

"How?" Alonso's mom snaps.

"He just had surgery!" Aunt Emilia says.

YeaLee takes a small capsule out of her purse. "This is ground willow bark and bone of stag—"

"Ick."

"It's in a capsule. You won't taste anything."

Alonso frowns. "What does it do?"

"If there is another entity inside of you, this will force them to reveal themselves."

"And if there's nothing inside of me but me?"

YeaLee shrugs. "A little pain."

"Will I die?"

"If I was here to kill you, I would've done it already."

Alonso shivers, but he holds out his hand.

The pill feels like a pill going down. Alonso blinks and waits.

"It will take a moment," YeaLee says.

"Clearly." But as soon as the word leaves Alonso's lips, he feels it.

It's as though horns are blooming within his stomach and stretching out into his every limb. "Oh fuck," he says, doubling over. Tears come to his eyes, but there's an antler in his throat now, and he can't speak.

Then, all at once, it subsides.

Alonso gasps, struggling to breathe.

"Look at me," YeaLee says.

He wasn't prepared for her to have her glasses off. Once again, he's thrown off by the ashy violet of her eyes, but he can't look away from them, even when she reaches out and touches his hand.

"Hm," YeaLee says, and she steps back.

"Well?" Aunt Emilia says, wringing her hands.

"It appears that the poltergeist is gone."

"Wait," Alonso says. "If you're able to see the future, why are you here? Wouldn't you already know the poltergeist was gone?"

"As I said yesterday, I see many possible futures. A large part of my job on the Council is risk mitigation. If the paths that branch off from the one that you're on show a high likelihood of death or destruction or miscellaneous chaos, that is how I make my decision." She cocks her head at him. "It appears, Alonso De Luca, that you are very lucky."

"Lucky?" Alonso scoffs.

"Yes. Based on what I saw yesterday, the odds of you defeating the poltergeist were less than one percent. If Penny Emberly hadn't discovered the Barrions' connection to your coven—"

"Connection?" Alonso's mom says. "What connection?"

YeaLee raises an eyebrow at Alonso.

"I was gonna tell them," Alonso mutters. "That's not the kind of thing you can just drop on a person. Plus I'm recovering from anesthesia."

"Your coven needs to recognize its new members," YeaLee says.

"New…" Vera's face falls. "What new members?"

So Alonso tells them the truth: that James isn't just an asshole. He's also their half brother. Alonso has avoided thinking about this; the pain meds have made that easier. But now that he's saying it out loud, he thinks about Corey being…

Family.

By the time he's done, they're all exhausted. Except YeaLee, who's acting like she deals with crises like this every day.

"I spoke with James and Corey this morning," YeaLee says. "And Penny."

"You did?" Alonso says, almost choking on his words.

"Yes." YeaLee slides her sunglasses back on. "Corey Barrion managed to change his family's fate. It's impressive. They all vouched for you, as we knew they would."

Alonso feels a big reveal coming. "But that doesn't matter to the Council."

YeaLee drums her fingers on her knee. "There seems to be something in the water here in Idlewood. Some significant events in the world of witches have taken place in this town over the last six months. You're creating a lot of chatter. After everyone dug themselves out of the motel rubble last night—'

"Sorry. Even though that wasn't me."

She ignores him and continues. "They got to talking. They are intrigued by your power, and your innate sense for spells. Some of them say you're the next Park HaeJung, which I find deeply offensive."

"You're the master of backhanded compliments, huh?"

YeaLee examines him. "Do you want to hear what we've decided?"

"I don't know," he grumbles.

"While you are indeed guilty of necromancy, the murders were not your doing. That perpetrator has been banished, and the police have been taken care of."

"Taken care of?" Donna mutters.

"Clay Thornberg's death has been ruled accidental. He was heavily intoxicated."

"No. That's not right. He was murdered."

"Do you want to serve time in prison?"

"No, but . . . but should I?"

"There is something you can do," YeaLee says. "So I think you should let me finish."

That's ominous, but he nods.

"We had an emergency Council meeting. Marley and Milton Pierre attended, and they both argued quite enthusiastically in your favor. We found them convincing."

"Milton?" Alonso says. "I thought . . ."

"I believe he was always on your side. Once he learned the poltergeist was gone, he said killing you would be cruelty, and the Council agreed. But necromancy is still a crime. It shows a huge amount of power in your blood, and we don't want to lose that. The Council has spent hundreds of years fearing power instead of honing it. Which is why the Council decided to transmute your sentence."

Alonso sits up, flinching as his shoulder throbs. "You're not going to kill me?"

"She said transmute," Aunt Donna says. Her

fingers are twitching, probably aching for a cigarette. "That means your sentence isn't gone. It's
changing."

Alonso's heart dips low in his chest with
dread. "Changing to what?"

84

Penny

AS PENNY AND HER MOM PULL INTO HORIZON Café's parking lot, Penny stares at the trees, which are covered with a light dusting of snow. It's two days before the new year, and the streets of Idlewood are quiet. The town is still reeling from the news about the upcoming sale of Barrion Heating & Cooling. The headlines, national and local, all paint a very specific picture:

Workforce shrinks at Barrion Heating & Cooling after employees claim unsafe conditions

Union sues Barrion Heating & Cooling for endangering members

Fallen from grace: What's the future of the Barrions' influence in Idlewood after they let go of their company?

Penny wanted to text Corey about it, but as usual, she didn't.

Corey and Alonso have both been MIA these past weeks. After they returned from the Second World, Penny spent the night in the hospital waiting room with Corey, desperate for news about Alonso and Mr. Barrion.

Alonso's surgery was quick. Penny didn't see him at the hospital, but he texted her afterward to tell her he had to leave town for a couple weeks. Penny hasn't heard from him since.

But Corey's dad was in the operating room for fifteen hours. Finally, the doctors told them Mr. Barrion would live. But nothing would ever be the same.

Penny pulls up one of the news articles on her phone again. The photo shows Mr. Barrion giving a press conference about the sale of Barrion Heating & Cooling to an investment firm. In many ways, he looks like his usual self: perfect hair, pressed suit, haughty gaze. But one big thing has changed.

Mr. Barrion is in a wheelchair. And, as the doctors told them, he will be for the rest of his life.

After that, Corey told Penny he needed some

space. Penny wanted to ask him so many questions, but she held them in.

Now she's starting to wonder if she'll ever hear from him again.

"Penny?" her mom says. "You coming?"

"Sorry," Penny says, and she hurries inside after her mom.

There's a man waiting in the café, dressed in wide-leg pants and a camel-colored coat. He's examining the burns on the walls.

"You must be Andrew," Penny's mom says.

"Indeed I am," he says, shaking her hand. "What a great space you have here. I'm so sorry about the fires, of course, but I already have a million ideas for how we might rebuild and refresh it."

"I'm all ears," Penny's mom says.

As they talk, Penny walks around, touching her fingers to the scorch marks on the walls. Tonight, she's going over to Naomi's to finish her college applications. It used to be that she couldn't picture leaving Idlewood, but now, she's started having daydreams about another life. One on a leafy college campus, where she'll walk through green quads to get to her classes and her dorm. A year ago, the idea of sleeping anywhere but her childhood bedroom would've scared her. Now leaving Idlewood feels inevitable, but not in a bad way. In a way that means she wants it. And her mom will still be here, in the café, living out her dream with Ron by her side.

A car passes outside, and Penny glances through the glass front door.

Her stomach drops.

The blue Shelby is parked out front. Alonso leans forward in the driver's seat, and when he sees her, he lifts his hand in a wave.

"Sweet pea?" Penny's mom says. "You okay?"

Penny nods. It's a blatant lie.

Her mom follows her gaze outside. Penny filled her in on the basics of what happened. She had to address it after the car accident, and especially after Clay's death. Her mom took it as well as any normal person would—which is to say, she cried. Penny suspects her mom doesn't want her around Alonso, so she's not surprised when her mom asks, "Do you want me to tell him to leave?"

"No. I'll talk to him."

Penny wonders if this will be the moment her mom puts her foot down. If she'll finally forbid Penny from talking to her dangerous witch ex-boyfriend.

But that's not Anita. She nods once and says, "Okay. I'll be right here if you need me."

Penny tries to keep her hands from shaking as she walks to the car, but as she slides into the passenger seat, she ends up sitting on them to hide how nervous she is.

Hot air blasts from the vents, and the car windows are fogging up. She can't look at Alonso yet, so she just stares at the dashboard.

"Nimble says hi," Alonso says. "She misses you."

"I miss her, too."

Alonso shifts, his leather jacket squeaking against the seat. He's wearing a black sling, too, and it's strange to see someone as animated as Alonso be forced to move slowly, cautiously. When he speaks, his voice is barely louder than a whisper. "But did you miss me?"

Penny tears her eyes away from the glove compartment and lets herself really look at him. His eyes are bright. His skin is flush with color again.

But what Penny really sees is what has stayed the same. And this is what floods Penny's chest with longing.

"Where have you been?" she asks.

"New Orleans."

"New Orleans?" Penny can't even imagine it. "You've been across the country? Why?"

"It's where the Council is headquartered. They wanted to run some tests. See what my magic could do."

Penny's heartbeat picks up. "Since you're back, does that mean...?"

Alonso sighs, resting his head against the seat. "The Council isn't going to kill me, thanks to you and Corey and the Pierres. They confirmed my grandpa is gone."

"Is Marley in trouble?"

"No. I didn't give YeaLee enough credit, I guess. She and Marley see eye to eye on some things, though that isn't the case for all the Council members." Alonso turns his head, his gray eyes examining Penny's face as if he wants to memorize her every feature. Then he says, "But they're sending me away."

Penny sits up. "Away?"

"I'm moving there. To New Orleans. I leave tonight."

Alonso is moving to Louisiana. That's all the way at the bottom of the country. It's not a car ride away, it's a plane ride. And even then, it isn't quick, or cheap. Penny and her mom can barely afford one vacation every few years.

"There's a school," Alonso says. "It's for witches like me who have had trouble in the mortal world. They'll teach me better control of my magic. And since I'll be away from my coven's homestead…" He swallows. "I'll be less dangerous."

"For how long?" Penny whispers.

"I don't know. Could be a few months, could be a few years."

"Years?" He might as well have said he's moving away forever. "But you have to finish high school" is the only thing Penny can think to say.

"I'll be finishing school online."

"Then can't you just get training here? So that we—"

"So we what?" Alonso says. "We can get back together? We forget about all the spells I used, the people I killed?"

"That wasn't *you*."

"Maybe. But Clay is dead because of my magic. So is Corey's grandpa." Alonso's face screws up. He's trying not to cry. "I have the responsibility to make sure nothing like this ever happens again. I want to be a witch my coven can be proud of."

Alonso doesn't mention Penny. She hasn't factored into this plan at all.

The tears are already coming, and she can't stop them. She's too tired to do anything but let it all out, as embarrassing as this is.

Pretty soon, she's sobbing. All the pain and the worry and the heartbreak of the last few months bubbles up as if it's fresh, and it comes out with force, wracking Penny's body in a way she can't control.

Alonso doesn't say a word. He just pulls her to him.

This isn't how their story is supposed to end. She doesn't want Alonso to be a painful memory she learns to live with. She wants him. Just him.

"I could go to college in New Orleans," Penny says.

"Is that really what you want?"

Penny knows the answer right away: She doesn't want to leave Indiana. And her mom wasn't wrong all those months ago—she can't use Alonso as the deciding factor for college. This is a path she needs to create on her own.

Penny gives Alonso a sad smile. "I guess not."

Alonso lifts her chin up so she's looking him in the eyes. "And what about Corey?"

Penny's heart breaks, but in a new place. "I care about Corey. He's become one of my closest friends. I thought it could be more, but...when I thought I'd lost you forever, it became clear to me how different my feelings are for the two of you. I won't stop caring about Corey, even if he never speaks to me again. But I love *you*, Alonso."

Alonso closes his eyes, as if he's basking in her words. "I was so scared I lost you by pushing you away. And now I'm losing you anyway."

Penny pulls his forehead to hers. "So come back when you're done. Find me."

"What if you fall in love with someone else?"

"What if *you* fall in love with—"

Before she finishes that sentence, Alonso grabs Penny's face and presses his mouth to hers.

It's soft. Slow. Even when Alonso drags his teeth across her bottom lip, it's tender. Penny wraps her arms around his neck, pulling him close.

When they come up for air, Alonso leans his forehead against Penny's again. "I've loved you since before I understood what that meant. I've loved you like it was breathing. I couldn't stop if I tried."

Penny closes her eyes. She tries to clear her

mind, to use her third eye to see where they might be in a year, two years.

This time, there's nothing. Her gut isn't telling her things are going to be good, or bad. Maybe that's the most painful part of growing up—the security that you've felt your whole life goes away. You have to accept that you don't know what's coming, and actually, you never did.

"If you're leaving," Penny says, "are you going to end the spell? The one that ties us together?"

"Do you want me to?"

Penny shakes her head.

"Then I'll leave it."

She wants to believe that's a promise. But it feels like a concession.

Penny grabs his face in her hands. Now it's her turn to memorize him. His uneven haircut, his sharp jaw, the hollows under his eyes.

"I'll love you forever," Penny says.

"Just love me until I come back," Alonso says. "Then we'll figure it out. I promise."

"Okay," Penny says, and she pulls Alonso down for one last kiss.

Corey

IT'S NEW YEAR'S EVE AND COREY'S FINGERS are especially sore from the guitar strings. But the calluses are growing. Every day when he wakes up, he stares at them for a while. They look like someone else's hands, not his.

But they *are* his. And he's proud of that.

He's in the middle of playing one of Hozier's older songs when Aunt Helen walks in.

"Wow, that was you," she says. "I thought it was a recording."

"You don't have to give me fake compliments. I'm, like, really bad."

Aunt Helen laughs. "Since when do I give fake compliments?"

"Since never, I guess." He plucks a few strings. "How's Julian?"

"He called me today. On video."

Corey straightens up. "On video?"

"They're letting him have a little more access to technology during the holidays. He still doesn't know when he'll be able to come home, but the doctors have said there's some progress. His new medication is working much better for him."

Corey nods. Whenever Julian gets home from the hospital, they'll have a lot to work through. They've said the kinds of things you can never take back. Will they be able to salvage any part of their relationship?

Maybe salvaging isn't the goal. Maybe it's time for Corey and Julian to make something new.

Aunt Helen's expression is pained. "I'm sorry, Corey. Maybe I could've prevented what happened if I'd seen what Julian needed."

"This wasn't your fault."

"I have to own up to it in order to do better. I've been so lost in my own pain for so many years…" Aunt Helen's eyes grow distant. "I want to be more like Anita."

"Penny's mom?" Corey tries to sound casual. "You two are hanging out again?"

"Very subtle, Corey. When the entire house is talking about it, I'll know who to blame."

Corey leans on the top of his guitar. Aunt Helen's hair is loose around her shoulders instead of in her usual low bun. Her smile is soft around the edges.

"I'm happy for you," Corey says.

"Nothing is happening, so don't get all excited." Aunt Helen turns serious again. "Speaking of Penny, did you know she just got here?"

Corey stops strumming the guitar. His fingers hover over the strings. "Yeah. I invited her over."

"Mm." Aunt Helen considers him. "Do you want to talk about it?"

"Maybe later."

Corey finds Penny in the library. She's wearing a fuzzy blue sweater and staring at a ten-foot-tall Christmas tree, which blinks at her silently.

"That's Warren's doing," Corey says.

Penny looks at him, and there's such a mix of emotions in her eyes that Corey can't look away. So he keeps talking.

"He puts trees up in every room. They all have a theme."

"What's this one?" Penny asks.

"Uh…" Corey stares at the red and green lights, ornaments, garland. "Christmas?"

Penny laughs. "I think it's pasta." She points at an ornament, and Corey looks closer. There are red tortellini, green bowties, gold rigatoni.

"Definitely pasta," Corey agrees.

Silence stretches between them. Corey glances at Penny, who looks like she's in physical pain. He clears his throat. "You can sit down. Want anything to drink?"

"I'm good. Just came from work."

"Oh, the holiday drag show? You had it at the community center?"

"We needed the space. Holly Pocket won Christmas Queen this year."

And then she's showing him photos and videos of the show. As they watch a drag queen wearing red-and-white striped tights drop into the splits, it's almost like things are normal between them. Corey can almost forget about the bargain, and the revelations about his dad's biological father, and the car accident…

One thing feels different, though. That weight Corey has felt his entire life, but especially since his mom's death, is gone. Everyone in his family is free to fall in love.

And to have their hearts broken.

"There's something so sad about the holidays," Penny says as she locks her phone.

"Maybe it's because we miss people more than usual."

"Maybe." Penny looks out the window—at the De Luca house.

"He told me about New Orleans," Corey says.

Penny nods. "They all left yesterday. I guess they're spending some time together before they drop him off."

Corey nods, lacing and unlacing his fingers. "I'm sorry."

"For what?"

"That he's gone."

Penny smiles, but her eyes are sad. "Me too."

She's staring at him with the full force of her summer-blue eyes. He remembers looking into them that night in the hospital parking lot last July, when he told her about his family curse. That was the first time he'd realized that Penny Emberly was stronger than he'd ever given her credit for.

"I'm not here to make you my pseudo-boyfriend now that he's gone, by the way," Penny says.

Corey is so shocked that he laughs. "Okay."

"Just putting that out there."

"Thanks, I guess? But I didn't think that."

"Did you think I was using you before? When Alonso and I were broken up?"

Corey rolls out his neck. "No. But that doesn't mean I wasn't filling a void."

Penny pulls the sleeves of her sweater over her hands. "I wasn't thinking about it that way. I just liked being with you."

He's already given her up, so this shouldn't hurt. But it does. "Me too, Penny. But I don't think we can be friends right now."

Penny takes a breath. "I thought you might say that."

"It would've been easier if the Shadow just took all my feelings for you. I'd be a shell of a person, but at least I wouldn't be in pain."

Penny doesn't laugh. "You don't mean that, do you?"

"No," Corey says, trying to smile at her. When that doesn't work, he adds, "Mostly."

"I get it," Penny says.

Corey clears his throat. He doesn't want to ask this question, but he can't avoid it forever. "So you and Alonso . . . ?"

"We're not together."

"But you will be when he's back."

"He doesn't know when that will be." She shrugs. "I don't actually believe this right now, but maybe it isn't all bad."

610

"How so?"

"The breakup was a reminder of how big my insecurities are. My self-worth depended on being with Alonso, and then…it started depending on you." She glances at him, a blush rising in her cheeks. "So I feel kind of worthless right now."

"You're far from worthless, Penny."

"I know," Penny says. "I mean, *now* I do. I didn't for a while. And that's why I think I need to be on my own. Everyone at school thinks I got dumped, and I guess I did. But I need to stop caring."

"Exposure therapy?"

"Something like that." Penny's smile fades. "I guess I should go."

"I'll walk you out."

"It's okay," Penny says, walking backward. "Just enjoy the pasta tree."

Corey smiles. "Happy New Year."

"Happy New Year, Corey."

After the front door of Meredith House closes, Corey leans back in the armchair. His eyes wander to the photo of him, his dad, and his mom over the fireplace.

"Happy New Year, Mom," he whispers.

Corey's phone buzzes. He pulls it out of his pocket.

AD Alonso De Luca

Corey cringes.

AD Alonso De Luca

Alonso sends a selfie of him, his mom, and his aunts walking down Bourbon Street. Aunt Emilia's face is blotchy, and Aunt Donna is drinking from a tall green beverage that's definitely alcoholic.

AD Alonso De Luca

Corey snorts.
"Corey?"

His dad is at the entrance to the library. He's in his new chair, the one they got him after he hated the first two. He's still adjusting to it, and some days he's frustrated, but Corey's dad is still organized and determined, so he's figuring it out.

"You're in pajamas," Corey says.

His dad shifts uncomfortably. "I'm trying not to wear suits all the time. It's something Shelly recommended."

Shelly is his therapist. Corey smiles. "Matching set. Nice."

Corey's dad glares at him, but only a little. "What were you laughing at?"

Corey shows his dad the photo. He reads the text beneath it and blinks, slowly.

"One sister was more than enough," his dad mutters.

Penny

JANUARY ARRIVES. MOST DAYS ARE SPENT working on the café rebuild or watching reality dating shows in Naomi's basement. Penny wraps herself in these days like they're a warm blanket, but eventually, she has to go back to school.

The snow outside is layered and slushy. Penny digs her heavy snow boots out of the closet. When she pushes through the doors to Idlewood Central High School, people are laughing and screaming as they try not to slip in the water tracks on the floor. She can't help but listen to the whispers about Alonso.

"Is he really gone?"

"He moved to, like, Mexico, I heard."

"I won't miss him, he was such a mess."

"Are you joking? That man was fine as hell, can't believe I won't see his beautiful angry face anymore."

Penny tunes it out. As she puts her books in her locker, Naomi appears beside her.

"Hey—" Penny cuts off when she sees Naomi's face. Her eyes are wide, and her lips are pressed together as if she's barely keeping something in.

"Bathroom," Naomi says.

They go to the bathrooms by the woodshop classroom, where there are usually fewer people. When they're inside, Naomi checks for feet under the stalls. Then she leans against the sinks and says, "Did you hear about Dylan?"

Penny blinks. "What?"

"She just graduated early? She apparently had enough credits, so she applied and they approved it. She's already left Idlewood."

"She..." Penny tries to process this. "Left? Without saying goodbye?"

Naomi shrugs. "People are saying she went to New York or LA, I don't know. Yvonne Mason just told me."

Penny tries to make sense of this. It feels like déjà vu. Alonso is the one who dropped out and left town. How could Dylan be gone, too?

"Can't say I'm upset," Naomi says. "She's the most difficult person I've ever met."

"She also helped us with the exorcism. And with the spell last August."

"What, so you're going to miss her?"

Penny sighs. "Maybe. Even if I didn't like her most of the time."

"Me neither," Naomi says, but for the first time she looks almost sad. "She's funny, though."

"She is. Maybe you can look her up when you move to LA?"

"Manifesting," Naomi says, waggling her fingers. "The LA part, not the continued Dylan friendship part. I've had enough Dylan to last me forever."

Penny tries to forget about Alonso and Corey. It doesn't work.

There are many sleepless nights. Moments where the reminders of Alonso—a song, or a booth at IHOP, or any mention of bike polo— hit Penny like a brick. And she can't watch *Amityville High* or listen to her favorite Quicklime album without thinking of Corey.

Penny pushes through. She keeps going, day after day.

A month after Alonso and Dylan leave town,

Penny and Naomi are eating lunch. Talk about Alonso is already fading. Penny should be grateful for that, but it's only making her feel worse.

"This has been the most depressing winter of my life," Naomi says, "but there's nobody else I'd rather be depressed with."

Penny holds up her carton of milk, and they cheers. A second later, a tray slides onto their table. When they look up, Corey stands there, looking between them.

Penny sits up. "Hey."

"Hey," Corey says.

"Well hi," Naomi says.

Corey gestures to the chair. "Can I sit here?"

Penny isn't sure what this means. He said he needed space, and it hasn't been that long. But when he smiles at her, it feels good. He doesn't look like he's faking it.

"If you want," Penny says.

After that, Corey starts joining Penny and Naomi for reality TV. They're all sick of *Amityville High*, it turns out. They discover that they all enjoy nature documentaries, especially ones about the deep ocean. All the animals look like aliens, and it reminds Penny how much she doesn't know.

One day, when Naomi has fallen asleep and Penny's mom is reading in her room, Penny asks to talk to Corey out on the porch.

"Is this okay?" Penny says. "With you and me?"

Corey rubs his neck. "Yeah. It's . . . nice."

"I know," Penny says, and she means it. Things feel the same, but different. Like they're settling into a real friendship.

"You and Naomi . . . you're the only ones who I don't have to explain myself to."

"I think we feel the same way."

Corey sucks in a breath, and Penny braces herself for whatever is coming next. Then he says, "I got into Oberlin."

Penny gasps. "Oberlin?"

"I submitted my application back in November. I'm going to study business, but they have a music conservatory there. I can learn guitar for real. I'm going to take some classes and see what happens."

For the first time in a while, the horizon of their lives is visible, and it's bright.

"I expect videos of your progress," Penny says.

Corey beams. "I promise."

In early May, Penny gets accepted to Indiana University in Bloomington. And a few days later, Naomi gets her acceptance to UCLA.

"Los Angeles!" Naomi screams in the hallway at school, and she and Penny drop their notebooks and jump together, making everyone walk around them. Some people scowl, but most of them laugh and clap and ask what schools they got into.

They decide to drink champagne, and Penny's mom agrees to buy them a cheap bottle. Penny invites Corey over, too, and when the doorbell rings, she skips over to let him in.

"Hey!" Penny says. Someone steps out from behind Corey, and Penny gasps. "Helen! I mean, Ms. Barrion—"

"Helen is fine." She holds up a pie box. "I got lemon meringue."

Penny beams. "My mom's favorite. Come in. Mom! Helen is here!"

Anita appears at the entrance to the kitchen. There's flour in her hair and on her apron, and when she sees the pie box, her mouth falls open.

"You didn't drive to Indianapolis just to get my favorite pie."

"I might've," Helen says, smiling.

"Well, come in! I need a helper to put this chocolate chip cookie dough on a pan. I guess we'll be having pie *and* cookies."

"The dinner of champions," Helen says, and they disappear into the kitchen.

Later, after they all drink champagne, Penny feels like she could float on air. But their little house is hot with all the people, and Penny decides to sit on the porch. Out of habit, she takes out her phone to see if Alonso texted her—

But no. He hasn't texted her since December, and there's no message now.

The tears hit Penny out of nowhere. They're all being loud inside the house and she's sure they can't hear her, but the thought of them seeing her like this months after the breakup makes her want to run down the street, through the clicking sprinklers, and into the woods.

But she doesn't. And soon, the screen door opens.

Penny glances up as Corey sits down next to her. She's terrified of what he might say, but he just sits there with her as the moon appears in the evening sky.

When her crying subsides, Penny sits back in the porch swing. "Hey," she says.

He cocks his head. "You want to talk about it?"

"Not really."

Anita and Helen's laughter rings like a wind chime.

"How long until there's a wedding?" Corey says.

"I give it a year." Penny thinks back to December—to the car accident. To Corey's cousin. "How's Julian?"

"He called me today."

"He did?"

"He apologized. Said he's coming home soon."

"How do you feel about that?"

Corey shrugs. "We'll see. He sounds pretty different now. I guess we all are."

"Yeah," Penny says softly.

"Apparently your mom already offered him a job at the café. Said it'll help with his anxiety?"

"Ugh," Penny says, burying her face in her hands while Corey laughs.

The crickets and frogs begin their chorus, and

Penny closes her eyes and breathes in the smell of cut grass. "I'm really going to miss this."

"Me too."

"And you."

Corey puts an arm around her, and Penny leans into him.

She wants to ask if he's heard from Alonso. If he's okay. If he's already moved on. But she stops herself.

Ron arrives holding a foil baking tin. "Sorry I'm late. My oven and I are officially mortal enemies," he says, leaning over to kiss Penny's head. "Come and eat this barbecue. You're required to tell me it's delicious even if it isn't."

Corey gets up to follow him. "You coming?"

"In a minute," Penny says.

She counts to ten after Ron and Corey go inside. Then she closes her eyes. "I promise I'll remember what this feels like," she whispers to herself.

Penny gets to her feet, but as she opens the screen door, she lingers for another moment, looking up at the crescent moon.

Maybe Alonso is looking at this same moon right now. And maybe, just maybe, he's thinking of her, too.

Epilogue

ACT I

FROM THE BALCONY OF HIS SHITTY APARTMENT IN the French Quarter, Alonso stares up at the crescent moon.

The angry buzz under his skin is long gone. The teachers at the Laveau School taught him how to control that within his first few months. Every once in a while, Alonso's magic rears its head like a hurricane. But now, it knows Alonso is in charge, and it listens.

Alonso leans over the wrought iron balcony, which creaks in a way that should be terrifying but just seems normal after almost eight months in the city. Groups of people stumble past below, shouting and sloshing their cocktails around. This has become Alonso's white noise.

Will he be able to sleep without it?

The apartment door opens. "Hey, Alonso!"

Luz struts into their shared studio. Their dark hair is especially wild tonight, and when they take off their jacket, the tattoos on their arms dance over wiry muscles.

"How'd you do on the exam?" Alonso calls back.

Luz flops down onto their waterbed, which sloshes violently. "Failed again. I'm retaking it in a week."

"You'd pass if you studied."

"I ain't got time for that," Luz says. Ever since they started dating Bianca, studying is on the back burner. Luz leans forward onto their knees. "What's on your mind?"

Alonso shrugs.

"I know," Luz says. "You're thinking about Big Hair Girl."

Alonso glares at them. "How do you know what she looks like?"

"You have a photo of her in your nightstand."

"Since when are you going through my shit?"

"Brother, I *always* go through your shit. Your life has been interesting. Mine was boring."

"Boring? You've been farming super powerful crystals since you were thirteen."

Luz ignores him. "Are you seeing her when you go back to Indiana?"

Alonso sighs, looking up at the moon again. "Maybe."

"Can't believe you're already leaving."

"I can't take the humidity here anymore. I thought Indiana summers were bad, but swamps are worse."

Luz nods at Alonso's suitcase. "Bet the coven is excited to see you."

"I'm going straight to Bloomington for school. It's only like an hour away from Idlewood though."

"Wait, you're going to Big Hair Girl's school? Does she know?"

Alonso lobs his empty root beer bottle at Luz, who catches it easily and tosses it onto the floor.

"Stop interrogating me," Alonso says.

"*Meow.*"

"There's my number-one girl," Luz says as Nimble climbs onto their lap. "Did you know Alonso is taking you back to Indiana?"

The cat purrs, rubbing up against them.

"I'll miss you, too, you sassy ho."

After Alonso finishes packing, he considers the apartment. This place has been his sanctuary since he moved in eight months ago. Now it's August, and after working day and night to finish high school on time, he's leaving for college.

And Penny doesn't know.

He was planning to go to IU anyway, or at least that's what he's telling himself. It's a big enough campus that they'll never have to see each other if they don't want to.

But Alonso *wants* to see Penny. The only question is whether she'll want to see him.

Alonso hugs Luz. He forces Nimble into her cat carrier. Later, as his plane flies out of Louis Armstrong International Airport, he watches the city of New Orleans fade into the mist.

ACT II

For a kid who's been popular his entire life, Corey doesn't really make friends at Oberlin.

People know him. They say hi to him. But when Corey isn't in class, he spends every waking hour in the practice rooms.

He couldn't hear himself getting better at first, but one day he decided to play his old videos and compare them to his new ones. Corey felt sick when he saw the slow way his fingers used to move across the guitar strings. He actually sent these videos to Penny? What was he thinking?

To make up for it, Corey films himself playing "Battle Bouquet." He's gotten pretty good at it, so he makes himself play without the sheet music, too. When he sends it to the Cozy Mystery Book Club group chat—which Penny, Naomi, and Marley are still part of—he's met with immediate heart emojis.

PE Penny Emberly

Sending this to my mom

She's going to cry

NS Naomi Salazar

In a good way?

MP Marley Pierre

Damn Corey. That's hot.

Corey snorts.

The doorknob to the practice room rattles. "Hello?" someone says, knocking.

Corey puts his phone in his pocket and reaches over to open the door. "Hey, I have the room until—"

He stops.

"Oh," the girl says. She shifts her violin case from one hand to the other. "Sorry, I think we might've gotten double-booked? I'm on the schedule now."

But Corey can't speak. He recognizes her from campus. "You're..."

"Inaya." She adjusts her hijab. Her eyes are green, and they're lined with something dark. Corey doesn't understand makeup, but he understands that whatever eyeliner she's wearing makes it look like she can see right through him. "You're Corey, right?"

"Yeah." He stands up, gathering his sheet music. "Sorry, let me clean up—"

"You know what, it's fine, I'll use another room."

"No! You're on the schedule. This was my fault. I was just texting anyway." He slings his guitar case over his shoulder. "See you around?"

"Yeah," Inaya says. But as Corey is walking away, she calls out, "Hey, Corey?"

He turns around. "Yeah?"

"I heard that song," she says. "The one you were just playing. No idea what it was, but you should post it. You're, like, really good. And I normally hate the guitar."

Corey's heart thumps even as he laughs. "Who doesn't like the guitar?"

"Me," Inaya says, completely serious. Then she closes the door.

This time it's Corey who lingers outside the door, listening as Inaya plays the violin. The rooms are soundproofed, but the building is quiet right now, and he can just make out the song. It's something classical, maybe Bach.

Then, abruptly, the song changes. It melts from classical to something more modern. It takes a few seconds for Corey to recognize it.

She's playing Hozier. Corey's favorite.

ACT III

Classes have been in session for two weeks, and Penny is still getting lost.

"Dammit," Penny mutters, zooming in on the map on her phone. "I was going to Goodbody Hall. How did I end up in Dunn Meadow?" She turns around, ready to head back the way she came.

And she bumps directly into someone.

"Whoa!" Penny says, falling back. Two hands grab her by the shoulders, steadying her. "Thanks. Sorry, I was distracted—"

She forgets everything she was going to say next.

"I swear I wasn't following you," Alonso says. "I mean, I was, but I wasn't being weird about it. I was figuring out what to say."

Penny is still gaping at him, though. His hair isn't dyed anymore. It's longer, and it's pulled back in a bun at the nape of his neck. He's wearing black-framed glasses, and he's exchanged his dangly earring for a silver hoop.

This is Alonso, but he's not just the boy Penny knew in high school. He looks like a man—and somehow he's become even more heart-achingly beautiful.

"What?" Alonso asks, a small smile on his face.

"You look different," Penny says, unable to hold back the note of pain in her voice.

"I'm going for soft goth these days," Alonso says. "You, um. You cut your hair."

Penny snaps out of her daze. She grabs a strand of her shoulder-length hair. "I wanted a change. I don't know if it really suits me."

"You look beautiful," Alonso says, his voice low, and Penny's heart soars.

The sun is shining through the trees, making

this feel like a memory before it's even over. Alonso's eyes rove her face, and when her eyes drop to his mouth, his lips part. And god, does she want him to kiss her. It's been months since they've seen each other, but Penny doesn't care. She wants him just as much as ever—maybe even more than before. She's this close to throwing herself at him when Alonso tears his gaze away from her face and steps around her.

"I guess I should go to environmental policy," Alonso says.

"You...have a class?"

"Yeah. Since I go here."

"You go here," Penny breathes.

Alonso's smile fades. He looks bashful all of a sudden. "I hope that's okay."

That's all Penny can handle. She drops her backpack. She drops her phone. She takes three strides over to him and throws her arms around him.

Penny knows it's too much. Maybe he's with someone else already. Or maybe he isn't interested in picking up where they left off. She's about to let go when Alonso hugs her back, burying his face in her hair.

The sun creates dappled shadows on the grass.

Cardinals and sparrows fly between the trees, filling the air with music. Penny closes her eyes, listening to the sound of Alonso's heart beating in his chest.

"Penny Emberly," Alonso whispers, "you knew I would come back for you."

Acknowledgments

The time has come to say goodbye to Idlewood. First, I want to thank you, the readers, for being on this journey with Penny, Corey, and Alonso. Seeing your enthusiasm for this series has been motivating, joyful, and absolutely surreal.

Thank you to my team at Park, Fine & Brower Literary Management, especially my remarkable agents Pete Knapp and Stuti Telidevara. They manage my anxiety without even having medical degrees, folks! Thank you also to Danielle Barthel and Jalynn Knight—I don't know how you stay so organized, but it inspires me to make a better calendar. And to Kathryn Toolan, thank you for finding new homes for this duology around the world.

Thank you to my US publisher, Little, Brown Books for Young Readers, and especially to my brilliant editor Ruqayyah Daud, who asked all the right questions and helped make this duology exactly what I wanted it to be. Thank you also to the rest of the LBYR team: Alvina Ling, Megan Tingley, Jackie Engel, Dael Ki, Esther Reisberg, Martina Rethman, Stefanie Hoffman, Alice Gerber, Savannah Kennelly, Christie Michel, Victoria Stapleton, Melanie Rapoport, Danielle Cantarella, and Patrick Hulse. Additional thanks go to copyeditor Chandra Wohleber and proofreaders Jessica Lack and Kelley Frodel.

A huge thank you to Colin Verdi for the appropriately spooky artwork that graces the cover of the US edition of *The Neon Sky* and the US paperback edition of *The Glittering Edge*.

Huge thanks to my lovely UK team at the Soho Agency: Philippa Milnes-Smith, Lydia Silver, and Eleanor Lawlor.

Penguin Random House UK has been an incredible champion of this series. Thank you to my team there: India Chambers, Carmen McCullough, Awo Ibrahim, Alicia Ingram, Romilly King, Tom Rubira, Mollie Schofield, Millie Street, Libby Thornton, and Adam Webling.

Thank you to Philipp Beck for the gorgeous cover art for the UK editions of *The Glittering Edge* and *The Neon Sky*.

Thank you once again to FairyLoot for choosing *The Glittering Edge* for your YA box and designing a stunning edition of *The Neon Sky* to match it. To Anissa de Gomery and the rest of your team: You made this duology look as magical on the outside as I wanted it to feel on the inside. I can't count the number of readers who have discovered this series because of FairyLoot. My gratitude is truly bottomless. And an especially big thank-you for commissioning the *Glittering Edge* tote bag. I now own three and will probably make my husband buy more of them secondhand on Mercari.

Thank you so much to my international publishers: Hachette Livre (France), HarperCollins Deutschland (Germany), and Knigolove (Ukraine). And if more publishers join them after I submit these acknowledgments, I'm so grateful to you, too!

I also want to thank the Bookstagrammers and BookTokers who have boosted *The Glittering Edge*, drawn fan art for it, and generally been excited for the series. It's been a joy getting to know all of you, and I'm so grateful for the time you've taken to draw these characters, edit posts, make videos, and shout about this book from the rooftops of the internet.

Thank you to all the booksellers and librarians

out there who have made space for *The Glittering Edge* and *The Neon Sky* on their shelves.

Thank you to the authors who blurbed *The Glittering Edge*: Stephanie Garber, M. K. Lobb, Angela Montoya, Ginny Myers Sain, and Emily J. Taylor. I'm in love with the many worlds you've created, and I still pinch myself that your words are on my debut novel.

Thank you to Molly Wagner, dear friend and critique partner, who provided the feedback I desperately needed as I was revising *The Neon Sky*. Your brain is gigantic. If you ever decide to use your powers for evil, the world doesn't stand a chance.

Thank you to Brian Welk and my husband for schooling me on football. I now know that professional games are rarely played on Wednesdays and that 12–18 is not a realistic score at the end of the game. I call that progress! (Corey would be shaking his head in disbelief right now.)

Thank you to my friends for movie nights, long phone calls, and laughter—and for always hyping me up. You totally don't have to read what I write, but it means the world when you do.

Thank you to Grandpa and Grandma for the endless support, and an extra thank-you to

Grandma for trying to strong-arm readers into buying my book at her local Books-A-Million.

Thank you to my family for all the excitement and support over the many years I've been writing books. To Alec, Andrew, Micaela, Aidan, Annaliese, Adam, Omma, Yealee, and the rest of the Villaires, Songs, and Brokaws: I love you.

Thank you, Mom, for letting me vent to you, but also for celebrating with me even when the publishing wins are tiny.

Thank you, Dad. I know better, but I still feel you all around.

Finally, thank you to my husband, Joon. I used to resist the idea of relying on anyone so deeply, as if I had something to prove to myself or to the universe. But now that my first series is complete, I can say with certainty that these books wouldn't exist in their current form without the meals you cooked, the sleep you encouraged me to get, and your deep well of love. You inspire so many of the words that I've written and will write. Nobody shines brighter than you.

About the Author

Alyssa Villaire is the #1 *Sunday Times* bestselling author of *The Glittering Edge*. She writes fantasy books with eerie magic, complicated friendships, and lots of yearning. Alyssa is based in Los Angeles, where she lives with her husband and a steadily growing library.

CELEBRATING 100 YEARS OF PUBLISHING

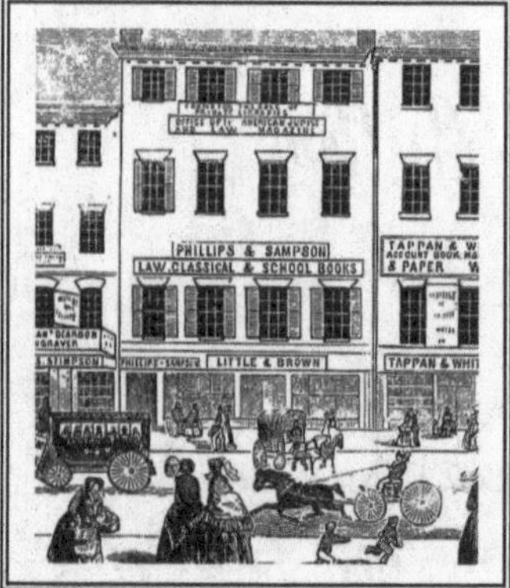

Dear Reader,

You may have noticed the words "Little, Brown and Company" on the title page of this book and wondered what they mean. Well, Charles C. Little and James Brown were the founders of this publishing house, and the "and Company" is all the editors, designers, marketers, publicists, salespeople, and more who help produce each book and bring it to readers like you. Little, Brown was founded in Boston, Massachusetts, in 1837, and some of its early publications included *The Writings of George Washington* and *The Works of Benjamin Franklin*. The catalog grew to feature works by Emily Dickinson and Louisa May Alcott, among many other notable authors. In 1926, recognizing that the literature we read when we are young has a deep and lasting influence and requires expert curation, the company appointed an editor to lead a dedicated children's department.

In 2026, Little, Brown Books for Young Readers celebrates one hundred years of excellence in publishing. Today, we are a division of Hachette Livre, the third-largest publisher in the world, and we are based in New York City. Our staff has grown from a team of two to more than one hundred people. And with the changes in technology, our books are read by more readers, in more ways, and in more countries than ever before. However, one thing has not changed: our commitment to providing a supportive home for all creators and superb stories for all readers. Thank you for being one of them.

Megan Tingley
President and Publisher

To learn more about Little, Brown's history, authors, and books, please visit LBYR.com.